The
Heartbreaker

ST. MARTIN'S TITLES
BY REXANNE BECNEL

The Bridemaker
The Troublemaker
The Matchmaker
The Mistress of Rosecliffe
The Knight of Rosecliffe
The Bride of Rosecliffe
Dangerous to Love
The Maiden Bride
Heart of the Storm

The Heartbreaker

REXANNE BECNEL

St. Martin's

For Clifford Rex Chauvin
Thanks, Dad

PROLOGUE

The London Tattler—January 18
After nearly two years' absence from town society, James Lindford, Viscount Farley, has returned from his second sojourn to the Orient. His mother and stepfather, Viscount and Viscountess Acton, hosted an exclusive dinner party for him at their home on Portman Square. He plans to make his first social appearance at the Edgerton Ball, Tuesday next.

The London Tattler—January 22
The Earl and Countess of Basingstoke have formally announced the betrothal of their youngest daughter, the beauteous Lady Catherine to James Lindford, Viscount Farley. Though some were surprised by the announcement, your faithful correspondent has long suspected that the pair would wed. After all, Lord Farley has a strong interest in the foreign affairs of our great land, and the Earl of Basingstoke is one of the king's most trusted advisors in such matters. It can only be hoped that Lord Farley will be content now to reside in his home country and make foreign policy, and leave the actual adventuring to unattached young gentlemen.

The London Tattler—January 30

The lovely Lady Catherine Winfield was spied arm in arm with her fiancé, James Lindford, Lord Farley, at the French Opera House. They are widely agreed to be the handsomest couple presently on the scene, and word has it that their wedding celebration will surpass that of the Duke and Duchess of Ashbourne.

The London Tattler—February 4

Half the ton ought to be sick in bed today, for despite the blizzard attacking the city last night, the engagement party at the Basingstoke manse was a veritable crush, with more bared arms, shoulders, and bosoms on display than at a midsummer ball. Lady Catherine, shortly to become Viscountess Farley, was aglow and the undisputed star of the evening with her admiring beau circling close attendance on her.

The London Tattler—February 6

An ugly rumor has arisen, only to be proven no rumor at all, but rather, the unadulterated truth. Your faithful correspondent has learned that less than three weeks after the formalization of their betrothal, the much feted Basingstoke–Farley union may dissolve before it has rightly begun. It seems the proper Lord Farley has behaved in a decidedly improper manner—not that most young men abroad have not. But he has the apparent effrontery to bring the results of his indiscretions into his own household. Poor Lady Catherine has taken to her bed in shock.

The London Tattler—February 9

The latest word on the Farley brouhaha is that the viscount's bachelor household now boasts both a small girl and a baby as its newest residents. Two children from his past. Could there be more? Your faithful correspondent has seen them, and regrets to report that one of them is a dark-skinned infant, obviously the result of a dalliance with some exotic eastern creature. There can be no doubt now about Lord Farley's scandalous escapades while abroad. Inquiring minds wonder, since his itinerary took him to Lisbon, Naples, Cairo, and Bombay, does he intend to present his fiancée with a byblow from each of those ports?

The London Tattler—February 14
Saint Valentine sends felicitations to lovers everywhere. But the patron saint of love cannot mend the damage Lord Farley has inflicted upon the heart of the woman who so faithfully awaited his return from his lengthy sojourns abroad. Your faithful correspondent is the first to report the legal dissolution of the betrothal contract between the grievously wounded Lady Catherine and the philandering Lord Farley. Rumor has it that Lord Farley's political aspirations cannot help but suffer as well: Lord Basingstoke is not known for his forgiving nature.

The London Tattler—February 19
The Fleet Street Haberdasher's near Chancery Lane was the site of a near brawl between the widely castigated Lord Farley and the Honorable Mr. Peter Wilkerson, middle son of the Marquis of Gorham. Were it not for the cool head of Mr. Kerrigan Fairchild, blood surely would have been spilt. It seems Lady Catherine has many defenders who cannot forgive Lord Farley the grave disservice he has done his former fiancée.

The London Tattler—February 24
Two longtime servants in the Farley town house have abandoned their posts. Although neither felt at liberty

to discuss the tumult that reigns in their former place of employment, neither denied that a front window was shattered three days ago, that the laundry shed was set afire, and that the curtains in one of the downstairs rooms were ripped down from their hangings.

It is abundantly clear to this correspondent that Lord Farley has taken complete leave of his senses. Perhaps his foreign travels have fevered his brain. Whatever the cause, it is fortunate for Lady Catherine that she has discovered his moral weakness prior to binding herself to him in perpetuity.

And speaking of the beauteous Lady Catherine, on Monday evening she made a triumphant return to society at the Dowager Countess Bedham's annual rout. Wearing a spectacular gown of golden gauze overlaid on a darker golden silk underskirt, and adorned with rosettes of embroidered seed pearls, she entered on the arm of the Honorable Mr. Percival Langley, widely known as her staunchest defender and admirer...

CHAPTER 1

The wailing could be heard throughout the entire house. Though the nursery was on the third floor of Farley Park's east wing and the master's apartments occupied the second floor of the west wing, the baby's crying carried there, faint, but no less distressing. Even when James Lindford retreated to the book-lined estate office on the first level, he could not entirely blot it out.

What was wrong with the child that she spent every night screaming? Frustrated, he ran one hand through his disheveled hair, then turned and stalked away from the tall window and its view of the night-shrouded countryside.

More to the point, what was wrong with the nurse he'd hired that she could not appease the poor babe?

He ought to be able to sleep through the din. Young Clarissa had no trouble doing so. But then, the older of his two daughters *had* to sleep at night. She expended so much energy creating chaos during the day that she collapsed exhausted every night, only to begin the cycle anew come the morn.

He paused before the liquor cabinet, straining to hear. Was that silence?

Then it came again, little Leya's angry, sobbing wail. So far away, yet she might as well have been in the same room, for her cries pierced his heart and tortured him with guilt.

How had he gotten himself into such an insane situation? What had possessed him to think he could be a good parent to the two little girls he'd so casually fathered? If the investigators he'd hired ever located his third child and she turned out to be even half as unruly as these two, he'd end up in Bedlam.

Somewhere a cock crowed, though dawn was only a hint upon the horizon.

He would get no more sleep this night than he had any other during the past week. Rather than console himself with whisky, he ought to go up to the nursery and comfort his poor motherless child. Perhaps if he were lucky, Clarissa would sleep later than usual, and he would only have to deal with one unhappy daughter at a time.

In the nursery a solitary candle burned, but it revealed more than enough. The nurse lay on her cot, hidden beneath a heavy counterpane with a pillow clasped over her head. Meanwhile Leya sat in her bed, sobbing as if her heart were broken.

Guilt poured over James like frigid winter rain. The poor little girl was nine months old, yet already her mother had died, her mother's family had rejected her for her mixed Indian and English blood, and she'd been dragged halfway around the world to live in a chilly foreign land nothing at all like her warm native India. Cared for by strangers and an inept father, was it any wonder she wailed? Her heart *was* broken.

It was his responsibility, however, to mend it. So with another sigh, this time of resolution, he crossed the room, vowing to discharge the coldhearted, incompetent nurse and find someone—anyone—who could ease his little daughter's unhappiness.

"Hello, Leya. Hello," he said, hoping his raspy voice sounded more soothing to her ears than it did to his own.

Startled, she looked up, a sob catching in her throat. Her little chin trembled as if she were about to let out another wail. But a yawn overtook her first, and before she could work herself back up to a scream, he lifted her, tangled bed linens and all, and began to waltz her around the slant-ceilinged nursery. "One, two, three. One two three. It's time to dance with me."

He held her snug against him, for he'd learned that she cried less that way, as if the security of his hold was some sort of comfort. "One, two, three. One two three. We're just fine, you and me."

Leya yawned again, a huge, trembling exhalation, and after a moment the weight of her head came to rest on his shoulder. James smiled and nuzzled his cheek against the baby's silky black locks. Notwithstanding her unhappy temperament, she was the most amazing little thing, incredibly beautiful with blue-gray eyes set within thick black lashes. Right now those lashes were clumped together with tears, and even in sleep her little chin and baby lips trembled from her emotional storm. So he kept on waltzing, though slower now, and reduced his singing to a humming version of Strauss's latest offering.

Despite the pandemonium her presence had introduced into his life, James freely admitted that Leya was his child and his responsibility. So were Clarissa and another child whom he hadn't yet located.

It wasn't as if he hadn't known about his children. He'd supported every one of them from the moment of their births. For years he'd convinced himself that he was meeting his obligations by providing their respective mothers with adequate income to house, clothe, feed, and educate them. But two years ago his complacency about his role in their lives had been shaken when Marshall MacDougal had arrived from America looking for the man who'd so casually fathered him, then abandoned him.

That man had turned out to be James's first stepfather—his sister Olivia's father. But even though his stepfather had been dead for years, the man's long-ago actions might very well have ruined Olivia and their mother, as well as cast serious shadows on James's reputation and that of their other half-sister, Sarah.

But instead of ruining them all by claiming the inheritance that was rightfully his, Marsh had fallen madly in love with Sarah. After a tumultuous courtship they'd married and he'd taken her back to America with him. A happy ending for all involved. But James was acutely aware of the catastrophe barely averted. Property, money, inheritance claims—they had all teetered precariously near disaster, and all because Olivia's father had selfishly chosen to ignore one of his children.

Marsh's situation had started James thinking about the two children he'd fathered—especially since he finally had begun to seriously consider taking a wife. But James hadn't gone so far as to do anything about his daughters. Then he discovered he had sired another child, for on one of his trips to Bombay, Leya's grandfather had appeared at his door, announcing Senita's death from a sudden fever and shoving her baby into James's arms. His baby . . .

That day had changed everything. From his refusing at first to take the babe, to his coming to love her, the transition had been swift, if not smooth. It had taken two months to return from Bombay to London with the little girl, enough time for him to decide it was time to locate his other two natural-born children.

No child of his would have reason to destroy his legitimate family's life or reputation, he'd resolved. He would meet his daughters, get to know them, and supervise their education. He meant also to see to their future needs by providing adequate dowries for them.

Like all his business decisions, it had been a course of action based on practicality and his conviction that the investment of his time and money would someday prove to be well spent.

He could never have anticipated, however, the Pandora's box that simple decision would open. For when he'd located Clarissa, he'd discovered a creature as unlike innocent little Leya as possible: a ten-year-old street urchin whom he'd mistaken for a dirty little boy. A dirty, foul-mouthed pickpocket of a boy.

Her mother, once a gorgeous opera singer, had become over the years a drunken, abusive harlot. From what he could tell, she drank up every penny of the money he'd sent her for Clarissa's expenses.

Worse, he didn't doubt that given another year or two, Clarissa would have been pushed into the same line of work as her mother. It had sickened him to even imagine such a thing. But it had made his decision easy. He had no choice but to remove her from her mother's care and the threat of a life earned on her back.

Her mother had driven a hard bargain, but he'd paid her off. Only he'd found, to his daily despair, that Clarissa—Izzy, as she demanded he call her—was far more difficult to deal with than her pitiful, grasping mother. As determined as he was to educate her and make her presentable, she was even more determined to oppose him. She was like a feral kitten with her claws always at the ready, always hissing and looking for a way to escape.

To complicate matters further, it had proven impossible to hide the child's presence. Before he could explain the situation to Catherine and to her father, the truth had come out in one of those rags that called themselves newspapers. By then it was too late, for neither his humiliated fiancée nor her enraged father would listen.

Like a speedy galleon come to ruin on uncharted rocks, both his social and political careers had been wrecked. Basingstoke had known precisely whom to talk to in government, while the gossip rags had done the rest. In frustration James had retreated with his daughters to Yorkshire to wait for the gossip to die down and reconsider how best to gloss over the situation.

As bad as the situation was, it was only a detour on the path to his ultimate goal of becoming the King's Counsel on Foreign Affairs. It wasn't a dead end; he wouldn't let it be. For now all he had to do was wait— and deal with his children.

He eased into a rocking chair, careful not to jostle Leya awake. Removing Clarissa from London had been a good idea, he told himself, as he leaned back in the rocker and closed his eyes. She'd run away twice in London, but she couldn't do that here. In the countryside she was completely out of her element. By the time she was brave enough to try another escape, maybe she would have come to trust him enough not to want to escape.

Meanwhile he had to find a governess for the child and hire another nurse for Leya . . .

High noon was not the best time for fishing, but the early spring day was so warm and lovely that Phoebe Churchill could not resist her niece Helen's entreaties to go afield. After all, the household chores were done, and they'd seen to the goats, the chickens, the bees, and the garden. There was no reason why seven-year-old Helen could not do her daily lessons outdoors just as well as she could indoors.

"How about things that begin with an *l*?" Phoebe suggested as she cast her line toward the deepest part of the pond.

"Hmm." The golden-haired little girl's brow puckered in concentration. "Ladybirds."

"Very good."

"And licorice sticks."

"Even better," Phoebe said, as she played the lure deftly across the surface of the quiet pond.

"Let's see. Love, and loons, and . . . lucky four-leaf clover!" Helen crowed, holding one up. "Look, Phoebe. Look what I've found!"

A strike on Phoebe's line just then prevented her looking. "I've hooked one. A big one too!"

"Don't lose him!" Helen shouted, scrambling to Phoebe's side.

"Come along, Master Trout," Phoebe coaxed as she fought the game creature, moving down along the pond bank. "You shall make a lovely meal. Or two," she added. He felt that big and strong.

It took several minutes of teasing him to the bank before she could land the silvery creature, and they were in high spirits as they made their way back to their lunch basket.

Except that their old willow basket was gone.

"What in the world?" Phoebe stared around in confusion. Not only was the basket and its half-loaf of bread, jar of pickles, and hunk of cheese gone, so was the tattered old blanket they'd spread in a grassy area near the trees.

"What happened to our lunch?" Helen asked, looking around as if their picnic were only misplaced.

"I don't know," Phoebe muttered, glaring toward the woods, searching for any sign of the guilty party. "Maybe Gypsies."

"Gypsies?" At once Helen pressed up against Phoebe's side. "Let's go home, Phoebe. Gypsies are bad. Grandma said they're murdering thieves who steal bad children right out of their beds."

A little shiver coursed through Phoebe as she scanned the familiar, yet now threatening forest. But to Helen she said, "Then you've nothing to fear, do you? For you're a very good child. The best."

They left at once. At least they had the trout, and her fishing rig. But that was little comfort to Phoebe. Maybe Mr. Blackstock was right, she fretted. Maybe they did live too far from town for safety. For if a thief could steal from them at midday, what might he do at night?

Or when they were away from the house!

"Hurry," she said, breaking into a trot.

"Are they after us too?" Helen asked, squeezing Phoebe's hand so hard it hurt.

"Oh, no, sweetheart. I'm just hungry, that's all."

Everything at home appeared fine. The three goats were still in the meadow; the chickens ranged around the yard and garden, and none appeared missing. But even so, Phoebe's worries did not abate. She would have to inform the magistrate about this the next time she went into Swansford, even though she knew Mr. Blackstock would point to this as one more reason why she must sell her cottage and farm, and move into town. But Phoebe refused to do that, at least not until she'd exhausted all her resources.

Come the morning, however, the bucket at the well came up missing, as did her little gardening bench. She could see the marks in the grass where it had been dragged away.

But why would Gypsies steal a bucket and a bench when a goat would be so much more useful to them? It made no sense. Perhaps it wasn't Gypsies at all. But then who?

"Put on your mourning dress," she told Helen. "We're going to town." She didn't have to explain why when she turned the barely used key in the ancient door lock. Too bad she couldn't lock up the carrots and turnips in the garden, or the tools in the shed next to the chicken house.

Dew still clung to the grass and heather as they made the two-mile walk to the small village of Swansford. Phoebe carried three dozen eggs, and Helen carried a round of soft goat cheese. They meant to exchange them at Leake's Emporium for flour, soap, and thread. She also had two books to return to Mr. Blackstock, who had the only library in town.

Outside Leake's, three old women with shopping baskets propped against their hips stood in earnest conversation with the vicar. A large farm wagon stood outside the store. Phoebe recognized it as belonging to Farley Park, though she hadn't seen it often. Already it was half full of supplies.

"Goodness, they're buying out the shop," Phoebe muttered. "Hurry up, Helen."

Inside, the normally quiet shop was abustle with activity. "D'you have the cakes of soap in there?" a wiry woman asked.

"Yes, ma'am. Right here, ma'am," Mrs. Leake's son, Martin, said, bobbing his head beneath the teetering load of flour sacks balanced upon his shoulder.

"And the molasses?"

"Already in the wagon, ma'am, beside the candles."

"Good. Now there's the matter of cake flour. I'll need some extra fine milled flour for my cakes."

Just then Mrs. Leake came out from the storeroom, her arms overflowing with bolts of linen. Spying Phoebe, she gave her a quick nod. "I hope you're not in a hurry, Phoebe girl."

"No. But will there be any flour and soap left for us?"

"I'll see there is. Meanwhile, just set your goods over there." She indicated one corner of the counter. "Mayhap you'll prefer to come back in a half hour or so."

"Perhaps I should. Is something going on at Farley Park?"

"Indeed. Himself has decided to take up residence. Not just a visit either, or so I hear. That's his house-keeper come to oversee the purchases. 'Scuse me, but I can't talk now."

As they wove their way past the scowling house-keeper and her two assistants, Helen tugged at Phoebe's sleeve. "Who's Himself? I never heard of anyone named that."

The wiry woman must have had ears like a cat, for she turned her sharp gaze on Helen, then Phoebe. "For your information, James Lindford, Viscount Farley, has taken up residence in his ancestral home after many years away. I'm certain he'll introduce himself to the mayor, the vicar, and the magistrate once he's settled in. Until then, I'll thank you and the rest of the villagers not to speculate on the reason for his return, or the du-ration of his stay."

Then with a pinching grip she halted poor Martin. "Let me see that salt. I'll not pay good money for salt with grit or chalk mixed in."

Outside Phoebe and Helen shared a look of conster-nation. "My goodness," Phoebe said as they started to-ward Mr. Blackstock's residence. "She certainly was cross, wasn't she?"

"Just like Grandmother used to be," Helen remarked. "That's what happens when you get old."

Phoebe shook her head. Out of the mouths of babes. But it was true. Phoebe's mother had died less than a fortnight ago, but already the difference in their home life was apparent. Without Emilean Churchill to disapprove and scold, there was no longer a need to tiptoe about, burying any hint of ebullience or joy or just plain silliness. No more excessive adherence to the polite manners her mother had demanded of her and her sister, Louise, and more recently, of Helen.

Duty, obedience, moral exactitude. Those were the bulwarks that had formed her mother's life. Their household had been a silent, unhappy place. But not any longer.

If only Phoebe could escape this nagging sense of guilt. She should be sadder that her mother had died. But her sadness was more for the way her mother had chosen to live.

She shook off those thoughts and said to Helen, "If Lord Farley's housekeeper is cross, I suspect it's because the viscount didn't notify her that he was coming. Just like a man," she added, under her breath.

Though she'd never met Lord Farley, Phoebe had heard talk of him all her life. For the most part he was considered a fine gentleman with quite the head for business, especially considering that he'd come into his title so young in life. His mother's pride and joy. A good landlord, according to his tenants, albeit an absent one. Apparently he'd had to be the man of the family for his mother and his two half-sisters, and had managed all their estates until they'd married.

Left unsaid, however, were the facts that he was past thirty and not yet wed himself. The gossips held that he preferred the excitement of town life and traveling abroad to the pastoral quiet of the Yorkshire countryside. It was also whispered that he was quite the ladies' man, and that he'd cut a considerable swath through society.

As the properly raised sister of a baron, Phoebe's mother had been prone to forgive the titled almost any sin. But even she had cautioned her two daughters that, rich or poor, men were lustful creatures who could never be trusted. A marriage contract was a woman's only insurance. Consequently, a man still not committed to marriage by the ripe age of thirty must be looked at with some mistrust.

But whether the viscount was an upright bachelor or a debauched rake was none of Phoebe's affair, so long as she could still trade for what she needed from Mrs. Leake.

Phoebe and Helen made their way up the steep brick road to Mr. Blackstock's grand two-story residence to find that even he was in a dither over Lord Farley's return to the district. It seemed that in his youth he'd been the previous Lord Farley's confidant. As a result, the return of the younger Lord Farley had stirred up a wealth of memories in him.

" 'Tis a grand day for Swansford. A red-letter day. There's nothing like having the lord in residence. It benefits the whole countryside," he gushed, taking the books Phoebe returned to him.

"Mrs. Leake shall certainly benefit," Phoebe remarked. "Farley's housekeeper was purchasing everything in sight. How many people are in his party, anyhow?"

It was an innocent question, perfectly logical. Yet for some reason Mr. Blackstock averted his gaze and began restlessly to search the disorganized surface of his desk. "He, ah . . . I understand he has two, ah . . . guests. And of course, several additional servants to assist them."

"Two guests? Are they from London also? We haven't had any toffs in these parts in a very long time."

Mr. Blackstock cleared his throat. "I'm not certain about that. Here, Phoebe." He located what he was searching for on his desk and presented a neatly penned document to her. "This establishes you and your sister as your mother's heir—just as she was your father's heir. You and Louise are each half-owners of your family property on Plummy Head. You haven't heard from Louise yet, have you?"

"I doubt she's even received the letter I sent her in London." It had been over two years since they'd had any word from Louise. Not a Christmas letter, nor a note to Helen for her birthday. And of course, not a penny to help support the fast-growing child. No matter how many letters Phoebe sent, pleading for Louise to write her daughter even if she couldn't send money, the letters were never answered.

If Phoebe hadn't become inured to her sister's selfishness, she might have worried that something dreadful had befallen her. But Louise would always land on her feet, to the detriment of anyone standing too near. Louise was more likely too involved with her latest lover and her acting career to care about any of her family. Louise's response to the news of their mother's death would probably be little more than a shrug and an "Oh, well."

So much for being Emilean's favorite daughter, the beautiful one who, as a child, could do no wrong. The irony was that Louise had fled Plummy Head and Swansford just as soon as she possibly could, leaving Phoebe to deal with their aging parents.

Repressing a spurt of resentment, Phoebe scanned the document Mr. Blackstock had prepared, then signed as he indicated. Louise would write or show up when it was convenient for her to do so, and no sooner.

Meanwhile, Phoebe wanted to inquire further about the goings-on at Farley Park. But it was plain to her that Mr. Blackstock had no intention of gossiping about the exalted son of his exalted friend. Phoebe was no fool, though, and she drew her own conclusions. She might be a country bumpkin, well on her way to becoming a spinster. But she read widely, and she knew something of the world. Besides, her sister was an actress on the London stage and the most notorious woman to ever hail from Swansford. During her last visit four years previously, Louise hadn't minced any words—at least when their mother wasn't around—and the still impressionable Phoebe had soaked in every scandalous conversation.

So it seemed obvious to her now. If a bachelor lord had arrived unannounced at his country estate with two guests that a respectable gentleman like Mr. Blackstock could not acknowledge to an unmarried young woman like Phoebe, well, it must mean something improper. Most likely, women of questionable reputation.

Phoebe considered that a long moment as she stared blankly at the painstakingly penned document in her hand. How shocking if that were true. Certainly it would account for that housekeeper's short temper.

But it was no concern of hers.

"Now, Phoebe," Mr. Blackstock continued, clearing his throat. "Have you given any thought to what I said about selling the farm?"

She gave him an impatient look. "I'm sorry, but I'm still not ready to make that decision."

"You may be forced to do so. I cannot much longer ignore the fact that the taxes on your farm are seriously in arrears, child. How are you to assemble such a sum unless you sell out—" He broke off, then his lined face brightened in a hopeful smile. "Or perhaps if you were to settle on a husband? That's what you need, you know, a good hard-working husband to take care of matters like this for you—"

"Mr. Blackstock," she interrupted, barely repressing her frustration. Her mother hadn't been made particularly happy by marriage to a hard-working man. "I appreciate your concern for my financial predicament, but I came to town for another reason entirely. It seems we have a thief in our midst."

He blinked. "A thief?"

Though Mr. Blackstock was duly outraged by Phoebe's tale, his conclusion did not jibe with Phoebe's. "We haven't had a thief in Swansford since that Thornley lad was arrested eight—no, nine years ago. Robbed Leake's till he did, but we figured it out fast enough. No, he's the only thief from Swansford, 'less you count Dirty Harry and his habit of overcharging his customers once they get too soused to notice. So you see, Phoebe girl, it must be Gypsies. They're known to head up along the coast once the weather begins to warm up."

"It hasn't warmed up very much. Besides, Gypsies are more likely to steal chickens and goats."

"Well, now, I'm sure Gypsies use baskets and buckets like anybody else."

"And garden benches?"

He frowned, turning his bushy brows into one long gray line overhanging his eyes. "Maybe they took it for . . . for firewood."

"With a forest full of wood available for the taking? Besides, have Gypsies been seen anywhere in the district of late?"

"Well, no. But then, they're a sneaky lot," he said, clearly not willing to have his judgment overridden.

Phoebe let out an irritated sigh. "I don't believe it's Gypsies," she insisted. "The only new faces around Swansford are ensconced at Farley Park, and they're hardly suspect. So my thief must be someone local. Perhaps it's only a prank," she went on before he could disagree. "I know boys can be a troublesome lot. But I want my basket back, and my bucket and my bench."

"Yes, yes. Perhaps it was a prank," he admitted. "I'll look into it and see what I can find out. But you know, Phoebe girl, if you moved to town or got married, you wouldn't have this problem."

"I'm not moving. Not yet," Phoebe said, trying to remain pleasant. "And in order to marry, one must first find a willing partner."

Frowning, Mr. Blackstock leaned back in his chair and crossed his sausage hands across his tightly stretched waistcoat. "As you wish." He thought a moment, then his expression lifted. "There is another solution. Not for the taxes, of course, but for your protection. Indeed, I believe I made the very same suggestion to your mother after your father passed on—God bless them both. But she didn't like dogs, she said. Nor cats neither."

"A dog." As soon as the idea was planted it took immediate root in Phoebe's head. "A watchdog."

Mr. Blackstock nodded, well pleased with himself. "A watchdog," he echoed. "And it just so happens that Martin Leake's bitch whelped nearly a dozen pups. 'Course, four of 'em died. But there's seven or eight left. I 'spect he'll be glad to give you one."

A dog. When Phoebe fetched Helen from the Blackstocks' kitchen and her treat of blackberry jam on scones, she gave her the news. The girl's eyes lit up with delight. "A puppy? For us to take home?"

They found Martin behind his mother's store greasing the axle of their delivery wagon for Monday's trip to Louth. In a small pen near the store's tilting back steps were the wriggling puppies with their mother complacently nursing them.

"You come at a good time, Miss Phoebe. They're just about ready to leave their ma." He held up his hand. "They was born on St. Simon's day. Since then we've had St. Oswald's day and St. Frances's day. Then there was St. Maud's and St. Basil's." One by one he ticked off his fingers. "The vicar says they'll be ready on the feast of St. Rupert, and that's tomorrow."

"I see. I wonder, do you think it would be all right to take one of them a day early? Please?"

A silly grin came over his face and his ears turned red. "Well, I guess. I mean . . ." The red crept onto his already florid face. "For you, Miss Phoebe. Only for you."

"Oh, thank you. Thank you so much."

Martin Leake might look like a man, and his exacting mother certainly worked him like one. But he was a simple fellow, more like an overgrown child than a man. Still, he was good-natured, a diligent worker, and he had a gentle way with both animals and children. Phoebe sometimes suspected he had a bit of a crush on her, but then, he blushed when any woman paid particular attention to him.

"Well, Helen. We may select a puppy today. Which one will you have?"

It was a hard choice, but in the end, with Phoebe's encouragement, they selected the smallest of the litter, a little brown and white spotted fellow with a stumpy tail which nonetheless beat back and forth with feverish excitement every time Helen petted him.

"He's going to fuss the first few nights," Martin said as he placed the pup in Helen's arms. "But if you let him sleep with you he'll keep quiet. Plus, the closeness will make you his family, and he'll guard you extra special good."

Martin tied a length of string about the puppy's neck

for the walk home, and though she'd not really accomplished her goal of finding their thief, Phoebe did feel better. She'd always wanted a dog. So had her father. But her mother had forbidden it. If Louise had wanted one, no doubt their mother would have relented. But Louise was no more enamored of dogs than their mother had been. Animals were for providing meat, milk, cheese, and eggs, she'd always said.

But their puppy was going to provide something just as important, Phoebe decided. Protection and companionship.

"What shall we name him?" Helen asked as they made their slow way home through the advancing afternoon chill.

"Whatever you like. Here, don't pull on the string so hard, sweetheart. Let's untie him and teach him to follow us. That way he'll learn the way home should he ever wander off."

They decided to call him Bruno, after rejecting Laddie, Brownie, Spot, and Mister. When Bruno's little legs would carry him no farther, Helen did. And when her arms grew tired, Phoebe took over the task. As they rounded the last craggy outcropping before their cottage, however, she put him down, and she and Helen ran the last slope of the stony path, with the little fellow trailing gamely behind.

"You're home now," Helen said, falling to her knees beside the front stoop, waiting for Bruno to reach her. "And you'll keep those mean old robbers away from us, won't you?"

It couldn't happen too soon, Phoebe decided. For to her dismay, she could see that someone had been there while they were gone. A small muddy footstep outside the kitchen door, a broken stick, and a scratch on the shutter at the side of the house verified that someone had tried to pry the shutter open.

But she didn't reveal any of that to Helen. At least it was only children, she consoled herself. The footstep was too small to be anything else. If she stayed close to home for the next few days, perhaps the little hooligans would give up and go bother someone else with their not so amusing pranks.

Three days later, however, the pranksters went too far. For when Phoebe finished washing Helen's hair and went outside to brush it in the first sunshine they'd had after two days of drizzle, she discovered that the thieves had struck again. And this time they'd stolen the watchdog meant to protect the household. They'd taken Bruno.

Phoebe had to swallow a very unladylike oath. Helen started crying, but Phoebe shushed her as she examined the scene. Sure enough, a trail of small footprints led across the muddy yard to the field, and probably the woods beyond.

"You've gone too far this time," she muttered. "Too far." She didn't pause to fetch a shawl or even lock the door. "Come on, Helen. They can't be that far ahead of us. If we have to, we'll capture these nasty little thieves ourselves."

For once Helen conquered her timidity. She dashed her tears and followed Phoebe without complaint as they tracked the line of footprints in the damp ground and across the crushed grasses in the meadow. It was more difficult to follow the trail through the forest. But Phoebe had grown up traipsing through these woods and she remembered every dip and hollow that had attracted her as a girl. Slowly they crept beneath the arch of the oak trees, following a narrow deer path until she heard something and froze.

For a moment there was nothing but the sough of the

breeze in the newly greened trees, and the everyday rustle of birds and beetles and burrowing spring creatures. A nervous Helen crowded up behind her.

"Shh," she cautioned the child.

Then it came again, the high-pitched yip of a puppy. As one, Phoebe and Helen hurried on, following the yapping until they heard also the voice of a child.

"Are you hungry, then? Don't worry, Georgie. I'll swipe you a nice joint of mutton from the kitchen. You'll like that, won't you, my Georgie boy?"

The only answer was the puppy's enthusiastic barking. Was it just the one child? "Stay here." Phoebe mouthed the words to Helen. "Don't come out till I summon you." Then slow step by slow step she inched forward, past prickly holly and unfurling ferns.

"Fetch," she heard the child order the puppy. "Fetch."

But of course, the fat, stubby-legged little dog hadn't yet mastered that trick.

Around the trunk of a massive oak tree Phoebe finally saw the child. To her surprise it was a girl, a very dirty girl in what looked like a well-made coat but which had a torn pocket, and a dangling hem, with a pair of ruined stockings sticking out beneath. Even more surprising than her appearance, however, was that Phoebe didn't recognize the child. With her pale complexion and sandy-colored hair, she was definitely not a Gypsy. Nor was she from Swansford or any of the surrounding farms or cottages.

That was neither here nor there, however. The little thief's identity could be determined later. Right now Phoebe just wanted to nab the light-fingered hooligan before she could get away.

"If you won't fetch, what *will* you do?"

Phoebe watched as the girl sat down cross-legged in front of the panting puppy, then lifted it gently into her lap. "Are you tired, poor baby? Is it time for your nap?"

This was her chance, and Phoebe took it. She sprang from behind the tree and latched onto the girl's arm with the same strength she used to hold the occasional recalcitrant goat.

The little girl was stronger than she looked, though, and even wilder. The puppy went flying as the child twisted away. But Phoebe lunged forward, tackling her in a patch of newly budded wild blueberries. It took all her weight to trap the struggling child and pin her to the ground. Nothing, however, could halt the stream of filthy curses that spewed from the little girl's mouth.

"Let me go, you bloody arse! You stinkin' cunt! You stupid bitch!"

Phoebe could scarcely believe her ears. "You'd better hush that sort of talk right now!" she hissed.

"I'll cut out your bloody heart!" the girl screeched, trying to buck Phoebe off. "Just see if I don't, you whore!"

"And I'll wash your mouth out with soap. Where's my bucket and my bench?"

"Go to bloody hell!"

Had she not heard the words, Phoebe would never believe a child could speak so horridly. And a girl at that. She was sorely tempted to slap the nasty-mouthed creature, if only to silence her. But she'd been slapped often enough as a child to know such punishment only bred a fiercer sort of resentment. She'd never once hit Helen, and she wouldn't allow this poorly raised wretch to start her doing such things now.

"Where we're going," she muttered as she dragged the child upright, "is to the magistrate's office. Then we'll see how brave you are, my tart-tongued little friend."

"Rot in hell!"

"It'll be you who'll rot in gaol if you don't change your ways," Phoebe snapped back, manacling the girl's wrist with one hand while with the other she tried to smooth out her own skirts. And what a skinny wrist it was, she realized. She peered at the child, trying to see past the tangled mat of hair that fell over her face. "Who are you?"

"Bugger off!"

Phoebe's nostrils flared with distaste. As angry as her own parents had made her, she'd never said the sort of things this girl did, nor thought them either. It took every bit of her forbearance to remember that for all her bravado, the little girl was probably terrified.

"Tell me who you are, and perhaps we can settle this with your parents instead of the authorities."

At that the girl looked up. Slowly her angry glare shifted into a smug sort of cunning. "Do whatever you want. My father *is* the authority around here. He's the most important person in these parts, and *you're* the one as will end up in the gaol. Just see if you don't!"

Two things registered in Phoebe's mind. First, that the girl must be from London, for no one around here spoke with that peculiar sort of tough, clipped manner. Second, since Phoebe knew the child didn't belong to the magistrate, and since only one other person in these parts outranked a magistrate, that meant her father must be . . . Lord Farley?

But no. That couldn't be right. Lord Farley had no children. He wasn't even married, for she would have heard if he was. The entire district would have been abuzz with the news. And anyway, this child appeared to be a little older than Helen.

Then again, as she well knew, some children were born on the wrong side of the sheets. The fact was, the stealing had only begun after Lord Farley's arrival, and hunter, the man looked more like a reckless highwayman than a peer of the realm, and Phoebe felt a distressing shiver of fear. He wore neither coat nor hat, and his golden hair fell in disarray over his brow.

But she had no doubt he was Viscount Farley, for there was an arrogant, lordly bearing about him. He rode his elegant steed with that easy carelessness that bespoke privilege and education and a worldliness foreign to these parts.

But lord or not, Phoebe fixed the much-gossiped-about viscount with a censorious gaze. If he thought he could foist his unruly London ways on the good people of Swansford, well, she was just the one to set him straight.

As he pulled his animal to a plunging halt right before them, she took a steadying breath and tilted her chin up to an arrogant angle. She kept a close grip on his thieving little girl as she glared at him. "Could it be that this is *your* child?"

the child was heading toward Farley Park. Th
could have brought his natural-born child to li
ley Park. That would explain the fine qualit
clothes, if not the condition.

But the idea of so privileged a child stealin
infuriated Phoebe more than anything. "What rig
a girl like you to steal from poor folks like us?"

In short order they were marching through the w
Phoebe dragging the nasty little beggar while H
struggled to keep up with Bruno in her arms.

"Wait, Phoebe," Helen pleaded.

"Phoebe, the evil one," the other girl taunte
"Phoebe, the seedy. Phoebe, the frumpy, frightfu
looking fool."

It was all Phoebe could do not to snap at either of the
children. By the time they traversed the forest and the
long hill that was the shortcut to Farley Park, Helen was
crying and Phoebe was cursing under her breath. At least
the wretched little thief she'd caught was huffing too
hard to cast any more invective at them.

Just when Phoebe thought she'd have to tell Helen to
sit and wait for her, she spied the chimney pots of Farley
Park rising beyond the hill. And no sooner did she see
the chimney pots than a horseman charged over that very
same hill.

Upon sighting them, the rider drew up, then changing
direction, spurred straight for Phoebe and the bedraggled
pair of girls.

"You can sit down now, Helen," she said over her
shoulder. "As for you," she said, holding tight when her
captive tried once more to wriggle free. "You'd better
hold still."

Then pushing back the tangled mess her hair had become, she straightened to her most imposing height and
waited for the rider. Though mounted on a magnificent

CHAPTER 2

James flung himself off his horse before it came to a complete halt. "Clarissa! Thank God. Where have you been?"

"Skulking around my farm is where," the woman holding the girl's arm retorted when Clarissa remained mute. "Trying her very best to steal me blind."

James's gaze went to the woman, a somewhat disheveled, obviously angry woman with a little girl of her own peering from around her skirts. Bloody hell. It wasn't enough that Clarissa wreaked havoc on one household. Now she'd started in on another.

"I assure you, madam, that I will compensate you fully for whatever trouble my daughter may have caused you. Come here, Clarissa."

Clarissa shot the woman a smug, taunting smile, then yanked her arm free. But the look she sent James was even more unpleasant. "I told you to call me Izzy."

"And I told you to come here," he snapped. He'd reached the end of his patience with her three days ago, not that it had done any good. If anything, Izzy's—*Clarissa's* behavior had gone from bad to awful to unbearable. Everyone seemed to have different advice: threaten her with punishment; bribe her with presents; shower her with attention; ignore her when she misbehaves; spank her; lock her in her bedroom; send her to boarding school.

Return her to her mother in the Seven Dials district, one of London's seediest quarters.

That last one he'd refused to consider, for Seven Dials guaranteed only one sort of future for a child: a sordid, lifelong mire of thievery, drunkenness, drug use, and prostitution. No matter the hell Clarissa put him through, he'd never let her anywhere near that place or her mother again.

But the suggestion about a boarding school, that one was beginning to sound like his only remaining choice. Especially now when the girl pointedly ignored his command and instead went over to pet his horse.

Bloody hell!

He thrust both hands through his hair, anything to prevent him from landing a firm swat on his aggravating firstborn's rear end. An impatient "Ahem" drew his attention back to his aggrieved neighbor.

"Yes, madam. I haven't forgotten about you. Tell me what Clarissa has done and I'll see that you're compensated for your trouble."

"She stole my well bucket, my lord. Also, a market basket, a blanket—admittedly an old, oft-mended one—and my garden bench. What she could want with that I cannot hazard to guess. Then today—today she stole our dog!" She drew the blond-haired child who was holding the puppy in front of her. "It nearly broke Helen's heart when we discovered him gone."

"A bucket, a blanket, and a bench. I believe one pound should cover the cost. Or perhaps a guinea?" Guineas were not often used in the country, and he'd learned long ago that it carried a certain cachet for someone to possess one.

But the woman seemed little impressed. "You're forgetting the basket. My grandmother wove that basket herself, my lord. *Her* great-grandmother," she added, indicating the silent child leaning against her legs.

James gave her a narrow-eyed gaze. Was she trying to squeeze him for a larger sum? Because if she was, her timing couldn't be worse. He'd thought his last week in London god-awful, what with the messy dissolution of his marriage contract, the painful death of his political aspirations, and the gossips having a field day with both. But this first week in the countryside had been holy hell. Not enough sleep, impossible children, contrary servants. Now his daughter, whom he'd saved from the vilest sort of future in Seven Dials, thanked him by proving herself to be a foul-mouthed brat, an unrepentant liar, and a common thief.

Not that he should have expected anything else given that her mother had drunk every penny of the generous allowance he'd sent her the past ten years. Still, he hadn't expected the child to hate him.

"I'm sorry," he said to his neighbor, too annoyed by the situation to inject any real apology into his tone. "It seems I've forgotten my manners. You've obviously deduced my identity. Might I inquire to whom I am speaking?"

She lifted her chin to a pugnacious angle. "Phoebe Churchill," she answered with no less asperity than he. Even her curtsy managed to convey her disdain.

For a simple country woman with her hair awry, her skirt streaked with mud, and bits of leaves and grass clinging to her bodice, she had an awfully haughty bearing. Half the grand dames of London would envy her.

But it was not his intention to bandy words with the

chit. "Thank you, Mrs. Churchill, for returning Clarissa to me—"

"Izzy!" the child shouted.

He ignored his mouthy street urchin of a daughter, and dug into his purse. "Here's a guinea. If we can't locate your basket for you, I'll send my man with another coin. Where do you reside?"

She gave him a long, even stare. It gave him the uncomfortable sensation of being weighed, measured, and somehow found wanting. "Plummy Head," she answered. Then without taking his coin, she turned to Clarissa, summarily dismissing him. He frowned at her audacity, then waited with smug knowledge of what was to come when she approached his feral child.

"I would like my things returned," she said to the child. "Tomorrow would be a good day. When shall I expect you?"

For once Clarissa was speechless.

"Well?" the woman prompted. "What time? I'll be baking in the morning, so you may wish to come after the apple tarts are done."

Though the girl's only answer was a scowl, it could not entirely disguise the fact that Mrs. Churchill's invitation had Clarissa completely flummoxed.

Having had the last word, the woman took her little girl by the hand. "We'll be home all day, Izzy, whatever time you choose to come. I believe you know the way." To James she only gave a curt nod.

She and her daughter started back across the fallow field until Clarissa cried out, "Wait!"

They all turned to the girl. "You're not leaving me here with him, are you?" the dirty-faced child exclaimed.

The woman's arching brows knit together and she shot a suspicious glance at James. "Shouldn't I? He is your father."

"Because . . ." The child met James's baffled expression with a hateful glare. "Because he beats me."

"I do no such thing! I've never once laid a hand on her," James swore to Mrs. Churchill. "Though I've been sorely tempted to," he added, advancing on Clarissa.

But his neighbor stepped directly between him and his devious offspring. Shooting him a suspicious look she said to Clarissa, "What do you mean by 'he beats me'?"

"I don't beat her!" James bit out.

"He does! He does!" Like a chameleon Clarissa changed from accused thief to pitiful victim—and right along with her Mrs. Churchill turned from irate neighbor to protective mother.

She crouched in front of Clarissa. "Has he hurt you?"

"I have not hurt her!" James protested.

Mrs. Churchill stood and rounded fiercely on him. "Be quiet, Lord Farley. Just be quiet and let me handle this." Then once more she turned her back on him.

James almost choked on his rage. By damn, but he was sorely tempted to throttle the gullible, interfering wench!

"Now Izzy," she said, as if he weren't even there. "Tell me exactly what occurred."

James could not believe this was happening. His guttersnipe child, whom he'd saved from a wretched fate, was accusing him of treating her badly. Clutching her puppy, the other little girl stared wide-eyed at him, as if he were a demon complete with horns, a tail, and cloven feet.

"He hit me with a strap," Clarissa lied, sending him a resentful glare. "An' he wouldn't give me any supper. Nor any breakfast neither."

"You certainly are thin," the woman commiserated with her.

"She has a kitchen full of food," James said with barely controlled temper. "Anything she might want."

Mrs. Churchill held up a hand to silence him, but her gaze remained on the child. "I'll bet that strap must have hurt."

The child nodded, the very picture of desolation. "It was terrible; just terrible. I cried and cried, and begged him to stop. Only he wouldn't."

"I never—" James began.

"The bruises must be awful," Mrs. Churchill went on.

"Yes, and they hurt something fierce—" The girl broke off in mid-lie. In the same moment James realized where Mrs. Churchill's line of questioning was headed.

He studied the woman with grudging respect as she smoothed a hand over the child's head. "Let me see those bruises, will you?"

Frowning now, the girl shrugged her off. "I don't want to."

"Why not?" Mrs. Churchill stared steadily at the now scowling child. "Could it be that perhaps you're making this up?"

Judging by the mulish expression on her face, James was sure Clarissa would maintain her lie. But she was nothing if not unpredictable. Without warning she spat, "Bugger off!" and started running up the hill toward Farley Park.

For a moment he just stared after her. At least she was running toward her home and not away. But the confrontation depressed him anew as he recognized the magnitude of the task he'd set himself. Clarissa hated him. She fought him at every turn, and he didn't know what to do about it.

Beside him Mrs. Churchill cleared her throat. "We'll be off then," she said when he looked over at her. "I meant what I said when I invited her to visit me. I hope you'll let her come."

He nodded. "Of course. And thank you." He hesitated, then went on. "I want you to know that I've never laid a harsh hand on her. Never."

She gave a faint smile, just enough to make him study her more closely. "I know." Then her smile faded. "The fact remains, however, that she doesn't seem to like you very much. Not at all, in fact, and I have to wonder why."

Then not allowing him time to explain the situation, she turned, took her daughter's hand, and left.

James stared after her, noticing almost too late the details he'd not seen before. Her straight, slender back as she marched down the hill. The curve of her hips and the hidden length of her legs wading through last year's knee-high meadow grass. Her hair was a rich brown hue, streaked red by the strengthening midday sun.

Her eyes had been, what? An amber-brown, flashing with temper, he recalled. Not a beautiful woman, but striking all the same. And memorable. Especially when she smiled.

Only the reminder that she was married with a child of her own made him look away from her departing form. But even that took an act of strong self-will. It was dallying with too many women that had landed him in his current situation; he couldn't afford to resume that sort of activity here, especially with the entire country-side watching his every move.

Then again, if he didn't find some sort of outlet for the frustrations besetting him, God only knew when and where he would explode.

Meanwhile, there was his hooligan daughter to deal with.

Muffling a curse, and feeling far older than his thirty-four years, he collected his grazing animal, heaved himself into the saddle, and started after his child.

"Was that Himself?" Helen asked when they were halfway down the hill.

Lost in her own thoughts, Phoebe was slow to respond. "Yes. But his proper name is James Lindford, Viscount Farley. If he should ever address you, you must curtsy to him and say 'my lord,' and use your very best manners."

Helen digested that as they wended their way down the hill. Ahead of them crickets, gnats, and other buzzing creatures sprang up in an insect cloud, while the dried stalks of last year's grass swished against their skirts. "His girl, that Izzy girl, she doesn't use very good manners. And she's a liar, too, isn't she?"

"I'm afraid so. But I think she only acts that way because she hasn't been taught any better."

"Does that mean her father isn't a very good father?"

It would seem not. But all Phoebe said was, "I'm not sure what the situation is between them." She was curious enough, however, to want to find out.

"I wonder where her mother is."

Her mother, who was *not* Lord Farley's wife. So far as anyone knew, the viscount was still a bachelor. And yet he freely claimed Izzy as his daughter. That meant Phoebe's first guess was right: the girl must be natural born.

Like Helen.

Phoebe's sympathy for the unhappy little girl immediately increased. Given her wild appearance and appalling behavior, could it be that the child had not been a part of Lord Farley's home until recently?

To Helen she said, "Judging by her accent, the girl and her mother probably lived in London."

"In London? Oh, maybe she knows *my* mother!"

Phoebe reached down and gave Helen a hug. Her niece's ever-present longing for her absent mother was a constant source of pain for them both, and it fomented a simmering resentment in Phoebe's chest. She would never understand Louise's utter neglect of her daughter. Never. "I'm afraid it's not likely they know one another, sweetheart. London is a huge place, you see, as big as a hundred Swansfords. Maybe even a thousand."

"A thousand?"

Phoebe nodded. "Say, how about a piggyback ride down the hill?" Anything to distract Helen from the subject of London and a mother who never came to visit.

Izzy didn't come for apple tarts the next day, much to Phoebe's disappointment.

"I'm glad she didn't come," Helen said as she licked the sweet residue of a tart from her fingers. "She's mean and I don't like her."

"What she *did* was mean. But I'm guessing she's not always mean. It's probably just that she doesn't have any friends around here."

"I don't have any friends and I'm not mean."

"You have me."

Helen giggled. "That's different. You're my aunt." Then her face puckered in a thoughtful frown. "I wonder if *she* has an aunt like you."

Phoebe shrugged as she finished off her own tart. "Izzy seems like a very lonely little girl. Maybe all she needs is a friend or two."

Helen wrinkled her nose. "Not me, though."

Phoebe let the matter drop, but the idea did not go away. Izzy and Helen were alike in more ways than one. Both natural born and likely to suffer for it at the hands of other children. Though the children of Swansford only repeated the words they heard from their parents, they were words with the power to hurt a sensitive child like Helen, and to continue hurting her long after they were said. That's why Helen hated going to school in Swansford, and why Phoebe had taken over educating her.

Two motherless girls, scorned by their peers. Despite the fact that one had grown up too tough and the other a little too sheltered, they might each be precisely what the other one needed.

Perhaps she should approach Lord Farley on that matter, she thought as they made their way to Swansford the next morning. It was a misty day with fog hunkered down in the hollows and low spaces between the hills. As they passed Nester Hill, Phoebe stared down the road that led to the three-story limestone edifice at the center of Farley Park. But the memory of the viscount's stern face put an immediate end to that foolish idea. With an effort she turned her attention to the widening path before her. She was better served staying strictly out of Lord Farley's way. No doubt he had a proper governess or nurse, or some other personage to attend to Izzy.

"Hurry, Helen," she called to the child as Helen chased after Bruno, who scampered after a yellow butterfly. "Mrs. Leake likes to get the eggs early, before all the shoppers have been and gone."

In the neatly stocked store, Mrs. Leake sat on a stool working a column of figures in her ledger book. But she put the battered book aside when she spied Phoebe and Helen. Waving Phoebe over, she distracted Helen with a hard butterscotch candy.

"Is it true?" she asked Phoebe without preamble. "You accused Lord Farley's child of stealing from you?"

Phoebe set the egg basket down on the waxed wood counter. "She *did* steal from me. I caught her in the act. But I expect to eventually—"

"But surely you didn't really march her home and demand restitution from him?"

"No. That is, I didn't demand anything. And I didn't *march* her there. I simply returned her home. That's all. Indeed, he was out searching for the child even as we approached the park. Where are you hearing these things, anyway?"

Mrs. Leake sat back on her stool. "That's neither here nor there. I'm just relieved to know you haven't taken complete leave of your senses." Then before Phoebe could respond to that remark, the shopkeeper leaned forward, a conspiratorial gleam in her eyes. "It's all over the countryside, you know, about those children of his."

"What about them— *Children?* Are you saying he has more than the one?"

"Indeed. That tough little Londoner and," her voice lowered a notch, "a dark-skinned baby. Both of 'em natural born," she added with a knowing nod.

Phoebe pursed her lips. So she was right about that. But Mrs. Leake must have forgotten to whom she was speaking, and Phoebe was not above reminding her. "I'm reasonably certain that it's not the children's fault who their parents are."

At once Mrs. Leake's leathery cheeks turned pink. "Gracious, I'm sorry, child. You know I don't hold it against Helen what that wild sister of yours did. Why, everybody knows that Helen is the sweetest little thing in the world."

"Yes. She is."

"And it's all to your credit, your good influence upon her. You raised your niece right, not like that light-fingered guttersnipe at Farley Park. You should hear the tales coming from the Park. Why, one of the upstairs maids has quit her position, and she told us that the nurse they brought from London was sent packing yesterday."

She pressed a finger to her cheek. "Or was it the day before?"

"Good Lord."

"The way I hear it, the baby wails all night, and the other one runs wild all day." Mrs. Leake shook her head. "Seems the gossips ran Himself out of London. That's why he's here after so long away from the district."

"I doubt the gossips shall run him away from here," Phoebe said with some asperity. But the irony of her remark was lost on Mrs. Leake. Though she was at heart a kind person, Mrs. Leake had a strong need to know everyone else's business. It probably came of running the main store in town. The men gossiped at the pub or the blacksmith's, while the women gossiped at Leake's Emporium. And right now the primary subject of gossip was Lord Farley. Phoebe supposed she ought to be glad there was someone in the district whose bad behavior exceeded even Louise's.

"How's a bachelor to raise two little girls?" Mrs. Leake went on. "That's what I'm wondering. And what's he intend to do about that little thief he's thrust into our midst?" She broke off when the bell over the door tinkled. With an innocent air and lips clamped tight, she commenced scrubbing the already spotless countertop.

A man entered the shop and, removing his hat, approached them. He gave Phoebe a nod, then addressed Mrs. Leake. "Good day, mum. I'm up from Farley Park with a notice from Himself. He asks if you would be good enough to post it in a conspicuous location."

He handed a sheet of paper to her, and after she scanned it, she nodded. " 'Twill be my pleasure. Be sure to tell your master that Mrs. Leake is happy to post any notice he should like. Anything at all."

"I will, mum. Thank you, mum."

Once he was gone, Mrs. Leake turned, and with an expectant look on her face, thrust the notice at Phoebe.

He needed a governess; and if she was to keep her farm, she needed a better income than eggs, cheese, and honey brought in. Should she apply for the position? And if she got it, would she have to live at Farley Park? She certainly didn't want to do that.

But if she didn't pay her land taxes, she'd have to sell out and move to town, and she didn't want to do that either. Better to be someone's governess, she decided, than someone's laundress or kitchen drudge—although being governess to Izzy, trying to teach her and mold her into a proper young lady, sounded like a horrendous undertaking.

Then again, her mother hadn't exactly been easy to take care of. Maybe she should take the position.

"You're getting ahead of yourself," she said out loud.

"What?" Helen asked as she dangled a bit of rope in front of Bruno. He leaped and snapped to get it, without much success. But it was a game he and Helen played endlessly, and it made Phoebe smile.

"Bruno is getting bigger already," she said, changing the subject.

"Not as big as his other brothers and sisters. Martin let him play with them today."

"Bruno may not be the biggest of the lot, but I'm sure he's the smartest. Aren't you?"

Helen grinned, leaping along like the happiest child in the world. "Yes, he's the smartest puppy of them all!"

They skipped and danced the rest of the way home, pushed by the wind and barely beating the onset of a fierce spring storm. Only the next morning when Phoebe went out to milk the goats did she discover the three-legged milking stool gone.

"Izzy!" she exclaimed under her breath. She fumed the whole while she milked the goats on her knees. Not

Governess required to supervise the care of
two children.
References required. Inquire at Farley Park.

Mrs. Leake raised her brows until her forehead was as furrowed as a newly plowed garden plot. "Didn't I say so? The nurse is gone and the household is in an uproar." She harrumphed, then added, "Seems to me they're more in need of a gaoler. You know, Phoebe, you're the most qualified person to take on that position. Such a good, God-fearing girl. And a natural-born care-taker. That's what I always said. First your ailing father, then little Helen and your mother too. And then there's all the fine manners your mother taught you, the book-learning and the way she brought you up so proper and la-di-dah."

She rummaged around for a tack and hammer. "Your mother might not have been the easiest person to know— God rest her soul. But no one can argue that she was the closest thing we had to a proper lady around here— at least since the young lord's mama moved away."

She tacked the notice onto a post, then turned and faced Phoebe directly. "You're already teaching Helen at home. Why not take on Lord Farley's young ones as well? It's no secret around here that you could use the money."

So everyone knew about her financial difficulties. Phoebe wasn't surprised, but it was humiliating all the same. Still, Mrs. Leake's suggestion haunted Phoebe all the way home. Her, supervising the care of two children? A viscount's children?

She'd never before considered taking on work as a governess. Then again, there'd never been such a posi-tion available in the neighborhood before.

But there was now.

only had the girl not returned the other items, she'd stolen yet again.

They managed the chores in record time, and the morning shadows were still long as Phoebe stormed toward Farley Park, Helen hurrying to keep up. It was less than three miles, yet until two days ago Phoebe had not taken this route in many years. There'd been no reason to do so. Her meager acreage bordered the Farley properties, but the forest kept the Farley retainers away from her cottage on windswept Plummy Head.

Somewhere in that forest, well hidden, no doubt, were her pilfered possessions. But why would Izzy choose such oddments to steal? A blanket and a dog she could understand, and perhaps even the basket. But the bench and stool and bucket were household items. Of what use could they be to a child—

She sucked in a sudden breath. Of course! Izzy made no secret of her disdain for her father and how he'd stolen her away from her old life. Could the child be trying to set up a household of her own, a secret hideaway where she could live—or thought she could live— all on her own?

The idea was so touchingly sad that it doused every bit of Phoebe's fury. What an unhappy little girl. Nonetheless, Phoebe could not allow such thieving to go on. It wasn't good for Izzy, and besides, Phoebe needed her things back. She used them every day.

She glanced around her as they went on. What sort of place would a little girl like Izzy choose as her hideaway? Somewhere well hidden. And near water. Perhaps along the rocky little beck that ran eventually into the river. Or perhaps near Wildfen Pond.

Wherever, Phoebe vowed that before the day was out she would reclaim her goods, with or without Izzy's assistance.

The grand house at the center of Farley Park looked still and peaceful as Phoebe and Helen crested the hill. The rare March sunshine glinted off the triple row of windows that faced the eastern horizon, and a handful of horses grazed a sloping meadow to the west. A pair of swallows circled overhead, but Phoebe saw no people anywhere. No one in the walled garden, no one in the kitchen plot. Beyond the house, even the stables appeared deserted. If not for the single plume of smoke rising from the kitchen, Phoebe could have believed the house empty—or at least still asleep.

But as they neared the forecourt, she heard a shout, followed by a crash—pottery smashing upon stone, she would guess. Directly after that came the high-pitched wail of a baby.

They were definitely *not* asleep at Farley Park.

Feeling as if she were eavesdropping, Phoebe hesitated. Front door or back?

Front, she told herself. She was an aggrieved party come on important business—at least it was important to her. "Wait here by the fountain," she told Helen. "This shouldn't take long." Then up the wide stone steps she went, and gave the door knocker three smart raps.

Four minutes and twelve additional raps later, the door jerked open.

"I've come to see Lord Farley," she said to the maid who answered the door. Then she just stared. The maid was a disheveled mess, with her hair falling down from her mob cap and a big green stain on her apron.

"He's gone for a walk," the girl said, wiping her eyes. "Around back, I believe." Then she shut the door—slammed it, really—leaving Phoebe aghast at her rudeness.

What in the world? The situation here was worse even than Mrs. Leake had described.

But she hadn't come this far to be turned away. So around the house she strode, her boots crunching the gravel as she wondered where Viscount Farley had gone off to on foot when his household was so obviously falling apart.

The baby's wails, weaker, but just as heart-rending, led her to him. At first when she came around the clipped yew hedge, Phoebe just stopped and stared. He was so tall and broad-shouldered, and in his grasp the baby seemed tiny. Or maybe it was the other way around: the tiny child made him appear bigger than she remembered.

In any case, it was a profoundly moving sight. Phoebe had never seen a man playing at nursemaid before. To her best recollection, her father had never once cradled the baby Helen in his arms like that. He'd certainly never shown any particular attention to her or Louise.

But here was the high-and-mighty viscount once again in his shirtsleeves, with his hair mussed and the shadow of a beard on his face, pacing back and forth on the gravel walk, jiggling a dark-haired baby on his shoulder and singing some song that didn't sound like any lullaby she knew.

". . . the ships sail in, the ships sail out; they never bother me . . ."

His voice was hoarse and tired, and whether he was in tune, she couldn't determine. Still, the sound of his singing to the child loosened some tight little knot in Phoebe's chest. He was trying so hard to comfort the unhappy child. From the weary look of him, he'd been trying a very long time.

"May I?" she asked, approaching him with arms extended.

He looked up, startled, then obviously relieved. Without a word he passed the baby to her and sagged back onto the stone half-wall that encircled the herb garden.

"She won't sleep," he said, rubbing one hand across the back of his neck. "She won't sleep more than an hour or two at a time, and unless you're walking her or jiggling her, she cries."

Phoebe did a quick check but the baby wasn't wet. "Does she have a rash? You know, on her bottom?" Not that she actually expected him to know.

"No. Nor any fever. The doctor has been out twice to check her and he says she appears healthy. He reckons it's the change of climate."

Phoebe shook her head at that. "Is she eating well?"

"She acts hungry. But then she fusses."

Phoebe hugged the baby, a sweet-smelling little armful, and nuzzled her silky hair. "What's her name?"

"Leya."

"Leya." Foreign sounding. But it suited the olive-skinned little girl. "Hello, Leya," she crooned to the momentarily silent child. "Aren't you the beauty."

At once Leya's face screwed up. But before she could let out a fresh wail, Phoebe turned the child in her arms, balancing Leya's backside against her hip, and holding her steady with a snug arm across her belly. To her relief, the wail never came.

Continuing to walk back and forth, Phoebe smiled at Lord Farley's amazed expression.

"What did you do?"

"My niece was a fussy baby, but she always felt better when I held her like this. Leya's stomach is probably upset and the pressure of my arm eases the pain. What has she been eating?"

He stood and began to walk beside her. "I don't know. Some sort of gruel. Mashed vegetables. But mostly milk."

"Cow's milk?"

"I assume so. Isn't that what you're supposed to give

them—I mean if they don't have a mother to . . . ah . . . to tend to those things?"

She looked up at him, amused by his embarrassment to be discussing "those things."

He had extended his hand to Leya and the child now held fast to his finger. At once a quiver of heat shot through Phoebe, unexpected and unnerving. He was too close. That was the inane thought that went through her head. He was too close, and though this was his baby and he had every right to be touching her, it felt as if he had somehow touched her too.

Wholly undone, she stopped and handed Leya to him. "Here, you try it."

In the transfer his hand grazed hers, and again she felt that startling frisson of awareness. Sucking in a sharp breath, she stepped back, averting her eyes from him to his child.

For a moment the baby looked ready to cry again, but once Lord Farley had her positioned just right, she instead let out a little sigh. As if Leya knew the source of her relief, she stared straight at Phoebe, her baby eyes wide and unblinking. And just that fast, Phoebe fell in love with her. She was so perfectly, exotically beautiful with her blue-gray eyes, golden skin, and shining ebony hair.

Leya's gaze was so trusting, so accepting. So content. Life had not yet tarnished her soul and, God willing, it never would.

"Once again I find myself in your debt, Mrs. Churchill," Lord Farley said, drawing her attention back to him. His smile, overlaid so sincerely upon his weary, rough-hewn features, disoriented Phoebe. For a moment she could only stare at him. Against the stubble of his unshaven face his teeth gleamed too white. The chest hair that curled up at the loosened throat of his shirt made him look elementally masculine. Indeed, his disheveled appearance made her feel strange, in a way she'd never experienced—small and feminine and vulnerable, though that made no sense.

Then an echo of her mother's strident voice came to her, reminding her that under no circumstance should a woman ever allow herself to be alone with a man dressed only in his shirt sleeves. Not even if it *was* perfectly innocent.

Phoebe knew she must state her business, then be gone from here.

So, pulling herself together, she crossed her arms and frowned. "You are hardly in my debt, Lord Farley. However, I did come here today on an urgent matter. It seems Izzy has struck again."

"What?"

"She stole my milking stool—at least I assume it was she."

His expression fell from gratitude to frustration. "Bloody hell," he muttered.

Needing to find some flaw in him, Phoebe latched at once onto that. "If you curse in the presence of your children, you cannot fault them when they echo your words back to you. I believe Izzy's language is foul enough already."

Even to her own ears she sounded stiff and prissy. Stifling a groan, she realized that it was worse than that. She sounded just like her own stern, fault-finding mother.

To his credit Lord Farley didn't respond to her criticism. Instead he began again to walk. After a moment, she followed.

"I don't know what to do with that girl. She hates me and all the staff too. No matter what we ask of her, she does the opposite. She curses, she refuses to bathe. She screams and breaks things. She runs away and—as you know—she steals anything that isn't tied down."

Despite her wariness of the viscount and the awkward circumstances, Phoebe's tension eased a bit. At least he was trying to do right by his children.

She tucked her chin in and took a steadying breath. "At the risk of appearing too bold, could I ask how long you've had your daughters with you?"

He glanced at her, then away. "I've had Leya several months. But Clarissa . . . six weeks or so."

"I see. Might I inquire further about their mothers?"

He smoothed his hand over Leya's hair, then kissed the dark crown of her head. "Leya's mother died when she was two months old. Clarissa's—" His jaw stiffened. "Clarissa's mother is a—" He broke off. "She lives a life unsuited to raising children." A muscle in his jaw flexed. "She used Clarissa to . . . to run errands, shall we say. To tend her needs and mind her other children."

"I see," Phoebe murmured, though she didn't. Not entirely. But whatever those "errands" were, they must not have been appropriate for a girl only ten years old. "So . . . So Izzy has other siblings?"

"Yes. And Izzy is her old name, from her old life. I want her to be called Clarissa now."

Phoebe sighed and wove her fingers together. "What you're doing for them seems commendable, Lord Farley. But I wonder if you might be trying to accomplish too much too fast with the girl."

"What I'm trying to do is save her from the wretched sort of life her mother chose."

"Yes, and that's most commendable. But can't you see how frightened she is?"

He snorted. "Frightened? I've yet to see that child frightened of anything. Even the threat of a good switching doesn't faze her."

She gave him a sharp look. "You said you'd never laid a hand on her."

"I haven't." He stopped and turned to face her. "I'm not generally inclined to beat children, Mrs. Churchill. But so far nothing else has worked—and now you tell me she's stolen yet again."

They stood at the far end of the clipped lawn, where the gravel walkway gave onto a mowed walking strip through the rougher meadow. Though the man managed to rattle her with just the force of his eyes, Phoebe tried to ignore that. How could she be frightened of a man who held a happy, babbling baby in his arms?

But there was more to him than merely the struggling father, she reminded herself. He might be trying to do right by his daughters, but he'd not behaved so nobly with their mothers. The very thought of what he'd obviously done with each of them turned her mood black. But then, hadn't her mother warned her incessantly about just such self-indulgent male behavior?

Determined not to dwell on him or his wild past, she plucked a long stalk of grass, waved it in front of Leya, and steered her thoughts back to the matter at hand. "I've been trying to figure out why Izzy would steal from me again, when she knows I would guess she'd done it. I'm beginning to think—" She shook her head. "It will sound perverse, I know. But I wonder if she *wanted* me to come back here and accuse her."

"Why would she want that?"

"I'm not sure. Perhaps because I'm the first person who has called her Izzy? After all, that's the name she knows herself as. Try to put yourself in her place. She's lost every aspect of her old life. As bad as it may have been, it nonetheless was all she knew. Is it asking too much to allow her to keep the name she wants?"

He frowned, but he didn't argue.

"Also," Phoebe went on, "I think it may have confused her a bit when I tried to befriend her by inviting her to my farm. And intrigued her. Actually, I was quite disappointed that she didn't come."

"You think she wanted to come?"

"Perhaps."

He heaved a sigh. "Perhaps. One thing I've learned: the child is smart as a whip despite having no education to speak of. You're right. She knew you'd come charging over here when your milking stool went missing. The question is, why did she want you to come?" Again he sighed. "As you can tell, I've reached the limits of my patience with Clarissa. With Izzy," he amended, a wry twist on his lips. He jiggled the baby who seemed content on his hip. "You seem to have solved Leya's problem. Maybe you're right about Izzy too."

He smiled at her then, a half-smile, really. But there was a warmth in his clear blue eyes that touched her.

At once Phoebe averted her gaze. Just that easily he made her far too aware of him, too aware of the physical nearness of him. It was unsettling and confusing and she didn't like it one bit. She was grateful when he started back toward the house.

"Let's find Izzy," he said, "and see what she has to say for herself."

It was only then that Phoebe remembered that she'd left Helen and Bruno beside the fountain in the forecourt. And only when she discovered them gone, did she realize what a dreadful mistake that had been.

CHAPTER 3

Phoebe's brow creased in worry as she scanned the empty forecourt. "It's not like Helen to wander off alone."

"Izzy," Lord Farley muttered. "Damn that child."

Phoebe didn't bother to rebuke him for the oath this time. She felt like echoing him herself. This was Izzy's doing. Still, she couldn't believe that Izzy would go so far as to harm Helen. "Maybe Bruno ran off and Helen followed him."

"Or maybe Izzy took him again."

Still holding the baby, he strode to the front door, shoved it open, and bellowed for someone named Benson. Within seconds a stocky man arrived, pulling on his coat as he shuffled up. "Here. Take Leya," Lord Farley ordered. "Like this." He positioned the baby as Phoebe had showed him in the man's reluctant grasp. "Alert the staff that Izzy and Mrs. Churchill's daughter, Helen—"

"She's not my—"

"—have gone missing. Also, a puppy named Bruno. And whoever you give Leya to, have them hold her just this way." Then, still in his shirt sleeves, he strode toward the far side of the house and the myriad outbuildings beyond.

After only a moment's hesitation, Phoebe went after him, holding up her skirts as she ran to keep pace with his long, angry strides.

"She likes the stables. And also the ice-house," he muttered. "Don't ask me why."

"I'm beginning to think she might be trying to furnish a little hideaway of her own, somewhere in the woods near my house."

"I don't understand that girl."

"Nor I. But as you are her father, you must learn to," Phoebe said as they entered the stable.

He shot her a sharp look, causing her to turn away from those disturbingly direct eyes. It reminded her, though, of something she *needed* to be reminded of: that he was a viscount and she a mere farmer's daughter. She didn't need her exacting mother here to tell her that she had no business instructing him about what he should or should not do.

The problem was that she had no actual experience dealing with the nobility. Despite her mother's endless lectures on the proper way to behave in polite society, she'd had very few opportunities to put those lessons to the test.

On the other hand, it was *his* daughter causing all the trouble, not Helen—whom he still thought was *her* daughter. Eventually she would have to disabuse him of that notion.

In the main section of the stable they found no evidence of the children. While he checked the several stalls and the tack room, Phoebe scurried up the ladder to the hayloft. Again she found no children, but there were signs of Izzy's presence in the past. An empty cup. A sheet. A doll and a doll bed.

"Look at this," she called down to Lord Farley.

In a moment he was beside her in the dusty, low-ceilinged portion of the loft. He picked up the doll with her cracked face and faded gingham dress. "If I remember correctly this is one of Sarah's dolls."

"Sarah?"

"My youngest sister."

Phoebe recalled from Mrs. Leake's remarks that Lord Farley had two sisters. Half-sisters. Just as Izzy had a half sister in Leya, and other half siblings through her mother in London.

"Poor Izzy," she said, taking the nearly hairless doll from him. "She must be very lonely. I'm guessing she misses her family, even if they aren't ideal. You know, I'm beginning to think she's trying to create something of her own here, a family she can feel safe with." She looked up at him. "That could be why she took this doll, and it's probably why she tried to take our puppy."

He ran a hand through his hair. "If she wants a puppy she has only to ask me for one."

"But don't you see? To her, *you're* the one who stole her life from her. *You're* the one she's trying to defy."

His eyes held with hers, and even in the dim light of the loft, she saw the anguish that shadowed them. "I can't return her to that god-awful life," he growled. "I won't."

"Of course not. But the two of you can't go on like this. It's up to you to find some common ground with her."

Phoebe stooped to replace the doll in its toy bed. When she stood, he was nearer than before, staring intently at her. "Will you help me?" he asked. "I need a governess. Will you take the position?"

A nervous flutter started in Phoebe's stomach. "I . . . um . . . I don't know."

"I suppose you have to discuss this with your husband. But I can make it well worth your while." He stepped nearer still. "And if you like, you can bring your daughter with you."

"She's not my daughter," Phoebe said as the flutter increased. Then abruptly she turned and started down the ladder. "We'll never find them if we don't look."

"She's not your daughter?"

When they reached the stable floor, it was she who strode ahead and he who followed in her wake. "Helen is my niece, my sister's child whom I have raised."

"I see. Have you other children of your own?"

"I am not wed, my lord." Why did her stomach tighten in a knot to tell him that? "Could we please concentrate on the task before us?"

But he was not to be put off. "You're not wed? So . . . that means you're available for the position as governess to Izzy and Leya."

She sighed. She was very available and she should be ecstatic at the opportunity offered her. Indeed, she ought to agree this very moment before he could change his mind. Here was the answer to her overdue taxes, a way to keep the house and farm, meager though they were.

But something inside Phoebe, some unfamiliar little buzz of alarm, centered deep in the nether reaches of her belly, warned her away from this man. Somehow she knew this would be no simple position in a large household. Not if Lord Farley were involved.

"I . . . I shall have to think about that. Let's find Izzy and Helen first, though, shall we?" For a moment Phoebe expected him to argue further. But though his expression remained sharp, with a little nod he conceded the point.

She had forestalled him, but not for long. In truth, she feared that Lord Farley had only begun to pursue the subject of a governess for his two difficult children.

As they approached the ice-house, they heard Bruno's high-pitched barking. Just beyond the squat, thatch-roofed building, Izzy stood holding the puppy, keeping him away while a weeping Helen tried futilely to take him back.

"He's mine," Helen wailed. "Give him to me."

"I'm not going to hurt him," Izzy swore.

"You're hurting him now!"

"I am not! If you would just stop acting like a baby."

"I'm not a baby!"

"Izzy!" Lord Farley bellowed as they strode up.

Without thinking, Phoebe laid a cautioning hand on his arm. "Gently, my lord. Gently."

At once Izzy jerked around to face them. But whatever alarm the girl felt, she swiftly hid beneath a sneering expression and a pugnaciously tilted chin. She didn't put down the dog, nor did she retreat.

Beneath her hand, Phoebe felt the muscles of the viscount's forearm tense. Then, as if by an act of supreme will, he relaxed. She promptly pulled her hand away, but it didn't help. There had been an odd intimacy to their little exchange, her hand on his arm. She'd sensed his emotions and counseled him, a man—a viscount!—with whom she was barely acquainted. And he'd listened to that counsel.

It was a wholly unsettling experience.

"Izzy," he began again. "You must return Helen's dog to her."

Upon spying the two adults, Helen ran crying to them and buried her face in Phoebe's skirts.

"I wasn't hurting him!" Izzy shouted at her father.

"I didn't say you were. But you can't go around taking things that don't belong to you. And now Mrs. Churchill—Miss Churchill tells me that you've taken—"

Again Phoebe stopped him with a hand on his muscular forearm. "I missed you, the day before yesterday,

Izzy. I was so hoping you'd come up to visit us at Plummy Head."

Izzy's scowling eyes darted from her father to Phoebe. "That's a stupid name, Plummy Head. I didn't see any plums there."

"That's because plums don't ripen until the fall. But that's not why it's called Plummy Head."

The child wanted to ask why. Phoebe could see it on her face, and it gave her renewed hope for finding her own common ground with her. She turned to the viscount, only then realizing her hand still rested on his arm. She snatched it back, but the look in his vivid blue eyes told him he'd noticed the familiarity.

Thank God the viscount couldn't tell how profoundly that simple touch affected her. At least she hoped he couldn't tell. Her heart's pace had trebled, her mind had gone blank as a white canvas, and her mouth felt as dry as chalk.

Thankfully she managed somehow to find her voice. "If it pleases you, my . . . my lord, perhaps Izzy might like to accompany Helen and me back to Plummy Head."

"No," Helen cried, lifting a wet face and horrified gaze up to Phoebe. "I don't *like* her."

"An' I don't like you either, you big blubber baby," Izzy spat right back. "How old are you anyway? Two?"

With renewed weeping Helen buried her face once more in Phoebe's lap, and for a moment Phoebe was torn. Were two children ever more different?

Lord Farley cleared his throat. "Perhaps Izzy and I could *both* accompany you home."

Him? In her simple four-room cottage?

Phoebe's heart renewed its painful thudding against the wall of her chest. How had things spiraled so utterly out of control? This was hardly what she'd had in mind when she'd set off so angrily for Farley Park. All she'd wanted then was her milking stool returned, along with the rest of her purloined goods. But here she was, grabbing a viscount by the arm, forcing unsolicited advice upon him, and becoming entirely too discombobulated by his presence. And now he wanted to come calling at her humble little cottage.

"Um . . . I don't believe that's necessary," she stammered.

"But I'd like to," he insisted. One of his brows arched, as if to say, surely she would not turn him down.

And of course, she could not. "Oh. Well. I suppose, then. That is . . . if you're sure."

"I'm sure." When he finally turned that dark probing gaze on Izzy, Phoebe took a long overdue breath. "So, Izzy," he went on. "What do you say? Shall we escort them home?"

The child shoved a tangled lock of fair hair back from her brow, studying him with a suspicious scowl on her face. "Whyn't you calling me Clarissa anymore?" She sneered the hated name out.

He shrugged. "I know now that I shouldn't have done that. If you wish to be called Izzy, then Izzy it is. So," he continued. "Are we off to Plummy Head?"

She hefted the complacent puppy in her arms. "Can we take the pony cart?"

"The pony cart?"

"I saw it in the stable. Can we ride in it? Can I drive?"

Phoebe slanted a look at the viscount. *Say yes,* she silently willed him. *She's throwing you a little twig of the olive branch, so say yes.*

"Do you know how to guide a horse?"

This time it was Izzy who shrugged, a gesture so similar to her father's that it made Phoebe smile.

" 'Course. How hard can it be?"

"It's not hard at all," he said, strolling up to her. "But a good driver knows how to guide his animal without hurting it. Horses have sensitive mouths, you see." He scratched Bruno behind the ears. "Come on, then. Let's have a look at that cart and harness one of the horses."

Izzy put Bruno down and at once the puppy started off, nose to the ground. Only then did Helen break away from Phoebe to follow him. But all the while she shot black frowns at Izzy.

Lord Farley started for the stables, and after a moment Izzy followed. But at the corner of the ice-house he slowed and looked back. "Do you want to help us, Helen?"

Helen ducked her head and shook it no. But Phoebe had other ideas. "We'll both help. Come along, Helen. Come on, Bruno."

Izzy scowled. "Why does *she* have to help? She's probably scared of horses."

"Am not!"

"Hunh." Izzy broke into a trot. "Then I want to bring Leya too," she demanded. "She hates it here as much as I do."

They made an incongruous group. The viscount, as casual as a farmer with his wide shoulders encased only in his shirtsleeves; Phoebe with her everyday apron still pinned over her plain worsted wool dress. Dirty, uncombed Izzy drove the horse while Helen, looking like an affronted angel, held tight to the squirming puppy. Leya, bright-eyed and gurgling, perched on Phoebe's lap, leaning forward with her stomach pressed comfortingly against Phoebe's arm, chuckling with delight every time the cart lurched through a hole or over a rock.

Phoebe was relieved when they did not encounter anyone on the road that wound around the hill and through a short stretch of woods. The last thing she needed was the people of Swansford gossiping about her and the viscount, especially given her sister's wanton reputation.

On the other hand, it occurred to her that anyone not knowing who they were might have thought them merely a regular little family out for a ride—father, mother, and their children.

Gnawing the inside of one cheek, she turned away from the far too virile viscount and stared off to the east, to where the restless sea lay beyond the last of the green, treeless hills. It gave her a peculiar feeling to think about Lord Farley that way. A peculiar, churning feeling centered low in her stomach.

It was on account of the children, she told herself. She loved children—babies like Leya, angels like Helen. Even difficult little devils like Izzy were lovable if you were patient enough to see beneath their hard-edged exteriors.

Her tumultuous feelings about Lord Farley and his children were perfectly normal for a woman of her age, she told herself, for one day she hoped to have children of her own.

But first you need a husband.

A husband. Mr. Blackstock would certainly agree with that. However, she was no more enamored by the prospects in Swansford than her mother had been, albeit for different reasons. Her eyes darted to Lord Farley, then away. Her mother would certainly have approved of a viscount for one of her girls. But Phoebe dismissed the idea before it could form. Her mother had always had unrealistic expectations for her daughters. But Phoebe knew that a wealthy viscount was beyond the realms of possibility for a country girl like her, even if her mother's estranged uncle had been a baron.

More importantly, though, was the fact that she

couldn't possibly be happy with a man possessed of such a reckless romantic history as Lord Farley.

Searching for a distraction from such thoughts, she turned to Helen who sat crowded up beside her in the open wicker vehicle. "Would you like to hold Leya on your lap?"

Helen's unhappy little face lit up in a brilliant smile. "Oh, yes."

From the front of the pony cart Izzy glared back at them. "Leya is my sister, not yours."

Helen looked up at Phoebe with new tears in her eyes. "But she held Bruno, and without even asking."

Phoebe smoothed the top of Helen's golden head. "You know, it's very hard to share the things we love. You love Bruno; Izzy loves Leya—You do love her, don't you?" she asked Izzy.

The girl scowled and looked away, but after a moment she gave a reluctant nod. Phoebe couldn't help smiling. What a momentous concession! Without thinking, her gaze sought Lord Farley, who stared down at Izzy in amazement. Then he raised his eyes to meet Phoebe's and grinned, and again Phoebe felt that unsettling curl of heat deep in her belly. The situation was turning dangerous.

At once she focused back on Helen. "The point is, Leya will go home with Izzy, and Bruno will stay with us. If you wish to play with Leya today, you must allow Izzy to play with Bruno. And vice versa," she added to Izzy. "Do you know what that means?"

An irritated Izzy slapped the reins to make the sturdy cart horse increase its pace. "It means the crybaby has to let me play with Bruno." She gave Helen a smug look. "I hope Leya wets your dress."

Phoebe sighed. It was a beginning. And at least Lord Farley had conceded the issue of Izzy's name.

As they came up the last rise to Plummy Head she scanned the grounds surrounding her home, the place she'd lived her entire life. It looked as it always did, never changing save as dictated by the seasons.

But today she looked at it with a different eye, trying to see it as *he* might, and in the process, seeing all its shortcomings, just as her mother always had. The slate roof sagged on one side of the chimney; the exposed tails of the roof could bear a fresh coat of paint, as could the windows and doors. The narrow path up to the house was overgrown and rutted with water standing in puddles. The well house needed a new roof, and the lean-to barn was gray with age and had listed to the left ever since that fierce storm last August.

But the garden was neat and orderly, she told herself, as was the orchard. And the early roses beside the front door were greening up very nicely. In the near meadow, Posie and the other browsing goats lent a contented aura to her little farm.

The cottage on Plummy Head might be nothing when compared to the expanse and grandeur of Farley Park. But for all its shortcomings, it was snug and sturdy, the chimney drew well, and she had no reason to feel ashamed. Her mother might have been bitterly disappointed by her reduced circumstances, but Phoebe loved the place, peeling paint and all.

Bruno started barking when he spied his now familiar haunts, and he and Helen jumped down together once Phoebe took Leya. Izzy jumped down too, but Lord Farley caught her by one arm.

"Just a minute, young lady. It's part of your responsibility as the driver of this conveyance to tend to your horse's needs. Where may we water him?" he asked Phoebe.

"I've a pot tied to the well rope. A pot, because my

bucket is still missing," she added to Izzy. "I need it back."

"Yes. What about that bucket?" the viscount asked. "And all the other things you've stolen from Miss Churchill?"

Izzy rolled her eyes. "They're in the woods." She gestured vaguely with one hand. "I don't know 'xactly where."

"You know where," he accused the child.

"Yes. I'm sure she does," Phoebe interjected. "In fact, why don't you go fetch the bucket and the milking stool right now, Izzy, and later I might show you how to use them. I'm sure it won't take you long, and while you're gone I'll make sweet milk and spread some plum jam on fresh bread. It should be ready for you just about the time you return."

Leading the horse, Izzy sauntered to the well without answering. Lord Farley stared after her frowning, with his fists on his hips. "If you're trying to bribe her with jam and bread, I don't think it will work."

"It's obvious your threats haven't proven successful with her. Perhaps my rewards will."

He turned to study her. "Yes, but jam and bread? She had puff pastries with chocolate sauce for dessert last night. Why should bread and jam tempt her when she can have cake and other sweets as soon as she returns home?"

Phoebe gave him an irritated look. "Because you haven't tasted *my* plum jam and bread." Without warning she thrust Leya at him. "I believe your daughter needs her nappy changed."

Phoebe could have groaned as she fled to the kitchen. What was she thinking, bragging about her plain cooking when he had a cook to prepare him whatever he desired? And then to hand the baby to him so waspishly? This was no cloddish farmer's son for her to order about. This was Viscount Farley, the richest landowner in these parts. He was highly educated, a world traveler, and wealthy beyond her imagination. Born to every privilege the English aristocracy offered.

Who was she to treat him so familiarly?

It was only that he rattled her so, with his direct gaze and too casual garb. But that was still no excuse, and she knew it. Resolving not to let him affect her, she busied herself in the kitchen. First she stoked up the fire with two added logs, then she drew fresh goat's milk from a jug she kept cool in the deep water basin. She cut four crusty slices of bread and toasted them as she warmed a small portion of jam.

But as she glanced out the window and saw Lord Farley holding Leya and talking to Helen, her confused emotions rose right back up to torment her. How could she be expected to treat him with the deference his title required if he insisted on acting like an ordinary man? One minute he was Mr. Shirt Sleeves, driving a simple pony cart and in desperate need of her help. The next moment he was Mr. Puff Pastry and Chocolate Sauce, too good for her fare.

Well, just see if he didn't find her bread and jam as good as his snooty old desserts. And if he knew so much about what children wanted, why was he begging her help anyway?

And why are you so angry? another, saner voice in her head demanded to know. The man might know nothing about raising children but at least he was willing to try. Helen's father had never evinced *any* interest in his daughter.

Then again, did Helen's father even know he had a child? Considering Louise and all the escapades she'd boasted of, she might not be certain *who* had sired Helen. Wasn't that a sad and distasteful thought?

Beset by too many conflicting emotions, Phoebe resolved to just deal with the task before her, nothing else. So she pulled the toast back from the hearth and set the slices on a large platter. While they waited for Izzy to return, perhaps she should check on Leya before Lord Farley made a complete muddle of things.

She found him bent over Leya on the cart, struggling unsuccessfully to fasten a fresh nappy around the squealing baby. At least they were happy squeals. Helen sat perched beside Leya, dangling a knot of grass just above the baby's head. Every time she tickled Leya's nose the baby laughed out loud, and so did Helen.

So did Lord Farley.

The deep sound of his laughter rumbled all the way through Phoebe, rattling her nerves and making her stomach knot. It was almost like nausea, except different. Worse.

Suddenly Phoebe understood just how dangerous this man was. He acted like such an ordinary fellow. But in truth he was anything but. He might not put on airs; he might even lower himself in ways few other men would. But that only made him more attractive to her, and that's why he was so dangerous. A simple country girl had no business becoming attracted to a wealthy lord like Viscount Farley. Only disappointment—or disaster—could come of it.

She wrapped her arms across her stomach, hugging her unsettled feelings inside her. She could not let his low laughter affect her, nor his handsome face and easy ways.

But knowing that did little to help her, for she continued to stand there watching as Lord Farley, with some assistance from Helen, finally managed to bundle Leya properly. He lifted the baby up, then after a pause, tossed her high over his head.

Phoebe gasped, but Leya squealed her delight. Helen clapped her hands and giggled uncontrollably. He did it again, laughing along with them, and a third time as well. He only stopped when he heard Izzy's cry from across the yard.

"Don't you hurt my sister!" The little girl charged past Phoebe, tossing the milk stool and bucket down as she ran by.

"But she liked it," Helen said. "Now who's the scaredy-cat?"

"Shut your bloody trap," Izzy shouted, her chest heaving from her exertion.

"I didn't mean to frighten you, Izzy. Here," her father said. "You can hold Leya if you want. And if you like," he added after Izzy took Leya from him, "I can toss you up in the air like that too."

Izzy turned away without answering. That's when he looked over and saw Phoebe. Once more he grinned at her. "So. Is your famous bread and jam ready?"

Phoebe tried not to smile back, but it was no use. Reason was not going to win out over emotion. "It's ready," she answered, feeling color flood into her cheeks. "It's ready."

CHAPTER 4

James watched Izzy grab the goat's udder, then snatch her hand back when the animal turned her head and let out a loud, plaintive bleat. Helen laughed, which drew a scowl from Izzy. But it also seemed to bolster the child's resolve.

She might be a liar, a thief, and the most contrary being he'd ever encountered, but Clarissa Elizabeth Lindford was brave. Adversity seemed to strengthen her determination. If only she could harness that willpower of hers into a more positive direction.

"Not so hard, Izzy," Phoebe instructed. "Bella is an old dear, and she likes to be handled gently."

Like most females. James turned his focus from Izzy to the woman kneeling in the straw beside her.

What was he to make of Phoebe Churchill—*Miss* Phoebe Churchill? Though she spoke with a Yorkshire lilt, there was something in her speech that gave the impression of a greater sophistication than he would expect from a country woman. But it was more than that.

He allowed himself to study her as he hadn't before. As he *shouldn't* do now. But he did it anyway. She dressed like a country woman, in sturdy wool and practical shoes. And her apron was ever-present, pinned at bodice and waist.

Had he ever seen his aristocratic mother wearing an apron? He laughed inwardly at the thought of Augusta, Lady Acton even owning such a common garment. His sister Olivia owned them, and employed them too. But then, for all her success in society, Olivia was perfectly content to be the wife of a Scottish baron, and more than willing to roll up her sleeves and go to work when necessary.

Even his youngest sister, the beautiful and obstinate Sarah, was not above getting her hands dirty—at least she would if her beloved Marsh was involved. No doubt his sisters would like Phoebe and her practical approach to life.

But there was a difference. His sisters might be less fastidious than his mother when it came to running their households, but they were that way by choice. They still had servants at their beck and call.

Judging by the simple cottage and outbuildings that comprised the Churchill home place, Phoebe didn't have that sort of choice. Nor had she ever. She milked her goats, cooked her meals, and tended to all the other chores as well.

His gaze followed the line of her graceful neck, slipping down her slender back to the trim waist and flaring hips hidden by her plain twill skirt. She possessed little and seemed to expect little more. How might she respond to a bit of flattery, a few small gifts, the promise of a quarterly allowance, and perhaps a generous stipend for clothes and the other gewgaws women adored?

His breeches grew tight at the thought and he shifted uncomfortably from one foot to the other. What was he thinking? He could hardly make such a proposition to a respectable woman like her.

Assuming she *was* respectable.

Perhaps he should make a few discreet inquiries.

As if she sensed his thoughts were on her, she looked up and smiled. "She's getting the hang of it."

Fortunately she turned back to Izzy who was diligently shooting short streams of warm goat's milk into a metal pot. But the vision of Phoebe's uptilted face, and that lovely mouth curving in such an artless smile fired James's imagination anew. Though she did nothing overt to entice him, this winsome country girl had nonetheless started an ache in his loins. He ought to banish it, but he could not.

Did she know what she was doing to him?

Unfortunately, he suspected she did not. It would be far better for him if she did. Mothering her niece and his girls might come naturally to her, but flirting with randy young lords did not. It had been wishful thinking to imagine otherwise. No matter how frustrated he felt and how appealing she looked, she was not that sort of woman. He didn't have to make any inquiries to be certain of that.

It was up to him to get his base thoughts under control, and to remember what he *really* needed from this woman. If he really wanted to, he could find female companionship anywhere. But a good governess who could deal with a finicky baby and a belligerent ten-year-old? That was a damned sight more rare. He'd best consider what he needed most from Phoebe Churchill and not ruin matters just because his Prince Charming stood at attention every time she was near.

"I'm going outside. To check on the horse," he added when Izzy's gaze jerked up to him.

"Don't you think Izzy's doing well?" Phoebe asked, staring intently at him. "I think she has a natural talent for animal husbandry."

"Ah . . . Yes. Yes, she does," he agreed, only belatedly understanding her silent message. "You're very good at milking," he said to Izzy. "Very smart to catch on so swiftly."

But the girl had turned away, her skinny back hunched as if to ward him off.

Damn, but he was a clod when it came to this fathering business. Thinking about sex when he should be thinking about his children. Too much thinking about sex—and engaging in it—was how he'd come to have three natural-born children in the first place. If he was to avoid having any more, he'd better keep himself focused on what was important. Phoebe Churchill would make the perfect governess. No more. No less.

"Can we come back tomorrow?" Izzy asked Phoebe a half hour later. The sun had begun its downward arc to the west and it was time for them to return to Farley Park.

James waited without speaking for Phoebe's answer.

"I'm sure your father has better things to do than spend the day here," she finally said when he didn't respond to her pointed looks.

"No he doesn't." The girl didn't even glance at him for confirmation. But James refused to become nettled by her presumption. It had taken only one short afternoon for him to determine that children were Phoebe's weakness. When it came to coercing her to become their governess, Izzy and Leya were his trump cards.

"Besides," Izzy went on. "You're the only one who can keep Leya from crying all the time. She likes you better than she likes all those bitches—I mean witches— I mean grouchy old women at Farley Park." She smiled impishly.

Helen giggled nervously at Izzy's impertinence, but

at Phoebe's stern look the younger girl went quiet. James wished Izzy were half so easy to repress.

"If they're grouchy, I suspect it's because you've given them ample cause to be," Phoebe said.

"But you're not grouchy."

James hid his grin behind a contrived cough. *She's got you there, Miss Phoebe Churchill.*

But Phoebe ignored the child's last remark. "Leya was only unhappy because she had a stomachache. She's going to be much more content now that she'll be given goat's milk instead of cow's. You will make sure to check on that, won't you, Izzy?"

"Oh, yes." Izzy hugged the bladder of goat's milk Phoebe was sending home with them. "Anyone who gives her cow's milk will have me to answer to. But I still want us to come visit again tomorrow."

Tenacious as a bulldog, James thought. He cleared his throat. "I have an idea. If you're interested, Izzy, I could start your riding lessons tomorrow."

The girl eyed him with cautious interest, but not nearly so much enthusiasm as she directed to Phoebe. He went on. "You're old enough to learn how to ride, and perhaps we can come by here to get more of Miss Churchill's goat's milk. Would that be convenient?" He directed that last to Phoebe.

Under Lord Farley's intent scrutiny Phoebe felt a spurt of confusing emotion. Unwonted pleasure; unwonted panic.

She knotted her hands beneath her apron. "Of course you may come. And I would be happy to provide all the goat's milk Leya needs." Then like a goose she just stood there, as gauche and awkward as he no doubt expected a simple dairymaid to be.

He nodded once, then turned away. What else did she expect? She would not let herself weave foolish fairy tales over a man like him when the proof of his indiscreet manner of living stood squarely in front of her.

She and Helen watched as he sat with Leya in the cart and let Izzy once more handle the horse. They waved when he waved, then silently watched as the cart and its passengers made their slow way along the seldom-used cart track up to the main road.

Helen leaned her head against Phoebe's arm. "D'you think Himself will teach me how to drive a cart?" she asked. "And maybe, one day, how to ride a horse?"

Phoebe heard the wistful note in her niece's voice, and wished she could banish it. This was Helen's first real interaction with any man other than Martin and the Reverend Peggerson at the church. Martin was as simple as a child, though, and the vicar was as stern and intimidating as Helen's grandmother had been.

Lord Farley, however, had been kind and gentle with his daughters. Phoebe had noticed; impossible for Helen not to notice too.

"Lord Farley is an important man and probably very busy, sweetheart."

"Yes, but . . . maybe, if I ask very nicely."

"Yes. I think maybe he might. Especially if you tried harder to be nice to Izzy."

Helen wrinkled her nose, then gave a great, put-upon sigh. "All right, I'll try. But she's not very nice to me."

"She seems to be getting better though. Don't you think?"

After a long while the child nodded. "A little."

The next morning dawned raw and cold, with an angry spring storm goading the sea into a frenzied thrashing against the cliffs below the house. For Phoebe the wet boom and crash was as familiar as a lullaby, more wind than rain.

Helen and Bruno stayed indoors while Phoebe tended

the goats and chickens. There would be no laundry today. But that didn't mean there would be no chores. Her winter firewood was nearly used up, which meant she would need a new load from Martin—which meant she would have a lot of sewing to do in exchange.

Perhaps today she could clean out the cupboards so at least that would be out of the way when she tackled the rest of the spring cleaning. And she could start a new batch of cheese.

So she gathered up the egg basket and the milk bucket, and ducking her head against the cold sting of the erratic rain, she hurried across the muddy yard and back to the house.

Inside all was snug and warm, and she and Helen passed the morning in quiet activity. Given the weather, she doubted they would have visitors, and as the day wore on, she became doubly sure.

After their midday meal Helen dozed in the big overstuffed parlor chair, her book forgotten in her lap, while Phoebe turned her attention to the cheese. Rennet, ripening milk, cheese cloth. The pleasantly sour fragrance was like the crashing waves, part of the fabric of her life. Her mother had hated both, as had Louise. As for her father, it was hard to say, for he'd spoken so seldom, and then primarily for utilitarian purposes.

Would Helen grow to cherish the everyday sounds and smells of their simple life? Or would the child one day want to escape, like her mother before her?

Phoebe stirred a spoonful of sour milk into the fresh milk, then fastened a cheese cloth square around the top of the bowl to keep out any stray insects and dust. Outside, the rain had begun in earnest, tapping a lively pattern on the two glass windows, beating more dully on the shutters and door, and making a soft whooshing noise on the thick slate roof.

Phoebe smiled to herself as she wiped her hands, then cleaned off the sturdy kitchen table. Being alone in her own house was still a novelty, a stolen pleasure she reveled in.

Of course she wasn't alone. The sleeping Helen had curled up in the chair near the hearth with Bruno squeezed in beside her. But her little-girl snores and those of the dog only added to the ambiance of the snug cottage. It was a spartan life with few luxuries, but it was safe and secure—or at least it would be, did the threat of their unpaid taxes not weigh so heavily upon her.

Thinking of those taxes led her to considering Lord Farley's tempting offer of a paying position. She should say yes. Why was she so afraid to do so?

She just was. No logical reason, but there were lots of illogical ones. The manly figure he cut, especially upon his horse; his gorgeous eyes which seemed to see far beyond the surface of her skin; his sincere efforts on behalf of his children.

Phoebe muffled a groan. She refused to waste an afternoon daydreaming about a man like him: one she could not have and should not want. So she settled cross-legged on the floor in front of one of the cupboards and went to work.

She'd hardly begun when a sudden bang on the kitchen door jolted her alert. Before she could react, the door swung open, carrying in a gust of cold, wet air, and an equally cold, wet Izzy.

"We're here!" the child cheerfully announced from beneath a red muffler and a dark green oversized rain hood.

Phoebe stood. "We?"

"He's putting the horses in your goat shed," the girl said, thrusting back her dripping hood.

That fast, Phoebe's contentment fled. Lord Farley was here. Why on earth would he ride out on such a dreadful day to come to her simple abode? "Close the door, Izzy, before we all catch our death. Come, let's get these wet things off you."

"I see the baby's taking her nap," Izzy said with a smirk. "I can play with Bruno all by myself now."

Phoebe took Izzy's cape and shook the rain droplets from it, then hung it on a wall hook. "Two points, Izzy. As a visitor, first you knock. Then you wait for the door to be opened rather than bursting in as you did."

"But it was raining and I was cold."

"And second, you ask your hostess before you assume you may entertain yourself with any of her possessions."

Izzy frowned at her and Phoebe braced herself for an outburst. But to her surprise, Izzy composed her face into a pleasant, if forced, expression. "Sorry. *May* I play with Bruno?"

"Yes. Of course you may. Go sit near the fire. Are your feet wet?"

"A little."

"Then take off your shoes and set them on the hearth to dry." She was busy situating Izzy when the second knock came. She froze, crouched before the hearth, when he knocked again and cracked the door open.

"Is anyone home?"

Phoebe drew back when he peered around through the opening. Goodness, she was dressed like a household drudge.

"It's cold," Izzy called. "Close the door."

Then he was in, stamping his feet, shutting out the cold and wet, and filling her cozy cottage with his unfamiliar masculine aura. For a moment Phoebe's head spun. She knelt on the solid floor, and yet still she felt dizzy, as if she might tilt right over.

"Good day, Miss Churchill," he said, when she continued silently to stare up at him.

Somehow she rose awkwardly to her feet, smoothing her skirt and apron—anything to avoid looking at him. How ridiculous was that? "Good afternoon, Lord Farley." At least her voice didn't tremble like her hands did. She knotted her fingers at her waist. "May I take your coat?"

"Thank you." In one easy movement he swung his heavy caped riding cloak off and she reached for it.

That's better. Just remember all Mother's instructions on manners and visitors and small talk and such.

Unfortunately she hadn't counted on the effect of his coat, its lingering warmth and the subtle scent that lifted from it. Wool and saddle leather, horses and rain. But there was something else she couldn't name, something heady and powerful that made her dizzy all over again.

She clutched the cloak to her too long, pressing it to her chest while she tried to catch her breath. *You're acting like a fool!*

As she turned and hung his beautifully cut garment on a peg beside her own plain cloak, she resolved to cease this foolish overreacting to him. The disparity between the two garments summed up the situation so well. They had business to do, that was all. He'd come for milk and perhaps for more insight into raising his children. She was perfectly amenable to supplying both. Beyond that they had nothing in common.

Taking a breath, she turned back to him. "I had quite given up on you both, the weather is so horrid."

"We didn't mind the rain," Izzy said from her place by the fire with Bruno. "I'm used to it. In London it rains all the time."

"Indeed." Phoebe's gaze flitted back and forth between father and daughter. "Tell me, how did Leya fare last night?"

"She slept through the night," Lord Farley answered. He rubbed the back of his neck and gave her a wry smile. "I'd forgotten how good it feels to sleep a whole night through without interruption. Thank you for that. I'm eternally in your debt. We all are."

Pleased by his sincerity, Phoebe tried not to let her smile stretch too wide. "I'm relieved to hear it."

"Such a simple solution to Leya's misery," he said. "May I sit?"

"Of course. Would you like tea?"

He pulled out a chair at the table. "Anything warm will do."

Phoebe turned to the hearth and swung the kettle over the fire. He might need something to warm him, but she most certainly did not. Indeed, her cheeks must be fairly glowing.

"The only problem we had with Leya," he went on, "was when we left to come here. She cried to come with us, but the cook warned about bringing a baby out in such weather."

"The cook was right. And I'm not so certain about Izzy being out either."

"But you don't mind my getting a good soaking?"

She looked up from measuring out the tea. "That's not what I meant."

"No." He smiled at her again, holding her gaze captive this time. "I know that's not what you meant. I'm only teasing you."

It was more than just teasing, though—or it affected her more. Phoebe had never been so aware of anyone in her entire life. He was like a force unto himself, like a powerful wind, unsettling everything in its path. He scattered her wits and her good sense like a spring gale scattering the winter's leftover leaves and grasses.

That wasn't necessarily a bad thing, she told herself. Not so long as she kept a strict control on herself.

So she smiled, then looked back at her task. "Izzy," she called. "Come have tea with us."

It was easier with Izzy at the table with them. "Should I awaken Helen?" Lord Farley asked.

"No. I'll make her a cup later. So, Izzy. How are you occupying yourself? Are you behaving any better?"

Izzy concentrated on her tea, stirring three generous dips of honey into it. "I haven't lifted anything else, if that's what you want to know."

"That's reassuring. I'm enjoying having my bucket and stool back. When might I expect the return of the other things you took?"

Izzy shot her a fierce scowl. "When it stops raining."

"Good. Then perhaps one day you can join Helen and me at our outdoor lessons."

"Lessons?" She'd looked interested until Phoebe mentioned lessons. "I don't need no lessons."

"*Any* lessons," Phoebe corrected. "And yes you do."

Without warning the girl leaped up, overturning her chair with a great clatter. "No I don't!"

With one swift move Lord Farley caught her by the arm. "Izzy! That's no way to behave. Pick up that chair and apologize."

With a jerk the girl pulled the chair upright. But her face was a study in childish mutiny. "I'm not having lessons. I told you I wouldn't an' I meant it."

"What about today's riding lesson?" Phoebe put in, keeping her tone mild.

Izzy shot her a suspicious look. "That's different."

"Really?" Phoebe took a sip of her tea. "I don't see how. And yesterday you had a driving lesson, as I recall. Why not a different sort of lesson tomorrow?"

" 'Cause you mean reading. And ciphering. And all that other stupid stuff that stupid teachers try to cram into your head. Well, I don't need any of it."

Phoebe felt Lord Farley's gaze on her as he awaited her response. But she kept her gaze locked with his daughter's. "You think it won't be any fun. But it will be. Just ask Helen."

"That baby?" Izzy sneered. But instead of running off, she sat down in her chair again. Beneath the sturdy table one of the girl's feet swung back and forth, thumping an agitated rhythm against the chair leg. Above the table she reached for her oversweetened tea and added yet another dipper of honey from the round honey pot.

Phoebe hid a smile. Izzy was intrigued. She didn't want to be, but she was.

For a moment they were all quiet. Outside the insistent rain slackened, and when Bruno stretched, then whimpered to be let out, Phoebe rose to open the door.

"I'll go with him," Izzy said, jumping up and snatching her cloak. Before they could stop her, she was out the door and splashing across the muddy yard after the puppy.

Standing in the doorway watching them, Phoebe didn't realize Lord Farley had come up behind her until he spoke. "Does your offer to Izzy to join in Helen's lessons mean you've decided to take the position as her governess?"

She startled, then forced herself to remain very still. "It's one thing to include the child in our casual lessons, and another thing entirely to step in as her governess. Though I appreciate the compliment you've given me, I don't think I'm adequately qualified for the position."

"Well, I think you are. So does Mrs. Leake down at the store. She specifically recommended you. Besides, every time I watch you deal with Izzy I have all the proof I need."

In her throat Phoebe felt the heightened racing of her heart. He was flattering her and it was working. Still, she demurred. "I couldn't possibly act as governess to Izzy and still manage my farm." *I couldn't possibly be in the same household with a man like you all day.*

"With the salary I'm prepared to pay, you can afford to hire a maid or even a farm worker. Please, Phoebe. Miss Churchill," he amended at her quick look of consternation. One of his hands curled around her arm, forcing her to face him. "I need your help." He paused, staring steadily into her eyes. "Izzy and Leya need you."

It was a powerful plea, playing to every one of her weaknesses. Between the heat of his touch, his familiar use of her given name, and the entreaty in his mesmerizing eyes, Phoebe could hardly catch her breath. And hanging over all was the irresistible temptation of finally having a reliable income.

On the other hand, however, there was his reputation with women to consider. His shameful reputation. "I . . . I can't," she whispered. Why was she whispering?

"You can," he said, his blue eyes dark with insistence. "You offered to let her take lessons here with Helen. How is my request so different?"

Because it is, she wanted to say. Only how to explain it? Fortunately Helen's sleepy voice piped up behind him. "Phoebe?"

At once Lord Farley released her arm and stepped back, and with the break of his hold Phoebe gulped in a huge breath of air—and sanity. This man had the power to convince a woman to do anything, she reminded herself. Today she'd nearly agreed to work for him. If she did that and crossed paths with him on a daily basis, what else might he convince her to do?

She swallowed hard and stared past him to where Izzy romped with Bruno. She had only to look at Lord Farley's by-blow children to know the answer to that question.

She turned to Helen and took her gratefully into her arms. "Hello, sleepyhead. Look who's come to visit."

Helen peeped, shy and rosy, from her burrowed place in Phoebe's skirts. "Hello." She gave Lord Farley a sleepy smile. "Did you bring Leya with you?"

"I'm afraid it's only Izzy and I today. But you can come visit Leya any time you like," he added, shooting a glance at Phoebe.

Not fair, she wanted to scold him. Not fair at all.

Helen raised her head. "Izzy?" Craning her neck, she peered past Phoebe, and when she spied her nemesis, she stiffened. "She's getting Bruno all wet. And all dirty."

"Now Helen, Bruno needed to go outside. You should be proud of him. He stood by the door and whined, just like you've been teaching him to do."

Helen pulled away and stood on the edge of the stoop, halting when the rain began to pelt her. "Bruno. Bruno!"

Izzy looked up, but Bruno didn't.

"Bruuunooo!"

Lord Farley sidled through the doorway, brushing against Phoebe as he did. "I'll get him, Helen. Wait here."

Helen's anxious gaze followed him and only when he scooped up the dirty pup did the child's narrow shoulders relax. "He's nice," she said. "I like him."

"Yes. So do I," Phoebe murmured. *Too much.*

Izzy was exuberant once they all returned to the house, as much to taunt Helen as anything else, Phoebe speculated. While the girls squabbled in the parlor over drying off the little dog, Phoebe quickly filled the bladder with fresh milk. Of course, the viscount followed her into the kitchen.

"You're the right person to teach my children," he said, taking up right where he'd left off. "I'll pay you eight pounds per quarter, I'll provide you and Helen each a comfortable room at Farley Park, and I'll have the schoolroom there refurbished—whatever you might require."

"I couldn't live at Farley Park. What about my goats and chickens? My garden?"

"You can continue to live here or move into a room at Farley Park. And you can spend whatever amount of time you like in either place. Teach the girls there, teach them here. Just say that you'll take the position, Miss Churchill. We can work out the details later."

In the end she gave him the only answer that would hold him off. "I'll think about it. That's all I can promise."

"That's all I want." But as she turned away, Phoebe could swear he added, "For now."

CHAPTER 5

That night it stormed. The wind howled around the windows, the rain pelting at the ancient cottage as the sea raged against the beach and cliffs. By comparison, the previous day's dreadful weather seemed almost pleasant.

Helen lasted five minutes in her own bed before a hair-raising bolt of lightning sent her diving into bed with Phoebe. Once comforted, the child swiftly fell asleep. But Phoebe wasn't so fortunate.

It was the storm, she told herself. Noisy, angry—it was impossible to ignore. And Helen, all arms and legs and soft snores, took up more space in the bed than her slight, seven-year-old body should. Plus, Phoebe had the three goats in their rickety lean-to shed to worry about. What if this storm finished off what the one last August had begun, and that poor excuse for a stable finally collapsed?

Then you will have to take up Lord Farley's offer, if only to afford building a new goat shed.

Which brought her circling back to the real reason she couldn't sleep: Lord Farley. Not the offer he'd made her, but the man himself.

She let out a huge, frustrated sigh. Lord Farley. Viscount Farley. James Lindford.

James.

"James." She tested the name out loud. Thunder rumbled its long, low answer.

Annoyed by her foolishness, she twisted around to her opposite side, and tried to punch up her ancient feather pillow. She was not going to think of him as anything but Lord Farley, principal landowner in these parts and a man whom a woman like her absolutely could not weave any fanciful dreams around.

On the other hand, would it really hurt to think about him that way? Not act on it, of course. Only, perhaps, to daydream about him—or rather, a man *like* him.

She sighed. She was twenty-four years old and for the past eight years she'd been as responsible as any housewife, tending to aging parents, to her sister's abandoned baby, and to the farm and its myriad chores. The only thing she hadn't done was tend to a husband's needs.

Nor had she had a husband to tend to hers.

She shivered, a hot little quiver that had nothing to do with the cold, damp night. What *did* a husband do for his wife, beyond the obvious, of course?

She understood the mechanics of sex and procreation. From everything she'd seen of dogs and chickens, goats and even cattle, it looked none too pleasant for the female of the species.

Her mother certainly had made it sound horrid, with all sorts of dire consequences: a man could *ruin* a woman, but not vice-versa; he had his way with you, and a woman had to do her duty. She suffered the pain of the marriage bed. Then came the pain of childbearing, the sickness and backaches and fear. And never forget how many women died upon the birthing bench.

There were a hundred reasons to resist the temptations of lust, and Phoebe's mother had preached every single one of them.

But then, Emilean Churchill's life had been ruined by lust. Louise was the one who'd discovered the source of their mother's bitter discontent, thanks to the village gossips. It seemed their mother had been the only child of the younger daughter of a baron's brother. That much they'd already known. Though Emilean's connection to the peerage was not close, she'd been raised a lady and had expected to marry well.

But a handsome farmer's son had turned her head—though it was hard for Phoebe to picture her taciturn father either young or handsome. Nevertheless, in a moment of youthful indiscretion, Emilean's life had been forever altered. Forced to wed, she'd moved with her new husband into his parents' small cottage on Plummy Head, a refined and educated young lady living what she considered the coarse life of a rural peasant.

Of course, the Churchills weren't peasants. They'd owned their farm free and clear since the Civil War. But to Emilean, they'd been peasants and she'd never bent enough to see them any other way. Her life's goal since then had been to marry her daughters to men of better society than her own husband. So she'd adhered to the strictures of her own childhood and applied herself to the education of her girls with a vengeance. No rule was too minor to be ignored, no infraction too insignificant not to require prompt punishment.

And no young man was allowed anywhere near her daughters. Lustful, deceitful villains all. That's how she saw them.

Phoebe had tried hard to please her mother, and for a while so had Louise. But Louise had swiftly grown too beautiful to escape the notice of the local young men. With her lush figure and mane of golden hair, she'd attracted men like the beacon fires on the coast attracted smugglers.

The more they'd come around, the harder Emilean had preached, and the wilder Louise became. Phoebe had been fourteen when her sister ran off with a ship's captain, and sixteen when Louise returned to deliver a tiny infant into her mother's care.

That's when the bleakness had settled in earnest upon the Churchill cottage. The bleakness and shame and silence.

Again Phoebe shivered and rolled to her other side. She pulled the heavy wool blanket up to her chin. The problem was, despite her mother's bitter denunciation of men and their vulgar, lustful ways, Phoebe had heard enough talk from other sources to know that some women enjoyed the company of men. Her sister obviously did. On her last visit Louise had dropped all sorts of hints about the private goings-on between men and women, laughing at Phoebe's shocked blushes and embarrassed curiosity.

Just to remember Louise's ribald stories started the knot in Phoebe's stomach churning, sending a wave of heat through her. She turned over again and thrust the blanket down from her chest. Unfortunately, it wasn't only Louise's frank words that were heating her; rather, it was Lord Farley. Lord Farley and her overactive imagination.

But why was she having such a foolish reaction to such an unobtainable man?

She hadn't reacted so when Osmund Shepherd had kissed her on market day three years ago. Then she'd been more worried that he might want to marry her, and how was she to decline his offer without hurting his feelings? He hadn't asked, though, and six months later he wed Eliza Perkins, the baker's oldest girl.

She hadn't responded to Thomas LeFarge either, the ship's captain whom everyone knew was smuggling

French wines and laces. He was handsome and dashing, but not her sort at all. Three kisses and no reaction save, perhaps, for mild disgust.

But Lord Farley . . . He had but to look at her with those intense eyes of his, so blue and hot and perversely distressing—

She kicked the blanket off her legs and lay in the cool blackness of her attic bedroom and let Lord Farley's image play across her mind.

James . . .

If only he were an ordinary man, a farmer, say. He certainly had the shoulders and arms of a man who hefted hay bales and handled dray animals. But he was too worldly for a farmer.

A solicitor, then. After all, he was educated and well read with the sharp gleam of intelligence in his eyes. But the solicitors she knew were fussy sorts, mired in detail, and pasty-looking from long hours spent indoors, bent over their desks.

Somewhere between an obscenely masculine farmer and a keenly intelligent solicitor. Not a merchant. That seemed too mundane. Perhaps a bailiff?

She curled onto her side. A bailiff. Yes. The overseer of a large estate which required he be an expert horseman and well read, at least on matters pertaining to land management and animal husbandry. He would know about managing people too—servants and tenant farmers and field laborers. If a bailiff were to wed he would want a woman of some refinement and education, but who also knew about farming. Someone who loved living in the country.

She would make the perfect wife for a bailiff.

If he were a bailiff.

Only he wasn't.

Lord Farley was a lord. A viscount. A peer. A man who could have his pick of women from the highest strata of British society—and the lowest strata, if what he implied about Izzy's mother was true.

A woman like her, set somewhere in the middle of his wide-ranging tastes in women, had no business yearning after a man like him.

"Lusting, you mean."

She cringed to speak the words out loud. But there was no other explanation for this hot sleeplessness that plagued her.

Remember Mother and all her warnings.

Except that her mother could have been happy with the fruits of her personal lust if she'd just allowed herself to be.

All right then, remember Louise and her shameful behavior.

But if Louise had focused her lust on one man instead of such a variety, she, too, might have found contentment.

Phoebe frowned into the darkness of her low-ceilinged bedroom, trying to make sense of her mother's troubles, her sister's, and now her own. Lust was a real thing, clawing at the insides of a woman. Directing it upon the right man—the *one* right man—seemed the only solution. And since Lord Farley could never be the right man, it behooved her to restrain this unruly lust that so lately beset her.

But despite her dire warnings and earnest intentions to shield herself from the wicked direction of her secret desires, when Phoebe slept, it was to dream of a lust fulfilled by a sun-browned, shirt-sleeved bailiff of a man. A lust fulfilled in a sweet-scented hayloft, and punctuated by a true and deep-felt joy in the fulfillment.

• • •

They awoke to watery sunshine, a storm-strewn yard, and a partially collapsed goat shed.

Phoebe surveyed the damage. She and Helen could clear the yard of broken branches, and drag off most of the broken boards of the precariously tilted shed. They could sweep away the rivers of mud and replant any uprooted shrubs. She could even put the ladder up against the house to check for loose roof slates.

But she'd have to hire someone to rebuild the goat shed, and she had to do it soon. Though winter was over, there was no guarantee against another storm like last night's blow. Posie, Bella, and Fern deserved some sort of shelter. Short of bringing them into the kitchen, she had no choice but to approach Martin—or accept Lord Farley's offer.

"We're going to town," she told Helen as they ate their morning porridge. "Put on your mourning dress."

At Leake's Emporium, Helen went around back to see the last of the puppies, while Phoebe went inside. A cluster of women looked up when she entered. Their guilty expressions turned to relief when they saw her. "Oh, it's you, Phoebe. Good. Come look at this," Mrs. Leake said. "You need to see this."

The miller's wife and the Widow Watling moved aside to reveal a small stack of newspapers spread open on the store counter. "Here," Mrs. Leake said, stabbing a finger at an article set off by a decorative border. "And here. And here." She flipped to several other issues. "My newspapers came last night, the monthly bundle I always get from London. But I didn't look through them till this morning. I tell you, I could hardly digest my breakfast when I read it."

Phoebe scanned the articles, a series of gossipy columns in the aptly named *London Tattler*. It was the sort of scandalmongering she normally wouldn't bother with, or if she did read it, she would laugh at the pretensions and foibles of both writer and subjects.

But today she couldn't laugh. Lord Farley—their Lord Farley—had been formally betrothed until just weeks ago. But that betrothal had been broken by his fiancée due to the revelation of the existence of his several natural-born children. Well, only two. But according to the articles, there was good reason to suspect he might have others.

"Now didn't I say there was something odd going on with that young man?" Mrs. Leake asked. "Didn't I? Two such children is bad enough. But more? And then expecting this poor Lady Catherine to raise them in her own household, with her own children, which he'd obviously get on her quicker than an old tomcat gets a litter on a—"

She broke off with a chagrined glance at Phoebe. "Sorry, child. I always forget that you're still unmarried." She patted Phoebe's hand. "It's a good thing you didn't take that position in his household. You didn't, did you?"

"No. No," Phoebe repeated, still in shock. She'd known about Lord Farley's natural-born children. Already she was half in love with both of them. But could there be more?

In truth, however, the children weren't why Phoebe's hands were curled into fists, her short, practical nails pressing into her palms. It was the betrothal.

Though it made no sense, the fact that he'd recently been betrothed to this Lady Catherine Winfield seemed almost a betrayal.

Forcing herself to a shaky calm, Phoebe read the articles again, deaf to Mrs. Leake and her cronies' buzz of speculation. He'd been abroad, come back with Leya,

located another child—Izzy—and then been hounded
out of London.

Part of Phoebe admired him all the more for his te-
nacity in the face of such public censure. But another
part, the stupid, unworldly part, was furious at him. Furious!

But why?

She folded the papers and pushed them away. She
was furious because he'd been engaged. Worse, he'd
been engaged to a beautiful, titled young woman whom
everyone obviously admired. No doubt he'd been madly
in love with her, but she'd swiftly found a new suitor in
that Percival Langley fellow.

Perhaps Lord Farley had retreated to the countryside
not because of his children, but to mend his broken heart.

The very idea made her head hurt. She'd spent most
of last night imagining him falling in love with her,
knowing it was stupid, but recalling every fairy tale
she'd ever read, and believing that maybe such tales
could come true.

But the real truth was that her fairy-tale hero was
probably still in love with the beautiful Lady Catherine.

He had no business affecting her so perversely when
he was otherwise attached!

". . . and the butler's wife's sister told me he had a
letter from one of those Bow Street fellows. You know,
the ones that all the well-to-do hire to investigate whatever they need investigated." Mrs. Leake gave a knowing nod. "Now why would he spend good money on a
person like that? I'll tell you why. Because there's more
children where those two come from. Mark my words.
He'll be running a regular orphanage up at Farley Park
before you know it."

"But they're not orphans," Phoebe said. The three
women swiveled as one to face her. "They're not or-

phans; they have a father willing to see to their needs."

"That's true," Widow Watling said, nodding her gray head. "I suppose there's something to be said for a man who doesn't shirk his responsibilities. On the other hand, that particular man changes women more often than the post coach changes teams. What about the womenfolk around these parts? How can any of our young women be safe from such a man?" Her face settled into lines of disapproval. "Doesn't Mrs. Phillips's eldest girl work over to Farley Park?"

"You know, I believe you're right," Mrs. Leake said. "We'd better warn her to stay strictly away from that man, or before she knows it she'll have a bun warming in the—" Again she broke off with an apologetic look at Phoebe.

But Phoebe was too unsettled to care about the other woman's slip of the tongue. As soon as she could, she abandoned them to their unpleasant gossip and sought Martin in the backyard. She did not want to think about Lord Farley or his fiancée or any of the countless maids in his employ who might be more eager to succumb to his deceitfully appealing manner than she.

All she wanted was her goat shed rebuilt and to pretend she'd never met Lord Farley.

Nor did she want to ponder why she was so upset by any of this news. It wasn't her business, and most of it wasn't even news to her, except for the fiancée part.

To her relief, Martin promised to come up to Plummy Head the very next day to repair her shed, and to bring both his and his mother's mending with him in exchange. Back inside the store the gossip continued about the viscount with a new cast of village women and a new set of opinions. Ignoring them, Phoebe checked the mail basket. Nothing yet from Louise. Then she set off, despite Helen's pleas to linger.

"But there's two puppies left," the child pointed out. "Once they're given away Bruno won't have anybody left to play with."

"He has you now, Helen. Come along."

"But it's not the same. I'm not a dog. If we took another puppy home with us—"

"One is enough."

"But Bruno would—"

"No!"

Inside Phoebe cringed at the overly sharp tone she'd used. Helen was not the source of her bad humor. "I'm sorry, Helen. I'm just a little cross today."

Helen glanced at her sullenly, as if to say, "Cross, just like Grandmother."

What a dreadful thought, yet Phoebe knew she deserved it. As they trudged the wet path home, she made an extra effort to prove herself nothing at all like her never content mother. She made up a song about a colony of toads and pollywogs who lived in a pond called Big Muddy, and charmed her way back into Helen's good graces. And she convinced herself that she was perfectly content with the life she led.

But when they turned the corner past the ancient lichen-streaked boulder that marked one corner of their farm, Phoebe's contentment shredded, like an old burlap sack. Even from this distance she could see that her goats' feeble housing now lay in complete ruin. Only it was not due to the storm, but rather to the efforts of two burly workmen.

They'd already sorted the wood into two stacks, one of straight reusable lumber, the other of splintered, rotten wood. And next to those rested a third stack of freshly cut boards.

"What are you doing?" she cried, hurrying across the muddy yard.

"Don't you worry, miss," the elder of the two men said. "We'll have it back to rights by tomorrow evenin'."

"But I don't understand. Who told you to do this?"

The man grinned. "Lord Farley. The viscount. He said he owed you a debt."

Lord Farley? Phoebe turned away before the fellow could notice the color that flooded her cheeks. She feigned interest in the stack of freshly cut boards while her mind spun in frantic circles. What did Lord Farley mean, he owed her a debt? Even more important, what did the workmen *think* he meant?

While Helen and Bruno watched the workers dig new post holes, then lift up the posts and pack them in with gravel, Phoebe prepared tea for the men and worried. When she was calm again, she brought the tea, honey, and cream out to them.

"No. I must thank you," she said when they expressed their gratitude. "I never thought my meager assistance to his two children would warrant such a generous gesture from the viscount."

"Well, he was clear in his orders to us, miss. He says to us that he don't think your old shed could've withstood last night's blow—and it seems he was right. So he says to us, he says rebuild that shed so no wind can blow it down again."

She gave them lunch and a cold supper as well. By then it had become clear that the new structure would be almost twice the size of the old one. It was equally clear that she must go up to Farley Park and thank her benefactor.

The next day Martin arrived, loaded down with his mending and his mother's, but with no shed to fix in exchange. Instead Phoebe set him to cutting firewood, painting the front door, and watching Helen while she went alone to Farley Park.

She selected an apple-green dress, her favorite, though she usually saved it for Sundays. It was only good manners to dress well when you called on the highest-ranking personage in the district, she told herself. Her mother would certainly have demanded it of her.

But Phoebe suspected her choice was caused more by vanity than proper manners. Lord Farley was accustomed to fine ladies dressed in the most fashionable designs. She wanted him to know that in spite of her limited living circumstances, she'd been raised a lady— and that he must treat her as one.

Upon her arrival, the butler ushered her directly to the master's office, as if he'd been instructed to do so even before she got there. Lord Farley probably expected this call. It didn't help her mood any to know how easily he predicted her behavior. Nor was her confidence bolstered by this first view of the interior of Farley Park. The entrance hall alone was twice the size of her entire cottage, and everywhere her gaze touched was further proof of his wealth and lineage. Portraits, statuary, jewel-tone carpets that silenced their footsteps.

His butler knocked at a heavy door, opened it for her, then closed it, shutting her, a silly, awestruck country girl, in with him, a powerful lord of the realm.

Lord Farley looked up when she entered, then stood. He was garbed in a collarless white shirt, an open waistcoat, and buff-colored breeches. "Good morning, Miss Churchill. I'm glad you're here. Have you come to accept the position of governess?"

"No," she said, taken aback both by his directness and his appearance. Didn't he ever dress in the finery of the peerage? She cleared her throat. "I came here to thank you for sending your carpenters to rebuild the goat shed. How could you have known it was necessary?"

"You forget that I tethered my horse in there. I supposed it hadn't improved in condition during the storm. Do you have any other damage?"

"No."

"Because if you do, just direct the men to it."

Frustrated, Phoebe crossed her arms. "I can hardly repay you for what they've already done. Certainly I can't afford—"

"I don't expect payment."

He came around the desk and that fast the conversation tilted in his favor. If he'd seemed excessively masculine and overwhelming in her small kitchen, he seemed impossibly so here, surrounded by the trappings of his noble title. Once more he smiled at her. "Your advice for Leya about the goat's milk has made life at Farley Park infinitely more pleasant. By comparison, repairing your shed is nothing."

The sincerity of his expression and the appreciation in his eyes made mincemeat of the arguments she'd constructed during her march here. She'd helped him; he'd helped her. Put that way it seemed like neighborliness at its most simple.

But then his eyes flicked over her. Very fast. Very brief. His expression didn't change. But in an instant, everything else did. For no reason that Phoebe could explain, he managed to light an unruly flame inside her—just as he'd obviously done to all sorts of women, all over the world, she reminded herself. The irony was that she was beginning to understand why so many of those women had succumbed to him.

But that didn't mean she would succumb. If anything, it warned her to stay strictly away from him. That meant she couldn't let this man do her any more favors. None. She had only to recall the vicious gossip those newspaper articles had started, and how easily such gossip could transfer to their little outpost of society.

After all, Martin would tell his mother about Lord Farley's carpenters at work on her farm. Phoebe shuddered to think how that fact might be misrepresented. Mrs. Leake liked her well enough. But the woman never forgot that she was Louise's sister. Nor did anybody else in Swansford. Guilty by association. Cut from the same cloth.

No. She had to keep her relationship with Lord Farley as circumspect as possible, and allowing him to rebuild the most important of her outbuildings was simply too much. For years she'd struggled to rise above the stain of her sister's reprehensible behavior. She refused to let this man ruin her good name, even if his intentions were proper—which she wasn't at all certain they were.

"Lord Farley, I appreciate the kindness you intend. But the time I spent with Leya cannot compare to the work your men are doing. I insist on repaying you for their labors."

"Very well. Come look at the schoolroom with me." He advanced to the office door and held it open. "Perhaps you can give me some advice on how to refurbish it."

Too late Phoebe realized that she'd fallen into his trap—his very well thought out trap. Not budging, she stared at him. "I was thinking more of mending. Some task like that."

"I don't have any mending."

"Izzy does."

"I'm purchasing her a new wardrobe, something less fragile." Once more he gave her that smile, the one that unsettled her down to her toes. "Farley Park is a self-sufficient household, Miss Churchill. The only things we're really missing are a nurse and a governess." One of his brows arched in expectation, and she could swear she saw a glimmer of smugness in his eyes.

She jutted out her jaw. "Very well, then." She stalked past him, through the door and out into the hall. "I'll have a look at your schoolroom and give you my opinion. But I cannot be governess here. I haven't the time."

"Whatever you say," he murmured. But she knew he meant the exact opposite. He was humoring her for now, but he hadn't given up his campaign to have her in his employ.

To her everlasting shame, Phoebe felt a perverse thrill. He was a force to be reckoned with, this man with his natural-born children. But so was she. He thought he could waltz back to Yorkshire and command the will of every woman he met. But she was wiser than most women.

He might have won this particular skirmish, but he would never win the battle.

CHAPTER 6

The schoolroom at Farley Park took up the entire end of the top floor of the east wing. With monstrous windows soaring nearly to the ceiling on three sides, it commanded a spectacular view of the Yorkshire countryside. On one side meadows and forests spread as far as the eye could see. On the other Phoebe picked out the stables, laundry sheds, and all the sundry outbuildings required to support an estate the size of Farley Park. Beyond those buildings, a narrow lane meandered to a cluster of whitewashed cottages that were sheltered by a row of elm trees. She picked out the largest cottage, that of Farley Park's bailiff.

Phoebe stared at the sturdy, thatch-roofed structure, made toy-like by the distance. It had its own garden with a fence around it. Clothes hung drying on a line in the backyard.

Twice now she'd spent the night beset by dreams of a tall, handsome bailiff, lovely disturbing dreams that left her restless with unnamable longings. Only those longings weren't really unnamable. In her mind she heard the word "lust," spoken in her mother's scathing tones, tormenting her with shame. Lust was at the root of those forbidden dreams, and lust would bring her to disaster if she let it.

But how was she to silence the nighttime wanderings of her poor, fevered brain?

She turned from the windows only to face an even more distressing view. Lord Farley stood in the middle of the long-abandoned schoolroom, surrounded by the forgotten remnants of his childhood, but studying her, not the schoolroom. His fists rested on his hips—lean hips, as it happened, with powerfully sculpted legs encased in buckskin breeches. That, coupled with the tweed waistcoat, his casual shirt sleeves, and the open throat of his collar, absent of a stock, made him look every bit the hard-working bailiff of her midnight longings.

"What do you think?" he asked.

I think you're seducing me without even trying. And doing a very good job of it.

"I think it's perfect," she said in a strained voice. She turned to circle the room, nodding too vigorously and feigning interest in everything she saw. A globe. A dictionary. An inkwell long dried of its contents. "All it wants is a good cleaning." She picked up a useless, splintered quill pen. "Do you intend to have Leya spend her days up here along with Izzy? If so, you might want to section off a play area for her, and also provide a little bed where she can nap."

"What about books?"

She stiffened her shoulders and took a breath. *Be firm, Phoebe.* "I would leave that decision to the governess you hire. She may be particular in that regard."

He stared at her. She didn't have to look at him to know he was watching her every move; she could feel the power of his eyes.

"Sixty pounds," he said.

She wasn't sure she'd heard him right until she spun around and spied the smug smile on his face. He'd just offered her sixty pounds to work for him? Although he didn't look in the least affected by the princely sum he'd so casually thrown out, Phoebe certainly was. She gaped at him, aghast. "Sixty pounds? Are you mad? You can hire three governesses for a sum like that."

"You would think so. But the woman I have in mind drives a hard bargain."

Phoebe shook her head. "I assure you, if you post a notice in any of the York newspapers with that sum listed, you'll be besieged with eager applicants."

But he only shook his head. "I want you to teach my children. No one else."

Their gazes held and clashed. But though Phoebe wanted to be angry at his high-handed persistence, she perversely felt flattered. How could she not be? Sixty pounds was a veritable fortune. With that sort of income, she could easily afford a maid-of-all-work, as well as a man for the garden, the animals, and general repairs. She could purchase new clothes for Helen instead of always remaking old garments for the child, and she could afford to set aside enough money to one day send the girl to a proper finishing school.

They might even decide to take a holiday down to London, and while they were there, visit Louise. Wouldn't that shock her older sister, to see Phoebe and Helen dressed fine, with money to spare?

But as quickly as that satisfying scenario came, Phoebe quashed it. Helen was far too young to be exposed to how her mother lived.

Then Phoebe blinked and realized how foolish she was to imagine any of those things. If she took the position of governess for Lord Farley's children, then started employing servants of her own and dressing above herself, the gossips would work overtime to link her to her employer in a less than exemplary light— especially should the outrageous amount of her wages ever be disclosed. Everyone in Swansford would be convinced that her newfound wealth was in fact the wages of a sinful life. After all, everyone knew that he'd lived the life of a profligate. As for her, she'd spent the last eight years trying to live down the scandal of being Louise's sister. She couldn't afford any slips in her behavior.

She cleared her throat. "I'm sure you mean your generous offer as a compliment, Lord Farley—"

"It's not a compliment at all. That's not how I do business. Sixty pounds is a practical, well-reasoned offer of employment. Nothing more, nothing less."

"Maybe to you," she said, deciding it was time to speak more plainly. "But to the folk around here it would look considerably worse. To put it bluntly, you have a certain . . . reputation, shall we say. Should you suddenly overpay any female working for you, her reputation would be cast in a less than favorable light."

A crease formed between his brows. "Are you saying the reputations of my housekeeper and the numerous parlormaids and cooks and laundrymaids—well paid, I might add, and several of them single—are now in question?"

"No. Not at all. Everyone knows they've worked here for some time. But a new employee . . . especially a governess."

"Haven't these same people known you all your life? Why should they think any less of you?"

He was determined to be obtuse, wasn't he? Her temper riled, Phoebe planted her fists on her hips. "Why? I'll tell you why. Because my older sister ran away with a man without bothering to marry him first. Because she promptly left him for someone else, and him for someone else. Because my niece, Helen, has no father."

She should have stopped at that. But in for a penny, in for a pound. "And then there's the fact that due to one youthful indiscretion, my mother was forced to marry beneath her. Even so, she always considered herself superior to everyone else in the district. Her uncle was a baron, you see. Despite the fact that her entire family turned their backs on her, she never let anyone in Swansford forget her lofty beginnings. As a result, even after all these years, discussing her daughters' shortcomings gives those people a great deal of satisfaction. I'm sure you'll understand, Lord Farley, why I can't afford to have any shortcomings, real or otherwise."

The silence that followed her outburst fairly echoed in the dusty schoolroom. Somewhere three floors down a man called out, and after a moment a woman answered. The wind carried the piercing cry of a hunting bird. But in the hollowness of the long-neglected chamber, there was only her, Lord Farley, and the ringing silence.

She heard when he took a long breath and released it. "I appreciate your situation, Miss Churchill. But you've met my children; you know they're in dire need of a governess. I assure you, the offer I made you is legitimate."

Phoebe nodded, a tight movement of her head. "I'm sure it was. And I wish you well in locating the right person for them." She took a breath. As far as she was concerned, the subject was done with. "As for the classroom, I can't imagine a nicer location for children to spend several hours a day."

She turned for the door, then stopped. She'd almost forgotten her main purpose in coming here. "Thank you for sending your men to rebuild my goat shed. In the future, however, it would be better if you let me manage my farm as I see best."

To her relief he didn't argue. With head held high and poise intact, Phoebe glided to the door. *Mama would be so proud.*

Her perfect, self-righteous exit was ruined, however, in the barreling form of Izzy. With a clatter of boots upon the uncarpeted floor, the skinny child burst into the room and plowed into Phoebe, nearly toppling them both to the floor.

"There you are," Izzy said, righting herself, then shoving a tangled lock of hair back from her brow. She scowled at her father. "Whyn't you tell me she was here?"

"I'm sure Miss Churchill wasn't planning to leave without visiting with you. Were you, Miss Churchill?" He deflected Phoebe's look with an unrepentantly smug smile.

Ignoring him, Phoebe reached out and tucked the wayward lock behind Izzy's ear. "I was just coming downstairs to find you." A fib, but a harmless one.

"To tell me you're going to come live here and be my governess?" Eyes sparkling with anticipation, the girl danced back and forth from one foot to the other. "Mine and Leya's?"

Phoebe pressed her lips together. Was this the same wild child from just a few days ago? She glanced at Lord Farley but found no help there. He, too, was waiting to hear her reply.

"I . . . You see, I can't live here and be your governess, Izzy. I just can't. But you can still come up to Plummy Head. I'll teach you about the goats and my bees—you haven't seen my beehives yet. And I'll show you how to fish."

Izzy's expression fell. It wasn't the answer she

wanted, and she rounded on her father, glaring at him. "This is all your fault. Whyn't you give her enough blunt so she'll say yes?"

"I did—"

"It's not about the salary," Phoebe interrupted. She caught Izzy by the arms and crouched down so they were on eye level. "It's just that I have other responsibilities."

"You mean Helen. It's all because of her. You don't like me 'cause of her."

"No. I do like you, Izzy. Very much."

But the girl jerked away and sneered. "You're a liar. You only wanted to get your stupid basket and other junk back. That's the only reason you were nice to me!"

"Izzy! That's not true."

"Shut up! Shut up! Shut up!" She darted past Phoebe and dashed out to the stairs. "I hate you, you whore! You slut!" Her shrill cries echoed as she stormed down the stairs. "I hate all of you!"

Phoebe stood there, too stunned to react. From sweet, childish hopefulness to a rage too bitter for any child to feel—and all on account of her.

As if he read her thoughts, Lord Farley came up beside her. "She didn't really mean what she said. If anything, I suspect she feels exactly the opposite."

Phoebe knew enough of children to suspect he was right. Yet still, painful emotions clouded her eyes with tears. Was she being selfish, denying Izzy the comfort she desperately sought and Leya the mothering she deserved? Was she more worried about what the gossips might say about her than what two little girls needed? Three little girls if she included Helen, who could only benefit from the financial security Lord Farley's offer would provide.

Impatiently she dashed her tears away. "The last thing I want is to hurt her."

"I know that, Phoebe."

Through damp eyes she looked up at him, and this time, instead of their differences, what she saw in him was their similarities. They both wanted what was best for Izzy and Leya. He was willing to buck the London gossips for his children's welfare. Was she willing to do the same with the Swansford gossips?

She shivered at the dangerous truth. Though it contradicted years of guarding her every word and action, a small part of her *was* willing.

As if that truth leaped through the air from her to him, his hands caught her arms and turned her to face him. There was something else they both wanted, and the crackling awareness of it stole the air from her lungs. Her eyes grew huge as she stared up at him. They wanted each other. He wanted her as much as she wanted him.

And he was going to kiss her.

Phoebe stood very still, not even breathing, as his head lowered. She'd been kissed before. It didn't mean anything more than what it was, she told herself. A momentary giving in to desire. He wasn't going to ravish her; she wouldn't allow things to progress that far. She only wanted him to kiss her, to discover what it was like and why she wanted it. And then she wanted to kiss him back.

His fingers tightened on her arms. Strong, clever fingers. Warm, possessive fingers. He tugged her nearer; she caught her breath in anticipation.

His eyes were so intensely blue. His lashes seemed too long and thick to belong on a man.

She sighed. He was the man of her nighttime imaginings, just a man, not a peer. Her bailiff. She closed her eyes and all those impossible dreams came true. His lips met hers, so warm and hungry, and they ignited some latent fire deep inside her. Then he shifted and slanted his mouth on hers, and it was both terrifying and thrilling. One of his hands slid up her arm to cup her cheek, a long, slow stroke that worked like a bellows upon hot embers.

She wanted more—more closeness, more of something—and he accommodated her. With an almost imperceptible pressure at the corner of her mouth, his thumb coaxed her lips apart and all at once the fire roared out of control.

She wanted to recoil. She *should* recoil. But even more, she wanted to embrace the fire, to feel the flames lick higher. Already they licked at her thighs and belly and—

"Bloody hell!"

He thrust her an arm's length back. His breath came in harsh rasps, while a stunned look darkened his face. "Bloody hell. That was not supposed to happen."

Disoriented, Phoebe backed farther away and wrapped her arms across her stomach. "No . . . It . . . it wasn't."

"It won't happen again. That I promise you." In frustration he raked one hand through his hair. "Don't use this as a reason not to be governess to my girls, Phoebe. Don't do that."

My girls. The way he said those two words cut through the tumult of emotions that beset her. For him his daughters came first. He would resist the inclinations of the flesh—inclinations he'd obviously succumbed to in the past—if that was best for his girls.

But she . . . She was the one who hadn't wanted to stop. Though she was filled with a strange clawing yearning for him, he'd been the one to pull back, determined not to give her the excuse she needed to stay away from Farley Park.

He had pulled away when she had not.

If she needed proof of his sincerity, that was awfully good. Could it be that she was the untrustworthy one? He might have gone through a world of women in the past, but it seemed he didn't mean for her to become one of them.

Disappointment knifed through her; painful and perverse. Why didn't he want her?

Though she fought them, every insecurity she'd ever felt rose to bludgeon her self-esteem. She wasn't beautiful like Louise, nor rich and titled like his former fiancée and the other women he'd known. Why should a man like him want a woman like her?

"No," she said. Was that the only word left in her head? She cleared her throat. "No, I would never blame Izzy and Leya for what you—What we—" She crossed her arms over her chest and huffed out a breath. "For what just happened."

"Then say you'll reconsider my offer. You name the salary." Again he swept a hand through his hair. "You can see how attached Izzy has become to you."

Phoebe forced herself to think about the children instead of the man who'd just curled her toes with his kiss. "She's so attached to me that she hates me."

"She doesn't hate you."

It was hard to know what Izzy thought. "Perhaps you can convince her to come up to Plummy Head for lessons there."

He scowled, hunched his shoulders, and shoved his hands in his pockets. "If she comes to your farm for lessons, then I wouldn't be anywhere nearby and you could preserve your reputation among the old biddies around here. Is that the idea?"

She raised her chin and met his brooding gaze. "I believe it would be for the best. After Helen, the most important thing I have is my good reputation."

Dark and brooding, his eyes moved over her, head to toe and back again. It was unnerving, mainly because Phoebe couldn't tell what he was thinking. Did he like her more for herself or for what she could provide his children?

More importantly, which way did she *want* him to like her? *Stop being so perverse!*

"Very well," he said. "I'll have her brought to your house every day for lessons."

Phoebe nodded. It was for the best, she told herself. Everyone got what they wanted this way: financial security for her and Helen; an education for Izzy.

But as they walked down the stairs side by side, it occurred to her that Lord Farley had not gotten what he wanted. He was a man accustomed to the company of women. Since she would not be that company, did that mean he'd find someone else?

Phoebe stumbled, but caught herself on the handrail.

"Are you all right?" he asked.

"I'm fine," she answered, keeping her eyes trained straight ahead. "Just fine."

CHAPTER 7

Lord Farley's workmen had finished constructing the goat shed except for shingling the roof. Martin had cut and stacked half a cord of wood near the kitchen door. He'd also taught Helen how to train Bruno to sit, lie down, and come when called. By the time Phoebe arrived home after a long roundabout, soul-searching hike along the cliffs, she had only to restoke the fire and prepare supper before the chill of night crept over the land.

She sighed as she stared down at her plate of stewed carrots and cheese bread. "What would you say if we hired a maid-of-all-work for our household?"

Helen looked up from her supper. "Does that mean I wouldn't have to sweep the stairs anymore?"

"That's right. Or haul water from the well, or carry in the milk from the goats." Helen tended to spill more than she carried in.

The little girl grinned. "Then I say yes."

"There is a catch."

Helen looked up from licking melted cheese from her thumb.

"Lord Farley has offered me a position teaching Izzy, and I think I must accept his offer."

"No." The excited grin dissolved into an obstinate frown. "I don't like her."

"Now Helen. I'm sure you'll learn to get along."

"But it's too far to walk every day."

"She'll be coming here."

That turned Helen's plaintive expression desperate. "No. Not here. Not her."

"Her father has offered me a very good salary, Helen, and we certainly need the money. With it I can hire that maid and we'll be able to spend all spring doing our lessons outdoors. In the meadow, or perhaps at Wildfen Pond, or even down upon the beach. Think about it. I'll have so much more time to spend with you if I don't have to do all the cooking and washing and tend all the animals."

She could see the struggle on Helen's perfect little face: freedom from chores versus Izzy's constant presence. Phoebe leaned forward, pressing the point. "I think Izzy is already getting nicer. I'm sure you've noticed. I predict that within another week or so the two of you will be the best of friends. I promise, Helen. You'll be glad of this. By the time of the May Day Festival, you'll have forgotten you ever disliked Izzy."

Helen slumped back in her chair, the very picture of dejection. "Will Leya be coming with her?"

"Perhaps not at first. She is, after all, still an infant. But I'm certain we can convince Lord Farley to send her now and again."

Mention of Lord Farley perked the child up. "Do you think Himself would teach me how to ride?"

Phoebe reached over and stroked her niece on the cheek. "If you want him to, I'm sure he will."

"Will you ask him?"

Conscious of an unseemly warmth rising into her face, Phoebe returned her attention to her supper. "I think it best if you ask him, Helen. He seems a very accommodating man. When it comes to children," she added under her breath.

James had supper alone in his office, eating at his desk before a sputtering fire. The room was dark and cold, just like his mood. Just like his life.

He'd had four letters today. One from his friend Kerry inquiring about life in the hinterlands, one from his mother assuring him that the gossip in town was beginning to ease, and a third from one of Lord Basingstoke's cronies stating that James's expected appointment as the King's Counsel on Foreign Affairs had been rescinded. No surprise in that. Still, the slight rankled. How long was he to be shunned for his indiscretions, which were no less than those of three-quarters of the House of Lords?

He knew, though, that he wasn't being punished for having fathered his children. His crime was acknowledging them and daring to bring them into his own household.

He let out a frustrated oath. It had been a stupid, ill-considered decision, moving Izzy and Leya into his London home. Yet even now he didn't think he'd do any different.

He stared moodily into the fire. Perhaps he might have married Catherine before telling her about his children. Perhaps.

Bloody hell, what was the point in rehashing any of it? What was done was done. He'd closed the door on any alliance with Lord Basingstoke when he humiliated the man's daughter. No use to stew about that anymore. At the moment his most pressing worry was what to do about Izzy.

All day long the child had fled in the opposite direction every time she saw him, like a feral cat determined to remain free, even as it skulks around the barnyard hoping for a stray bit of food. According to the cook, Izzy had filched two apple tarts, a half-loaf of bread, and a small crockery tub of butter from the pantry. Then she'd disappeared to some hiding place or another.

At least Leya was asleep. Goat's milk had made a world of difference in the child's temperament, and without her stomachaches, her bright eyes and cheerful smile had swiftly charmed everyone who came in contact with her. Everyone, that is, but his housekeeper. Mrs. Gatling's sour disposition matched her sour expression.

Eventually she'd have to go. It was clear to him that the nature of his children's births was a barrier the woman would never be able to climb over. She didn't want to climb over it. But he'd be damned before he subjected his girls to her constant disapproval, no matter how subtle.

If only the woman could be as accepting of his children as Phoebe.

He pushed back in his chair, forgetting his meal. Phoebe. The whole day he'd struggled to put those few minutes in the schoolroom out of his mind. But damn, if that kiss hadn't tormented him at every turn.

He took a long sip of wine. He'd spent the better part of his adult life being stupid when it came to women. Or maybe impulsive was a better word. The fact was, he liked women, whether tall, short, voluptuous, or waif-like. He liked blondes, brunettes, and red-heads, and he'd never understood men who limited themselves to a particular type.

Added to that, between his mother and two sisters, he'd been raised on the vagaries of the female mind. So you'd think he'd be wise to their inconsistencies.

But the only truth he'd ever learned was that women made no sense at all. They didn't think the same way men did. He'd learned, though, that if a man was patient and observant—and determined—he could discover a woman's weakness. For some women it was elaborate flattery, for others the need to be pursued. Some desired extravagant gifts, others needed a hint of danger, a taste of the forbidden.

The most dangerous women, however, were the ones who demanded love.

He untied his cravat and flicked the cloth onto his littered desk. Naturally, Phoebe Churchill fell into that category. That was reason enough for an honorable man to maintain his distance. On top of that, she was inexperienced when it came to men and was essentially alone in the world. Far too vulnerable for a man like him to dally after.

But the main reason he should never have kissed her was because of his girls. Izzy liked Phoebe, notwithstanding the child's rantings to the contrary. Izzy instinctively trusted her, and so did he. The simple fact was, he needed Phoebe Churchill to take care of his children, not to take care of him.

He threw back the last of his wine, then glowered into the waning fire. Another long night in his cold, lonely bed. But it would be worse tonight; he could tell. For he still tasted the wonder on Phoebe's lips when he'd deepened their kiss. He still felt that sweet pliancy when her young, lithe body had arched against his. Her skin had been as soft as buttermilk, her hair fragrant with some sort of flowers.

He groaned at the urgent rise of desire, firing his blood and fighting the stricture of his breeches. He needed a woman to relieve this frustration, and soon. But besides his own servants—whom he never indulged with—there were no other convenient women to be found. Another reason to hate the countryside.

"Bloody hell." He lurched to his feet, determined to quash these pointless yearnings. First he would search out Izzy. Wherever she'd hidden, she must have fallen asleep by now. He'd awaken her and explain that Phoebe wanted to be her governess, but at Plummy Head, not Farley Park. Then he'd carry her to her own bedroom.

After that he'd open the last envelope, sent by the investigator he'd hired in London. With any luck that man had finally located his other child.

He just hoped that this one didn't complicate his life as much as the first two had.

Izzy arrived at ten in the morning, carried in on a fierce wind that promised a cold day but no rain. She knocked once, let herself in, then slammed the door and scowled at Phoebe and Helen. "I'm here like you wanted. So let's go fishing."

Helen scowled right back. "Fish don't bite in a storm. Don't you know anything?"

"Kiss my arse."

"Izzy!" Both girls looked up at Phoebe's stern tone. "Young lady, you can just march yourself right outside and begin this morning anew. Or you can return home. The choice is yours to make. However, you need to understand one thing: I do not allow foul language or bad manners in my home."

The girl leveled her with a lethal stare. "I didn't want to come here anyway."

Phoebe rebuffed the glare with a regretful smile. "That's too bad. Because I really wanted your help with the goats today. They're a little leery about their new shed and are off their milk. But I suppose Helen and I can manage without you."

Phoebe watched from beneath sheltering lashes as Izzy struggled between what she wanted and what she thought she wanted. When the girl yanked the door open and stormed out, Phoebe's heart sank. But after a long, breath-holding moment, a single rap sounded.

Phoebe swung the door wide. "Come in," she said, and ignoring the determined scowl on the child's face, gave her a warm, welcoming hug. "I'm so glad you're here. Why don't you put your shoes over there, by the hearth? And look, this peg is for your cloak." She smiled down at Izzy. "So. I assume Leya isn't coming today."

"Cook says she has a fever." Izzy set her gloves on top of her shoes, then donned her inside clogs. "She only felt a little warm to me, and she didn't act like she was sick. I wanted to bring her anyway, but Lord Farley said no."

From the kitchen table Helen said, "Whyn't you call him Father or Da' or Poppa like other children do?"

" 'Cause he wants me to," Izzy said, slanting Phoebe a sly look.

Phoebe hid her smile. "How wise of you, Izzy. I completely agree. You should only call him Father when you begin to feel as if he really *is* your father. I have to say, though, that I'm reassured by how hard he's been trying. Did you know, even though I initially declined his offer to become your governess, he refused to give up until I agreed? But tell me about Leya. When did her fever start?"

"I don't know." Izzy wandered over to Bruno who was energetically gnawing an enormous old ham bone.

"Is anyone else at Farley Park sick?"

Izzy shrugged. But when Phoebe pressed her hand to the child's forehead, Izzy let her. "How did you get here?" Phoebe asked once she was reassured that Izzy wasn't feverish.

"He brought me."

He. Phoebe cleared away their breakfast dishes. There was only one *he* in Phoebe's life—and hers too, it seemed. "I'm surprised he didn't come in to say hello."

"He had business in town."

It was just as well, Phoebe told herself as she pulled out two slates and an old book of letters and rhymes. It was better than well. He meant to keep his distance, just as he'd said. He would pay her wages; she would instruct his daughters. With a bit of luck they might go weeks without ever crossing paths.

Months even.

It was an ideal arrangement. The answer to her prayers. So why did she feel as if a black storm cloud had just settled over her head, turning everything in her life colorless and bleak?

Then a thought occurred to her and she brightened. He'd brought Izzy here; eventually he'd have to retrieve her.

But late in the afternoon a servant came to fetch Izzy, driving the closed coach up the rutted lane. It was raining and cold as they waved Izzy off, and low-hanging clouds threatened to engulf Plummy Head in a chilly fog. The dreariness mirrored Phoebe's mood perfectly.

You should be happy. She forced herself to count her blessings, ticking them off in her mind. The goats were dry in their new shed. There was plenty of stacked wood in the yard. She and Helen were warm and snug in their cottage with the possibility of eviction no longer a threat. Most of all, she now knew that she could trust Lord Farley.

But therein lay her discontent. She could trust Lord Farley to keep his distance, to respect her person, to never kiss her again.

She stared out into the empty, prematurely dark sky.

How was she to live out the rest of her gray, colorless life if she never expected to be kissed like that again?

Izzy arrived early the next morning, alone and on foot, with her hair streaming in tangles, no gloves on her icy hands, and without a scarf to warm her throat. Again she barged in without knocking, but the look on her face forestalled any scolding.

Alarmed, Phoebe dragged her next to the hearth. "What's wrong? Has something happened?"

A hard shiver racked the girl's thin body. "Leya woke up really sick. Her skin feels just as hot as a fire brick and she's puking her guts out. She's too sick even to cry, Phoebe. She just lies there whimpering." Izzy stared at Phoebe, her face pale with the cold, and a stricken look in her huge blue eyes. "She needs you. I know she does. Will you come back with me? You have to come."

Fear chilled Phoebe to her soul. Babies died of fevers; it happened all the time. "Did your father send to Swansford for the doctor?"

"Yes. But Leya needs *you*. You're the only one that can make her better."

"I'm sure the doctor will know what to do," Phoebe said, trying to console both Izzy and herself.

But Izzy was adamant. "You made her well before. You have to come right now. Hurry. Get your cloak and boots."

"All right, we'll go. But first you need a hat and gloves. Helen, find something of yours for her."

Once bundled up they made the three-mile distance in record time and with no complaints from Helen. It began to sleet as they started down the last hill, but the vigorous half-walk, half-run kept them warm. Izzy hurried them in through the kitchen, then up the servants' stairs to the nursery where the housekeeper stood in the hall, issuing orders to two maids.

When the woman spied the three of them still in their coats, with a frosting of ice crystals on their shoulders and hoods, she crossed her arms and glared down her nose at Phoebe. "Are these the manners you would teach this child? To barge in unannounced, uninvited, and without even removing your outerwear?"

"Bugger off," Izzy said, charging past the woman.

But the black-garbed harpy caught Izzy by the arm. "Oh, no you don't. This is a sickroom. No visitors allowed."

"Take your hands off her," Phoebe demanded. "Izzy has every right to be concerned about her sister."

The housekeeper gave Phoebe a scornful once-over. "I shouldn't be surprised that you'd take up for her. You're all of a kind. You. Her. That niece of yours."

At the first cross word Helen had ducked behind Phoebe, and in the face of this woman's undeserved scorn, she clutched at Phoebe's skirts. It was the only thing that prevented Phoebe from slapping the odious woman silly. How dare she imply anything so sordid!

She drew herself up. "I suggest you release that child, get out of my way, and keep yourself well beyond my reach when I go through that door. For I assure you," she added, starting forward. "I *am* going through that door."

Bullies were all alike, Phoebe thought as she strode unchallenged through the door. They backed down at the first sign of opposition. But her satisfaction at besting Farley Park's vile housekeeper disappeared the moment she entered the nursery. The sour smell of vomit, the overheated room, and the glum expression on the rumpled doctor's face as he spoke to Lord Farley foretold an enemy far more difficult to defeat than a hateful, dried-up old woman.

"What is it?" she asked, focusing on the doctor as she removed her cloak and bonnet.

"Hallo, Miss Churchill," Dr. Ward said, as if it were the most ordinary thing in the world to find her at Farley Park. "I'm thinking she's contracted some sort of pox. But the high fever has me a trifle baffled, as does the vomiting."

Pox. That was Dr. Ward's catch-all phrase for anything he couldn't otherwise diagnose. Leya could be suffering with anything.

Phoebe glanced at Lord Farley who stood over Leya's bed. He looked as if he'd been up all night—his hair stood up in dark blond spiky clumps; his unfastened waistcoat hung open; and his shirt gaped at the throat and was stained with who-knew-what. Most distressing of all, his face sagged in lines of worry and exhaustion. How awful he must feel to have no clear diagnosis for Leya's illness.

With an effort she tore her gaze from him and turned to the girls, who stood warily just inside the tall doorway. "Izzy, I want you to take Helen to your room. Or down to the kitchen. Whatever you like."

Izzy frowned. "What about Leya?"

"She's very sick, but I'm going to stay with her and do all I can to help. Only I can't have you and Helen getting sick too. If you want to help your little sister, you must stay healthy and do exactly as I ask. Can you do that for me?"

Izzy's fearful gaze darted from Phoebe to the tiny bed where her half sister lay, then back. "Will you come tell us how she fares?"

"Of course I will."

"All right, then." Izzy nodded. She caught Helen by

the hand. "Come along, Helen. We'll go to the kitchen and tell Cook to prepare tea for everyone."

Phoebe smiled encouragingly at Helen, who looked frightened to death. "That would be lovely." She glanced at Lord Farley, who stood over Leya's bed, staring down at his listless child. "Have her also send up breakfast for your father."

When the girls left, Dr. Ward drew Phoebe aside. "It may simply be the same childhood pox that comes around every few years. Most children survive with no repercussions. We'll know for sure if blisters begin to form. Take care not to touch them. And keep everyone well away from this room. Meanwhile, my advice is to try and make her as comfortable as possible. And keep that fever down."

Then he collected his coat and hat and let himself out, leaving Phoebe and Lord Farley to tend the now eerily silent Leya.

"Thank you for coming." Lord Farley's voice was a low rasp against the crackling pop of the fire. "How did you know to come?"

"Izzy." Phoebe moved to stand next to him beside the bed. "I assume you didn't send her to me."

"No."

Phoebe stroked Leya's burning cheek. "I do believe Izzy loves this little girl. She's known Leya, what, two months or so?" She lifted her gaze and studied his profile. "And yet already she loves her little sister with a fierce intensity."

"So do I." He turned to face her. "I never expected to. But I do. And I can't—" His voice broke and she saw him swallow hard against the emotions that flailed inside his chest. "I can't lose her. I can't."

"Don't talk about losing her. Children survive illnesses like this all the time."

"But not always," he said, his voice dark with fear. "Not always. She's from India, you know. What if she's more susceptible to whatever sort of pox this is?"

Phoebe didn't know how to reassure him except to say, "I'll help. However I can, I'll help."

His hand caught hers and without thinking, she clasped it. It was totally inappropriate for more reasons than she cared to consider. Yet it felt achingly right. Palm to palm, fingers entwined as if in a solemn pact, they joined their hands, their wills, and the strength of their bodies to fight for Leya.

It proved to be a very long day.

They fell into a natural pattern, sharing ideas and efforts, and never ceasing their vigilance. Phoebe knew the importance of dribbling water down the baby's throat, for a fever could quickly parch her tiny, burning body. One slow spoon at a time she fed water to Leya, so that her stomach wouldn't revolt.

In India Lord Farley had seen a dangerously feverish child immersed in a cold bath, anything to reduce the killing heat. In the Orient, he told her, the healers advocated cleanliness for both patient and caregivers. Also for bedding, clothes, dishes—anything that came or went in the sickroom should be kept scrupulously clean with hot water and lots of soap.

And in the midst of it all, Izzy and Helen brought tea and broth for Leya, plus bread and meat for them.

"You must discharge that housekeeper," Phoebe murmured much later in the afternoon while Leya slept. Lord Farley sprawled back upon a settee, his eyes closed in exhaustion, his long legs draped on the floor. She had collapsed in a large upholstered chair.

"I know. Unfortunately I have to wait until I can secure a decent replacement."

Working side by side with him, worrying and praying

and battling the same demons, had broken down enough barriers between them that Phoebe hesitated only a moment before saying, "I don't think you should wait. That odious woman's poisonous attitude is far worse for this household than hobbling along a few weeks or even months without a proper housekeeper. The woman makes no bones about the fact that she despises both Izzy and Leya—and probably you as well for forcing her to deal with them."

A weak cry from Leya forestalled his reply. They both leaped up to find the baby shivering, her lips trembling, her few teeth chattering. At once Phoebe picked her up, bedding and all, and hugged her close. Lord Farley draped a blanket over Phoebe and his child, tucking it close around her on the chair. They'd been through this twice now. Fever, then chills. Cool water, then warm broth.

Together they fought for Leya through the long hours of the night, taking turns, dozing intermittently. Near dawn Phoebe went out to use the necessary, and discovered Helen and Izzy sleeping just outside the nursery door on a mattress hauled from one of the nearby bedchambers. The two were curled up together, under a mound of blankets, for the hall was cold and drafty. A welcome smile curved her lips. They reminded her of puppies, like Bruno and his litter mates. It seemed that, faced with Leya's illness, they'd put away their animosity toward one another. At least something good was coming from this dreadful night.

When she returned, Lord Farley stood over Leya, a lamp in his hand and a worried frown upon his face. "The blisters are spreading. Look at her cheeks."

"But remember, Dr. Ward said that was good. It means the illness is progressing as it should. The sooner they come, the sooner they'll leave, and the sooner she'll recover. We may have to bundle her hands, though. If she scratches them she could scar."

"I won't care if she scars, so long as she lives." He was silent a moment, then turned to face her. "I'll never be able to repay you for what you're doing."

He said no more; but then, he didn't need to. The power of his feelings, the utter sincerity of them, was there in his eyes. It was in the very air between them. They were connected now in a way that transcended this one day and night of struggle. They'd fought together for this child's life, and Phoebe was beginning to believe they'd won. No matter what the future held, she and Lord Farley would always share this night, this victory.

But it went deeper than that; it was more pervasive, more primitive. Their gaze clung. Bone weary though she was, Phoebe felt the moment stretch out, taut and crackling, until the inexplicable undercurrent grew too hard to fight.

She ran a shaky hand through her disheveled hair. She'd never been drawn to anyone like she was drawn to him—and he seemed equally drawn to her. It couldn't merely be lust, she told herself. It couldn't. No sane man would lust after a woman as unkempt and drooping as she was.

Could there be more between them? Might he actually care about her?

Her poor beleaguered heart was long past sorting out the truth from wishful thinking. As she began to sink into the sea-blue depths of his eyes, she could only say, "You needn't thank me, Lord Farley. I've grown to love Leya too." She was drowning in his eyes, hardly able to breathe. "And . . . and also Izzy."

The entire world shrank down to just the two of them, now, in this room.

"I've never met a woman like you."

She let out a strangled laugh. "No?" Of course he hadn't. He traveled in very different circles than she.

He shook his head. "Will you stay here at Farley Park until she's well?"

"Of course." Her voice faded to a whisper.

"I can discharge Mrs. Gatling today."

She nodded.

"But I'll need your help."

Again she nodded. A team of wild moor ponies couldn't drag her away.

He stepped nearer, a mere foot closer to her. Yet in that one step he breached a wall, he crossed some line that up to now had kept them fellow soldiers in the battle they'd waged. But no longer.

Instead of soldiers fighting the good fight, they were stripped to their most basic selves: a woman and a man, excruciatingly conscious that the attraction they already felt had suddenly strengthened. No longer a flickering flame of heat, it had become a raging fire. An inferno . . .

CHAPTER 8

It made perfect sense to James. This woman, so unlike Catherine, so unlike any other of the many women he'd known, made perfect sense to him. He pulled her closer. She was the perfect height, and the ideal size. He felt her melt unresistingly in his arms. She was kind and generous and she adored his children.

But best of all, she wanted him.

He tilted her chin up and searched the unblinking hazel depths of her eyes. She was so innocent. That was the only contrary ripple in the tidal wave of certainty that rushed over him. Too innocent to know what was best for herself.

But he ignored that ripple. He wanted her.

No, it was more than that. He needed her.

"Phoebe." He murmured her name against her lips and felt her mouth answer.

"James."

One syllable, yet he'd never heard anything so erotic. His name in her low, breathy voice.

"Ah, damn," he muttered. He was well and truly lost. His weariness fled, replaced by full-blown desire. Her breasts, pressed soft and warm against his chest, and yielding. Her supple waist fitted the curve of his arm, and her mouth . . .

Her sweet, luscious mouth was created for him and his pleasure. Innocent and seductive, her lips met his, slanted to fit better, and opened to accept the greedy thrust of his tongue.

He wanted to devour her, to consume her for his own selfish pleasure. At the same time he was determined to make her burn with desire for him.

Somehow he moved them to the settee, sitting down with her on his lap. Her arms circled his shoulders; her fingers tangled in the hair at his nape. He shifted her so that her legs draped over the arm of their seat and tilted her backward in his embrace. She was his for the taking, his to sate his ravenous hunger upon, and then to savor a second, a third—an infinite number of times.

In his breeches his arousal demanded more and he thrust against the warm fullness of her bottom.

Her answer was to kiss him as he'd been kissing her, to explore the depths of his mouth with increasing boldness, increasing demand. It was a demand he was fully prepared to meet.

He slid her off his lap. She flexed to accommodate him, and without even pausing for a breath, he lay over her upon the narrow settee.

Beneath him Phoebe felt the change, like a shift in the wind, like a tilt in the axis of the earth. Up to now she had wielded the power. Sort of. Now he held it.

Or maybe he'd always held it. Maybe it had been her delusion, thinking she could say yea or nay to this man, and control the restless beast he'd loosened inside her.

Lust. In her head she heard the word spoken in her mother's harsh, disapproving voice.

Then another voice, young and rebellious—her own, she realized—pointed out that if her unhappy, critical, friendless mother so vehemently disapproved of lust, it must be a marvelous thing.

Though contrary to a lifetime of belief, once considered, the heretical thought would not go away. Emilean Churchill had hated so many things: music, laughter, anything bright or exuberant or filled with emotion. But her mother had been wrong about all of that. Could she be wrong about lust as well?

Phoebe needed to know, for above all else, she did not want to turn into a bitter, critical woman like her mother.

So she accepted the hard masculine weight pressing down on her, and she gloried in the knowledge that James Lindford wanted her, Phoebe Churchill. He could have any woman he wanted, but he wanted her because, despite their differences, at heart they were alike. They knew what really mattered, and they fought for it. He'd left London for his children; she raised her niece. And then tonight they'd worked together to keep Leya safe. A man who loved his children as intensely as James loved Leya and Izzy surely would love a woman just as intensely. He would cherish her.

As if to prove her right, he began a trail of kisses, warming her neck, heating the shell of her ear, rousing a fire of epic magnitude in the nether reaches of her belly.

"James," she moaned, moving restlessly beneath him, wanting things from him she could not rightly put into words.

But he knew. He knew and he answered her silent pleas with a touch here, a caress there. The inside of her elbow. The palm of her hand. The place beneath her ear that had no name. When had these common, everyday parts of her become so sensitized?

Then one of his knees parted her legs and pushed

between her thighs. It was a strange, invasive movement. Possessive. Thrilling. At the same time one of his hands skimmed up her waist and ribs, then palmed the side of her breast.

Oh yes. Don't stop, was her shameful, greedy response.

He heeded that too, sensing it though she could not form the words. Then he smoothed his thumb over the crest of her breast, and someone groaned. Could that be her?

When he did it again, using the tip of his thumbnail to tease her nipple to excruciating awareness, she again groaned.

"Phoebe," he said, murmuring her name against her lips, against the curve of her neck, and the hollow of her throat. And all the while he increased that sweet torturing of her breast until she was panting with need, a human inferno thrashing beneath him, churning on the inside and threatening to explode from the violence of her emotions.

When a surge of cool air swept over her legs, she felt one blessed moment of sanity. The lower half of her was entirely bare. How had that happened?

She had her answer when his palm, hot and bold, curved behind her knee. But that sensual, wholly improper caress felt too right for her to bid him cease. If this was lust, she feared she would never deny it again.

When he ground his hips against hers she thrust back in instinctive acceptance. How had she ever thought this a repulsive act? How could she have disdained it? Feared it? Dreaded it?

He shifted to one side and his hand moved higher. She sucked in a sharp breath when he reached the apex of her parted legs. Fear and longing pounded through her veins as he cupped that most private part of her.

Fear. Longing. Need. She *needed* to know the rest of this.

"Are you chaste?" He murmured the words hot and hoarse in her ear.

Inside she had melted into a roiling brew of emotion. But somehow she managed to nod. Speaking was impossible. Yes, she was chaste. But for how long?

Maybe she should stop him.

But then he parted the curls down there, parted them and touched her, and any thoughts of stopping these wondrous feelings burned right out of her head.

Oh yes. Oh there. Oh, this wonderful . . . marvelous . . . unbelievable . . .

He made a tiny circling movement, like he'd done with her nipple. Only this little circle was so much closer to the boiling center of her longing. Of her lust. He circled her and it felt hot and wet—and then she erupted.

"Yes. Yes." She heard her cries over and over as her body arched in spasm beyond her ken. He urged her on, stroking until it was unbearable, until she was sobbing, her face wet with unknown tears. That's when he moved his finger farther back, someplace deeper, filling her with new feelings even as the tremors still rippled through her. He thrust in and out, rousing her anew. Though the sensations were the same, they were somehow different.

For just a moment he stopped, just long enough for her to gasp for breath. Had she died? Was this heaven?

Then once again he shifted over her, and she felt a new probing, harder and larger.

Phoebe opened her eyes to find his face an inch from hers, his eyes dark and unnervingly blue, and fixed intently upon hers. "It may hurt," he murmured. "Just a little. But that will pass. I promise." He pressed harder, filling her in a new way, a frightening yet necessary way.

"Phoebe?"

She nodded, never removing her gaze from his. In he came, short probing strokes, each one bolder, each one deeper. He filled her, stretched her. Possessed her. Then a pause, a sudden thrust, and he was fully in her.

It didn't hurt. Not really. But she gasped at the finality of it, the unimaginable sense of completeness. She was his now and the thought filled her with joy.

His. And he was hers.

Their eyes held as he pulled slowly out, then came into her again. "Oh my." She breathed the words.

A faint smile curved his mouth and she felt the strongest urge to kiss that mouth. He stroked into her again, faster, deeper, beginning a rhythm she instinctively recognized and rose to. She accepted him into her body, into her heart, and pulled his head down to hers, fastening their lips as erotically as their loins.

This pure pleasure, this utter completion—could this be what she'd so feared? She vowed then never to fear it again, for this was perfection. This was joy. This was love and lust and need and forever. And when he rushed her back into that wild chasm of freedom and victory and physical abandon, she took the leap eagerly, exploding around him in the same moment that he exploded into her.

Afterward Phoebe wasn't clear about exactly what happened and in what order. She could believe that she'd fainted, except that she never fainted. All she knew for certain was that he was heavy and replete upon her, and then, without her being aware of it, he was gone.

She sat up and a dampened cloth was pushed into her hand for her to clean herself. It was awkward and totally disorienting. But then he was there, kneeling before the settee, smiling at her. He caught her other hand and kissed it, then studied her with a serious expression.

"That wasn't—" He broke off and released her hand.

"I didn't plan on that, Phoebe. The long night together—"
He broke off again. "I won't make any excuses. What's
done is done. Though I should, I can't regret it. I hope
you don't either."

Phoebe cleared her throat. Her cheeks were scarlet
and she wanted to look away from him. But there was
no escaping his scrutiny. "I don't regret," she said.
Should I?

"Good. We need to talk about this. But not now. Not
here in the nursery. I'll summon a maid to find you a
bed."

"What about Leya?"

"She's sleeping. No need for both of us to sit up with
her. I'll sleep later. And once we're sure she's all right,
we'll talk about what just happened."

He was right, of course. Phoebe wanted to talk now,
to figure this out, except that she was too befuddled and
overwhelmed and exhausted to think straight. And then,
Izzy and Helen were asleep just outside the door—

She went rigid with horror; the last of her confusion
fled. She *hoped* they were still asleep. She remembered
being awfully noisy. Added to that, dawn was near; the
housekeeper and some of the maids might already be up
and about.

So she agreed to his suggestion, ducked her head, and
was grateful when he departed to summon a maid.

She stared about the silent room, then, testing her
shaky legs, stood. Good Lord. She'd really done it this
time, taken an irrevocable step in a direction she could
not change. Not ever.

And though she was glad and would never wish this
night different, as the seconds stretched into long
minutes, a new fear crept over her. This might have been
a first for her, but that wasn't the case for him. He'd
done this selfsame act with any number of women. At

least three, but probably more. Many more.

She frowned and drifted over to the small iron bed and gazed down at his sleeping daughter. He hadn't married any of the women who had borne his children. Why should he behave any differently with her?

And what if they, too, had created a child?

Her hand flew to her stomach, but with an exercise of will she tightened her hand into a fist and drew it away. It was pointless to worry about that possibility now. Still, she couldn't help counting back to the last visitation of her monthlies. Two weeks? No, three. At any rate, it had been before she ever met James—Lord Farley. Before he'd returned to his country estate with his oddment of a family.

A weight of fear began to lift from her chest. She should be safe then, with only a few days to wait to be sure.

She looked back at Leya and felt an unexpected pang of regret—utterly perverse, of course, but nonetheless real. There would be no baby Leya for her and she should be grateful. But if they ever did this again . . .

No. She could not let that happen. It was far too dangerous. Unbidden, however, a ripple of remembered passion coursed through her, like an echo of a favorite melody. If they never did this again—if she never married anyone or ever lay in a man's arms for the rest of her life—she would have to remember the music they'd made this night, the melody of passion and love. Physical love if not true love.

Phoebe hugged her arms around herself and shook her head. If she let herself think like this she would drive herself quite mad. She was simply too tired and too overwhelmed by the last few hours to think clearly. She needed the reprieve of sleep; she needed to escape her thoughts, at least for a little while.

A still sleepy maid came into the room and silently led her off, past the two little girls slumbering in their makeshift bed in the hall, and away from James, who settled in a chair next to Leya's bed. The chamber given her was on the second floor, small but pleasantly appointed, with a newly laid fire struggling to beat back the chill. The maid said little, only turning down the bed and pointing out the chamber pot and a ewer filled with water.

Phoebe was relieved when the girl left. It was too hard speculating on what the girl did or didn't suspect, whether she could tell just by looking what Phoebe had done tonight, how drastically she'd been changed.

Far easier to be alone, to undress herself and suffer the icy penance of her cold-water ablutions. Even the sheets were frigid despite the mountain of bedding she pulled over herself. But in the stillness of the featherbed her memories kept her heated. Before the bed had fully warmed from her body heat, Phoebe was asleep, exhausted in body, spirit, and heart.

When she awoke it was to utter bedlam. The first jolt came when Helen threw herself across Phoebe's bed, sobbing hysterically. Through the open door came the screaming of an outraged Izzy. "Get out of my house! You bitch! You whore!"

Phoebe jerked upright in absolute panic. They knew what she'd done! Guilt exuded her every pore. They knew what she'd done last night with Lord Farley, and soon everyone in Swansford would know!

Meanwhile, Helen continued to sob. "I won't stay here. I won't! He can't make me."

"Helen. Helen." Phoebe drew the shivering child into her arms, trying to understand. "Hush. It's all right now. I've got you."

The girl curled into a terrified ball in Phoebe's arms,

and for a moment Phoebe's panic turned to confusion. Why was Helen so upset? Surely this wasn't all on account of Izzy's fury. And why should Izzy be so angry? "What on earth is going on, sweetheart?"

"I won't leave you." The little girl sobbed as if her heart were broken. "I hate her. She can't make me leave you."

Phoebe could make no sense of that. "Helen. Listen to me. You know Izzy won't really hurt you. Whatever she's angry about, you mustn't let it frighten you like this."

"Not Izzy." The words came out wet and muffled against Phoebe's chest. "Not Izzy."

Somewhere downstairs a piece of pottery crashed. A door slammed. Phoebe tried to think. It must be the housekeeper, that horrible, unfeeling tyrant of a housekeeper. If Izzy was raging and Helen was weeping, it could only be on account of Mrs. Gatling.

"You just hush your crying, Helen. I'll take care of everything. Just let me get up and get dressed." Untangling herself from the child's clutches, Phoebe clambered from the bed and threw on her clothes. Helen hid under the covers. Meanwhile Izzy's tantrum echoed from somewhere on another floor. Though she couldn't decipher the exact words, Izzy's fury was unmistakable.

Good for her, Phoebe thought. As she followed the sound of the tirade, she strode down the hall, pinning up her hair as she went. Phoebe meant to take up right where young Izzy left off. She was tired to death of adults belittling children for matters not of their making.

At the bottom of the stairs the ancient butler stood blinking, the absolute picture of bewilderment. Two maids huddled together in the niche beneath the stairs, while the housekeeper hauled two carpetbags furiously to the door. The woman gave Phoebe a venomous glare as she stalked by.

"Two of a kind," she muttered. "Sluts all." Then she slammed the door behind her.

Phoebe started after her, determined to lambaste the hateful old biddy before she could escape. But the butler shook his gray head and with a trembling hand pointed toward one of the parlors. "I believe you're needed more urgently in there, miss. Please."

Phoebe halted, staring from the pleading butler to the front door to the parlor and back. What was going on in this household? She swung around when she heard Izzy.

"—and you're the worstest of all! I hate you!"

The parlor door crashed open and Izzy barreled out, a wiry knot of rage and frustration. Not even sparing Phoebe a glance, she bolted for the rear of the house.

From inside the parlor Lord Farley's voice carried. "Bloody hell. Izzy? Come back here! Bloody, bloody hell!"

But it was a woman's laugh that raised the hair on the back of Phoebe's neck. A woman laughing? A new form of disorientation rooted Phoebe in her spot. Surely not one of the maids. Then a horrible thought occurred to her. Horrible to the point of nauseating. Could it be that Lady Catherine from the newspaper? The one he'd been betrothed to?

"My, my," the woman continued. "It seems, my lord, that you've been quite a busy man. But I'm not complaining. In fact, I was thrilled when your man of business contacted me. At least now my little girl will have two sisters to grow up with."

Not Lady Catherine, Phoebe thought with a sinking heart, but someone else. Izzy's mother—but no. The woman referred to her little girl having *two* sisters.

Something inside Phoebe's chest turned to lead. This must be yet another of his women.

She swallowed the absurd disappointment that clogged her throat. The gossips were right. He *had* been searching for another of his children, and it seemed he'd found her. Or rather, the child's mother had found him.

Phoebe's first instinct was to turn around and leave, just like Helen had done. To leave and go home and try to pretend she didn't care that another of his many women had just landed on his doorstep.

When he appeared in the doorway, however, one arm outstretched to close it, she froze. When he saw her, he did the same.

He looked utterly done in, was her first thought. Weary beyond the telling. But there was more, a shock in his eyes, as if he couldn't believe the woman was here. And when he continued to stare at Phoebe, a dark flush, as of shame, covered his face.

She wanted him to feel ashamed. Yet a fair part of her knew that this was none of her affair. His past was his own business. It was his present and the future that she was concerned with, and then, only insofar as it applied to her.

But that fell under the purview of logic, and Phoebe was far from feeling logical.

"Are you listening, James?" came the woman's voice. Then, "Is someone out there?"

Again Phoebe felt the strongest urge to run, especially when she heard the light, tapping footsteps crossing the parlor. She wanted to run, but even more, she wanted to hold her ground.

This means nothing to me, she told him with the stiffening of her spine and the lifting of her chin. *Your messy life and the women in your past are your business. I'm going home.*

Then an enormous hat sheltering a wealth of blond curls poked past Lord Farley, and a pretty face peered out at her. "Why, it's Phoebe," the woman said, throwing Phoebe completely off kilter. How did this woman know her name?

"I was hoping it might be you," the gorgeous creature continued, sidling past Lord Farley with her arms stretched open and a smile on her obviously painted lips. "Oh, but it's been ages, Phoebe. Come, give your sister a hug."

For a moment the world seemed to stop. Louise. Phoebe blinked, only belatedly recognizing her sister. Louise was here? But that made no sense. She'd obviously come in response to the letter about their mother's death. But how would Louise know to find them at Farley House?

Phoebe started forward, a confused but welcoming smile on her face—until the full impact of her sister's conversation with James hit her.

Like a vicious blow it struck, hurting her as no mere physical blow could ever do. For it struck at her heart, a dagger of ugly truth tearing into the only part of her still vulnerable.

What had she said? "My little girl will have two sisters . . ."

Her little girl. Helen. Sweet, fatherless Helen who had been Phoebe's child in every way except by her actual birth. Izzy and Leya were her sisters?

Which meant . . . Lord Farley was Helen's father.

Louise had created this child with . . . with *her* Lord Farley?

Phoebe stumbled back a step, reeling from the hideous realization, yet unable to escape it. It couldn't be true. It couldn't!

But of course it was. As the silence in the foyer

stretched to the breaking point, she knew it was horribly, insanely true. Helen was Lord Farley's child, the one he'd been looking for.

And if Louise had come back to Yorkshire, it must be to give Helen to him—and to take Helen away from *her*.

CHAPTER 9

"Let me explain," James said, advancing into the foyer. But Phoebe retreated, her horrified gaze darting from him to her sister and back. Then with an anguished cry she turned, and fled up the stairs.

He started to follow her, to try to make her understand. But at the foot of the stairs he stopped. Understand what? That many years ago he'd made a child with her sister? Unfortunately for him, she already understood that now. Only too well.

From the doorway to the parlor Louise laughed, the same amused laugh that had charmed him so easily when he'd been a young man about town with only one thing on his mind.

It didn't charm him now. If anything, it raised the hackles upon his neck. Louise LaFleur, she of the golden hair and golden voice—and golden aura of sexual promise—was actually Louise Churchill, sister to Phoebe. Son of a bitch!

He should have made the connection. He'd met Louise in London, at a party given after a play she'd been in. He'd overheard her saying she was originally from Yorkshire and he'd used his own birth in that shire as a reason to approach her. It had worked, and for a few months they'd been frequent companions—until she'd announced her pregnancy, and the next comely woman had turned his head.

Had he truly thought the money he'd thrown at his peccadilloes could fully absolve him of the selfish choices he'd made as a cocky young rooster strutting through town?

He shook his head, disgusted at his own perversity. He was reaping the results of those days now. Louise was Phoebe's sister. God, had ever a man been so cursed?

"Really, James," came that golden, laughing voice. "You must not understand women very well if you expect my prudish little sister to tolerate any explanations from you." Louise came up beside him in a cloud of some overwhelming musky scent. "I expect she's even angrier at me than at you. But she'll get over it. She always does."

James glared at her, wanting to strangle her as much for her careless selfishness as for her spectacularly bad timing. But there were servants watching, and anyway, the damage was done. Phoebe didn't want to have anything to do with him. Izzy had stormed off in a rage; Helen had fled in terror; and Leya—

He started up the stairs, taking them three at a time. In the confusion of Louise's arrival he'd forgotten about Leya.

"You don't know Phoebe like I do," Louise continued, mincing up the stairs behind him. "She'll have to pout and sulk a long while before she comes around. But it will all work out. You'll see. My little sister is nothing if not dependable. You can hire her to be Helen's governess. The situation will hardly be any different than it already is. In fact—"

"My youngest daughter has a fever," he broke in. "Some contagion the doctor has not yet identified." He turned on her at the top of the stairs, and drew a grim satisfaction that she halted mid-breath. "I know you don't want to risk becoming infected and perhaps ending up with pockmarks on that face of yours."

Hastily she composed her expression into one of maternal concern. "Oh. The poor dear." She backed down a step. "I hope my darling Helen hasn't already been exposed?"

"I hope not also."

He left her there, a beautiful but soulless creature come to capitalize on the child she'd obviously neglected for years. He strode for the nursery. How had he ever admired her?

But he had more important problems to solve than that. Leya. Phoebe. Izzy and Helen. Every female in his life from infant to girls to women was a problem right now. Each one required his immediate attention. But Leya had to come first.

He stepped over the two girls' abandoned bedding and into the warmth of the nursery. Phoebe stood in the window, holding the whimpering child and swaying back and forth.

She was nothing like Louise. Like a cudgel to his head, that fact struck James. He halted in the doorway. Phoebe was slimmer than her sister, taller and not as fair. But it wasn't those physical differences that most impressed him. Few women could compete with the physical beauty of the actress Louise LaFleur. Inside, though, where caring and goodness and selflessness resided, that's where Phoebe outshone her older sister. That's where she outshone any woman he'd ever known.

He closed the door silently behind him. He wanted to

make love to her again. Right now. Here, with the rest of the world shut out.

It was insane, of course, and not least of all because now she hated him.

"Phoebe?"

She shook her head but didn't turn around. "Don't try to explain any of this to me. I don't want to hear it. Just tell me the truth: is Helen your daughter?"

He took a deep breath and blew it out. "Yes."

He saw her shoulders sag, just a little. But as if to negate that, her chin tilted up. "How long have you known?"

"I just found out. I mean, I always knew I had a child. With her," he added, hating the pain his every word inflicted on Phoebe. He raked one hand through his hair. "But I didn't know Helen was that child. Nor that you were Louise's sister."

Slowly Phoebe turned to face him. He braced himself to see tears. He'd never dealt well with women's tears. But Phoebe wasn't crying. She looked shaken, but not undone, as if, perversely, holding the vulnerable Leya gave her strength.

"All these years you neglected her—you and Louise. And now the two of you want to take her away from *me*, the one person who has always cared for her."

"I didn't neglect her. She had a generous monthly allowance—" He broke off when an ugly suspicion occurred to him. "Have you and Helen not been receiving that money?"

Phoebe shook her head, a bitter smile twisting her lips. "It seems Louise has lived very well at your expense, Lord Farley. I suppose she's here now to demand even more of your largesse."

Leya startled, then began to cry. At once Phoebe turned her attention to the baby, saving James from answering. He moved closer. "How's she doing?"

Phoebe shrugged. "Less fever, but more blisters." She began to sway and make soft shushing sounds to comfort the child. "I suppose that's a good omen."

He nodded, relieved on that score. He'd just found his third child; he didn't want to lose this one. "Do you think she'll eat?"

"I don't know. We can try."

"I've had someone go milk your goats."

She looked up and for a long moment their eyes held. Then she broke their gaze and turned back to Leya. "That's a good idea, but even goat's milk may not agree with her. First I'll try water, then milk. If she tolerates that, we can try a thin gruel."

James consoled himself that at least they were united in their concern for Leya. For now he would have to be satisfied with that. So he rang for a maid and sent orders to the kitchen, while Phoebe changed Leya's clothes and checked the spread of the pustules.

"You feed her," Phoebe said when she handed him the lethargic baby. "I need to find Helen. She was awfully upset."

He nodded. Phoebe was so calm, so organized. Perhaps Louise was right: Phoebe just needed some time to get used to Helen's new situation. Then everything would be all right. "Will you talk to Izzy too?"

"Of course." She paused at the door, glancing at him, then away. "Why was Izzy so enraged by Louise's arrival?"

He clenched his jaw. "Izzy was there when Louise arrived. It seems that Louise thought Izzy was Helen. Of course, Izzy set her straight. When Louise saw Helen though, she told her that I was her father and she could—" He broke off. "She told Helen that she could live here all the time now. That's when Helen got scared.

She said she wanted to live with you, but Louise said no, that she had to live with me now. Helen started to cry, and that's when Izzy jumped to her defense."

Finally Phoebe met his gaze. "Izzy was protecting Helen?"

James nodded. "She's got a streak of loyalty—at least to her younger sisters." He stared down at Leya and stroked her dark, sweaty hair. "She's back to hating me, though."

Phoebe stared at Lord Farley's head, bent over Leya. She wanted to hate him too, for luring her in, for making her admire him, for making her want him.

For giving her last night.

She gritted her teeth against the memory. She wouldn't think about last night. And she wouldn't console him about his daughter either. He'd made this mess; let him find his way out of it.

So she turned away, silently leaving him in the nursery. Helen and Izzy might hate Lord Farley; certainly she wanted to hate him. But what was the point? What had occurred between him and Louise had happened a long time ago. It had nothing to do with her. Nothing.

But Phoebe couldn't dismiss her pain with logic. Just knowing he'd done with Louise what he'd done with her . . .

She bit down on her lip, forcing her foolish emotions away, folding them up, never to examine again. She'd be better served seeing the man for what he was, by realizing that she meant no more to him than Louise had, no more than any of the many other women he'd seduced. It was time for her to end this stupid, romantic vision she'd created of him. Her bailiff. Again she shook her head.

The truth was, Lord Farley was very good at this business of lust. Very good. Sad to say, but her mother was more right than she'd guessed. Instead of being angry, though, Phoebe told herself that she should be relieved. At least she'd learned the truth about James Lindford, Viscount Farley, before she could be *entirely* taken in. She may have given him her innocence, but at least she hadn't handed over her heart.

Her most important task now was to concentrate on Helen. Nothing else. Phoebe had always known her sister was a negligent mother. But it was plain now that Louise cared about Helen only insofar as the amount of money she could pump out of the child's father. It infuriated Phoebe to even think how poor Helen must feel. For so long she'd idolized her absent mother, and Phoebe hadn't tried to stop her. But now the ugly truth was exposed. Not only had Louise deprived Helen of the mother she'd pined for, she'd stolen the money meant to benefit her own child.

A cold, shaking fury gripped Phoebe. How could anyone be so selfish and cruel?

She fully intended to have an answer. Once she found the two little girls and reassured them, she would go after Louise. Phoebe had too many years of repressed disappointment and disgust and rage pent up inside her. She didn't intend to repress it anymore.

It was cold and they hadn't taken the time to grab their cloaks. But running kept Izzy and Helen warm.

"Come on," Izzy called when Helen began to lag behind.

"I can't run anymore. I'm too tired."

"Well, I'm tired too. Come on." She grabbed Helen's hand, dragging her along.

"But my side hurts," Helen wailed. "I have to rest."

Disgusted with Helen—angry at the world—Izzy stopped. She rolled her eyes. "You're such a baby."

"I am not."

"I'm doing this for you, and you don't even cooperate."

"What do you mean? Where are we going anyway?"

Izzy planted her fists on her hips. They'd crested the windswept hill and were out of sight of the big house and its multitude of window eyes. But they were still exposed in the open field where anyone might see them. "We're running away from there until we get what we want."

Helen blinked her damp lashes and wiped her nose on her sleeve. "What *do* we want?"

Izzy opened her mouth, then closed it. What *did* she want? After a moment she said, "What I want is for people to stop always ordering me about. Everybody telling me what to do, where to live. Isn't that what you want?"

Helen nodded. "I just want to live with Phoebe at Plummy Head."

Izzy gnawed on her lower lip. "Me too. And we have to bring Leya with us. Once she's well, anyway."

For a moment the two girls stared at one another. "Are we really sisters?" Helen asked, her voice small and timid.

Izzy looked her over. Helen wouldn't last ten minutes in Seven Dials. But . . . She shrugged. "I suppose we are. I mean, if he's *your* father and he's *my* father . . ." She paused. "Your mother's a bitch, you know. You should be glad you never had to live with her."

Helen gave a little sniff. "I used to want to live with her in London. But now I'm glad I always lived with Aunt Phoebe right here. Do you have any aunts?"

"No. Well, yes," Izzy amended. "My father—*our* father—he has two sisters. At least, that's what he says. So they're my aunts and they're your aunts too." On impulse Izzy grabbed Helen's hand. But this time it wasn't just to drag her along. She smiled, a little shyly. "We're sisters, all three of us. That means we have to look out for each other. All right?"

Helen smiled back and squeezed her hand. "All right."

"Come on, then. Let's go."

They started for the forest, but stopped when they heard a high-pitched bark. "Bruno!" Helen shouted as the valiant puppy labored over the hill. "He followed us."

"I forgot to tell you, someone brought him to Farley Park last night after they milked the goats," Izzy said, scooping him up, with no complaints from Helen. Then together they trudged down the faintly greening hill. "I have a secret hideout," Izzy said. "We can go there."

"All right. Or we could go to Plummy Head," Helen said, her teeth chattering. "There's a fireplace and a stove, and wood. And food too. I'm hungry. Aren't you?"

"Good idea," Izzy said, changing direction. She cast Helen a small, approving smile. "Good idea, little sister."

"How could you?"

After a frantic search of the house and grounds didn't turn up either of the girls, Phoebe had returned, looking for her pitiful excuse of a sister Louise. She faced Louise now in the second parlor, a grand room warmed by a roaring fire. But no amount of heat could melt the icy rage that encased Phoebe's heart.

Louise glanced up smiling from her comfortable perch on a gold damask settee. She had the gall to look perfectly at home in the handsomely appointed receiving room, as if she deserved to be served tea and biscuits, and be brought pillows and lap throws, and otherwise be attended to by the butler and the parlormaid. A beautiful, feckless creature who lived to be admired and complimented.

But Phoebe was not of a mind to cooperate. All she saw was a hard, amoral creature whom she was ashamed to claim as a sister.

In the face of Phoebe's scorn, Louise's smile faded. "How could I what? Come home after my poor, old mother died? Come to visit my own daughter? Search for my sister here when I couldn't find her at Plummy Head?"

"Don't try to pretend you don't know what I mean." Phoebe stalked into the room and glared down at Louise. "I heard what you said before. You only came here because Lord Farley had you searched out. What I want to know is how you could steal from your baby, your own flesh and blood? How could you?"

A mulish expression turned Louise's face hard. "It was *my* money too. I'm the one who had to bear her, to get thick and ugly and fat. My figure has never been the same. Never! You'd understand what I meant if you'd ever had a child of your own."

Phoebe's nails dug into her palms; it was the only way to prevent herself from slapping Louise. Could anyone really be that self-centered and uncaring? Could any mother be? "You might have borne Helen, but I raised her. I was the one who saw how she pined for her real mother. For you. But all the while you were off entertaining yourself and worse, depriving her of the support her father thought he was providing."

Louise jerked to her feet. "It's not like it was that friggin' much! D'you have any idea how much it costs to live in town?" She tugged on the frilly cuffs of her stylish gown. "No. Of course you don't. 'Cause you've lived your whole life in that stupid cottage with your stupid goats and that stupid garden. Meanwhile I've had to work like a fiend just to keep up appearances."

"Yes. And I can see just how you've suffered. Is that Belgian lace?" Phoebe flicked the extravagant ruffle at Louise's throat. "And the gown. Is it French silk or Italian?"

Louise's green eyes narrowed to slits. "You couldn't possibly understand what's required to get by in London."

"No? Maybe that's because I was working so hard to get by in Yorkshire. Maybe it's because I was making over my old dresses to accommodate a growing child's needs. Oh, what's the use?" Phoebe threw her hands up and turned away. Louise had always been vain and selfish—and greedy. Phoebe had just never realized how much so. She would never change, nor could the past be altered. But the future . . . She turned back to face her.

"So, I suppose you're here to hand Helen over to him. How much is he paying you for her?"

Louise jutted out her jaw. "He's her father, you know. He doesn't *have* to pay anything to take custody of her, him being a viscount and all. Any court in the land would give her over to him. I really don't have any choice in the matter—"

Phoebe raised a hand to cut her off. "How much?"

Louise gave her a hard smile. "All right. All right. He's giving me a lot. That's all you need to know. A lot." She patted her elaborate coiffure. "Honestly, Phoebe. I don't know what you're so upset about. Look around you." Her hand gestured around the room. "The girl will be growing up in the lap of luxury now. Mother would be so pleased." Then, "Poor Mother. I was positively devastated when I received your post. Do you plan to sell the cottage?"

"Good lord," Phoebe exclaimed, aghast at the extent

of her sister's avarice. "First you steal from your own child, then you sell her away from everything she knows. Now you want to sell our family home out from under me? Well, the answer is no. I'm not selling Plummy Head."

"It's half mine, you know."

"I'm not selling!"

Louise rolled her eyes. "Oh, very well. You don't have to shout. And I didn't sell the girl. Lord Farley is just generous, is all."

Phoebe made a rude noise. "Yes. Generous."

Louise smoothed an imagined wrinkle in her bodice. "If you dislike him so, why are you here?"

That quickly, guilt rose to compete with Phoebe's fury. "He needed help with his children, so he offered me a position as their governess."

Louise's eyes narrowed and her expression turned crafty. "Are you sure that's all he wants, little sister?" Then she laughed. "You're such an innocent. I know you're angry with me, but take a bit of advice from one who knows. There are certain men who are simply impossible to resist. Once they set their sights on a woman, there's nothing she can do to resist him—and Viscount Farley is just such a man."

She strolled around Phoebe, studying her with an assessing eye. "Should he ever develop a taste for rustics, I fear you might be in grave danger."

Every word struck Phoebe like a blow, like the hammer strike sealing a coffin, confirming the terrible truth she wanted to deny. She swallowed past the lump in her throat, relieved Louise was behind her now and couldn't see her face. "I assure you," she stated through clenched teeth, "I could never approve of a profligate like Lord Farley."

Louise laughed. "So you say."

"I mean it." And she did. At that moment Phoebe hated James Lindford. He was manipulative and shallow and self-serving. A perfect match for her sister.

"Very well then," Louise said. "But there's no reason you cannot profit from his situation, Phoebe. If he wants you to be governess to his burgeoning brood, be sure you make him pay. Now that there's three children to mind, you must ask for a higher salary than whatever it is he's proposed. And consider. If he weds, he's bound to have even more brats." She gave a knowing chuckle. "The man's very good at making babies. A veritable baby maker. Of course, there was all that mess in town with his fiancée. Did you hear about it?"

Numbed by everything that had happened, Phoebe barely managed to reply. "Yes, I heard." From guilt to rage to desolation, then back to rage, her emotions pummeled her like an angry sea venting its all against a crumbling dory. This last surge of guilt, however, managed to swamp her, turning rage to exhaustion and resignation. Her shoulders slumped, and shaking her head, she turned to leave. She still needed to find Helen and Izzy. Since she hadn't found them at Farley Park, they must have run off into the woods.

"Where are you going?" Louise demanded.

"To find Helen."

"She's not your responsibility anymore, Phoebe. Her father has servants for that. They'll find her."

Such a complete inability to comprehend the love of family for family didn't warrant a response. Like a desperate creature gasping out its final breath, the last bit of affection Phoebe felt for her sister died.

"I should think you'd be grateful she'll be taken care of forever," Louise went on, following her into the foyer. "Now that you don't have to care for her every minute of the day you can afford to spend a little time on yourself. Fix yourself up; maybe even find a beau of your own. You're still young enough to catch a man, you know. You could get married and have your own children."

Phoebe just shook her head.

"Come now. Don't be angry with me, Phoebe. Let me help you. I can show you how to fix your hair. You're not that bad looking, you know. A few tricks with kohl and carmine. A little powder to whiten your skin. Why, I can make you beautiful."

All Phoebe wanted was to escape—from Louise, from this house, from this nightmare she'd somehow blundered into. Then from the corner of her eye she detected a movement. Above them Lord Farley had paused at the top of the stairs—Helen's father and the primary source of her pain and disillusionment.

Swallowing the sudden rise of unwonted emotion, she turned to face Louise who stared expectantly at her. "I don't want to look beautiful, as you term it, not if it attracts the lowly sort of men you cavort with. You know, the sort who gets a woman with child, then abandons her."

She left with her cold words hanging in the air, damning them both for the selfishness of their careless behavior.

Only one of them felt the sting of her accusation, however. Only one of them felt any guilt or shame.

And only one of them recognized that in finding his long-lost child, he might have lost his one hope for pulling his fragile little family together.

CHAPTER 10

James paid Louise to leave early.

He gave her fifty pounds for her journey home, as well as a letter to his London man-of-business authorizing a considerable amount to be transferred into her account once she legally signed over all parental rights to Helen. To sweeten the deal and hasten her departure, he offered her the use of his traveling coach complete with driver and footman to take her back to London. Anything to get her out of Farley Park and far away from Phoebe and Helen.

But as the heavy coach lumbered down the long driveway, with specific instructions to the driver not to take her anywhere near Swansford Village or Plummy Head, James found no relief. He stood at the window, blindly following the carriage's progress, and pondering his dismal situation. The problem was, he was deluding himself with details, and that only worked for so long.

Yes, he wanted Louise LaFleur—once Louise Churchill—as far away from him and his family as possible. The very sight of the woman sickened him. But she wasn't the villain here. It was him. Louise's shallow self-absorption was merely a weak reflection of everything he'd been in his life. Smug. Confident. Careless. Plowing through life with never a thought for the damage he left in his wake.

Money solved all problems. That had been the central philosophy of his life. And it still seemed to be. Just as Louise relied on her feminine charms to get what she wanted, he relied on his title and money. If you don't like the mess you've gotten into, throw money at it until it goes away.

The truth was, they were two of a kind, pitiful examples of the human race at its very worst. From the outside they looked fine. But inside, where it counted, they were rotten to the core.

And together they'd succeeded in devastating the two people least deserving of pain.

Outside, a bank of low clouds scudded across the late afternoon sky. An ugly day all around. God, would spring never come?

He rotated his neck, then rolled his shoulders, trying to loosen the knotted muscles there. Finally he turned and, head sunk low, he trudged up the stairs.

At least Leya was asleep. In the midst of all this chaos she had somehow managed to have a good day. But where had Izzy gotten to? And Helen?

He stared down at his sleeping child, the youngest of his three. But for the first time that day he allowed himself to think about his middle child. Helen. That shy little girl, so exquisite and delicate, was his, the third of the daughters, the one he'd been searching for.

It was a comfort to know that at least she had received a good upbringing, that she'd been safe all these years and surrounded by love. But her first seven years were still lost to him.

What a fool he'd been. If nothing else, he should have visited his children, made an effort to know them sooner.

He could have prevented Izzy living the wretched life she'd been forced into. He could at least have given each of them the image of a father to hold on to, the face of a man who cared about them.

Instead, he'd paid off their mothers, pretending he'd done his duty by his children when in reality he'd just been ignoring them. Was it any wonder they hated him?

He stroked Leya's baby-soft cheek, and smiled at the automatic sucking motions her little rosebud mouth made. At least he'd come to his senses in time for Leya. He would make certain she always knew that her father loved her.

As for the other two . . . He looked back at the window, out at the dreary afternoon sky. He owed it to them to be their father. Better to start late than to abandon them altogether. And the first thing he needed to do was find them.

Smoke from her cottage chimney swept west on the wind. Phoebe sighed as she hurried across the muddy field. They were here. For the first time that day she felt good.

When she burst into the kitchen the stench of scorched food assaulted her nose. They'd obviously burnt something on the stove. But she was too happy to see their startled faces to care.

"I've been so worried!" She flung herself to her knees between their two chairs at the table and hugged each of them to her. "Don't ever frighten me like that again. Do you hear me?" She gave Helen a severe look, then Izzy. But she ruined the effect by hugging them again so tight that Helen yelped.

"Sorry."

"I'm not going back there," Izzy said, ducking out of Phoebe's embrace. "You can't make me."

"Me neither," Helen said.

Izzy picked up a hard, scorched biscuit and slathered it with butter. Helen mimicked the action. "I'd rather live here," Izzy said. "You'll let me, won't you?"

"Say you will," Helen pleaded. "She's my sister, you know."

Izzy paused with the biscuit halfway to her mouth. "But I'm not stayin' if that bitch comes to live here."

"Izzy!"

The girl rolled her eyes. "All right. Not if that . . . that *woman* decides to live here too. If she comes to Plummy Head, I'm running away and this time nobody will find me. Not ever."

"Me too," Helen echoed, though a trifle less certain than Izzy.

Despite the utter seriousness of their threats, Phoebe had to swallow a smile. In all the drama of this dreadful day, the one fact she'd overlooked now stared her straight in the face. Helen and Izzy were sisters. Leya too. And happily, it seemed that the startling revelation had drawn the two little girls together.

She watched as tough Izzy smiled at sensitive Helen, and Helen smiled back. Just as Izzy had become fiercely protective of Leya, so had she now accepted this newest half sister and brought her into the fold of her odd little family. Likewise, it seemed that Helen had found an older sister to look up to.

They were becoming a family. It was only a father and their mothers that they lacked.

At the moment, however, Phoebe didn't want to think about the troubling adults in this awful muddle. She had the girls safe here; Lord Farley would take care of Leya. For now she just wanted to sit down and rest.

"Izzy's sleeping in my room with me," Helen said as Phoebe put away her cloak and boots.

"All right."

They were asleep long before dark, however. In front of the fireplace with Helen reading a story to Izzy—a happenstance Phoebe had at one time wished for—they slowly dozed off on the rug with Bruno curled happily between them.

Standing in the doorway between the kitchen and parlor, Phoebe wondered if she and Louise had ever shared that strong a sisterly bond. She couldn't recall ever being as close with Louise as Izzy and Helen had so swiftly become.

Inside her chest the aching hole she'd tried to ignore yawned like a terrifying, bottomless chasm. They were here now, two innocent children, their lives subject to the whims of their fickle parents. Unfortunately, not being a parent to either of them, Phoebe had no say in how long they would remain under her roof. Eventually Louise or Lord Farley was bound to come for them, and she would have to let them go.

As if she'd conjured up just such a visitor, a noise in the yard alerted her to someone's approach. Bruno lifted his head, but lazy puppy that he was, he flopped his tail once, sighed and rolled to his other side, then went back to sleep. Bracing herself, Phoebe unpinned her apron and smoothed her hair. If it was her despicable sister Louise, she would bar the door. Just see if she didn't.

But if it was Lord Farley . . .

"Are they here?" he asked, still astride his steed when she opened the door.

Staring up at him Phoebe nodded. Her throat had perversely become too tight to speak.

He stared down at her. His animal snorted and stamped. "May I come in?"

"They're napping."

"I'll be quiet."

She wanted to turn him away, but they were his children. Both of them. Phoebe's fingers tightened on the door. "Very well."

She didn't watch as he dismounted his horse and saw to the animal's needs. But even in the warm comfort of her familiar kitchen the image of him on his horse stayed in her mind. He looked tired. Also, perhaps, a little contrite. She pressed one hand to her knotted stomach. He was not a terrible father, she reminded herself. Not entirely. And he was trying to improve. He was just a man who continually allied himself with the wrong kind of women.

But that made her stomach hurt even worse. It had been bad enough knowing he had a world of experience with women. But to put a face to one of them, to know one of them had been her sister . . . Phoebe trembled with conflicting emotions.

She wanted to hate him, and until just now, she had. But at the sight of him, seeing that his concern for the children was real—somehow her hatred thinned and weakened and wanted to retreat.

Only she couldn't let it.

When the front door opened Phoebe busied herself in the kitchen with filling the tea ball and pouring simmering water into a cup. She heard him remove his greatcoat, hat, and gloves, then peek into the parlor. Bruno whined a greeting, but from the children no sound came. Then he strode to the table, each footfall an ominous sign that the time had come for her to face him.

"Louise is gone," he began.

Thank God. But even that happy fact couldn't lighten Phoebe's mood. She carried the tea to the table. "How did you manage that?"

His eyes were dark, shuttered against any display of emotion. He shrugged. "I gave her what she came for:

money. Then I sent her back to London in style."

Phoebe frowned. "In style? Oh. In one of your coaches."

"The big one."

She looked down at the teapot and gave the tea ball a jiggle. "I'm sure that pleased her enormously—although you may never see either the coach or your driver again."

"Even if that were true, I'd still believe that I got the better of the bargain."

They stood on opposite sides of the ancient table, solid English oak. But more than old wood separated them. The gulf between them was created by society, by custom, and now, by Louise.

They were still connected through Helen, though—Helen and the unfortunate physical attraction between them. Despite her rioting emotions, Phoebe knew she had to be forthright.

"What happened before—" Her face heated with color and she shook her head, breaking the hold of his eyes. "It can never happen again."

She waited, and when he didn't respond, she noisily pulled out a chair and sat. "Now that we agree on that, I suppose you've come to take Helen away from me."

She heard him sigh, then also sit. "Helen needs you, Phoebe. And so does Izzy. I'm not fool enough to think otherwise. I came here to make sure they were all right. And that you were."

"I'll manage." She lifted her gaze to him. "You needn't waste any time worrying about me, Lord Farley. I've managed very well all these years, and I'll continue to do so—unless it is your intent to take Helen off to London or some distant place like that."

"No. I won't do that. At some point, of course, she'll need to go to finishing school."

"Yes. I want that for her too."

"Meanwhile, I want you to continue as governess to them all."

"Here at Plummy Head. Not at Farley Park." She was in no position to make demands, but she knew she couldn't go back there, not to the scene of her capitulation to him. Still, she knew the balance of power had shifted today. He held all the cards, as he surely knew. For he could eventually hire another governess, whereas she could never find a replacement for her darling Helen.

Slowly he nodded. "Yes. For now it might be best if you continue to give them their instruction here." He paused. "How angry are they with me?"

She let out a humorless laugh. "Izzy vows she'll never return to Farley Park again. And Helen's going along with anything Izzy says."

"I see. Are you going to help me regain their trust?" His long fingers turned his cup in a restless circle upon its saucer. "Or will you encourage them in their anarchy?"

"It's up to you to earn their trust."

His hand stilled on the cup; his eyes remained fixed on her. "Do you think I can?"

Phoebe was slow to answer. "They're just little children. In time, yes, I believe you can win their trust—if you don't do anything stupid."

A long silence stretched between them. Then he said, "Can I regain your trust?"

She shook her head. "No."

It wasn't the answer he expected. Phoebe wasn't certain it was an answer she believed.

"No?"

She steeled herself against the traitorous emotions fomenting in her own chest. Only the most foolish of women would ever trust this man. "I trust you to do your best for your daughters. You've already shown more concern for them than most men in your position would."

His mouth twisted in a half-smile. "But you don't trust *me*. With *you*."

"Why should I?" She stared challengingly at him.

"What if I said I wanted to change the sort of life I've been living? I'm trying to make a good home for my girls. Doesn't that count for anything?"

Phoebe swallowed hard. *Not when you're seducing the hired help.* But she wasn't ready to discuss that. "If your Lady Catherine doesn't have faith in you, why should I?"

His eyes narrowed. She'd scored a direct blow with that one. It didn't make her feel particularly good, but still she pressed her advantage. "Tell me this, when your daughters come of age, what sort of men will you want for them?"

His brow creased in irritation. "That's not fair, Phoebe. As you said, they're only little children."

"Not for long. In a few years young men will be calling on Izzy, and soon after that, Helen. Will you approve of men like yourself?"

He leaned forward, his elbows on the table. "All men are like me, Phoebe. All of them."

"They are not."

"Yes. They are."

"Maybe in London. But not here."

"Everywhere."

"If that were true I would have lost my—" She broke off, confused and embarrassed. Angry. "They're not all like you."

"Trust me, they are. The difference is in the women. Some say yes more easily than others."

Her face went scarlet. "Are you saying I'm the easy sort?"

"No. No, not at all."

"Yes you are. Two weeks is all it took." Trembling, she pushed away from the table. "This isn't going to work. I think you'd better leave." She stood, tilting her chin belligerently even as she knotted her shaking hands within the folds of her skirt. If he didn't leave, she was afraid she might burst into tears, making an utter fool of herself.

He stood too, slowly pushing upright. "I'll leave. But you're wrong, Phoebe. This *is* going to work. My girls need you. And I think you need them too."

Something inside her started trembling anew, something that shook her so violently she feared her knees might collapse. But it was something he must not detect. She managed to keep her voice cool and aloof. "Perhaps you also need them, otherwise you wouldn't have gone to such extremes to find them. So it seems we share a similar weakness, Lord Farley. You may possess the legal power over those girls," she added. "But it's me that they love."

Cruel words, and they struck home. She saw the flinching pain in his eyes. But to his credit he only nodded and studied her with a cool, assessing expression. "Believe it or not, I didn't come here to antagonize you, Phoebe. Nor to insult you."

"All right then. You came to find your children and you have. You can see that they're safe, so now you're free to go."

"I'd hoped to talk to them."

"They're asleep. Besides, it's too soon. They need time to digest all that's happened. We all do."

She sounded like a shrew, sharp and accusing, and once again his eyes narrowed. "Very well. But I'll be back tomorrow. In the morning."

"Fine." She crossed her arms, wanting him to go—

wanting this entire convoluted mess to go away. Only it wouldn't. Helen was his now, not hers. She'd never really been hers, but at least there had been no one with a stronger claim to her.

Unfortunately there was someone now.

Phoebe wanted to despise him, but somehow she couldn't. This was the man who was taking Helen away from her, and the man who'd stolen her innocence, the two most valuable parts of her life. Yet he was also the man who'd given her a glimpse of something she'd never known existed. Absolute joy. Temporary, but absolute.

Phoebe's trembling grew worse; she had to clench her teeth and she feared her voice would reveal all if she spoke.

"Will you at least tell them that I came looking for them?" he asked. "That I care about their safety—and their happiness?"

His face looked as stern and impassive as ever. But his eyes—they were alive with emotion. Oh, God, she'd never be able to hate this man, not when he loved his children this much.

She gave a stiff nod. It was all she could manage. Then he left, snatching up his coat and hat, and stalking out the door, only pausing briefly to gaze upon his exhausted daughters. He shut the door softly so as not to disturb the children. But he might as well have slammed it, the impact on Phoebe was so strong.

What was she going to do? How was she supposed to survive the next ten years and longer caring for James Lindford's children yet *not* caring for him?

She sat there a long while, until a wet nose shoved its way into her hand. Bruno whimpered, then ambled to the door. Phoebe rose automatically to let him out.

"Good boy," she murmured as she watched him dart out into the chilly dusk.

Then beyond the low stone wall that separated the cottage yard from the lane, she spied a tall, dark silhouette, a man leading his horse through the gathering gloom.

Her heart stuttered to a halt. He was still here. She'd thought him gone by now, but he'd lingered. Bruno's nose came up as he caught the scent, and when the puppy barked, Lord Farley looked up. Like a blast of salty wind off the sea, the impact of his gaze struck Phoebe.

He paused, then raised a hand in farewell. Unable to resist, she raised hers in response. She pulled it back quickly, though, and turned for the safety of her warm, familiar house. But shutting the door couldn't shut out the image of him any more than it could shut out the oncoming cold of the night. Some of that cold had come in with her and it would take time for it to fade into the forced warmth of her kitchen.

But it *would* fade, she told herself. Just as the cold spring always gave way to summer heat, and fog crept away under the onslaught of the sun, so would this unseemly interest she had in the dangerously attractive Lord Farley fade. It had to.

For if it did not—if her perverse fascination with him was what she feared it was—then she was condemned to a lifetime of loving a man she could never have and certainly could never trust.

CHAPTER 11

James walked the three miles back to Farley Park, leading his horse, unconcerned by the cold, the dark, or the
rising mist from the sea. Everything was out of control—
his household, his children, his emotions. He didn't want
to return to his big, empty house. If it weren't for Leya,
he wouldn't go back at all. But where else was there to
go?

It was humbling to admit that though he'd never
needed anybody before, he needed somebody now. He
was angry, he was frustrated, but most of all, he was
lonely.

Lonely. It was a foreign experience, one he hated, but
didn't know how to fix.

At least there was one person who was always happy
to see him, and once at Farley Park he went straight to
the nursery. But he was disappointed to find Leya asleep.
"She fussed a bit," the maid who'd sat with her told him.
"She wants to scratch the blisters. But her fever is milder
and she ate well. This sort of pox don't affect the little
children as bad as the big 'uns."

That was welcome news. But Leya's peaceful slum-
ber left James even more alone. Hard to believe that only

a week ago he'd prayed for Leya to sleep. Now he wanted her awake, her dark eyes bright and trusting upon him. At least *she* loved him.

He retreated to his study for a whisky, but the house was too quiet for him to enjoy it. Too still. It needed children in it. It needed Leya and Izzy and Helen.

And Phoebe?

He rotated the amber liquid in the squat tumbler he held, fighting the urge to quaff the contents in one gulp and pour another.

His life was an unmitigated disaster with no one to blame but himself. But it wasn't just the enforced solitude of country life that was driving him mad, nor the bedlam he'd created with his children. If he was losing his mind, it was on account of some fresh-faced country woman with good manners, a better mind, and a winning way with children.

What he needed was some distance from the situation. Too much had happened, too fast.

But there was no distance to be had, and no escaping his thoughts—nor his guilt. He should never have kissed her. That was his first mistake. That kiss had led too fast to him making love to her, which had been another mistake. A monumental one. For Phoebe Churchill had been a virgin, and not only that, she wasn't the sort of woman a decent man fooled around with. She might be Louise's sister, but in every way that counted, she was her direct opposite.

He lurched to his feet, paced the claustrophobic space, then threw himself back into the chair. When the front door knocker echoed from down the hall, he leaped up once more, listening. When no one answered and it sounded a second time he cursed under his breath. Where in blazes was Benson? Propriety be damned, he'd answer the door himself. Maybe it was Phoebe.

Instead it was the last person he expected to see in such a rural locale. "Kerry? Bloody hell. What are you doing here?"

The Honorable Kerrigan Fairchild, youngest son of the Earl of Sanderly, strode into the foyer, all grins and good humor. "I thought I'd surprise you. But what's this about? Don't you employ a butler to direct this monstrous country abode of yours? I hope it's not some rustic custom in Yorkshire to answer your own door. Or has that wild child of yours caused the entire staff here to flee?"

"Some of them are still with me," James said, only half ironic. He closed the door. "God, am I glad to see you."

"Bored, eh? I thought you might be."

"Not bored. Not exactly."

"No?" Kerry scanned the quiet foyer and adjoining rooms with a discerning eye. "Nice place. Though you look like a fright. So. Where's the holy terror?"

"Izzy is staying with a friend."

Kerry grinned. "Pawned her off on some poor unsuspecting fool, have you? And it's Izzy now. I see she's won that battle—and probably several others as well."

In a way James supposed she had. At any rate, it was not worth arguing the point. "Leya is ill. It's best if Izzy spends as much time away from here until we're sure Leya's not contagious." He led Kerry into his study and poured both of them a drink, then waved Kerry to a seat and threw himself back into his chair. "Speaking of my daughters, I've located the third one."

"Indeed? Have you met her yet?"

"I have. In fact, she's here. That is, she's lived near Farley Park all her life."

"That's convenient." When James didn't respond, Kerry's dark brows rose. "It's *not* convenient?"

Once more James rolled his drink around in its glass, staring blankly at the amber liquid. "It's messy. Sit down; I'll explain the situation to you."

"Yes, maybe you should. Then I'll bring you up to snuff on what's going on in town. I'm sure you'll find it vastly entertaining."

An hour passed. Outside the closed doors of the study the house activities proceeded. Inside the study, the fire burned low. It was difficult to say which man's tale shocked the other more. Kerry reserved judgment on the restrained tale his friend revealed of a lost child found and a goat girl turned governess. He wanted to meet this properly brought-up farmer's daughter himself before he accused James of what he suspected the man was up to. Again.

As for James, he wasn't certain he believed the preposterous story Kerry related. "After the way she feels I humiliated her, why would Catherine change her mind?"

Kerry took a long pull of his drink, then made a face. "Perhaps the gay blades around town are beginning to wear on her nerves. Constant flattery and adoration can be trying, you know, even to someone as accustomed to flattery and adoration as our lovely Catherine."

"Catherine has that effect on men. Especially on those green fellows who consider themselves dashing."

"I'm afraid age is no cure for Catherine's appeal," Kerry said. "I heard Edward Altwood waxing eloquent about her, and he's got one foot in the grave. I've also heard that Percival Langley has become quite chummy with her and her father."

"Percival Langley." James shook his head. "Poor Catherine. But at least she has some balm for the disservice I did her."

Kerry stared at James from over the rim of his tumbler. "If adulation were a balm, I'm sure she would be happier than she is."

James set his empty glass down on the table. "I'm surprised you haven't thrown your hat into that ring. You and Catherine have always gotten on famously."

After a pause Kerry agreed. "Yes. We have. Unfortunately her father has higher aspirations for her than my paltry two thousand a year. I fear, however, that my greatest failing for him is that unlike you, I've no interest in politics at all."

James crossed to the hearth, threw on a log, then poked the sputtering embers to renewed life. "Speaking of her father, the last time I saw Lord Basingstoke he vowed to have my head on a pike if I ever approached Catherine again. He also said it would be his life's goal to see me ruined for any position involving foreign affairs."

"He certainly has the clout to do it," Kerry said. Then he shrugged. "What can I say? Notwithstanding her father's vitriol, Catherine told me that she misses you, and that she may have acted somewhat hastily. She's making a trip up to Yorkshire to visit you."

"To visit me? The hell you say. And her father has agreed to it?"

Kerry finished off the contents of his glass. "It seems so. Perhaps your political career is not ruined after all."

James raked a hand through his hair. This was the last thing he'd expected. "I'd given up on Catherine and her father. If she's coming here with his approval, that can only mean she wants to renew our betrothal. Did she say when she's arriving?"

"I believe her plan is to visit an ancient aunt of hers in Scarborough. That way she can decide on an impulsive side trip to visit you and thereby save face should your reunion not take," Kerry said, crossing one leg over the other. He studied James through narrowed eyes. "It will take, won't it?"

For a moment James didn't reply. If Catherine was willing to forgive him and accept his children—if she was prepared to renew their betrothal—then he still had a chance to someday succeed her father as the House of Lords' most influential member regarding foreign policy. His political goals would again be within his reach. All he had to do was regain her trust and convince her that his children were worthy of her concern.

But how was he to do that when Izzy and Helen had fled to Phoebe's cottage?

Phoebe. He straightened in his chair. If Catherine came to Farley Park, she was bound to meet Phoebe.

Bloody hell. Phoebe was already furious with him, and rightfully so. There was no telling what she might say to Catherine. Nor what Catherine might say to her.

The sound of a throat clearing brought him back to the moment. "You do still want to marry her," Kerry asked. "Don't you?"

"Of course," James reassured him. "Of course." But for a moment he wasn't certain. Marriage to Catherine would allow him to return to his old life in London. But living in London would put an end to the affair he'd just embarked on with Phoebe.

Not that she was presently disposed to continue it. But once Helen settled into life as his daughter, and life at Farley Park settled into a comfortable routine, he could bring Phoebe around.

The problem was, if Kerry was right about Catherine's imminent visit, he might be running out of time.

"We're not going back," Izzy stated. Beside her Helen nodded.

Phoebe stared at their twin expressions of determination. How had she not seen the similarities in them? Blond hair, blue eyes. But she'd been looking for Louisa's image in Helen, and Lord Farley's in Izzy. The truth was, however, that they both had their father's eyes. Even Leya, with her olive-toned skin, had inherited his brilliant blue eyes.

"We want to stay here," Izzy continued.

Coming back to the present, Phoebe nodded. She wanted them to stay with her too. But she knew Lord Farley would never agree.

During a long, restless night she'd come to the conclusion that she must not fight him anymore, at least when it came to the girls. As a child, she'd hated living in a family fraught with anger and animosity. She had no intention of letting that happen to these girls. So she'd decided to cooperate with the man—up to a point. That meant her first goal must be to improve him in his daughters' mistrustful eyes.

"More than anything I want you to stay here. Both of you. But your father loves you and he wants you with him. And he wants *me* to help all of you become a family."

"But we can be a family here at Plummy Head," Helen said. "Just like we were before."

"That's right," Izzy said. "Me and Helen never had a father before, neither of us. We don't need one now. Especially not him."

Phoebe saw Helen glance hesitantly at her new older sister. All her life Helen had felt keenly the lack of a father. Bad enough her mother had never been around, but at least she'd existed. Her father had never even had a name. Now, though, the situation was reversed. Louise might have washed her hands of her little girl, but James Lindford was here, very real and more than willing to be an active part of her life.

Phoebe cupped Izzy's cheek and stroked Helen's hair. "When your family is as small as ours, the loss of even one person is a very sad event. Your mothers have relinquished both of you to your father because they knew he can do a better job taking care of you—"

"They sold us," Izzy interrupted. "Like cows. Like goats."

"Like we sell a round of fat, white cheese to Mrs. Leake," Helen added, her little face somber.

Phoebe hugged them both, one urgent shared embrace, and reveled in the returned embrace of their skinny, little-girl arms. "Your mothers are both fools. But I'm glad they're fools, otherwise I wouldn't have the two of you here in my house with me. And I'll be even more glad when Leya's old enough for lessons too."

As she hoped, mention of their baby sister weakened the girls' resolve. "Why can't she come here now?" Helen asked.

"I hope she's not still sick," Izzy said.

"She's too young for lessons, Helen. As for how she's doing, we can ask your father when he comes. Do you remember how worried he was when she first fell ill?"

They both nodded, Izzy sullenly.

"That's because he loves her and worries about her, just as he loves you two and worries about you. I think it's time to stop being so angry with him. Just think about it, all right?"

He arrived just before lunchtime with a basket tied behind his saddle, and a man Phoebe didn't recognize riding alongside.

"I know who he is," Izzy said. "That's Mr. Kerry. I met him in London. He's one of Lord Farley's friends."

Already beset by nerves, Phoebe's stomach did a hard flip-flop. Why had one of his friends from London come this far north? He was a well-dressed nabob with a silver waistcoat peeking from beneath his navy blue frock coat, and gleaming Hessian boots in the stirrups. He appeared far too grand for Plummy Head.

What would a man like that think of her, a simple country woman? Even more unsettling, what might Lord Farley have told him about her? A lead knot formed in her throat. From the way the man's eyes studied her with such clear interest, Phoebe feared he may already have told him too much. How dare he!

"So you are the Miss Churchill who has wrought such a transformation in Farley's children," the man said once they were introduced. He smiled, and it seemed friendly and sincere. "Lord Farley didn't tell me you were even lovelier than you are capable. And you must be Helen," he added, bowing gravely as Helen peered at both men from behind Phoebe's skirts.

Then he winked at Izzy and executed a perfect curtsy before her. When he straightened up his droll grin turned challenging. "Can you do better than that?"

The girl's lips twitched, but she refused to smile. It was plain she was holding on to her anger with both fists. "I *could* curtsy better than that, if I wanted to."

"Hunh. Easy to say. How about you, Miss Helen? Can you curtsy that well?"

Somehow he coaxed a curtsy out of Helen, which goaded Izzy into doing one as well. Above the two blond heads Lord Farley's eyes locked with Phoebe's.

"That deserves a reward," Kerry said. He nudged his friend. "I said, that deserves a reward."

"Ah, yes. Indeed it does," Lord Farley said. He lifted the basket from his horse and set it on the ground. "Come see, girls. There's one for each of you."

Though she was suspicious, Izzy's curiosity was too

great for her to resist. She edged warily toward the basket, lifted the lid, then cried, "Kittens!"

How quickly the girls' mistrust fled, Phoebe thought, watching as they bent over and helped the kittens tumble free of their basket. How easily he bought their cooperation—just as he'd bought their mothers'.

She immediately regretted that thought. *Why are you being so ugly?* They might be like their mothers in some regards, but she, too, was turning out to be uncomfortably like her own. Sour and resentful. Critical. Never satisfied.

"Is the third one for Leya?" Izzy asked, clutching a gray fur ball with huge yellow eyes tight against her chest.

Lord Farley's clear blue gaze rested for one long moment on Phoebe before he turned back to Izzy. He crouched down and lifted the last kitten, a tiny mewing calico creature that barely filled one of his large hands. "Leya has a gray one like yours, Izzy, but with green eyes. This one I brought for Miss Churchill."

All eyes swung to Phoebe, awaiting her response. Helen's eyes sparkled with excitement, clearly delighted by his thoughtfulness. Mr. Fairchild also looked pleased, though not particularly surprised.

Izzy's expression was more speculative. Her eyes, so like her father's—and not just in color—darted from the kitten to Phoebe, then to her father. What was going on in that devious little mind?

As for Lord Farley, there was no mystery about his intentions. He was trying to make peace with her, and though giving her a kitten was small solace for taking away her niece, at least he was trying.

"Thank you." She took the kitten, trying to avoid touching him in the process. It didn't work. His thumb grazed her palm, and the heel of his hand bumped against hers. Momentary touches both.

Yet like the click of a key in a lock, they loosened the stranglehold Phoebe was keeping on her emotions. Fury and gratitude, panic and longing. Too much; too confusing. She pulled the kitten to her chest and stepped back.

"Well," said Mr. Fairchild. "Isn't this pleasant. I declare, there's nothing like a rustic holiday to refresh oneself. I say, Miss Churchill, are those goats in your shed?"

In short order she was giving him a tour of her little farm, or rather, Izzy and Helen were. For all his sophistication and impressive garb, Mr. Fairchild had an open manner that put everyone at ease. Phoebe found herself bringing up the rear along with Lord Farley.

Feeling his gaze upon her, she said, "Tell me about Leya. Is her recovery progressing?"

"She seems to be improving. Not so feverish. But the pustules are everywhere and she wants to scratch them. She's not very happy. Any suggestions?"

Phoebe kept her eyes on Izzy who was milking Posie with natural-born ease. "All you can do is try to keep her entertained. Distracted."

"I thought the same thing." He paused. "It would help if you came to visit her."

She forced down any show of emotion. "I'm sure the girls can keep her distracted."

"Phoebe, listen." Taking her arm, he turned her to face him. "When Izzy and Helen come home today, they'll need you with them."

Rattled by his touch, she shook off his hand. "You have a houseful of servants to tend their needs."

"It's not the same."

She tilted up her chin. "You should have thought of that *before* you decided to take Helen away from me."

She hadn't meant to say that. She'd vowed to restrain her resentment and hide her pain. But it was out in the open now. No use to pretend otherwise. She blew out a short breath. "You say you can give them a better life, but it's plain you can't, not if you have to rely on me for help."

"I never denied that I'd need help," he said into the sudden silence that gripped the new goat shed. Even the shooting sound of milk against the side of the bucket ceased. "I can't be a mother to them, Phoebe. I'm not equipped for it and, anyway, I don't know how. But even with my shortcomings, I can do a better job raising them than their real mothers did."

"At least Helen's *real* mother knew enough to leave her with me."

"Yes, and that's exactly why I want you to live in at Farley Park and be a full-time governess to them. You could be with her every day, just as you've always been."

Helen insinuated herself under Phoebe's arm, intimidated anew by all the stormy adult emotions.

Izzy, manipulative opportunist that she was, chose that moment to align herself with her father. "I want to see Leya. I miss her," she said, injecting a yearning ache into her voice. "Don't you miss her too, Phoebe?"

Phoebe's gaze went from father to daughter. What a conniving pair they were. "Of course I miss her. That's not the point."

"Don't fight," Helen pleaded, hugging Phoebe around the waist. "Please don't fight."

In the end it was easier for Phoebe to just resign herself and go along with them. Once Leya was well, this particular argument would no longer work, she told herself. Once Helen and Izzy were settled at Farley House with an established daily routine, her presence wouldn't be so necessary to them. She could live at Plummy Head and they could come for lessons. It wouldn't be the same, but at least she would see Helen every day.

For today, however, she conceded to join them at Farley Park.

Besides, she told herself as she walked alongside the horse which Lord Farley led with Helen astride, she *did* miss Leya.

Leya's sweet, splotchy face broke into a toothy grin when she spied Phoebe. "Mamamama," she chanted, bouncing up and down in her bed. "Mamamama."

"Hello, sweet thing. My little funny face," Phoebe crooned as she lifted her up. It felt good to cradle a warm, obliging baby in her arms, even one that smelled of camphor and felt suspiciously damp.

"What is this paste on her?"

Lord Farley held up a jar. "Something the cook said would hasten the healing."

"But it's so greasy. Something drying would be better. Izzy, Helen?" Phoebe called to the girls who stood in the open door, banned from entering the sickroom. "Have Cook prepare a pot of oat porridge and bring a big bowl of it to me. That will help dry her blisters," she said to Lord Farley. "And tell the kitchen to send up warm water; plenty of it."

James knew he should leave. Phoebe had matters well in hand, and besides, she didn't want him there. But he stayed anyway—for Leya, he told himself as he watched her examine the baby—arms, legs, tummy, backside. She even checked inside Leya's mouth, much to the baby's outrage.

"Now, now," she crooned, teasing Leya back into good humor. "You must be feeling considerably better if you can summon up such a strident temper."

All during the examination Phoebe had shot sidelong glances at him, looking away when he met her eyes. And throughout, she kept up an aimless chatter to Leya until the water appeared.

But if she thought she could pretend he didn't exist, he meant to show her she was wrong. "Here, let me help," he said as she began to undress Leya for her bath. But what started as a perverse form of belligerence, a determination to make Phoebe react to him, swiftly became something else. Leya was a slippery little eel, plump and splotchy, and playful for the first time in days. He'd never bathed her before, never even considered doing that sort of thing for a child.

But watching Leya splash and hearing her laugh warmed James's heart, even as the sight of the angry little blisters all over her body brought out an intense need to protect her.

That Phoebe felt the same was evident: the gentle stroking of her hands as she bathed the child; her delight in Leya's high jinks; her very presence at Farley Park at all. She loved his children, not just Helen, but Izzy and Leya too, and that was an advantage for him.

All night he'd considered the ramifications of Catherine's pending visit. If they renewed their betrothal, once they wed he would have the political clout he wanted and the career he'd been angling for. He had his children now too.

But that was no longer enough. He frowned at his own perversity. The fact was, he needed to fit Phoebe somewhere into his life, and the best way to do that was to keep her as the children's governess. Given her feelings toward him, it wouldn't be easy. But despite the damage Louise's appearance had done to the seedling trust between him and Phoebe, he refused to accept the situation as hopeless. In time he could maneuver himself back into her good graces, and the children were the best weapon in his arsenal.

For a moment he pondered what it was he was contemplating. A wife and a mistress. Could he juggle them both?

His gaze ran over Phoebe, lingering at the sweet pale skin of her throat as she tilted her head, at the thrust of her breasts against the plain green bodice of her workaday dress, on the narrow line of her waist before it flared into perfectly rounded hips.

She was not a showy woman like Catherine—or like Louise. No, Phoebe was beautiful in a different way, a quiet, unadorned way. She was made of sturdier stuff than the frothy sort of women he'd dallied with in the past. Yet somehow she seemed sweeter than all those others.

James swallowed hard, remembering how delicious she'd been, how fulfilling. He'd had only a brief taste of Phoebe so far, but it was enough to make him know he wanted more. He'd been gorging on confections all these years, never quite satisfied. It was long past time for him to sate his appetite fully.

CHAPTER 12

Phoebe teased Leya, distracting her from the oat paste drying on her widespread blisters. "I believe I'll take my meal in the nursery with Leya," she told Lord Farley. Anything to get him to leave. He'd been staring at her for the past hour, focused on every move she made, as if he were trying to figure her out. It was enough to rattle a girl's brains.

He was probably just trying to learn how to handle Leya, she told herself. He had no other reason to study her so intently. Certainly there was no reason for her heart to quicken or her stomach to knot up like this. But reasoning with her emotions didn't work.

"Shouldn't she be ready for her nap about now?" he asked.

"I suppose."

"Then we'll wait lunch until she's asleep so you can join us."

"That's not necessary."

"It is to me." He leaned one shoulder against the wall and crossed his arms, as if the matter were settled.

There it was again, that steady, unblinking stare. As before, a frisson of unwonted heat spiraled through her.

Phoebe set her jaw and said nothing. Meanwhile Leya took advantage of her distraction and caught Phoebe's hair in her tiny fist. "Mamamama," she again chanted, tugging in triumph.

"Let go, you little dickens. Ow!"

"She's stronger than she looks," Lord Farley said, coming away from the wall. "Here, I'll get it."

Unfortunately, the movement of his fingers in her hair did far more damage than Leya's, though of a decidedly different sort. More than Phoebe's coiffure had come undone by the time Leya relented and went eagerly into her father's arms. To Phoebe's relief, Lord Farley turned away from her and began to walk the baby, patting her back and jiggling her as he sang some low, soothing melody.

But Phoebe's hands nonetheless shook as she repaired her practical hairdo. Combs on the side; a tight twist in the back. Practical and easy to maintain without the use of a looking glass. She'd worn it in the same style for years.

Unbidden Louise's words came to her. "You're not that bad looking, you know. If you'd just fix your hair . . . A few tricks with kohl and carmine . . ."

She frowned and readjusted one of the combs, scraping it so tightly it hurt. "Botheration!"

"What's that?"

"Nothing," she muttered, refusing to meet his eyes. Nothing except that an unrepentant rake whom she ought to disdain possessed the ability to turn her insides to mush.

Nothing except that he had fathered her sister's child and now had taken Helen away from her.

Nothing except that she would always be tied to him through Helen. Always.

Phoebe stared out the window while he sang Leya to

sleep, and all the while she brooded over her situation. It was in this room she'd succumbed to him. On that settee . . .

"Shall we?"

Phoebe gasped at the low voice just behind her. "No." She whirled around, backing up until her rump hit the windowsill. "We can't."

Only inches away from her, Lord Farley tilted his head. "Of course we can. While Leya's asleep I'll have someone else sit with her so we can go down to lunch."

Oh. Lunch. Phoebe cast a guilty look at the settee, then away. She could not believe the direction of her own thoughts. For a moment she'd actually imagined that he was propositioning her again. Thank goodness she hadn't revealed more.

But James saw Phoebe's quick, furtive glance, and he knew exactly what it signified. He'd been avoiding that settee himself, avoiding looking at it or sitting on it. To remember that interlude was to want to repeat it. But he couldn't rush her. This was not the right time. Eventually, though . . . Eventually the right time would come to lay Phoebe down on that sturdy little settee and make good use of it again—

It was his turn to stifle a curse. *Down, laddie. Stay down.* But it was a painful walk to the dining room, following the sway of those sweet, rounded hips, knowing how easy it would be to slide those combs from her hair, imagining the heady pleasure of burying his face in those fragrant waves—and in other places as well.

"Phoebe—"

She turned at the bottom of the stairs, her eyes sharp with warning. "You must not address me so familiarly, Lord Farley. I must always be Miss Churchill to you. It's only proper. Otherwise the servants will talk." Her brow creased in a faint frown. "By rights I shouldn't even dine with you and your family. I'm your employee now, not just a neighbor."

"Nonsense. You're my daughter's aunt. That changes everything."

A shadow passed over her face, sad and resigned. "Yes. Your daughter's aunt. That *does* change everything," she agreed in a low voice that vibrated with emotion.

James stifled a curse. She was Helen's aunt because she was Louise's sister. That's what she was thinking: she was his former lover's sister. But that wasn't the point he wanted to make. She was more than an employee because she was family now: his beloved daughter's beloved aunt.

But she was focused on the brief fling he'd had with her sister, and she couldn't get past that. It had been the stupid mistake of a callow youth, and though it had given them Helen, whom he knew Phoebe loved, it still changed everything for her, in ways she wasn't yet ready to forget.

But he'd make her forget. He was getting his life back in order, and he meant to keep her in it. She started across the hall until he stopped her. "Wait, Phoebe. I have a favor to ask of you."

"A favor?"

"Yes." *I want you in my bed, to make you moan and call my name and forget how angry you are with me.*

He cleared his throat and tried also to clear his mind of such thoughts. He wasn't entirely successful. "I need to hire a housekeeper. Do you have any suggestions?"

She folded her hands together at her waist, the very picture, in her plain, dark dress, of an aloof governess. "No. You might inquire of Mrs. Leake. She knows about everything that goes on in the district. She'll know if someone suitable is available."

"Mrs. Leake. Of course. I'll send word to her."

But I'd rather you take on the task, tend my children, tend my country house—tend me when I'm in residence.

Phoebe's advice to Lord Farley haunted her throughout lunch. It was true, Mrs. Leake was the best person to consult with, for the woman had an uncanny ability to find out about anything going on in the district. No doubt she'd soon learn the truth about Helen's real father and, therefore, about Louise's long-ago tryst with Lord Farley.

The braised pork shanks sat like an indigestible stone in Phoebe's stomach as she contemplated the awful gossip that surely must follow *that* revelation. Maybe if she never went into town again she wouldn't have to suffer the censure certain to come: Louise and Lord Farley, and now her in Lord Farley's employ. Tsk, tsk, tsk.

Maybe she could hire that maid-of-all-work and have *her* do all the errands in town.

But later in the afternoon as Phoebe made the three-mile walk home, declining Lord Farley's insistence that she take the chaise, she found Swansford's nosiest citizen waiting for her, sitting in the store wagon right there in Phoebe's front court.

"Land's sake, child, where *have* you been?" Then before even climbing down from the high seat, Mrs. Leake leaned forward and added, "So, is it true?"

"Mrs. Leake. What a surprise to find you here. How long has it been since you've come up to Plummy Head? Three years? No, four."

The woman had the good grace to blush, but it didn't prevent her from pressing on. "You know perfectly well I was up for your mother's wake just last month. Anyway, the reason I came calling today is that the talk around town is just so unsettling. If it's not true, why, I want to quash it once and for all." She paused, her bird-like gaze scanning Phoebe as if she might be able to detect by the fall of Phoebe's skirt or the angle of her bonnet the truth of Helen's parentage.

Phoebe marched to the front door, trailed by the shamelessly curious shopkeeper. "Why don't you tell me exactly what you've heard, and from whom?"

"Very well. Mrs. Dickerson had it from Gladys Tinsdale that Helen—your Helen—is in fact the love child of Lord Farley. Our Lord Farley and your Louise. Is it true?"

Phoebe swallowed the bitter lump in her throat. It was pointless to lie. "I'm afraid it is."

"Land's sake! I can't believe you've kept such a thing hidden all these years."

Inside the cottage Phoebe turned around to face her harrier. "I assure you, I was as shocked as anyone when I learned of it. Now, is there anything else?"

Mrs. Leake paused in the midst of removing her bonnet. "You needn't be short with me, Phoebe girl. This is none of my making."

"Nor mine. Do you think any of this is easy for me? Do you? I love Helen as if she were my own child, and now I've got to relinquish her to her father because her mother says so—her mother who never once behaved as a decent mother should, and on top of that, who has lied to her family for years!"

Phoebe felt the sting of tears, angry, frustrated, heartbroken tears. She refused to cry in front of anyone, though. Especially Mrs. Leake or any other of Swansford's nosy citizens.

But she'd been holding too much in—too much and for too long—and the tears refused to obey. As she hung her bonnet and cloak upon a peg and made straight for the kitchen, the tears gathered and rose. And when she spied Helen's chair and Helen's slate, and the messy bouquet of early flowers Helen had plucked and arranged in a pretty blue bottle, the tears spilled free. She sank into the nearest chair, buried her face in her hands, and wept as she hadn't wept since she was a child.

"There, there." Mrs. Leake fluttered around, trying nervously to console her. "Don't cry so, Phoebe girl. You're only going to make yourself ill."

"What else . . . is there . . . to do?"

"It will be all right. You'll see." The woman patted Phoebe's back, then unsettled by so much emotion, she busied herself building up the fire and putting water on for tea. "You mustn't take on so, child. Helen loves you and she always will."

"Yes. I know." Phoebe sniffled and wiped her face with an apron folded upon the table. "I'm to be governess to them both. Well, to all three of them eventually."

"Well, then. You see? You'll be with her every day." She paused. "Does that mean you'll be living in at Farley Park?"

"No." Phoebe straightened up. "No. I'm staying right here. They'll come to me for lessons, and sometimes I'll go to them. But I live at Plummy Head."

Mrs. Leake served her a cup of tea, then patted her hand once more. "You're a good girl, Phoebe. Nothing like that wicked sister of yours. Nothing at all."

Phoebe wasn't so certain about that, nor would Mrs. Leake be if she knew what had passed between her and Lord Farley. But the woman would never know, because *no one* would ever know. And it would never happen again.

As for Mrs. Leake, she had much to brood over on the ride back to Swansford. Her several cronies, aware of her visit out to Plummy Head, awaited her at the store.

Once alone, with the door shades pulled down, they promptly bent their heads together.

"It's true," Mrs. Leake said. "Every word of it. As for Phoebe, well, she's devastated, the poor girl. If you could've seen her crying, grieving like her poor heart will never heal. It's a dreadful shame. That's all I can say. It's a dreadful shame the way he took that child from her. And as for that Louise!"

"Yes, but only think of the advantages little Helen shall now have," Gladys Tinsdale pointed out.

"Well, yes. That's true."

"A common bastard and a viscount's bastard, well, they's two very different things," Gladys said to nods all around.

"What Phoebe Churchill needs is a baby of her own to distract her from her troubles," Mrs. Stadler chimed in. "That's what every woman needs."

"But not like her sister did," Mrs. Tinsdale said. "A husband first, then a baby. That would solve all her problems."

A husband for Phoebe Churchill. Mrs. Leake smiled as an idea formed in her head. "You know, I do believe you've got something there. Phoebe needs a husband and a family of her own. Besides, we can't be too trusting of that Lord Farley. Three babies so far, and counting. Our Phoebe's not exactly safe in his employ."

The other women both nodded, their eyes wide and curious. So far none of them had even laid eyes on the rakish Lord Farley. Mrs. Leake went on, "I think we should put our heads together and come up with a list of men around here, good, reliable men, who are in need of a wife."

"Ooh." Mrs. Tinsdale smiled. "I believe I like where you're going with this."

"Indeed," Mrs. Stadler agreed. "You know, there's the

vicar over to Claymont. He's been widowed two years now."

"And the butcher's eldest son, he's of an age to wed."

"She's got land too, owned free and clear," Mrs. Leake said. "That ought to convince any bachelor to marry her."

Kerry Fairchild contemplated his friend over a glass of fine Scotch whisky. "I'm impressed by your skills as a parent. You're better at it than past history would indicate."

"My girls still need a mother."

"I suppose they do. How fortunate, then, that Catherine has changed her mind about you."

"Yes."

Kerry watched as James downed his whisky with one quick flick of his wrist. He went to pour another, but the decanter was empty, so he rang for a maid, then paced from bright hearth to darkened window and back. After a few circuits he yanked the bell pull again. "Damnation, where is everyone?"

The butler arrived, still pulling on his coat. His wispy hair stood on end, and the slippers on his feet revealed he'd already been abed. He blinked his bleary eyes. "Yes, m'lord?"

James frowned. "Are there no maids up to answer the bell?"

"Well, you see, the schedule is a bit muddled, what with—" He broke off and nervously cleared his throat. "It's a bit muddled," he repeated. He waited, and when James didn't say anything, again cleared his throat. "May I get you something, m'lord?"

A muscle ticced in James's jaw. "Another bottle of Scotch, if you please. Then go back to bed. I'm sorry I disturbed you."

The man left, James paced back to the window, and Kerry sipped his whisky. For a man who was about to regain the woman and the life he thought he'd lost, James seemed curiously agitated. "I say, James, I hadn't considered how difficult it must be to find decent servants out here in the hinterlands."

"Nor had I."

"I wonder, was your previous housekeeper truly worse than having no housekeeper at all?"

"Yes."

Kerry's brows rose at the curt response. "I see. Well, perhaps Miss Churchill could suggest someone to replace her. Perhaps Miss Churchill herself might be a good candidate for the position."

At the mention of the governess, James's gaze shot to Kerry. "She's already agreed to be governess to my girls."

So it was as he suspected. No sooner had James lost Catherine than he'd found someone to take her place. Catherine would not be pleased about that. Then again, maybe it was time for Catherine to recognize that James Lindford didn't love her—at least not to the exclusion of other women like Kerry did. Though it was churlish, he pressed on. "Yes, your governess. I wonder, though, how secure her commitment is. Besides, she seems a well-organized sort of woman. How hard can it be to issue a few orders to the staff and select a menu every day?"

"It's a big house. And what do you mean, her commitment?"

"I mean that Miss Churchill seems to be a born organizer. Plus, she wasn't born to be a governess. She's the sort that was bred to be a wife, to keep some man's hearth—and his bed—warm. Mark my words, if you don't hire Miss Churchill to manage things around here—you know, keep her *very* busy—some other man may well snatch her up."

James's eyes narrowed. "Since there are no other big households around Swansford in need of a housekeeper, and she's already agreed to teach the children, I doubt that will be a problem."

"I wouldn't be so sure of that. After all, she's still maintaining her own household, isn't she? Why do you think that is? Until she agrees to live in at Farley Park, anything could happen. Have you ever considered that she might have plans of her own?" He had to suppress a grin of satisfaction when James's mouth turned down in a frown. He went on. "I'm speaking of housewifery, James. Now that you've freed Miss Churchill of the responsibility of her niece's care, she's also free to see to her own needs. For a young woman like her, the number one goal is always finding a husband of her own."

With each point he made, James's expression soured more. Though James was his closest friend, Kerry had no compunction about twisting the knife. He'd loved Catherine from afar, suffering in silence as his friend courted and won her. It seemed more than fair for James to suffer as he had. "In case you haven't noticed, Miss Churchill is a damned handsome woman, with a surprisingly elegant manner about her. Perhaps too elegant for most of the country bumpkins in these parts, but all the same, eminently marriageable. You had better secure her and get her moved in here before she gets away, James." His eyes danced as he delivered the final blow. "Catherine will be eternally grateful."

Izzy and Helen sat up in Izzy's bed, the bed linens tented over their heads to create their own private domain. From the open curtains moonlight streamed through, illuminating the room. But it was still awfully dark compared to London at night.

"But I want my old bed," Helen said, fighting back tears.

Izzy put an arm around her. "You don't have to be scared. I'm here and you can sleep with me. Every night if you want. There's lots of room for both of us."

"It's too big." Helen bowed her head and fiddled with the ruffled hem of her night rail. "And this room's too big. And this house is too big. I want to go home. So does Bruno."

At the sound of his name, Bruno's tail thumped the bed between them.

"You'll get used to it."

"But I want Phoebe."

Izzy sighed. "So do I. Come on. Lie down by me." They snuggled together beneath the counterpane, two little heads on one pillow, with the growing puppy stretched between them, and their kittens curled together in a fluffy tangle at the foot of the bed. Izzy slid her arm around Helen and patted her shoulder. "There. That's better."

Helen sniffled. "You're nice. I'm sorry I didn't like you before."

"I'm sorry I didn't like you. I was just mad at everybody."

"That's how I feel. Mad at everybody. Except not you. And not Bruno. And not Mr. Fairchild either."

"Just Lord Farley and Phoebe, hunh?"

"Yes. How come she doesn't try to keep me at Plummy Head with her?"

Izzy shrugged. "She can't keep you. She's not your real mother."

"Then how come she doesn't come to live here with me?"

They lay in silence a long moment before Izzy said, "Did you ask her to?"

"No."

"I think you should. You know, if you cry and beg and act really, really sad and scared and lonesome, I bet you could get her to stay here with us. There's lots of bedrooms for her to sleep in."

"You think it would work? She would move here? But what about the chickens and goats?"

"There's lots of room for the goats and chickens too. And if she won't come even if you cry really hard, then I have another idea. We'll run away, just you and me."

"But I don't want to run *away*. I want to run *home*."

Izzy rolled her eyes. "Good thing you was born here and not in Seven Dials. You wouldn't've survived. You have to be sneaky, Helen. That's the only way to get your way. You have to trick people."

"That's not what Phoebe says. She says you have to be honest. To always tell the truth."

"Well, the truth is, we want Phoebe to live here with us and Leya. Right?"

Helen thought about that a long moment. Then in the dark of their moonlit bedroom she smiled at her new sister. "Right. We want Phoebe to live here with us."

CHAPTER 13

Phoebe stared at the impressive three-story mansion that was Lord Farley's ancestral home. Bolstered by wealth and history and political power, it was a mighty fortress indeed, one which the likes of her was not likely ever to pierce.

The smaller of Lord Farley's carriages had come just as she finished milking, bringing word that Izzy had a sore throat and that Lord Farley preferred not to have the child go out on such a raw, blustery day. Would Miss Churchill please come up to the Park?

She should have said no. But after Mrs. Leake's visit yesterday, she'd gone to consult with Mr. Blackstock regarding Helen's situation. Sadly, it was as she feared. She had no legal claim whatsoever to her niece. Neither her efforts, her time, nor her love counted one whit against the rights of Helen's natural parents.

During the long empty night that followed, she'd resolved to make the best of an unbearable situation. And her most important duty to Helen was to help the child find happiness in her new circumstances. She couldn't do that if she refused to go up to Farley Park.

So she'd made her hasty ablutions, changed her

clothes, and now she leaned out the carriage window and closed her eyes against the damp wind. It was a raw, blustery day, but not nearly so cold as it had been. Maybe spring had finally arrived.

Helen met her in the foyer, throwing herself weeping into her arms. "My goodness, what's all this?" Phoebe exclaimed, her voice warm and gently chiding, though she, too, felt like weeping. This was her own, dear child in every way except that which the law recognized. She forced a smile, and ruffled her beloved niece's fair hair. "Have they been treating you so badly as all this?"

"She missed you," Izzy said in a voice that didn't sound scratchy at all.

"I missed you." Helen hiccuped the words.

"She missed you," Lord Farley said from the open doorway to his study.

Though Phoebe had tried to prepare herself for this— after all, if she spent time with Helen, she'd be forced to see the man quite often—nothing could quite prepare her for Lord Farley leaning against the doorjamb, smiling indulgently at his girls. As seemed to be his wont, he was dressed casually, in doe-colored breeches, a chocolate-brown waistcoat over a crisp white shirt, and a simply tied stock. He looked every bit the fine country gentleman.

But beneath that façade lurked the dangerous allure of a pirate, of a marauding heartbreaker of a man. Though her heart thundered from the very sight of him, Phoebe knew she must keep herself under the strictest control. He was her employer, a viscount, and the father of her niece. The only emotion she could allow herself to show him was anger.

Behind him on a blanket in the middle of a rich red Aubusson carpet, Leya sat surrounded by toys and piles of crumpled paper. What a relief to have her downstairs with the other children. She was a strange sight, her delicate olive skin marred with red blotches and daubed over with pale oat paste. But her smoky blue eyes lit up when she spied Phoebe, and with a squeal and a toothy grin, she charged on all fours toward the foyer.

Thankful for a focus other than Lord Farley, Phoebe said, "Helen may be sad, and Izzy's throat may be irritated, but it appears that Leya is on the mend."

When the baby reached her father, she grabbed on to his high boot top, then pulled herself to a wobbly two-legged stance.

"That's my girl," he said, beaming down at the baby. "Isn't she something? Watch this." Bending down he let Leya clutch his fingers, then helped her stagger over to Phoebe.

Already Phoebe was hard-pressed to maintain her anger at him. But seeing him doting over Leya's ordinary, very natural triumph completely did her in. She crouched down, clapping with glee for the grinning baby.

"What a big girl you are. Look at you!"

"Mamamama."

"She thinks you're her mother," Izzy said. "Just like Helen does."

Phoebe's gaze met Lord Farley's, rising the long length of his muscular thighs, trim waist, and wide chest. If she was their mother and he was their father—

She banished the thought.

If he was embarrassed by Izzy's blatant remark, he hid it behind the dark intensity of his deep blue eyes. But then, he was an expert at hiding his emotions from view—all but one. For she saw a flicker of heat in his gaze, a spark of physical hunger that almost toppled her backward.

Fortunately, Leya teetered forward, drawing Phoebe's

attention away and allowing her to steady her own shaky self.

He still wanted her. He lusted after her.

She shouldn't be surprised; after all, a part of her still lusted after him. But she was done with that and he must be done with it as well. They were employer and employee now; that's all they could ever be.

The children took up the rest of the morning. Lord Farley kept to his study; Phoebe kept to the schoolroom. She told herself that was exactly what she wanted. She even sent word that she and the children would dine upstairs.

But Lord Farley and Mr. Fairchild came up along with the luncheon. "Hello, pigeons," Mr. Fairchild said to the girls. "I've treats in my pockets, but you must earn them. Show me what you've learned today."

While Izzy and Helen clamored around him, Lord Farley came over to Phoebe. "Are you all right?"

Phoebe looked at him, then away. "Of course." She placed the *First Reader* precisely in the middle of the table she sat at. "We had a very good morning."

"I'm not referring to the children's lessons, Phoebe. Miss Churchill," he amended when she sent him a censorious look. "How are *you*?"

"I told you. Fine. Very well. Never better."

He looked doubtful. "I worried that your first night without Helen might have been difficult."

Phoebe swallowed hard. "I managed."

"I almost rode over to check on you."

"There was no need." Lord preserve her if he'd come upon her in the state she'd been in last night. "You must never come there."

"Why not?"

Phoebe stood. "Because it would put my reputation in question," she hissed, though not loud enough to carry to the others. "As it is, this whole situation is the talk of Swansford."

"You'll only make yourself miserable if you listen to the talk of small-minded people."

"That's easy to say if you're rich and titled and male. Tell me, you have sisters and daughters. How would you feel if they had to work for a man like you?"

She stalked away, not allowing him to respond. But though she'd had the last word, Phoebe wasn't comforted. She didn't want to argue with him. She didn't want to interact with him at all.

Liar. She cringed at her conscience's painful honesty. The truth was, she wanted to interact with him all right, though it was generally known by another, coarser word.

After that she stayed as far from him as possible. After lunch, while Leya slept, Phoebe took the girls for a walk. They were in the herb garden, identifying the various plants and reciting their uses and spelling their names, when Mr. Fairchild rejoined them.

"Don't worry. James isn't with me," he whispered when Phoebe glanced warily beyond him.

At once she drew herself up and folded her hands tightly at her waist. "Worried? Why should I be worried?"

He gave her a knowing wink. "I've known James since our days at school, so I'm well acquainted with the sort of effect he can have on a woman."

If it were possible, Phoebe grew stiffer still. "You quite mistake the situation, Mr. Fairchild. Besides, I rather doubt any other woman has been in the same situation I find myself in with regard to Lord Farley. At least I certainly hope not."

"Are you saying you don't like him?"

Ahead of them the girls had plucked mint, rosemary, and bergamot sprigs, breaking the leaves and comparing the fragrances. She turned to Mr. Fairchild. "I'm just his employee. I don't have to like him."

"It's because of Helen, isn't it? You liked him until he took her from you."

She shot him an annoyed look. "How astute you are."

But he just grinned at her ill temper. "Perhaps this will make you feel better. It seems Lord Farley's former fiancée is having second thoughts—about being the *former* fiancée, that is. With any luck he and she will repair their differences and renew their betrothal."

That was the last thing Phoebe expected to hear, and in the sudden silence she went cold. But with Mr. Fairchild's shrewd gaze upon her, she knew better than to reveal her feelings. "I don't see how Lord Farley's plans to marry affect me, save perhaps—" She broke off when a horrible thought gripped her like a cruel hand around her throat. "You don't think he'll move to town and take Helen with him, do you?" If he did that, she would die. She would simply wither away and die!

Mr. Fairchild chuckled. "I assure you, Lord Farley's fiancée will not want to take his daughters back to town with her. Nor do I think that she'll be content to molder out here in the country. So you see, my dear Miss Churchill, should James wed her, it's very likely that you will spend most of the year alone here with the girls." He gestured with one hand back toward the towering house. "And you'll be living in far better circumstances than you have in the past."

"Yes." Phoebe found it hard to swallow past the lump of fear that lodged in her throat. "I see what you mean." Lord Farley would marry and go back to his old life. She'd been a fool to believe otherwise. So why was she so upset? This was a good thing, she told herself. It was. "I suppose then that I should be anxious for Lady Catherine's arrival."

"Oh, so you know her by name."

"Yes." Phoebe smoothed back a strand of blowing hair. "We do get the news from London, you know. Even out here in the moldering countryside."

He smiled at her, his eyes twinkling. "You mustn't think too badly of James, my dear. He only has his children's best interests at heart as, I assume, do you. In truth, the two of you seem in perfect alignment on that front. I suggest you relax and learn to enjoy your situation here, Miss Churchill. I certainly intend to."

A cloud sat over Phoebe's head all afternoon. The sun shone, the earth warmed, and the whole Yorkshire countryside seemed to stretch and bask in the face of the impending spring. But over Phoebe a dark winter hovered. James's fiancée wanted him back, the woman described as the beauteous Lady Catherine, the undisputed star of London society, widely admired, grievously wounded, and the sort of woman whom men fought over.

A man would be a fool not to want to marry such a woman. And Phoebe would be a fool not to want him to marry Lady Catherine, especially if Mr. Fairchild was correct about the three girls being left at Farley Park, in Phoebe's care.

But it seemed she *was* a fool, for the thought of Lord Farley wed to the perfect Lady Catherine with her politically powerful father made Phoebe's stomach tighten and lurch so violently she thought she might become ill.

When the girls had their tea at four o'clock, Phoebe decided to leave. She needed to be alone with her dismal thoughts, to grieve in private, though what she was grieving was hard to explain.

But the moment she reached for her cloak, Helen began to wail, "No. Don't leave me. Don't leave me!"

Phoebe ended up staying through the evening meal.

Once Helen fell asleep, however, with darkness fast upon the land and a bone-chilling fog creeping up from the sea, there was no choice but to accept the offer of a carriage to deliver her home. The last thing she expected was for Lord Farley to be her driver.

"Get in," he said when she balked.

Behind them the door closed, leaving them alone in the feeble torchlight of the rear courtyard. An owl hooted from near the stables, and the horse stamped impatiently, jingling the traces of the small chaise.

"I'd rather someone else drove me," she said. There was no need not to be blunt, for there was no one else to hear.

"Yes. I know. Get in," he repeated. When she hesitated, he grabbed her elbow and steered her to the conveyance. And when she balked at his high-handedness, he said, "Get in the chaise, Phoebe, or I will lift you in myself." To prove his point, his other hand patted her bottom in the most familiar way.

The nerve of the man! But it worked, for Phoebe hopped right in. Anything to avoid him actually picking her up.

"Do you treat all your employees so familiarly?" she spat when he climbed in beside her.

"Only the ones I've been familiar with in the past."

Her back went rigid. "I hesitate to speculate on how vast that number must be."

"Only one," he muttered. With a snap of the reins he urged the animal forward. "Only one."

They had driven to the end of the long driveway, almost to the road, before he broke the icy silence. "I needed to speak with you, Phoebe, and since you've made it clear that for your reputation's sake you don't want to be alone with me, I had no choice but to steal these few minutes when no one else could see us."

Phoebe kept her eyes fixed on the rump of the horse. Left, right. Left, right. Flick the tail. Left right. "Very well. I'm here. So what is it you want to say to me?"

He cleared his throat. "I want you to know that I appreciate how difficult this must be for you."

He appreciated her.

A wave of emotion rose in Phoebe's throat, but she ruthlessly squashed it down. What was not to appreciate? She'd made it easy for him to take her beloved niece away. Plus, she'd dived into his bed the very first chance she got. He'd be a fool not to appreciate her.

He went on. "I'll never do anything to separate you from Helen."

She made a rude noise. "You already have."

"She's my daughter and she needs to know that at least one of her parents wants her."

Phoebe didn't want to hear this. She wanted to clap her hands over her ears and not have to admit that he might be right. She stared fixedly on the horse's rump. Left, right. Left, right. "She cries for me."

"I know. But she wouldn't have to if you would live in at Farley Park, accept the governess position full time."

"I wonder how Lady Catherine would feel about that," she said, her voice too tart.

He shifted on the bench seat beside her. "What do you know about Catherine?"

"I know that a man should always let his wife make the major decisions about how to run their household."

"She's not my wife, nor even my fiancée. You've been talking to Kerry, haven't you?"

"He's been talking to me. But he was only trying to do exactly what you say you're doing. Reassuring me." She said the words as if they tasted bad.

"Did it work?" he asked. "Did he reassure you?" They

turned onto the road which led like a pale ribbon through the night, dipping into hollows of ground fog only to rise again, pointing the way south to Plummy Head.

Phoebe closed her eyes. "No."

She heard him sigh. "What would reassure you, Phoebe? Would you tell me that?"

Tell him what? That she wanted to keep Helen with her? He must already know that. Should she tell him that she wanted to make sure Izzy and Leya had a good life, that she wanted to be there every day to make certain it was good day? He would only say what he was already saying: live at Farley Park and be with them every day.

If only it were that easy.

"I want my old life back," she finally said. "The way it was before you came here. Before everything became so muddled." She concentrated on the little agate button on her left glove. "Before I had to admit how truly vile my sister is," she added.

"Life changes, Phoebe. And even when the change is for the better, it can still hurt."

"But this change isn't for the better. And I'm tired of it always hurting." She let out a frustrated sound. "Just . . . Just drive," she said, turning to stare out at the dark countryside.

Down the hill lay Swansford village, marked by the occasional light from an unshuttered window. Above them the sky was alive with stars, and the air smelled salty and damp. A night like any other—at least Phoebe tried to convince herself that it was. But when the chaise halted before her lonely little cottage—dark and probably cold—she knew this night was nothing like any other she'd known. Her life had taken an abrupt turn, an about-face, and from now on, everything would be new and different.

And frightening.

She climbed down from the vehicle before he could offer her a hand. He got down anyway.

"Good night. Thank you." She started for the door.

"Phoebe?"

She stopped. She knew she shouldn't. She should go inside—only three more steps. She should close the door, bar it, then climb up to her cold, lonely bedroom beneath the rafters, and resign herself to a life of spinsterhood. She could raise cats, lots of cats, and become an eccentric. The children of Swansford would point at her when she came to town, and she would laugh and they would whisper that she was crazy.

Frowning at that pathetic image, she stopped just short of the door. She didn't want to become a lonely spinster raising cats for companionship. She wanted more from life. She wanted something for herself. So she hesitated, and though she should not, she turned around.

As if on cue, he stepped forward. He was a tall, dark shadow conjured up by the swirling mists and backlit by the moon. Dark, dangerous, and oh, so appealing.

Before she could even think it through she said, "I accept your offer."

"You accept?"

Phoebe heard the surprise in his voice. He hadn't expected her to give in so fast. That was because he didn't understand how truly alone she now was. How lonely. "Yes," she went on before she could back down. "I'll come to live at Farley Park and take care of your children."

With that soft, breathy concession James won what he'd wanted from her. At least he had what he'd told her he wanted. But just as fast, like a single breath upon the wind, he knew it wasn't enough. With the moonlight illuminating her face, he could see every emotion she felt, every fear and every hurt. He'd bullied her into this. It was good for him; certainly it was good for his children for her to be a part of his household. But was it good for her?

He would make it good, he told himself. He would make her happy to be his lover. More than happy. Ecstatic.

Yet a part of him knew that as long as she lived in at Farley Park she would never have the freedom to build a life of her own. She would become a peripheral part of his life and his children's lives. His lover. Their governess. No room for a husband and family of her own.

But maybe that would be enough, he reasoned. Why couldn't it be? And it wasn't as if she couldn't have children of her own. His children.

He reached out to her, to take what he wanted. It was the habit of a lifetime. He came, he saw, he conquered—at least when it came to women. But he always made it worth their while, he told himself as he drew her nearer. Always.

"I'll make you happy you agreed to this, Phoebe. I promise. Will you come back to Farley Park with me tonight?"

She shook her head. "Not tonight. But tomorrow . . ."

Tomorrow was a long way off. Too long. Having achieved what he wanted, James immediately wanted more. He wanted her.

So he kissed her. Logic had nothing to do with it, nor kindness, nor anything but his own selfish need to possess her. He kissed her as he'd wanted to kiss her for days. Ever since that night . . .

He deepened the kiss and felt first accusation, then acceptance on her lips. He felt the pliancy of her body against his harder one, and the feminine strength of her that wanted to fight him, but instead relented. He reveled in her inner struggle, for it was like a storm from the sea striking the immutable shore. Violent. Magnificent.

They moved backward, her arched in his arms, him set on his course: to have this maddeningly delicious woman beneath him once more. Not on a settee this time, not hasty and secret. But slow and noisy.

His tongue probed within her mouth just as his erection wanted to probe her hot feminine core. Deep, rhythmic, hungry. When they came up against the door, he ground his loins against her belly.

"Damn you, Phoebe. You've been driving me mad." He was like a green lad, uncontrollable in his lust; like a stud horse denied too long. But not anymore.

Not anymore.

He found the door handle, turned it, and felt it give behind her. At last. At last—

"Wait!" Phoebe twisted her face away from his and one of her hands caught the door frame. "Wait. We can't do this."

CHAPTER 14

"We can. And we will," Lord Farley said, staring down at her. "We both want to."

Yes. They did. Yet even so, Phoebe knew she shouldn't want to. "No." She caught the edge of the painted door frame and hung on by the frantic tips of her fingers. But her objection was a dust mote on a windy day, there, then swept away when his clever lips moved to the shell of her ear, down to the lobe, then farther, to the exquisitely sensitive skin on the side of her neck.

"Yes." He bit the word into the hollow of her throat and slid it along her collarbone. "Yes." His palm smoothed along her arm to her hand, replacing the door in her grasp. Palm to palm, fingers entwined.

She dissolved beneath him, sandstone battered by the relentless sea. His will was greater, his skills undeniable.

But in the end it was her own passion that most undermined her. Her own perverse yearnings. For this man roused something inside her that no man ever had. That sweet, forbidden spice of lust.

"Yes," he murmured, and this time he lifted her off her feet and swept her into his arms as if she were the spoils of war and he some pirate plunderer.

She heard the door slam, kicked shut. He found the stairs and managed to climb the narrow passage without bumping her into a wall. Then they were in her bedroom, on the bed with her held captive between cool, creaking mattress and warm, throbbing male.

For one moment only, Phoebe thought of her mother. Emilean Churchill would die to know lust exploded like this within her meticulously managed household. But as fast as the thought came, it fled. He drove it out of her mind.

"First this," he said, rolling half off her onto his side and unfastening the clasp of her cloak at the same time. He shoved the heavy garment off her shoulders. "Then this." He began to unlace her bodice. But the whole time he kept his eyes locked with hers.

Had he looked away she might have found the strength to stop this madness. But he never looked away, not even to blink.

Her breaths came shallow and fast as the lacings gave ground to his clever fingers. "If we do this," she said, "I cannot come . . . come to live at Farley Park."

"Yes you can. You will." He folded back her bodice to expose her chemise.

She shook her head. "It would be too difficult, too complicated."

"No it wouldn't." With one simple tug her skirt strings came undone.

"What about . . ." What about Lady Catherine? she tried to ask. But he bent over and kissed her breast, kissed the very tip, right through the often-washed linen, and her objections turned into a groan.

After that she objected to nothing. He slid her skirt off and she helped by lifting her hips. He pushed her chemise up and she shifted to make it easier, to make it faster.

Then she lay back, embarrassed but too curious not to watch him remove his own clothing. Frock coat, waistcoat, shirt.

Ah, lust!

How glorious when the steamy heat in her belly flowed out to all her limbs, swamping her senses with desire. He kicked off his boots, peeled off his breeches, then stood tall and proud in the erratic shadows of the moonlit room. He looked so purely masculine that Phoebe wanted to cry.

He was here for her. Only her.

He returned to the bed, a powerful ghost lover intent on her pleasure. Hers. When had anyone ever cared about pleasing her? Never. Not once in her entire life had someone made any effort to please her. How could she protest it now, and why would she?

So with open arms and open heart she accepted him, relishing this moment of union and relegating everything else to some other part of her life.

Ah, sweet lust!

He came over her again, hot and hard and demanding.

But she was bolder than before, and she banished fear and shame. She pushed him back to the side and rolled on top of him, and kissed him with her whole being: mouth and breasts and belly and hands.

It was a heady feeling to be in charge, to be on top. She moved down, sliding on him and reveling in the coarse abrasion of his chest hair on her smoother skin, the solid flex of his muscles, and the ready prod of his erection.

His hands guided her to slide farther down his hard, mysterious body, so she continued her trail of curious kisses. She discovered his small, male nipples and flat stomach, his ripple of muscles and ribs, and concave navel. Then his arousal reared hot and hard between her breasts and for a moment she hesitated.

"Kiss me," he growled, hoarse and hungry. Needy.

He needed her to kiss him there just as, despite her initial shock, she'd needed that most intimate kiss from him. So she slid down farther still, pressing kisses along that strange, smooth skin. He jerked in response, not just his arousal, but his entire self.

It gave her an incredible feeling of power, and added a new facet to lust: *she* was driving *him* mad with lust. The knowledge fired her own need higher still.

She went to kiss it again, but with an indecipherable oath he grabbed her arms and dragged her up until they were once more face to face. Then clasping her head between his hands, he kissed her, a kiss so deep and possessive she felt ravished to her very soul.

"Phoebe." He groaned her name when they broke apart, gasping for breath.

"James," she whispered, loving the feel of his name upon her lips.

He responded with a hand at her knee, a shifting of his hips. Then he was there, poised to deliver her from this agony of trembling need, of crushing desire. Of endless, forever love.

No, she caught herself. She meant lust.

Not love, but lust.

Yet when he came into her, a long, slow stroke that filled her heart as fully as it did her womb, the unbidden truth vibrated through her. It was as real as this house, as solid as the granite jut of land that formed Plummy Head. She loved James Lindford.

The crushing knowledge left her gasping for breath, and tears seeped from between her eyelashes. She loved him and nothing in his past could change that. Not Louise, not Lady Catherine. The future was theirs to make into whatever they needed, and if they tried, they could make it wonderful.

But it was the present that filled her with joy. It was him in her arms now, the heated stroke of him—pulling away, pushing back inside her—that the whole of her being focused upon.

Oh, the joy of lust and love and hot, slick friction! He moved faster. He thrust deeper, an erotic empalement. Yet she didn't feel vanquished. If anything she felt victorious. On and on. Higher, hotter. Lust, love. Dominance, submission.

Searing heat, painful joy. Then it came, that wonderful, violent collision that shook her to her core, that wrecked them together, that fused them into one.

"Phoebe!" He shouted her name as he spent himself within her. Her answer was to clench him deep, to hold him and drain him and keep part of him forever with her.

James. Her James.

She would never give him up. Never.

He didn't leave her bed until very late.

Actually, it was very early if the truth be told, with the edges of dawn flirting along the dark horizon of the sea. But he didn't go before loving her again, slower, but no less intense. The initial desperation of need became instead a dance of discovery, a quest for perfection.

It felt as if it were the first time for them again, as if she'd never participated in this primal act of joining before. But at the same time, she knew now what she wanted and what he wanted. It was a dream that made no sense, segueing from one delicious moment to the next, with logic completely unimportant.

The little webs between her fingers were not supposed to be erotic spots, but they were. She should not desire the lick of his tongue beneath the curve of her buttocks, but she did.

He should not groan and buck when she smoothed the long strands of her hair over him and wrapped his throbbing penis in the tangled webs. But he did and he punished her—rewarded her—by pinning her immobile beneath him, not allowing her even to twitch as he brought them to screaming completion.

In the aftermath there was only the harsh sound of their gasping breaths and the soughing of the insistent night winds beneath the eaves of the house.

"If I had my way," he murmured into the sweaty darkness, "I would make you my captive, Phoebe. I would keep you hidden away for my pleasure only." His hand moved along her rib cage, up to the curve of her breasts. One of his fingers circled her nipple, bringing it to renewed awareness.

Her eyes closed in helpless surrender. Would this need for him never cease? This lust? Certainly her love would not.

"And every night," he continued, "I would come to you." He plucked at the aroused nub. "And every morning." He bent over and took the taut nipple between his teeth, teasing it with his lips and tongue until she whimpered for relief.

His hand slid down her belly toward the place that ached still for him, and she thrust eagerly up to his touch. One finger only he used, the merest touch of nail-tip over the fiery spot beneath her curls. Meanwhile his tongue flicked agonizingly over her breasts.

She reached for him, wanting a stronger touch. But he caught her hands and forced them over her head.

"Hold tight to the bedstead," he ordered. "Do it or I'll leave."

She did it. She didn't really believe he'd go, but she did what he ordered anyway.

Satisfied, he resumed those faint, tormenting caresses, so feather-light that she had to fight for the completion they promised. Every part of her struggled for that point of carnal saturation until even the trickle of sweat down her side was arousing, even the slide of her foot upon the soft, rumpled bed linens.

Each stroke became fainter still, each movement briefer and more tantalizing, until Phoebe was reaching deep within herself for the release she so urgently sought.

When at last it came, it was an explosion, arching her up from the bed, convulsing every bit of her from toes to nose to fingertips. It thundered through her body, caught on a tidal flood of fire and ecstasy. Then it left her, as if for dead.

"Dream of me," he said as he bent over her inert form and kissed her good-bye. "Dream of me waking and sleeping, Phoebe. And know that this is just the beginning for us."

Then he left, a herald of the dawn, if the warming light in her room was any indication. And a herald of a new dawn in her life as well.

She loved him.

"I love you," she called, a hoarse whisper in the sex-saturated air of her little room.

But he was already gone and she was too depleted to move. Too depleted, yet also too filled with emotions. Love, lust, happiness. Exhaustion.

She rolled over, feeling muscles she didn't know she possessed. But it felt so good. So good . . . She pulled the sheet and blanket over her—she'd never slept naked before.

But then, there was a first time for everything.

A distant rapping awakened Phoebe, followed by a shout from far, far away.

"Phoebe. Phoebe girl! Where are you?"

Mrs. Leake!

Phoebe shot out of bed, fueled by instinctive guilt. Mrs. Leake was here; that meant she must know!

"Aren't you awake yet?" The woman's voice came from inside the house now. "Have you taken ill?"

"I'm . . . I'm fine," Phoebe managed to call out. *And I'm naked.* Dear God! "Don't come up," she squeaked. "I'll be right down."

Like a madwoman Phoebe searched for her chemise and skirt and bodice. Her bedroom looked like a storm had torn through it with clothes and bedding and even the woven carpet thrown every which way. She frowned as she tugged her clothes on. Anyone who caught sight of it would know exactly what had gone on in here last night.

When she caught a glimpse of herself in the mirror, she was appalled at the sight. Puffy lips, sleep-deprived eyes, and knotted hair.

Anyone looking at her would have to know what she'd done last night. Done, then done again. Then done one more time still.

She paused, breathless and momentarily weakened by the impossible memory of last night. It had been so wonderful. So perfect. She hated that Mrs. Leake's presence made it seem tawdry.

"Land's sake," the woman called up the stairwell to her. "I've never heard the like, sleeping past ten o'clock. Are you well?"

"I'm fine. I'm . . . I'm coming." Phoebe slipped into clogs and wrapped her hair in a work turban. Then she closed the bedroom door and descended on shaky legs to the main floor. "I wasn't expecting callers today," she said when she came into the kitchen.

Her unsubtle rebuke flowed right off Mrs. Leake's back. The woman had already made herself at home, stirring up the embers and adding kindling to the firebox. "I was worried about you, child. All alone here." She looked up and squinted. "You don't look particularly well. Are you sure you're feeling quite yourself?"

Actually, no. Phoebe's legs were quivering, the muscles weak from last night's exertions, so she sat down hard in a chair.

"You've been grieving, haven't you? That's what's making you ill." Mrs. Leake pressed a hand to her forehead. "No fever. So I'm right. You're grieving over our Helen."

Phoebe braced an elbow on the table and rested her forehead on her hand. The awful truth was that during the long night of lovemaking with James, she hadn't once thought of Helen. Now, although she felt guilty for misleading Mrs. Leake, she could hardly correct the woman's misconception. So she let the woman bustle about, boiling water, fixing tea, and feeding the cat.

"Your goats will need attention shortly."

"Yes. I know."

"I take it you're not going up to the Park today."

Phoebe shook her head. "Not today." But perhaps she'd have a visitor later . . .

She lifted her head and rubbed her bleary eyes. "I wonder if you could help me, Mrs. Leake."

"Why, that's precisely why I'm here, child. To help you."

"I need to hire a maid, someone who'll mind the

house and tend the stock while I'm otherwise occupied."

"So he's paying you well enough that you can hire help yourself." The woman pursed her lips, weighing the matter in her mind. "I suppose that's good. As for finding someone, well, that shouldn't be too difficult, what with jobs being so scarce around these parts."

"If you hear of a suitable person, will you send them to me? I'll be either here or at Farley Park."

"Very well. But about you working up to the Park, I understand why you're doing it, child, what with Helen living there now and you being so alone here at Plummy Head. But you mustn't cut yourself off from your friends in Swansford." She poured the tea, then gave Phoebe an intent look. "I want you to come down to dinner after church this Sunday. I've invited a few friends, nothing elaborate, mind you."

Phoebe blinked in surprise. Mrs. Leake wanted *her* to come to dinner? That had never happened before, and it didn't bode well. "I, um . . . I'll probably spend the day with Helen."

"Nonsense. Everybody deserves a day off. Besides, you're spending enough time with the child—and you've done so every day of her life. It's time for you to seek a life outside of hers, Phoebe girl. Soon enough she won't need you anymore. What will you do then, all alone up here, too old to marry? You come to dinner Sunday. I'm not leaving here until you agree."

In the end Phoebe agreed. It was the only way to get rid of the woman. Mrs. Leake was up to something, and judging by her remarks, it probably had something to do with getting her married off.

"Thank you," she said, bracing herself on the door frame as Mrs. Leake climbed up into her wagon. Phoebe grimaced at the sight. If *she* had to climb into a wagon today, she'd never manage. Her legs were that weak.

Mrs. Leake lifted the reins, then paused. "Land's sake, I almost forgot. There's more goings-on at Farley Park, which you'll discover when you go up there today or tomorrow."

Phoebe's heart began to pound with dread. Not Lady Catherine. Not so soon. But she hid her fears behind a mask of polite curiosity. "Goings-on?"

"Oh, yes. A highfalutin carriage pulled by a high-stepping foursome came into town late last night. Very posh with two footmen and a maid to tend the two fine ladies who took rooms in the inn."

"Two ladies?" Of course. Lady Catherine wasn't likely to travel without a companion. "How interesting."

With a knowing tilt of her head Mrs. Leake said, "It seems one of them is that Lady Catherine we read about, that earl's daughter that your fine master humiliated so shamefully in London town. Well, it appears she must not have banished the troublesome viscount from her mind. Seems she's here to visit him, her and her friend, a Mrs. Donahue."

Mrs. Leake made a clucking sound as she shook her head. "Ooh, but that Lord Farley, he's a one, Phoebe girl. Very slick, very fast. After all, he took Louise in, didn't he? And we all know she's a woman of the world. So you just watch yourself with him. I don't trust him, and you shouldn't trust him either."

She huffed out a disapproving breath. "Given all that, however, I must say that I feel better about your situation as governess to those girls now that this woman's come back to claim him—at least, I'm guessing that's her intent. All the same, we don't need that man leading another one of our good girls astray."

Too late, Phoebe wanted to say as Mrs. Leake drove down the rutted lane. Too late. She watched as the heavy store wagon dipped and swayed like a foundering galleon.

Just so had Phoebe foundered on the slippery rocks that surrounded James Lindford. Love, lust. Three darling girls, and now a fiancée who wanted him back.

Shaken more than she wanted to admit, Phoebe returned to the house and sat down before her now tepid tea. Yesterday she'd agreed to live in as governess to his children. Last night she'd as good as agreed to become his mistress.

And now his fiancée had returned.

But despite Lady Catherine, as long as Phoebe loved James and his children, she feared there was no going back on either front.

CHAPTER 15

Helen and Izzy arrived in the afternoon, carried in the pony cart by a groom who'd been instructed to bring Phoebe's trunks and luggage back with them. Not that Phoebe had either a trunk or a valise to pack her meager possessions in. Her father's old carpenter's bag had to suffice, along with her mother's sewing basket.

In truth, it hardly mattered to Phoebe what she brought with her or what she carried it in. Her mind was too caught up with the dread of meeting the spectacular Lady Catherine, and the terror of seeing James gaze upon the elegant woman with admiration—and desire— in his eyes. He'd planned to marry her until she'd called it off. The London newspaper had made that plain. So why wouldn't he wish to marry her again? And why else would she have traveled this long way except to forgive him and take him back?

The most troubling aspect of the entire situation, though, was her own part in it. She had known about Lady Catherine's impending arrival before last night.

So why had she allowed herself to succumb to him?

Was she so desperate and pathetic as to think she could steal James's affections from his former fiancée by using her body as the lure? She already had three living, breathing examples that a physical entanglement would gain her nothing permanent from James. Nothing permanent except for heartache. Already she felt a distinct hole of misery growing in the vicinity of her chest.

"I don't think I've ever seen your bedroom in such disorder," Helen said, scanning Phoebe's attic bedroom, a surprised expression on her heart-shaped face.

"It looks all right to me," Izzy said, hopping onto the rumpled bed, then plopping backward. "Nice and soft."

"Get off there," Phoebe said. "You two go downstairs and find the kitten." Her activities with James in this bedroom—on that bed—were too fresh in her mind for her to be comfortable with the girls frolicking on it. It wasn't as if they could ever know. Still . . .

But as if thinking it made it so, Izzy turned her face into the pillow, then sat up as if stuck by a hat pin. Her sharp gaze flew to Phoebe's face; her suspicions were clear in her eyes. Then like a lamp being blown out, her expression swiftly altered from suspicion to innocent neutrality.

She knew!

Phoebe wasn't sure how she could—except that Izzy had been exposed to a very rough life in London. Could she know about what went on between men and women?

Inside Phoebe cringed. Of course she did. James had removed her from her mother because the woman was unfit. She could guess what that meant. It didn't help matters that the room fairly oozed the scents of lust and sex and the hundred other emotions released during those tumultuous hours before dawn's intervention.

Her heart thumped high in her throat as she watched Izzy slide with studied nonchalance off the bed. "We can make up the bed while you finish packing," she said. "Get on the other side, Helen."

"You needn't do that," Phoebe said.

But they did it anyway, and the whole while Izzy shot veiled glances at her. Phoebe concentrated on the contents of her armoire: chemises, nightgown, petticoats, five gowns, her good shoes, and her slippers. But she knew that Izzy had figured things out, and that changed everything. A governess was supposed to set a proper example to her charges. She most certainly was not supposed to act the harlot with her students' father.

Phoebe fretted the whole way to Farley Park, and when a sudden chilly rain caught them at the turn into the long driveway, it seemed somehow fitting.

They entered the house cold and dripping. Her bonnet drooped on either side of her face, and her hair hung in a wet hank over her eyes. Izzy and Helen promptly scampered up to their side-by-side bedchambers. But Phoebe remained in the foyer below, awaiting the ever tardy butler and wondering if there was any way to turn around and go home with no one the wiser.

Of course, as befitted the foulness of the day, it was Lady Catherine who first found her. Phoebe needed no introduction to recognize the woman. She was everything the newspaper had said: exquisite, elegant, every bit the fashionable young lady of society.

Phoebe almost gasped when, like a delicate, golden vision, the woman glided out of the billiards room. She was so genteel and ethereal in her movements she appeared almost to float. That she bore so many similarities to Louise was doubly depressing. The slanted, golden-lashed eyes, the blushing complexion, the perfect, Cupid's-bow curve of her lips.

For a moment she wondered if that elegant, fragile-looking beauty hid the same core of steel that Louise's did? But in the next moment she dismissed the possibility. Why should this powdered, pampered, perfume-scented woman be hard on the inside? She'd never wanted for anything in her life—except, perhaps, for the Viscount Farley.

Phoebe's already drooping shoulders sagged lower. No wonder James loved Lady Catherine. Which begged the question, what did he see in Phoebe?

Phoebe knew her limitations. She was tall and sturdy, with unfashionably dark hair and tanned skin sprinkled with freckles where she ought to be pale and soft. Her hands were rough and her nails short. Practical. Her hair was practical too, clean, but tautly pulled back and held in place with simple, unadorned combs.

Her mother had worn her hair in the same fashion.

Phoebe winced at that horrid realization. But it was true. She had all of her mother's worst traits. She was shrewish and judgmental, and she too often held a disapproving attitude toward others. Yet at the same time she was as wanton as ever her wanton sister had been.

Sick at heart, Phoebe shoved her drenched collapse of a hair arrangement back from her brow and faced this woman of impeccable appearance and morals.

"Good day. You must be Lady . . . Catherine." She stumbled over the words.

The blond beauty graciously inclined her head, then arched her delicate swooping brows. "And you are?"

"Phoebe Churchill. The governess."

"Oh. I see. The governess." The woman's cool blue eyes ran over Phoebe's bedraggled form, top to bottom, no doubt cataloging every single flaw.

Phoebe felt her first jolt of indignation. "Yes. The governess." She raised her chin a notch. "As you may have noticed, we were caught in the rain. Perhaps you could summon one of the staff to assist me?"

"Of course. I'm afraid, however, that you may find the staff at Farley Park wanting. But now that you're here to handle the children, and I'm here to assist James—that is, Lord Farley—perhaps we'll soon find him a proper housekeeper. If you'll wait here, I'll summon a maid to assist you." A faint smile curved her lips. "We wouldn't want you to catch a chill, would we?"

Alone in the foyer, standing in an increasing puddle of her own making, Phoebe felt a chill all right, but one entirely unrelated to her soaked clothing. That was the woman James loved, the woman he'd asked to be his bride. That was the sort of woman a man like him married, one with a well-connected family and a wide arc of social acquaintances. Phoebe's mother's extensive instructions in the social graces paled in the face of such a perfect example of the feminine arts.

Even Louise was but a weak imitation of the real thing. And Lady Catherine, by anyone's standards, was the real thing.

Clutching her mother's sewing basket to her chest, Phoebe peered about the magnificently appointed foyer and up the soaring stairwell. Here was the setting for a true lady: marble, mahogany, gold leaf, and fine art. She was more accustomed to plaster and sturdy oak, to whitewash and a simple crucifix upon the wall.

Just then the butler arrived, and at the same time, but from the opposite direction, so did James.

"My apologies, miss."

"There you are."

Behind the butler came Lady Catherine. James's eyes veered from Phoebe to the other woman, then back. After a momentary pause he said, "Miss Churchill, may I present Lady Catherine Winfield."

Like a golden cloud, Lady Catherine glided forward as before. Halting beside James, she tucked her beringed and braceleted hand into the crook of his arm, as if anchoring herself to him so that she wouldn't float away.

"Miss Churchill and I have just met, James. But rather than keeping her here to chat, perhaps we ought to send her up to her room so she can make herself more presentable."

"Of course. You must be freezing," he said to Phoebe.

Phoebe nodded, feeling as if she'd just been dismissed. Though relieved to quit the foyer and the humiliation of her embarrassing appearance, the trudge up the stairs behind the slow-moving butler offered no relief. She could feel James's eyes upon her the entire time. It only made things worse to know that he was attached to the perfect woman, someone Phoebe could never compare to, save unfavorably.

She waited an hour for hot water to be delivered to her room. The fire she built up herself, warding off the cold in the interim by wrapping a blanket over her damp chemise. By the time two fellows arrived with water for the tub, her hair was almost dry. She washed it anyway, and afterward donned her best gown. Foolish, of course. Her best gown was a turnip sack beside Lady Catherine's everyday one.

She was bent over before the fire, combing out her hair and mentally debating how to style it, when a knock sounded. "Come in," she called, expecting a maid. When James entered, however, she lurched upright, whipping her hair back in a half-dried tangle. "You're not supposed to be in here!"

"You invited me in." He closed the door with a portentous, delicious-sounding click.

"That's only because I didn't know it was you."

"Were you expecting someone else?" He grinned.

"No. Well, yes. A maid or perhaps one of the girls."

He shook his head. "I apologize for the disorganization of my household staff. At present no one seems to be in charge. As for the girls, they wouldn't bother to knock."

"You're deliberately ignoring my point," Phoebe said, flattening one hand against her nervous stomach. "You must not be in my private chamber. But since you know that, I can only assume you want to torment me. Well, I will not allow it."

In the face of her distress, James's taunting grin faded. "You're upset about Catherine, but there's no need. She's only visiting here for a few days." He advanced toward her and with his every step Phoebe felt her resolve falter. They were alone. Behind her was a bed, large and soft, and just waiting to be put to good use. On top of that, he wanted her—she could tell. And oh, how she wanted him.

But succumbing to their desire would provide only a false sort of reassurance. He wanted her in his bed just like he'd wanted an infinite number of other women. It was a fleeting need on his part. If she were to survive the coming weeks or months until he eventually returned to London, she must adopt a similar attitude. Their interludes—if there were any—could only be pleasant moments outside the strictures of their real lives. At least outside the strictures of *her* real life.

"Please. I beg you not to expose me to the censure of either your friends or the servants."

He stopped a single pace from her. "That's not my intention." Then he reached out and with his thumb lightly caressed her lower lip. One single stroke, then his hand fell to his side. "That's not my intention," he repeated. "But neither do I mean to ignore what we have, Phoebe."

"Miss Churchill," she said, but in a ridiculously weak and breathy voice. One touch and she dissolved. One touch.

Childish laughter, a clatter of feet, and a dog's animated bark put a swift end to their emotionally charged encounter.

"Phoebe! Phoebe—" Izzy broke off when she charged into the room. James was right, she hadn't bothered to knock. Helen piled in behind her with Bruno yapping at her heels. He had a blue ribbon tied prettily around his neck, and a smaller bit tied upon his tail. Once in the room he started to chase his tail and they all laughed. But Phoebe didn't mistake the suspicious glint in Izzy's eyes.

"Your room is a floor below ours," Helen said. "Why can't you be right next to us, like at home?"

"This is your home now, sweetheart. But that's a very good idea." Anything to put more distance between her room and James's. "Could I be moved into a room nearer the children?" She looked at him, her face as bland as she could manage.

One side of his mouth slanted down in wry acknowledgment of what she was up to. "I'm not certain there are any more suitably furnished rooms up there."

"Oh, yes." Helen earnestly nodded. "There are."

"The third floor is for children," Izzy countered. "This is a good room for Phoebe. She should stay here."

Izzy obviously was throwing Phoebe at her father, and Phoebe appreciated her good intentions. But the child didn't understand the complexities of the situation, nor the impossibility. All the little girl knew was that Phoebe would make a good substitute mother for her and her half sisters.

Though it seemed cruel to deflate her dream, Phoebe feared it was kinder than allowing Izzy to go on imagining a rosy sort of future that never could be. Phoebe was the governess and the viscount's current lover. She would never be his wife.

"Actually, I would prefer to be next to the girls. Why don't you two show me your rooms? You needn't worry, Lord Farley," she threw out as she took Helen's hand and started for the hall. "I'll make all the arrangements with the butler."

Izzy caught up with them at the stairs. "But that's such a nice big room. And all your things are already there."

"They're easy enough to move," Phoebe replied. As they started up the stairs she glanced down the hall. He was watching her, a speculative look in his eyes. She'd won the first round, but he was no less bent on seduction than before.

She was no less bent on it either. But she didn't intend to be walked on, not by him or by Lady Catherine. "By the way," she said to the girls, but loud enough to carry to him. "Have you met your father's guest yet, Lady Catherine?"

James heard the gauntlet Phoebe had thrown down, and he accepted the challenge with relish. "Dinner at eight," he called up to them. "At the big table."

If nothing else, dinner would be entertaining.

The dining room glittered, like the inside of rose-cut diamonds. The flames of three dozen candles glanced off the crystal, the silverware, and the gold-leafed mirrors that lined the walls. Phoebe's awed gaze swept the impressive chamber, though she tried hard not to gawk. Thankfully the table was set only on one end, with James presiding at its head. To his right sat Lady Catherine, Mr. Fairchild, and an overdressed woman who was introduced to Phoebe as Mrs. Donahue. On his left Phoebe took a seat between Izzy and Helen.

"Dining *en famille*," Lady Catherine said, smiling benignly. "I've always thought suppers of this sort one of the most charming aspects of country life. It's so pleasant an alternative to the more formal ritual of dining in town." She turned her clear gaze on Phoebe. "But I'm sure, Miss Churchill, that you will also instruct Lord Farley's children in the proper etiquette of formal dining."

"Of course." *To the limits that my own lack of knowledge can instruct them.* But Phoebe wouldn't admit that out loud for the world. It was obvious to her that Lady Catherine meant to prove her own superiority to Phoebe, which superiority of knowledge Phoebe reluctantly must concede—but only to herself. Phoebe sent a speaking look to Helen and Izzy, then nonchalantly unfolded her napkin across her lap. Like little echoes, they did the same and, to Phoebe's relief and pride, they continued to mimic her manners throughout the meal.

And what a long meal it became. The tight ship Mrs. Gatling had run had apparently gone aground in the several days since her dismissal. The leek soup came out in a timely manner, warm and fragrant and fairly tasty. But they waited fully fifteen minutes for Mr. Benson to pour the wine prior to the second course of pâtés being served. After the pâté came more wine, poured at an excruciatingly slow pace by the butler. Then came red mullet in cardinal sauce, served cold, though it wasn't meant to be. Another interminable wait led to an oyster dish; a good while later roasted venison arrived with peas; and eventually the final course: a duck sitting in its own congealed fat, surrounded by salad and root vegetables.

Lady Catherine kept a serene smile on her face, earning Phoebe's grudging respect. Phoebe could almost hear her mother's voice: a true lady never notices any shortcomings in her host's arrangement.

Her own expression was probably more like Mrs.

Donahue's, not nearly so calm and unconcerned. Before Phoebe went to bed tonight, she meant to detain Mr. Benson and make some very pointed suggestions about managing the staff. Meanwhile, had it not been for her competitive need not to be outdone by Lady Catherine, Phoebe was certain she would have stormed into the kitchen right then and there.

Fortunately Mr. Fairchild kept them entertained, enough so that the restless girls managed to make it through the meal, almost to dessert.

"My goodness," Phoebe said when Helen could not stifle a huge yawn. "It grows late. If you will permit it, my lord, I believe the girls ought to take their dessert in the nursery." She trailed off under his steady scrutiny. She'd avoided meeting his gaze as much as possible. Also Lady Catherine's. That had left Mr. Fairchild and Mrs. Donahue, who sat opposite her. But now she faced James.

Lord Farley, she told herself. She needed to think of him as Lord Farley, not James. But it was hard, given the level of intimacy they'd shared.

"By all means, Miss Churchill. The girls are free to go. Good night, Izzy. Helen." But when Phoebe stood to depart he said, "There's no need for you to leave early."

"I must see to the children."

"They know how to find their own bedchambers."

"Yes, but since I am their governess—"

"One of the maids will help them prepare for bed."

"But what of their dessert?" A pathetic argument to be sure, but Phoebe was becoming desperate. Somehow the children's presence in the dining room protected her. Once they left, however, her purpose here would suddenly seem suspect. The others might guess . . .

But James seemed determined to keep her here. "Mr.

Benson will see their apple tarts delivered to the nursery," he stated in a tone that brooked no disagreement.

Phoebe's heart sank. It was one thing to dine in this company with the children beside her. They were her buffer, her security, her reason for being here. With them gone, she was thrust out on her own, an oddity, a country fowl among city peacocks.

Phoebe had never regretted her lack of funds so profoundly as she did now. Why, Lady Catherine's dress alone would pay all her bills for a year at least. As for the value of the gold and amber necklace and earbobs that adorned the woman, they would probably see Phoebe into her old age.

But Lady Catherine was more than frothy salmon silk and sparkling gold and gemstones. For recognizing Phoebe's distress, she laid a perfectly manicured hand *sans* glove on Lord Farley's arm. "You must allow our Miss Churchill to govern the children as she deems best, James. If she feels she ought to accompany them, you must not overrule her."

The words were said sweetly and in such ladylike tones as to not imply any real rebuke. That made them all the more difficult for Lord Farley to ignore. "Very well," he conceded after a momentary hesitation.

But as Phoebe escaped the dining room with its rich fragrance of so many beeswax candles, instead of feeling victorious, she felt vanquished. Lady Catherine was the exact sort of woman a man like Lord Farley sought in a wife: beautiful, perfectly turned out, with impeccable manners and such grace, whether dealing with servants or a peer.

It only felt worse to acknowledge that Lady Catherine was also the precise image of what Emilean Churchill had wanted in a daughter. Louise had been beautiful; Phoebe had been dutiful; but neither of them had ever possessed the cool grace that Lady Catherine exuded.

Ahead of Phoebe on the stairs Izzy said, "I want to eat my dessert in bed."

"No. You'll make crumbs and stain the linens," Phoebe said as they climbed to the third floor.

"Bruno will lick them up," Helen said.

"And there's a washerwoman to clean the linens," Izzy pointed out.

When Phoebe didn't respond, the girls scampered ahead of her, leaving her to trudge heavily after them. A washerwoman, the upstairs maid, the cooks—she ticked off the staff, one for every step on the long run of stairs. The butler, the downstairs maids, the footmen. The groomsmen, the stable master, the gardeners. More staff than she'd ever considered, people waiting on you hand and foot, and someone assigned to every task. Louise was right. Helen would be raised with every comfort and every privilege.

The part of Phoebe that was small and mean-spirited took a nasty sort of comfort that chaos presently reigned at Farley Park despite all these people employed to run the house. But she knew it was only because no one was in charge of the staff anymore.

Though it was not her place to step in to rectify matters, neither was it in Phoebe's nature to tolerate such disorganization when she knew full well she could correct it. She might never have managed servants before, but she knew how a household ought to run. Difficult servants could be taken in hand much like difficult livestock—and difficult children.

Of course if she stepped in, she would be playing right into the viscount's plan to make her an indispensable part of his household. For now, though, she chose to ignore that fact. So she helped the girls make their ablutions and don their nightgowns, then settled them in the bed they now shared, with two tarts apiece on plates propped upon their laps.

Two impromptu stories about three little fairy children who lived in the attics of an enormous house were all it took to see the girls sound asleep. Dousing the candles, Phoebe made her way to baby Leya's room, and smiled down on the sleeping child. Leya was well on her way to recovery and soon would be chasing up and down the stairs and halls, exercising her newly discovered mobility.

Before then, however, Phoebe needed to make sure the floors of those halls were clean and mopped, and that the rest of the household functioned as it ought.

She returned downstairs to find the dining room dark and James and his guests retired to someplace else—which place Phoebe fully intended to avoid. Instead she sought the ancient butler in the kitchen, where he sat with several other members of the staff. They all looked up when she entered.

She folded her hands primly at her waist. "Lord Farley has suggested that you might need assistance in the management of his household until such time as he can hire a new housekeeper."

Mr. Benson blinked in slow comprehension. Standing next to the enormous hearth, the cook shot the older man a fulminating look and muttered, "Thanks be."

"Tomorrow," Phoebe went on, "I'd like to meet with you, Mr. Benson, as well as you, Cook, and also the most senior of the housemaids."

"There's two," the cook said sourly. "Sisters."

"Sisters?"

The other servants sent the cook cautionary looks, as if to say, watch what you reveal to an outsider. But the stout woman ignored them. "Yes, two sisters who've been with the family for years, and who disagree on everything. Everything," she emphasized.

When no one contradicted the disgruntled cook, Phoebe pursed her lips. She was beginning to understand. Sisters who disagreed on everything and who both probably aspired to the housekeeping position. This she could handle.

"Have them both join us, then. Eight o'clock in the housekeeping office." Then she left, pleased with the way that had gone. Except that she didn't know where the housekeeping office was. But it couldn't be that hard to find.

Taking up a candle from a small table in the service hall, she went into the butler's pantry, checking all the doors. She found the buttery, the pantry, and the linen storage, but no office. Closing a fourth door which led to a dusty, little-used storeroom, she turned, only to be startled by a looming shadow. James!

"Looking for someone? Dare I hope it is I?" he asked, advancing into the pale circle of light her candle offered.

Still startled, and with one hand on her throat, Phoebe said, "I . . . I was looking for the housekeeping office."

"It's here." He indicated a short hall behind her. "I'll show you."

Like a fool she preceded him down the hall, a willing fool who couldn't pretend not to know where that door really led.

Once in the compactly arranged office, he took the candle from her and set it upon the desk. "So, I take it you've decided to act as housekeeper for me?"

"Temporarily. Just for a few days, while you have guests. I . . . I thought but to ensure there are no more three-hour dinners and unanswered bells."

He stared at her, a bemused smile on his face, as if he hadn't expected that from her. With her stomach fluttering, Phoebe averted her gaze from his. "Well, perhaps I should go. I've arranged an early meeting here with the senior members of your staff."

"Your staff now," he corrected her. "But don't leave yet, Phoebe. I haven't thanked you properly for making this transition to Farley Park so easy for the girls."

Phoebe tilted her chin up and gave him an even look. "Did I really have any other choice?"

He shrugged. "I've known a lot of women who would never consider putting their wishes second to the well-being of those girls. So yes, I think you did have a choice. Come now, Phoebe. Don't pretend to be angry with me. You're here; I'm here. There's a lot to be said for the situation. Why not take advantage of the possibilities that presents?"

So saying, he advanced across the small office, unhurried, nonthreatening. Yet Phoebe felt as if the stability of her whole world was under assault. Everything she knew and relied on had been threatened by this man's entrance into her life. But instead of running away from him, she chose perversely to run straight to him.

He took hold of each of her arms and slowly, inexorably drew her to him. "I wanted to do this all evening," he murmured just before his lips met hers. "This and so much more."

CHAPTER 16

Phoebe had been wanting to kiss him too, no matter how much she tried to deny it. She'd wanted him to stand up at the dinner table, in front of his children, his friend, and most especially, his fiancée, and take her, Phoebe Churchill, in his arms and make love to her. To declare that she was his choice, no other, and to send everyone else away so that he could prove his love to her.

Such perverse thoughts. So sinful! But lust had turned her into a wanton creature, and love had driven the last vestige of logic right out of her head. So she accepted his kiss. She rose to it and gloried in the masculine invasion. Behind her the door closed. Ahead of her heat and passion beckoned. All she had to do was allow it to happen.

But they were in the housekeeping office. Worse, there were servants still about.

"Wait." She gasped out the word against his lips.

He shifted her up so that she sat upon a records cabinet. Then he leaned into her, and used his hips to press her knees apart. "No one will disturb us here."

"But Mr. Benson might hear us—"

"He's half deaf."

"There are the others—"

"Who are all seeking their own beds."

Sure enough, the sound of muffled voices carried from the hall. "G'night, then."

"See you in the morning."

Footsteps faded away, and Phoebe's fears began to ease. Then a step sounded nearer, and she tensed. Someone had stopped just outside the door to the tiny office. A low-pitched laugh carried to them.

"Why, Robert!" A young female voice giggled this time. "You wicked thing, you."

"C'mon, Peg. Give a good lad a toss, why don't you?"

"You're hardly a good lad," the girl protested, but with the sound of yes in her voice.

Robert chuckled and then something bumped against the wall, and someone gasped. "Oh, but I am a good lad, Peg. Very, very good."

Phoebe heard little else, only more bumping and heavy breathing. But it was plain what was happening in the shelter of the little hall behind the door. This Robert and Peg were making love!

Phoebe looked up at James, his face but inches from hers. A sultry light glittered in his eyes, sultry and dark, and clear in its intent. His hands moved from her waist to her knees, sliding her best skirt and prettiest petticoats up to bare her cotton stockings, her ribbon garters, and her naked thighs.

His hands were so hot and burning. Overcome by the wickedest sensations, Phoebe fell back against the wall.

"You're delicious," he said, staring down at the darker skin of his hands upon her pale flesh. "Delicious to touch." His clever fingers pushed higher, moving beneath the bunched fabric.

"They'll hear you," she warned. But it was a weak

protest, and if anything, it emboldened him.

"Delicious to taste," he went on as his gaze moved up to her mouth. With torturous restraint he bent to kiss her, and as his mouth captured hers, his palms slid higher still. His tongue possessed her mouth while one of his fingers possessed the seething center of her.

She cried out and arched against him, then turned her face away and clamped her lips shut. They would be discovered.

"Do you hear them?" he whispered hotly in her ear as his finger drew in and out of her. "Do you think he's doing this to her?" He made a deep, circular movement with his finger.

Phoebe's head thrashed back and forth. She was afraid to speak, afraid to groan, afraid to do anything but sit here, a boneless heap, and revel in the erotic sensations he roused in her. Beyond the door the faint rhythmic bumping increased, with muffled grunts accompanying it, and muffled gasps.

"Sounds as if they've already moved on to the main course," James murmured. "The feast." So saying, his hands glided around to her buttocks and slid her forward, to the edge of the cabinet. He lifted her legs to circle his hips, an action that felt utterly right to Phoebe. Then with a deft manipulation of the front of his breeches, he released his erection. With unerring swiftness he found the slick, demanding center of her. Found her and buried himself deep within her.

"Oh!" Phoebe breathed out the word while clutching at his shoulders. Her head fell back as he thrust again into her, certain and deep, a simple movement that nonetheless felt absolutely essential to her continued existence.

"Oh. Oh." Her moans became a breathy chant as he pulled her over and over to him. The movements were small but ferocious, made more urgent and powerful by their restraint. In a mad rush, on the housekeeper's record cabinet, with a housemaid and a footman echoing their behavior just beyond the door, he made love to her, and when the madness overtook her, she bit down on her lip to repress her scream.

"Damn," he swore against her neck as she clenched and clenched in involuntary spasms around him. "Damn!" Then he stiffened, raising her right off the cabinet top.

Phoebe clung to him, arms wrapped tight around his shoulders, legs fastened desperately about his hips. He jerked and thrust and spent himself in her, and she didn't want it to end. They were joined, made one. To pull apart now seemed impossible.

Then a sharp cry from the hallway returned her rudely to reality. The man swore in a breathless voice. "Criminy, but you're one fine bit of ass, Peg."

The woman giggled. "As are you."

Then a rustle of cloth, footsteps fading away, and Phoebe's world came back into focus.

James sat her down on the cabinet and pulled away. But though she slid back from him, disentangling arms and legs and skirt from their carnal embrace, he didn't entirely let her go. His arms were braced against the wall behind her, trapping her there, just as his hips trapped her with legs still apart, a most vulnerable position for a woman. She was fully clothed yet fully available to him—and not just physically. She averted her eyes as she struggled to control her breathing and control her expression. But Phoebe suspected he knew exactly how vulnerable her emotions were to him.

"Phoebe."

Slowly she lifted her gaze to find his vivid eyes boring into hers. The candle flickered behind him, casting his face in shadows. But she fancied she saw his eyes clearly, burning blue and midnight black.

"This is why I wanted you in a chamber well away from the children's wing."

Phoebe nodded. "Yes. I know. But . . . But was this so terrible?" she asked, shocked by her unexpected boldness.

He grinned. "No." He pressed a fervent kiss to her mouth, one that reignited every fire he'd just quenched within her. "Not so terrible at all," he said, once she was again melting for him. "But I'd prefer to make love to you as you deserve, in a big, deep bed where we can thoroughly exhaust ourselves on each other. You have to change bedchambers as soon as you can. Tomorrow," he emphasized.

"But the girls need me nearby. At least Helen does."

"I need you too."

She stared at him, moved by his words. Yet she hungered still for more. Why couldn't he love her?

Because he loves Lady Catherine, her mother's voice came chillingly to her. *Because men never love the women who give themselves away like sluts.*

Once more Phoebe averted her gaze, and after a moment he pushed away from the wall. There was an awkward silence as they adjusted their clothing. She started to slide down from the cabinet, but he helped her with a warm grip on her waist. He didn't immediately release her.

"This is not the way I planned it to be, Phoebe."

She straightened her shoulders and suppressed any self-pitying thoughts. "You needn't apologize to me, for I've never had any expectations of you."

He frowned. "None?"

She shook her head. "I'm not a simpleton, Lord Farley. I know what my place is within your household, and

I know how this ultimately shall play out."

"Do you?"

"I do. So you needn't make apologies for what we both participate equally in."

"It wasn't meant as an apology."

"Good." She sidled out of his embrace and on shaky legs moved to the door. "It's awfully late and I've arranged an early appointment with the senior staff."

He watched her with eyes which had been so clear and direct, but now were dark and shuttered. "Fine. I don't suppose you want me to walk you to your bedchamber."

A little tremble coursed through her, a perverse longing to have him walk her there and accompany her inside, then lie down and make love to her again, and afterward sleep naked in her arms, and her in his. It was utter madness. She wasn't certain people did such things. But she wanted to do it. With him.

"No." The word sounded strangled and none too convincing. She cleared her throat. "No. I don't think that would be wise."

"After you then." He gestured to the door. "I'll wait here a few minutes before I leave."

She nodded and left, but her legs threatened to collapse the whole long traipse up the stairs. On the second level candles burned in the hallway. Somewhere on this floor Lady Catherine slept. Phoebe didn't want to think about her, but she couldn't drive the other woman's image away. One day when James married Lady Catherine, he would do with her what he had just done with Phoebe.

Perhaps he already had done as much—

A little cry escaped her throat, and distress lent strength to her legs. She hurried up the last flight, the candle flame wavering fitfully. In the shadows of her bedchamber she hastily disrobed and made her chilly ablutions. Then donning her well-worn night rail, she slid between the icy sheets and stared up at the plaster ceiling.

She'd made her choice; it would be foolish to regret it now. Nor would she allow herself to envision a fanciful future that bore a closer resemblance to a child's fairy tale than to the reality of her life. She was no cinder girl raised up from the scullery by a beloved prince. At the moment she was the willing mistress of a viscount, that was all.

That some might consider her situation quite an accomplishment for a goat girl afforded her little comfort. The hopeless truth was that she wanted to be the cinder girl and have the prince love her and marry her and pledge eternal fidelity to her. She wanted the fairy tale.

A sob caught in her throat, but ruthlessly Phoebe fought it down. She would not cry over what she could not have. She'd never been the weepy sort; she wouldn't become one now.

Tea was served in the second parlor promptly at four o'clock, attended by James's guests and his older girls, both washed, combed, and handsomely outfitted. Luncheon had occurred with similar timeliness, a simple repast to be sure: roast chicken, a thick, warming, vegetable soup, and freshly baked rolls. But the food was good and, equally important, it was hot.

"What a difference a day makes," Kerry remarked as he bit into a sugared roll smeared with butter and plum jam. "Mmm. Or perhaps I should say, what a difference one woman makes."

James didn't rise to the bait, which, judging by his friend's avid gaze, was what that comment was.

Sitting beside Kerry, Catherine was not so observant.

"A good servant is indeed an invaluable commodity to any household. She makes life so much more pleasant."

"Indeed," Kerry said. "*So* much more pleasant."

James shot him a warning glare, only to be met by the most innocent expression.

"Where is our Miss Churchill anyway?" Kerry went on. He looked at the girls, who were working a puzzle on a low table near the hearth. "Izzy, Helen. Why didn't Miss Churchill accompany you to tea?"

"She told us she had to go down to the kitchen," Izzy said as she fitted a piece in the border of the puzzle. "Something about the maids."

"Although a governess is perfectly acceptable at tea, a housekeeper is not," Lady Catherine commented as she set her tea down.

James sent her a sharp look. At least she was making an effort with his children. But even so, her remark irritated him. "Miss Churchill is the girls' governess and Helen's aunt," he said. Catherine might not appreciate the reminder, but she'd better get used to it. "We're doubly in her debt since she has agreed to act as housekeeper until I can find a replacement."

Kerry straightened up, then patted Catherine's arm as if to lessen the force of James's reprimand. He shot James a speaking look. "So, why did the previous housekeeper leave?"

Tamping down his annoyance, James said, "I discharged her when I realized she was a humorless, coldhearted—" He broke off. "Let's just say that she wasn't very good around children."

"Come take your tea," Lady Catherine called out to the girls. She smiled in approval when the pair shared a look, then rose and marched obediently to her and accepted the cups she'd poured for them. She nodded when they carried their cups back to their table without rattling or sloshing tea into their saucers. Then she turned to James. "Miss Churchill is obviously very good with children."

Izzy smiled over at them, but it was a smile that didn't reassure James at all. "Miss Phoebe is a wonderful person and the best lady I ever met," the girl said. She glanced at James as if to be sure he got the message, then picked up her teacup again, sticking her little finger straight out as she sipped.

"Yes, she is," James agreed. "And you, apparently, are a very good student."

Izzy ignored him, as was her usual wont. Despite improvements in every other aspect of her bearing, the girl's frosty attitude toward him hadn't eased a bit. It frustrated him to no end. Why did she hate him so? If not for that, a casual observer would never guess that two months ago she'd been ratting the streets, begging, thieving, and living by her wits. Today she looked like a perfect little lady, dressed in a blue frock with white collar and cuffs, white stockings, and gleaming black shoes. Her shiny hair was clean and brushed, caught in a tortoiseshell barrette on each side. Though uncurled, it was thick and pretty, and recently trimmed of its ragged ends.

In short, Izzy looked every bit as pretty as Helen, save for that mulish glint in her eyes. But despite the war of wills he and she still fought, he had to admire the child. She might be a brazen, hard-nosed little thing, but no one would ever take advantage of her or her sisters, not if she had anything to do with it.

It was time, however, to lure her to him. He lolled back in his chair, steepling his fingers beneath his chin. "So. Would you girls like a riding lesson tomorrow?"

That perked them right up, like morning glories belling open at the first light of dawn. Their teacups rattled down upon their saucers, causing Catherine's brow to pucker. "Why wait till tomorrow? I want to go now," Izzy said, jumping to her feet.

Helen, too, leaped up in excitement. "Oh, yes. I so very much would like to learn how to ride." She hesitated. Then averting her eyes, she smiled and shyly added, "Father."

Father. One simple word. Yet its impact was monumental. James distinctly felt something in his chest turn over and melt. This was the first time one of his children had called him father. The very first time.

Standing in the doorway, poised to join the perfectly arranged tableau, Phoebe also heard the appellation. She hesitated, observing the play of emotions on James's face.

She knew she should think of him as Lord Farley, not as James. But it was hard to do that when she understood so intensely the feelings in his heart. He was utterly smitten with his girls, so mad for them that it was impossible for her to maintain a grudge against him.

" 'Scuse me, miss." The maid named Peg sidled past her with a fresh pot of hot water.

At once a faint stain of color rose in Phoebe's face. She watched as Peg swiftly exchanged the fresh pot for the tepid one, then withdrew on silent feet. She was a respectable-looking girl, neat in appearance and demure in manner. Phoebe would never have guessed her to be a wanton.

But then she, too, was neat in appearance and reasonably demure in manner. Did anyone suspect what she did when no one else was about? Peg hadn't guessed, nor had the footman—at least Phoebe hadn't intercepted any knowing looks or leers.

Then from across the room Mr. Fairchild looked up, his eyes bright and observant, and Phoebe's confidence plummeted.

He knew. She could swear it.

But he couldn't possibly know what was going on between her and James, and she had no reason to think he did. Surely James wouldn't have told him. Her certainty would not go away.

It didn't console her much that if he did know, he probably didn't think it so terrible. If anything it proved what she already believed. Wenching was a point of pride for most men, and sleeping with the help was common for men of wealth and social standing.

Beset now by doubt, she decided it better not to interrupt this little domestic scene. She should just trust Izzy and Helen to behave as she'd instructed, and slip back to the nursery or the schoolroom, or better yet, a solitary stroll through the garden.

When Mr. Fairchild smiled and waved her over, however, signaling her presence to the others, it was too late to escape.

"Phoebe, Phoebe," the girls chorused. "We're going riding." They ran up to her and each of them caught her by a hand. Then they dragged her into the parlor while everyone watched. The men stood. Mrs. Donahue gave her a taut smile, while Lady Catherine indicated a seat next to her.

Phoebe sat, overwhelmed by how perverse the situation was. The future wife and the mistress sat side by side where the object of their contention might contrast them at his leisure. She had no doubt who would suffer in the comparison.

Even without her beauty, her grace, and her status in society, Lady Catherine would fit right into Lord Farley's parlor. The room suited her, right down to its colors, Phoebe realized as she stared at the younger woman's skirts spread so artfully upon the settee. Her outfit matched the room's decor. Butter-yellow moiré skirts upon a cream and willow-green striped settee. Tasteful emerald earbobs and two bracelets complemented the collection of Staffordshire figurines and a large painting of Lord Farley's mother on the wall. And of course, Lady Catherine's fair hair and ivory complexion practically glowed in the sunny, cream-colored parlor.

Phoebe stared down at her unadorned wrists, and surreptitiously banished a dark spot beneath her left thumbnail. Did the woman mean to wear midnight blue in the darkly elegant dining room? Would her peignoir be the same color as the master's bed linens—

Stop it!

Phoebe knotted her hands to prevent them trembling. She didn't know the color of James's bedchamber walls and likely never would.

But his fiancée soon would.

"Tea?" Lady Catherine asked.

She tried to compose herself. "Thank you."

"Will you come riding with us too?" Helen asked.

"Riding." Phoebe was too overcome by the disparate forces rocketing about the deceptively peaceful gathering to think straight. She lusted after one of their company, envied another, feared a third, and in the midst of all that, had to be strong for the girls. It was all she could do to lift the fragile teacup to her lips and sip the unsweetened beverage. Riding was out of the question.

"Don't you know how to ride?" Izzy asked.

Phoebe set her cup on its saucer. "I'm afraid my experience is limited to bareback rides on a slow-moving draft animal."

"How unfortunate for you," Lady Catherine said. "I find nothing quite so invigorating as a ride on a fine-blooded creature. Don't you agree, my lord?"

"Indeed," James answered. But when Phoebe's gaze reluctantly met his, the glitter there bespoke another sort of ride entirely. Or perhaps it was only her wicked imagination at work. In desperation she refocused on her now unpalatable tea. She could not lead this duplicitous life. She simply could not.

As if coming to her rescue, Mr. Fairchild put down his cup. "I say, Farley, why wait till tomorrow? You ought to take the girls out to the stables now while there's still some daylight left."

"Oh, may we?" Helen pleaded.

Even Izzy, despite her misgivings toward her father and her blatant desire for him to pair up with Phoebe, didn't want to miss an opportunity to ride. "Yes. Tea is over, isn't it?"

"But they aren't dressed for riding," Lady Catherine pointed out. "If there is a decent dressmaker in your village we could order riding habits made for them."

"Phoebe sews all my clothes," Helen said. She smiled at her aunt. "Don't you?"

"Do tell," Lady Catherine said, smile still in place. "How fortunate for James to have such a clever person in his employ. Governess. Housekeeper. And now seamstress. Your mother must be very proud of you, Miss Churchill."

So there were claws beneath that sweet, kittenish façade. Phoebe gave Lady Catherine a strained smile but did not otherwise respond.

For his part James stood, as if belatedly realizing that his fiancée and mistress ought not be confined too long together. "It's too late to ride, but it's not too late for a lesson in saddles and bridles and the importance of attending to one's animal's needs."

The girls ran to the door, but halted when Phoebe

bade them wait. "Make your farewells as you've been taught."

They curtsied and thanked Lady Catherine for tea, then said good-bye to the others, turned, and walked hand in hand to the door. Once through it, though, they dashed as of one mind for the back door. Following them, James paused in the doorway. "Are you coming?"

To whom his query was directed was not entirely clear, at least not to Phoebe. But Lady Catherine understood it directed to her, and with a graciousness of movement that Phoebe was beginning to despise, rose and said, "That sounds lovely. Come along, Mrs. Donahue. You must join us." Then she turned to Phoebe. "Shall you accompany us as well, Miss Churchill?"

"No," Phoebe said. Then she added, "Thank you," in a voice strung as tautly as her nerves.

"Well. We shall miss you," Lady Catherine said with the utmost sweetness. But this time Phoebe caught a flash in the woman's pretty blue eyes. A hint of possessiveness? An inkling of triumph?

The moment ended when Lady Catherine turned to Mr. Fairchild. "Aren't you coming, Kerry?"

Mr. Fairchild stood and gave her a foreshortened bow. "No. I believe I'll stay here instead and keep Miss Churchill company."

Lady Catherine gave them a smile and a nod, then took James's arm, and the two of them, trailed by Mrs. Donahue, went after the children.

In the emptiness of the abandoned parlor, Mr. Fairchild raised a phantom toast to them. "What a handsome couple they make. Don't you agree?"

"Yes." *Handsome enough to give a jealous lover a pounding headache.*

"I have to wonder, though, whether or not they are truly suited to one another."

Phoebe swiveled her head around, unable to disguise her surprise. "Are you saying you don't think they are?"

"I'm not certain." His clever eyes narrowed when he grinned. "What do you think?"

Phoebe composed her face, and tried as well to compose her emotions. "I'm sure I'm not the appropriate person to venture an opinion on that subject." When he continued to stare expectantly at her, however, she grew flustered. "He is a lord; she is a lady. And as you say, they look exceedingly well together. What else is required?"

But Phoebe feared that Mr. Fairchild had an ulterior motive for this particular subject. She'd ascertained already that his idle manner hid a quick mind and sharp eyes. He suspected something. Once more she wondered if James had revealed the truth to him.

Abruptly she rose and strode for the door. "I've work to tend to," she muttered. "If you'll excuse me?"

"Work. My dear Miss Churchill, all you do is work. Surely you have time to sit and enjoy your—"

Phoebe left before he could finish. She could make time for tea, but not with someone who wanted to probe her thoughts and feelings as thoroughly as he wanted to.

And not while the children she loved were having a wonderful time with the man she loved—and with the woman *he* loved.

CHAPTER 17

James sat in a tall wing chair, listening to Lady Catherine play Chopin at the pianoforte, but thinking about Phoebe Churchill. On a rug before the fire Izzy and Helen teased their kittens with a length of ribbon, while Bruno napped. Kerry sat at a card table, hunched over a two-week-old copy of the *Times*.

"Damn," he swore under his breath. He glanced at James. "The *Skylark*—you know, that freighter I invested in. She's still not listed as having arrived in port. God forbid she's been lost at sea. Did you put any money in her?"

"No." James pushed to his feet, drawing a look from Lady Catherine. When she ended the piano composition, he said, "I'm going up to the nursery to bid Leya goodnight."

Izzy jumped up. "We'll come too."

"No." He stopped, then with a gesture he repeated in a calmer tone, "No. You girls must play the role of hostesses to our guests. I won't be long."

Helen started to protest. Though her shyness had eased around him, being left alone with their visitors was not something she was comfortable with. But Izzy's hand on Helen's shoulder and a reassuring smile silenced the younger girl. Phoebe had worked wonders with Izzy, James thought as he strode away. She'd turned his wild-cat of a daughter into an ally, and into a little mother to the other girls.

In truth, everything Miss Phoebe Churchill did was a wonder to him. Everything she touched, she managed to charm. His children. His household staff. Himself.

He exhaled, a sharp whistle of breath through his teeth, as remembered passion spiraled through him. Up the broad sweep of stairs he went, taking three at a time. He was heading for the nursery and he did want to check on the rapidly recovering Leya. But he wanted to see Phoebe too. He needed to see her.

Tea had been a disappointment and the visit to the stables only a brief distraction. At dinner she'd sat far down from him, accepting their compliments on the staff's prompt service with good grace. But she'd contributed very little to the conversation. When they'd repaired to the parlor, she'd excused herself—something about tomorrow's menu. Ever since, he'd found himself anxiously awaiting her return. Eventually she would have to come for Izzy and Helen.

But he wanted to speak to her in private before then, to steal a kiss and make arrangements for later.

He came upon her just departing the nursery. She looked up startled, and in the wavering amber light of the candle branch she carried, she appeared soft, inno-cent, and completely beguiling.

"Is Leya asleep?" *Come to me tonight.*

"Yes."

Yes, you'll come to my bed? Blood pooled seething and urgent in his loins.

"Yes, she's asleep. The blisters are beginning to dry." She sidled past him and started down the hall. "I haven't noticed any new blisters either. It seems the end of her illness may be in sight."

"Phoebe."

She slowed, then stopped, and after a long moment, turned to face him. "Yes?"

Her eyes were large and luminous, deceptively open. Yet he couldn't determine what she was thinking. Suddenly he felt as gauche as a lad of fifteen, finagling desperately to steal a kiss from a girl he'd long admired.

"I'd like to see you." His voice was thick and low. "Tonight."

She stood very still. Only the flickering of the candle flames and the dancing shadows gave any illusion of movement to her face. "Where?"

Here. Now. Anywhere. Anytime. "My study? We can be private there." He knew it was the wrong answer even before she blinked and looked away.

"Perhaps tomorrow would be better." Then she turned and fled, and he could only stare after her. It was Catherine, of course. Catherine's unexpected presence had Phoebe in a quandary and he couldn't blame her. He felt much in a quandary himself. He and Catherine hadn't yet spoken of their betrothal—about her willingness to renew it and his willingness to agree. But the signs were all there and he'd be a fool not to take advantage of his good fortune. Everything he wanted was within his grasp. He had only to reach out and take it. But at the moment all he wanted was Phoebe.

He was an idiot, thinking with his cock instead of his brain. But he couldn't manage to stop. No woman had ever interfered with his political aspirations before. But Phoebe was. She was wreaking havoc with them.

If only Catherine's change of heart had come at a more convenient moment. If only he'd had more time with Phoebe to cement their budding relationship. A week. A few days, even.

He raked a hand through his hair, then stared blankly around the room. He was an idiot risking his whole future because he couldn't get one woman out of his system. How in God's name had he dug himself into such a deep hole?

Phoebe also felt like an idiot, a maudlin idiot who must still believe in fairy tales. There was no other accounting for the emotional storm that beset her. Why not go to him? she wondered as she secured the safety of her bedroom. The dubious safety. She wanted to be with him. He wanted her to be. What had she expected, for him to invite her into the master's chambers? Why should he when she'd already proven herself willing in the nursery and in the housekeeping office? Men did not invite their mistresses into their private chambers in their ancestral homes. That was an honor reserved solely for a wife.

She leaned back against the door and let out a hysterical laugh. She wasn't sure where she'd acquired that bit of immoral etiquette, but somehow it seemed right. The master's chambers were for the wife to visit, for creating the lord's heir and all his subsequent children. A decent man wouldn't invite his mistress to the same bed his wife visited.

"God help me," she groaned. A decent man wouldn't maintain a mistress in the first place. And a decent woman wouldn't *be* that mistress. Had she made a terrible mistake coming to work here? Was it too late to change her mind?

She buried her face in her hands, but though she stood a long time with her head bowed and shoulders slumped, she wouldn't let herself cry. She couldn't. She was the girls' governess and so must go down to fetch them up to their beds. She would supervise their ablutions, and when she tucked them beneath the counterpane, she would tell them that on Sunday they must promise to be on their best behavior. For she'd been invited for dinner at Mrs. Leake's table, and she meant to go.

James was definitely avoiding being alone with Catherine.

For two days Kerry watched his friend dodge the bewildered woman, despite her increasingly unsubtle hints. No matter the occasion—a horseback ride, a stroll around the park, an afternoon in the library—James maneuvered like a chess master, making certain Kerry or one of his girls was always beside him.

Not that Kerry minded. It had been hard enough to watch his best friend win the affection of the woman *he* had come to love. When Catherine had broken off the betrothal, Kerry had been so happy he'd even allowed himself the foolish luxury of imagining her turning to *him,* falling in love with *him,* and convincing her rigid, unfeeling father to accept *him* as a son-in-law.

Pitiful hopes, and they'd been pitifully dashed when she'd begged him to precede her to Yorkshire. But he'd done it. He'd do anything for Catherine. The last thing he'd expected was James's lack of enthusiasm for resuming the betrothal. Despite Catherine's obvious misery, his hopes were once again raised.

It hadn't taken long to notice James's avoidance of Catherine. The question remained, was it deliberate, or unconscious? Even more curious, why did the man never use Miss Churchill as the buffer between himself and his would-be fiancée?

In the same manner Miss Churchill managed to avoid ever being alone with James. Very interesting.

But Kerry had grown bored with all this tiptoeing

about. He wanted to see sparks fly; he was ready for fireworks. If James couldn't be honest with Catherine, maybe it was time for Kerry to force the issue. Or perhaps Miss Phoebe Churchill should. Something was going on between the demure governess and his randy friend, and he needn't be a genius to figure out what.

But what if Catherine didn't care? What if she wanted James no matter the circumstances? After all, she was here despite his three natural-born children.

Muffling an oath, he put that thought out of his mind, and instead lifted his tumbler of whisky to the window and studied the light that poured through the gold-tinted liquid. Not for the first time he bemoaned the fact that he was a younger son—not that he wanted all the responsibilities that went along with becoming the Earl of Sanderly. But a younger son was considered second choice as a husband, at least among the first-choice ladies. And by every standard that counted, Catherine Winfield was first choice, as her father well knew.

Beyond the window a figure moved across his line of vision. Miss Churchill strolling with Leya on the child's first venture outdoors since the onset of her illness. He set down his drink. The day was quite fine, spring at its best, mild and sunny, with no storms queuing up along the horizon. Perhaps he, too, should avail himself of a little stroll.

As he departed the morning room he heard James's voice coming from his study. When Benson departed the study, nodding silently at Kerry, the first germ of an idea occurred to him.

"Benson, my good man. Might you be able to tell me where Lady Catherine is?"

"In the library, sir. With her friend."

"And Lord Farley?"

"He's tending to estate business, sir. All morning, he said."

"Good." Kerry glanced at the closed office door. He couldn't take the suspense. If James wouldn't willingly face the issue, then he would force him to. "Let the fireworks begin," he muttered.

The old butler cupped one hand to his ear. "What's that, sir?"

"Nothing, my good man. Nothing that concerns you."

James had a letter from his man of business, along with two recent reports on the situations in Paris and Bombay. For once he wasn't interested. Instead he was studying the crop reports and maintenance records for Farley Park, though not very effectively. He couldn't seem to concentrate on anything these days. When a soft knock sounded on his study door, he welcomed the distraction. A woman's knock. Phoebe's?

He stood in anticipation. "Come in."

But it was Catherine, Catherine alone, dressed in a pale blue morning gown of gossamer lawn that turned her eyes an impossible shade of blue. To his dismay he recognized a determined glint in those bluebell eyes.

She closed the door with a decisive click, then leaned back against it, all the while smiling at him in a manner he'd never seen before. It was a seductive pose, an I've-got-you-now pose, an aren't-you-glad-to-be-caught? pose. Except that he wasn't.

What was wrong with him? Back in London he would have been entranced, alert for any possibility of them being alone together. But this wasn't London and he wasn't entranced. And he knew why.

Phoebe.

When she didn't speak, he drummed his fingers on the desktop. "Did you need something?"

She took a deep breath, lifting her pretty bosom against the properly snug fit of her scooped neckline. Pretty bosom; pretty mouth; pretty, confused manner that should have him springing to her aid in the hope of stealing a kiss or maybe more. But all James wanted was to get back to estate business.

"Catherine?" he prompted.

"Oh, James," she burst out. "How much longer are you going to punish me? Must I grovel and beg your forgiveness? Is that what you require of me?"

Taken aback, James watched with increasing unease as two crystalline tears welled in her unblinking eyes, then spilled with magnificently restrained emotion onto her cheeks.

"Please. Sit." He indicated a chair, but she sank gracefully onto the leather divan. After hovering a moment, he came around his desk to sit beside her. He handed her a handkerchief which she took. But she didn't dab at her face. Instead she turned a heartbroken expression up to him.

"I know I'm behaving like a goose, interrupting you at your books, which I know men detest. Very likely I shouldn't have come to Farley Park at all. But somehow I seem unable to prevent myself from behaving the fool over you."

All James wanted was for this problem to go away. But it wouldn't. So he said, "You're not making a fool of yourself, Catherine. It's me. I should have addressed the purpose of your visit days ago."

She sniffled daintily and looked down at the handkerchief she clutched. "I suppose I shouldn't have made this journey to Yorkshire. But when Kerry didn't send word from you not to come, I took it as an optimistic sign."

"It's all right. I'm glad you came."

"It's just that matters were so awkward in town, with all the gossip and everyone counseling me. This way. That way."

"That was my fault," James said. "All of it was my fault."

"But I shouldn't have listened to them. Not to Papa nor to anyone else."

Papa. Lord Basingstoke. "Have you come here over your father's objections?" It shouldn't matter, but at that moment her father's opinion was vital to James. He might not be overwhelmed with desire for Catherine. But her father's good will was key to the advancement of his political career or the death of it.

She dabbed her cheeks, for the two tears had run their course down to her delicate jawline. "Papa was not at all pleased by your . . . your situation. However, once his initial anger was exhausted, he reassured me that, could you and I mend our rift, he would not stand in our way."

Mend their rift. The words made it sound so easy, as if James's children were simply a minor difference of opinion which could be discussed and reasoned away. "What of my three daughters? Will he accept them? Will you?"

Catherine blinked her damp lashes and gave him a brave smile. "Of course we will. He and I spoke about it and—" She hesitated, and a soft blush colored her pearlescent cheeks. "He admitted to a fling or two in his own youth."

Somehow James couldn't picture the stout, red-faced Lord Basingstoke ever having a fling. Nor of ever being young.

Catherine went on. "I've given it considerable thought. The baby—she's actually quite adorable and she could live with us while the other two attend school. If you wish them to eventually be presented into society, they will require far more instruction than their current governess can provide." She paused. "I presume you do want the best for them."

"Of course I do. But not right away. They need Ph— Miss Churchill. For now they need her."

Catherine dipped her head in quiet acquiescence, then looked up. "So we are in agreement." She smiled. "Father will be so pleased."

James managed a smile back, and when she placed one small hand on his arm, so small as to appear childish, he automatically covered it with his much larger one. If Lord Basingstoke was pleased, then James should be pleased. It seemed his three-year goal of courting the man would come to fruition after all.

But James wasn't pleased, not as he'd ought to be. When Catherine stood and apologized for interrupting his work, then took her leave, gliding away in that ethereal, floating manner of hers, he couldn't return to his work.

Without actually saying the words they seemed to have resumed their betrothal. There were questions still to be answered, decisions to be made, and all the legal papers to be redrawn and re-signed. The gossips were sure to salivate over every bit of it. But he was getting what he wanted. That's what mattered. He was back in the game. Once the marriage was done, the gossip would eventually fade away.

But what would his daughters think about this? What would Phoebe think?

He shoved the ledger book back from him, toppling over an Indian bronze of a tiger and its cub. It hit the carpeted floor with a dull thud, much like the sudden change of his circumstances had hit him. He'd just attained something he'd wanted a long time, something he'd lost, then anticipated regaining ever since Catherine arrived. But that something didn't bring him the satisfaction he'd expected.

Just a dull thud.

Phoebe saw Kerry crossing the back verandah too late to avoid him. He started toward her at a jaunty pace, swinging his arms and whistling like a plowboy. Were the circumstances of their acquaintance different, she would enjoy his company immensely. He was pleasant and good-natured, with just enough devilment in him to be entertaining. All in all, excellent company. But he was too curious about her—about her and Lord Farley—and she feared he meant to dig and burrow until he discovered that which she could never allow him to discover.

Unwilling to subject herself to his inquiry, she hailed the girls, who were hanging over the edge of the fountain. "Helen. Izzy. Look who's come to visit with you." He'd become a great favorite of theirs, and as Phoebe predicted, their heads popped up and at once they started a foot race toward him.

Izzy won. "There are pollywogs in the fountain." She grabbed him by one hand. "Come see."

Helen shook her head. "It's too early for pollywogs." She grabbed Mr. Fairchild's other hand. "They're probably just little minnows or insect larva."

Izzy shot her a withering look. "You don't know everything."

Mr. Fairchild waggled both their hands. "I'm afraid, though, that Miss Helen knows far more about the countryside than we city folk do, Izzy. It's no use to argue with her when her knowledge is greater than ours."

It was such a sweet scene, the normally timid Helen holding her ground while the usually irascible Izzy made a wry face, then conceded with a shrug. In her arms Leya

jiggled and laughed, and Phoebe hugged her closer to
her heart. Discovering they were sisters had been so
good for Helen and Izzy. The little family they were
forging had expanded both their horizons, and no doubt
would continue to do so. For all Phoebe's misgivings
about the situation, she was absurdly happy to be a part
of their newly blossoming lives.

"You might know a little more than me about country
stuff," Izzy said to Helen. "But if we ever go to London,
I'll be the one to teach you about everything." Then she
grabbed Phoebe's elbow, dragging her back to the fountain with them. "Come and see. If we catch some of
them in a jar of water, we can take them inside and see
what they grow up to be."

"Yes, indeed," Mr. Fairchild said. "Insects or toads.
Perfect indoor pets. The cats will enjoy the toads, I suppose. Batting them around. Eating them."

"No!" Izzy said, while Helen made a loud chomping
sound. They were a pleasant, laughing company, until
Lady Catherine and Mrs. Donahue found them. At once
Phoebe stiffened, Izzy scowled, and Helen retreated to
her hesitant silence.

Lady Catherine didn't seem to notice. Phoebe took in
the woman's beautiful sky-blue gown and perfect blond
coiffure, which were set off by a collection of gold and
aquamarine jewels she probably would dismiss as mere
baubles. Phoebe's mouth turned down on one side. Catherine was no doubt accustomed to bringing conversa-
tions to a crashing halt whenever she made an entrance.
She probably expected it.

"Good news," Mrs. Donahue announced, beaming at
her younger friend. "Grand news."

"Indeed?" Mr. Fairchild said. Phoebe sensed rather
than saw his good humor flee. "Pray, do not keep us in
suspense. Or perhaps I can guess," he added, an edge to

his voice. "Might it have anything to do with viscounts and weddings?"

Lady Catherine averted her gaze, but her satisfied smile revealed the accuracy of his words.

Like taffy candy, Phoebe's knees went weak. It was no more than she'd expected ever since the woman's arrival. Had she hoped they wouldn't eventually come to an agreement? Foolish girl. Foolish, foolish girl.

Mrs. Donahue laughed and clapped her hands. "Yes, a wedding, with a viscount—*and* a viscountess."

Mr. Fairchild glanced at Phoebe, a hint of accusation in his gaze. How was any of this her fault? Then he gave Lady Catherine a grave bow. "My congratulations. Farley is a lucky fellow indeed. Very lucky. And where is the bridegroom anyway?"

"I just left him in his office, hard at work," Lady Catherine said. "But I simply had to share my happy news with someone." Her eyes fastened upon Phoebe who had yet to move or speak or even to blink. "My dear Miss Churchill, I will need your assistance in getting to know James's children. I can count on you, can't I?"

Then not even waiting for a reply, she turned to Mr. Fairchild and, hooking her arm in his, started them back toward the house. "Come, I must tell the cook to prepare something festive for dinner tonight. And I need to pen a letter to my father about my good news. He shall be so pleased."

CHAPTER 18

It was all spiraling out of control. James stared out the window of his study, blind to the rolling, pastoral view. Over the course of three short months his life had lurched from one extreme to another. Betrothed, feted, and the toast of London society, he'd been so close to achieving his years-long goal. Then it had been yanked beyond his reach, the golden ring snatched back.

Now he had hold of it again, or he would once he and Catherine wed. If he was smart, he'd press for an early date, midsummer at the latest. That way he could salvage a small part of this year's season.

He rubbed one hand over the back of his neck. The problem was, he didn't want to go back to London. Not just yet.

His gaze focused on a pair of groundskeepers working along the driveway, then swept across the whole of his family estate. Farley Park was a handsome property. In the thirty years since his father's death and his mother's remarriage, he'd seldom visited the estate. But between the bailiff and his London solicitor, he'd seen that it was well managed. The income it produced was more than adequate to its upkeep, and the surplus had financed his many lengthy sojourns abroad.

He hadn't intended to reside here though, not until he was married and had sired a son who would inherit the property. When he had arrived, it had been under duress, with his personal life an unholy mess, and no real plan for his future.

Had it only been a month since he'd retreated from London? It felt like years ago. He could hardly remember his life before Leya and Izzy—and now Helen.

And Phoebe.

He needed to speak with Phoebe.

No. He needed to do more than speak with her. He needed time alone with her, without the threat of interruption either by children, servants, or anyone else. Phoebe felt uneasy around Catherine—which he understood. But he also got the sense that Catherine didn't particularly approve of Phoebe, which he didn't understand. You'd think Catherine would be happy to have some other woman tending to his children.

He supposed women were competitive in different ways than men. Nevertheless, he needed to reassure Phoebe that, unlike what she'd once predicted, the lady of *this* house would not be making the decisions regarding his daughters' governess. Phoebe's position at Farley Park was absolutely secure.

But as James left the study, he was met by his guests in the hall. One thing led to another, and Catherine never let him out of her sight. The children took their tea in the schoolroom, and tonight would be dining there as well. "So we adults may celebrate our betrothal," Catherine said when she told him the plans she'd made with the cook. "Miss Churchill said she understood and that she would sup with the children."

She understood? James clenched his jaw. Bloody hell. If Phoebe understood about the celebration Catherine planned, that meant she'd already been told about the renewed betrothal. Probably by Catherine herself. Damn, but he'd hoped to reveal that tricky bit of news to her himself.

Not until dinner was over—three bottles of wine consumed among the four of them, and his patience at a raging end—was James able to bid his guests goodnight. He made straightaway for Phoebe's third-floor bedchamber. Surely the children were asleep and would not disturb them. He eased open the door to her room. All was in darkness. "Phoebe?" He advanced to her bed. "Phoebe? Wake up. It's James."

She wasn't there.

As his eyes grew accustomed to the dark he scanned the room, baffled. The bed was still neatly made. She must be with the children. Was one of them ill?

In the room they now shared, Izzy and Helen were curled together beneath a mountain of bedcovers. Tucked amid the folds and curves were the three kittens as well as Bruno, who snored like a miniature bellows. But no Phoebe.

In Leya's room, however, he found the nurse's cot occupied. Impatiently he crossed to her. "Phoebe." He shook her by the arm. "Wake up. I need to talk to you."

"What? Who?"

James jerked back when one of the downstairs maids sat upright. Her bleary eyes bulged with fright, and she clutched the blanket like a shield to her chest.

"Holy damnation," he swore. "Where's Phoebe?"

The girl blinked. "Who?"

Bloody hell, would nothing go right for him ever again? Somehow James restrained himself from shouting. "Where is Miss Churchill?"

"Miss Churchill? Why, she said . . . she said . . ." the girl stammered. "She said she was going home, milord. That's right. Home." She pulled the blanket even higher, then added in a shaky voice, "I believe she lives over to Plummy Head."

He damn well knew where she lived. But why had she gone back there, and without telling him? James wanted to roar his frustration, to pound the wall or, better yet, put his fist through it. But the sleep-befuddled maid was staring at him as if he were a nightmare apparition. There was also Phoebe's reputation to respect.

So he reined in the unholy rage that gripped him and crossed to Leya's bed. The sight of her peaceful little face and the rhythmic rise and fall of her chest gave him pause. He tucked the blanket more securely around the sleeping cherub, then smoothed a hand over her silky head. Odd how the sight of her calmed him, how touching her seemed to connect him to Phoebe. But he wanted more than that vicarious connection. He wanted the real thing, to find her. Now.

"Keep up the good work," he muttered to the maid, who'd not budged from her terrified pose upon the narrow bed. Did the ninny actually think he meant to accost her?

Once out of the nursery, however, James forgot about the maid. He had to find Phoebe.

He caught up with her where the woods gave on to the field, then angled up toward her house. Off the sea the wind chased the strands of clouds and mist away, leaving the moon to light a chilly, colorless scene. Phoebe looked small in the vastness of the darkened landscape, like a lonely wraith wandering an inhospitable land that once had been a happy home to her.

But it was ruined now, and it was all his doing. The worst of it was that he couldn't undo it, not without either giving up Helen or giving up Phoebe. Even then it wasn't that simple. For Helen wasn't only a part of him; she was also Izzy's sister and Leya's, and the three little girls belonged together. Family, even one as messy and disjointed as theirs, was not something to give up without a fight.

He'd bet money that Phoebe felt the same way.

He reined in his blowing horse and watched as Phoebe hurried toward the hunkering shadow in the distance that was her cold, empty house. She walked the land without fear or hesitation. She probably knew every rock in the path, every dip and curve of rocky ground. This was her home, her life—or what he was leaving of it to her.

But no matter how badly she thought he'd ruined her life, he had to make it right. Somehow he had to try to make it right. So he spurred his horse forward from the edge of the woods, never taking his gaze from her.

He could tell when she first heard the thunder of hooves. She halted and turned, one hand to her throat, searching the dark. When she spied him, she stumbled back two paces. But she held her ground. She knew it was him. Who else could it be?

Phoebe waited for James at the stone wall, fighting for calm against a riot of emotions. She needed distance from him, that's why she'd needed to come home tonight. So why did her heart leap to know he'd followed her? The crushing wall of tears she'd fought and defeated rose now in absurd relief and gladness. He'd come for her!

But she had to turn him away.

When he brought his animal to a plunging halt not an arm's length from her, she tilted her chin up. "Go home to your fiancée, Lord Farley. There is nothing for you here."

He threw himself from the saddle with such violence his horse shied away. "You're here," he countered. And with that he caught her to him, as fiercely as a Gypsy thief bent on ravishing her.

"No—" She twisted and fought, furious at this newest example of his arrogant, high-handed behavior.

"Listen to me, Phoebe. That's all I want. Just hear me out—"

"No!" She turned away from the heat of his breath on her cold cheek. She tried to kick his shins, and to pry herself from the bear hug of his hold.

But he was too strong and too determined. With her arms trapped between them and her toes barely skimming the ground, she felt as helpless as a trout in one of her nets. She'd had every reason to be wary of him, yet still she'd unwisely taken the lure he'd dangled before her. There was no escaping the consequences now.

She wanted to scream her frustration, to revile him with her fury and her outrage. With her pain. How could he hurt her this way, deep in her heart where she was most vulnerable? How could she have let him close enough to do so?

"Be still, sweetheart." His embrace, though adamant, managed not to be cruel. He shifted her, sliding her down his hard belly and chest, until her feet found purchase. But it was the odd friction of wool on wool with warm bodies just beneath that resonated to her more than the pebbled ground beneath her boot soles.

"Phoebe," he murmured in a voice that vibrated through her, husky and warm. And as fast as her name disappeared into the night, so did he suck all the opposition from her.

"Phoebe." His gloved hand cupped her face; she felt the seams of supple leather caress her cheek. What she wanted, though, was flesh. Warm, naked flesh.

But the only uncovered portion of them was their faces. Like a being separated from herself, her head swiveled. Her sheltering eyelids lifted and her gaze fastened upon his clever, mobile lips.

That's what she wanted. His lips upon hers, that spiraling heat that turned her blood to lava, swamped every one of her senses, and pushed everything else out of her mind. She didn't want to think, not about anything.

For a moment only they were suspended between what they wanted and what they should want. On some level Phoebe sensed that he, too, hesitated. But then a rogue wind whipped her skirts against his legs. It tore her bonnet away and freed her hair to the tumult of the gusty night. His hand slid into her hair, his fingers curled into the tangles, and his mouth came down upon hers.

Lightning struck, not from the sky, but from the stormy center of her. Clean, hot lightning, surging with electric heat to meld them as one, to burn all but desire out of them.

"Don't run away from me," he said, a guttural command on her seeking mouth.

No. I won't, she answered with all the force of her yearning body. In this, at least, they were in utter agreement. He demanded the use of her mouth and she demanded that he use it well. Mouth and tongue; friction, invasion, and possession. She invaded him back, thrusting her tongue into his mouth in a rhythmic give-and-take that mirrored the other give-and-take she wanted.

A greedy moan vibrated between them. His or hers? One of his hands slid down to cup her derriere, pressing her to the ridge of his hardened male flesh. Her hands slid inside his open coat and circled his waist. He was so hot and so hard. Everywhere. He was muscle over bone, and all of it focused on her.

He moved his mouth to her ear, then her throat, nuzzling past the collar of her coat and dress. She felt the hard nip of his teeth, but instead of pain, it shot an arrow of intense desire to the churning place in her belly. As if it were a real caress on her nether lips, moisture rose inside her. Liquid want. Lust.

Lust. Phoebe struggled for logic and for breath.

"This . . . This isn't the answer. It solves nothing," she said, pulling her hands from inside his waistcoat. She pressed her palms against his chest and tried to push away from him. But he wouldn't release her.

"It solves one thing," he said. "It eases one pain. It scratches one itch. You feel that itch, don't you, Phoebe?" He caught her bottom lip between his teeth, not biting her, but tugging on it, teasing her with this possibility of a kiss until all she wanted was the fullness of his mouth on hers, the connection and invasion all over again.

It was the answer he sought.

"You see?" He pulled away just as she clutched him tight once more and arched greedily against him. Then without warning he scooped her up and, stepping over the squat stone wall, he strode across the yard to her cottage.

"Wait—"

"No."

"Your horse—"

"Will be there in the morning."

It was a maiden's dream, to be swept away through the dark of night by a man intent on giving her more pleasure than she could rightly imagine. The wind to propel you on, the moon to light the way, the stars to wink their approval.

Though she knew James wouldn't drop her, Phoebe clung to his neck and buried her face against his collar. She wanted this dream of stormy desire and fiery culmination, even though dawn would turn the dream to a nightmare of heartbreak and shame and despair.

He kicked open the door and, not bothering with the

stairs, made for the settee and the square of moonlight that lit the carpeting before the cold hearth. He set her on her feet but did not let her go. Even in the inkiness of the house she felt the force of his eyes.

"Where are the flint and steel?"

A shiver ran through Phoebe, though not of coldness. "I'll get them."

He knelt beside her layering wood upon the cold hearth, and when her shaking hands couldn't make a spark, he took over the task. A little fire, a pair of flickering candles. Then they faced one another, still dressed yet bared to one another in ways that terrified her. He knew her weaknesses. All of them.

No. Not all of them. She would never let him know that she loved him. That would be going too far.

She hugged her arms across her chest. Nor could she reveal how deeply his renewed betrothal had hurt her. For only a woman in love would feel betrayed by what he'd done. So she must be a woman *not* betrayed and *not* in love. Never in love. Only in lust.

He added several logs across the small, spitting flame, feeding it until its pale, yellow light drove the shadows back into the corners. Then he stood, shed his coat, and turned to her.

"Why did you leave without telling me?"

Phoebe lifted her chin, ignoring the tendrils of cold air on her neck that reminded her where his hot tongue had so recently trespassed. "I left a note on your chair in the morning room." When he only stared at her, tall and commanding in her little parlor, she went on impatiently. "Tomorrow is Sunday, my day off." Then, more angrily, "I have plans that don't include you."

"What of the girls?"

"They're your girls, remember? Not mine." She

clamped her lips together. There was too much hurt in her voice. Too much pain.

Unfortunately he heard it, for his tone turned from challenging to tender. "They'll always be yours, Phoebe. Especially Helen." He crossed to her. "You're her aunt. You're her family."

Something began to quiver inside her, something that made her next words come out strangled. "And what will I be to you?"

He lifted his hand to her and though she flinched, he slid the pad of his thumb across her lower lip, the lightest caress across the most sensitive part of her. "You are to me what I am to you, Phoebe. Nothing has to change between us."

She smiled, the most insincere smile of her life. "Your lover. I'll be yours and you'll be mine?"

The fire flared with renewed vigor. Pop, hiss. She felt the first wave of heat from the fledgling flame. But no fire of any size could thaw the icy dread that encased her heart. "I'll be your mistress and you'll be my protector?"

The firelight cast one side of his face in shadows, but still she saw his frown. "You make it sound tawdry."

"Isn't it?"

He caught her by the arms before she could back away. "No. Nothing about what I feel for you is tawdry." Then his eyes narrowed and he cocked his head. "You're the only one who sees it that way."

"Only me?" She gave him an incredulous look. "Me and anyone from Swansford who might suspect something between us. Oh, and then there's your staff." She was really working herself into a fine fit of pique. "Mr. Benson shall be so pleased to know your mistress is in residence on the third floor. So much easier than having to call for a carriage or a horse, and to dress his master to go off to meet his mistress. And then there's the small matter of your wife."

She jerked away from him, no longer pretending that this could be a civil conversation. "I'm sure the new viscountess won't see anything tawdry about her husband creeping about the house at night to carry on with the governess."

His brows lowered in a scowl. "Damn it, Phoebe! That's not what this is."

"Then what is it, James?" She threw her hands up in frustration. "What? Isn't it enough that you've taken Helen from me? Is it your plan to get a baby on me too? Another child to wield like a weapon against me?" Her voice broke, but when he tried to enfold her in his arms she shook her head and held him off.

"I'm sorry, Phoebe. Sorry about Helen. Sorry that Catherine ever came here. Sorry that your life has been torn apart because of me. But I can't be sorry about the time we've spent together."

Like the old oaks along the cliffs that quaked when the sea winds roared through, Phoebe shook from the force of his words. But they weren't enough. "You may not be sorry," she said—she lied—"but I am."

Their gazes clashed and held, until the intensity of it became unbearable. He was peeling away all the layers of her lie, and soon he would reveal every secret hope and foolish dream she harbored: She didn't want him to leave her alone; she wanted him to marry her, to be with her forever—only her—and need her above all others.

But he would never feel that way and she refused to let him see that pathetic need in her eyes. "It doesn't really matter," she said. "The truth is, now that I'm no longer burdened by aging parents and an orphaned niece, I've suddenly become more attractive to the local bachelors. Imagine that. I've been invited to dine in Swansford tomorrow. I wouldn't be surprised if by May Day I had a beau of my own."

It was an out-and-out lie, but Phoebe forced conviction into every single word, and it paid off. For the first time that night he looked flummoxed, as if the idea of someone else desiring her company was beyond the realm of belief. The very fact of his silence goaded her further.

"I plan to marry, you see. A woman who holds title to her own land is a rare commodity around here. Now that I'm not bound by family obligations, I expect to have men fighting for the opportunity to marry me. After all, as we both know, smart men always plot how to marry well." She gave him a curt nod. "I think you better leave now."

She was bluffing. It was patently false, everything she said. The last thing Phoebe wanted was to marry some sly fellow who wanted a farm more than he wanted a wife to go with it. But that was the sort of negotiations the Viscount Farley understood. You married the woman whose situation most improved your own. The others you simply slept with.

But bluffing or not, he must have believed her, for his jaw clenched and his eyes turned black with emotion. "Don't do it, Phoebe. Don't marry just to spite me."

"Spite has nothing to do with it. Like you, I'm making a practical decision."

"Practical, my ass. It's not the same thing. Catherine and I . . . You know we were betrothed before all this business about my daughters. But you, you're not being practical; you're trying to punish me." He stalked toward her, and to her shame, she retreated until the wall prevented her retreating any further. He trapped her there with a hand braced on either side of her. "The fact is, you said you'd take care of my girls. Were you lying? We agreed on a salary. Wasn't it enough?"

Phoebe was too furious to be cautious. How like him to behave as if she were at fault. "The salary of a governess and the salary of a mistress are two entirely different matters." With every word she poked him in the chest. "I cannot be *their* governess, the object of *your* lust, and *another* man's wife. I refuse to be!"

His face lowered to mere inches from hers. "Then just be the object of my lust."

"How dare you!"

She tried to slap him, but he caught her by the wrist. "Bloody hell, Phoebe. I don't mean that as an insult. I've never desired a woman like I desire you. I've never wanted someone so much."

A sob caught in her throat. He desired her. He wanted her. All well and good. But he didn't want her enough to marry her. It was past time that she accept the fact that he never would. So she collected herself, willing away every tear and every emotion except for a comforting anger. She lifted her chin and met him eye to eye.

"I'm flattered, Lord Farley. To be the object of lust to a man of your rank is quite a compliment for a mere farmer's daughter." Despite her every effort at control, sarcasm crept into her voice.

"You're more than a farmer's daughter," he growled. Around her wrist his grip tightened. "There's no reason we cannot continue as we have begun."

"I don't want to continue like that. Haven't you heard anything I said?"

He stared at her as if he couldn't believe she was serious. "Why the hell not?"

She shook her head. "I don't want to be your mistress."

A muscle in his jaw ticced. "That's not the right word for what we have."

"We have nothing."

"We're lovers. We have that."

"No. That's . . . that's not enough."

"Not enough?" He shifted just enough so that every breath she took caused her breasts to graze his chest.

She tried not to breathe.

Then he shifted again, easing one of his knees between her legs. She sucked in a hard breath, her breasts flattened against his chest, and she felt the shock arrow straight from her nipples to her womb. Like a spell, he cast his magic over her, melting her resolve and everything else. He moved his hand from her wrist, tangling their fingers, cupping her hand, then bringing her palm to his lips to kiss.

Oh, but she was a hopeless creature, a slave to lust, for the parts of her that had begun to melt, turned now to steamy lava.

"Don't do this," she whispered, knowing she didn't have it in her to resist that which she so dearly desired.

"I must," he said, lowering his head to kiss her trembling lips. "I must."

CHAPTER 19

They kissed forever. His mouth possessed hers fully, delving deep with his tongue, then sucking her tongue into his mouth. He tasted and probed and bit her lips almost to the point of pain. With his body he pressed her against the wall, meanwhile trapping her arms above her head. Hand in hand, mouths seeking and slanting, their bodies heaved in a desperate search for closer contact.

They were hampered, though, by wool and leather and muslin and twill. At some point Phoebe curled her calf around his. But too many layers of cloth hobbled her and all she could do was thrust her yearning hips against his thighs and loins.

She felt his erection, the hard ridge of male flesh that she feared and desired and seemed to have become addicted to. Since meeting him, she'd turned into a reckless wanton. Yet only in her lonely moments did she fret over it. In moments like this, with her flesh on fire and her mind consumed with him, wantonness became a galvanizing, essential thing. Her lifelong aim.

"Tell me what you want." He followed his words with the astonishing thrill of his tongue circling her ear.

No words would come. It took every bit of her concentration just to breathe.

"We're lovers, Phoebe. You and I." He slid his hips sideways, back and forth, so that she could feel every inch of his surging arousal. His breathing grew as labored as hers. "Nothing changes what we have. Nothing."

He was making her helpless with need. A dim part of Phoebe's brain recognized that. When he had her in his sexual thrall, she couldn't think beyond the moment, beyond the pleasure and promise of that mind-shattering culmination he'd introduced her to.

But he was in sexual thrall to her too. He caught her mouth in a wicked kiss, thrusting his tongue in and out along her sensitive lips, mimicking the action of his hips. He'd chased her across the moonlit hills, the hound on the trail of the evasive fox. In this case, a vixen. Oh, yes. He wanted her just as much as she wanted him.

So why couldn't she make him helpless with need? Why must she be the only one ever to give ground? Why couldn't she for once be the one to control him?

She broke the kiss, twisting her head to the side as she gasped for air. "I want . . . I want . . ."

"Yes?" His lips fastened upon her earlobe, tugging it in the most erotic manner. "What do you want me to do to you, Phoebe? Tell me. Anything."

"I want you . . . to take off your clothes."

She felt his smile as he kissed down the side of her neck. "I think I can manage that." But as he pulled away, it was her bodice he started to unfasten.

His hands were as quick and clever as a pickpocket's, but she slapped them away. "No. You first." She took a deep breath, holding his heavy-lidded gaze with hers. "I want to watch."

A predatory grin lifted one side of his face, the side

gilded by the strengthening fire. Already her little parlor seemed much warmer than before. "That sounds interesting," he said in that tempting, taunting voice that made her want to squirm. Then with slow, controlled movements, he began to disrobe. His coat he flung on a chair. His waistcoat followed, and then his shirt.

Phoebe watched every move with hungry eyes. His chest was beautiful. The erratic firelight painted him with moving shadows: planes, hollows, sinuous shiftings. With every flex she saw the smooth workings of his body, the body that he would use to give her every physical pleasure before this night was done.

Good heavens, did she really believe she could ever seek out some other fellow to marry when this man promised her such a cornucopia of carnal delights?

His eyes ran over her, as fiercely intent as if she, too, were naked before him. "I want to lick down the crevice between your breasts, Phoebe. To taste the sweet buds of your breasts, and to—"

"Don't talk!" She held up one shaking hand. "Don't . . . Don't say another word." *Otherwise I will suffocate from lust.* "Just . . . take off your clothes."

His eyes were alive with passion. He knew exactly what she was feeling. But he did as she ordered. His boots came off easily. Then he began the task of unloosening his breeches.

She watched with unabashed fascination. His arousal was huge, straining the twill fabric, trapped like a wild creature ready to pounce. Phoebe wanted to see it this time, not just feel it—though she wanted that too. But she also wanted to understand its power over her.

Finally the front of his breeches gaped open, revealing his linen undergarment stretched beyond its limits. For a moment he simply stood there, man at his most virile. Slick, golden skin stretched over taut, trembling muscle, with the tautest of those muscles rearing for release in the open vee of his breeches.

She could hardly breathe. This was all for her, the desire, the arousal. He'd chased her across a cold, midnight landscape so that he could have this moment with her.

Was she as willing to chase him? To make demands of him? To find a way to keep him for herself?

She was. To Phoebe's utter amazement, she was. Perhaps lust had made her bold—or more likely love and the thought of losing him. Whatever the source of her resolve, Phoebe knew she must fight to make him hers. She must become the hunter and him her quarry to chase down and capture for her own. It was the only choice she had.

"Take them off," she whispered into the supercharged air of her sedate little parlor.

He obliged, yanking off breeches and undergarment in one motion. Then he was naked. Magnificently naked. Like a virile god of old he stood, his erection huge and jutting toward her. No embarrassment colored him, no fear. If anything, he seemed emboldened by this most elemental revelation of himself. He was a man come to claim his woman.

"Your turn," he said, his voice a rough caress in the silent cottage. His chest rose and fell. He was breathing hard, as aroused as she. Phoebe decided to test his control.

She unbuttoned her bodice and, with a shrug of her shoulders and a wriggle of her arms, let it fall. She felt the fabric slither down her back, an unexpected stroke that might have come from one of his hands, it affected her so.

Unbidden, her hands went to her breasts. His eyes followed, and his erection jerked nearly upright.

Relying on instinct, Phoebe circled both of her nipples with the sides of her thumbs. Oh, yes. A faint moan slid past her lips, a vibration on her heated lips that aroused her further.

One of his hands went to his engorged penis.

"Show me what you like," she said, swallowing hard.

"I like you." He circled his shaft and slid his hand along it. Down, and then up.

She untied her skirt and let it fall. She'd not worn a corset, so only her chemise and stockings covered her burning skin. A single bead of moisture trickled down her side; another traced a path along the inside of her left thigh. Oh my, but the room had become unbearably hot.

When she bent to remove her stockings, James let out a guttural groan. She looked up. It was working. She might be fainting with desire, but so was he. His hand clenched convulsively around his erection. Then abruptly he released it.

"If you don't hurry," he said in a voice thick with desire. "I may waste this on the floor."

In answer she propped her foot on a chair and slowly rolled her stockings down. First one leg, then the other.

With a curse he was across the room.

"No!" She held him off with both hands against his damp, overheated chest.

He grabbed her by the arms. "I can't wait."

"You have to. You said you'd do anything I said."

"I didn't know you had torture on your mind."

"That's not my intention," she lied.

She felt him shudder. He closed his eyes and breathed deeply. She saw him swallow. Once, then again. She wanted to bite his throat and feel the workings of his Adam's apple on her lips. Instead she reached for his erection.

His eyes popped open.

"Do you like that?" she asked, stroking him as he'd stroked himself. *When had she become so bold?*

He didn't answer, not with words. But Phoebe felt his pleasure, she felt it in the smooth skin that burned against her palms. It was more than friction, more than fever. Whether she called it desire or lust didn't matter. She made him want her beyond every limit of his control. This time she wouldn't be the only one swept up in it.

So she stroked him and felt his whole being focus on the simple pleasure of her hand on his cock. His breathing sounded harsh and ragged. With his arms braced on the wall, he leaned heavily over her, looming like some fierce, predatory creature. So threatening; so overwhelming; so arousing.

She loved succumbing to him. Every single time, though she'd resisted, she'd also loved the sensation of being vulnerable to him, of being taken by him. But she loved this too, having him in her control and knowing he was swamped by feelings she'd aroused in him.

She switched hands, stroking down the fiery length of him, squeezing tighter than before.

He groaned. "Wait—"

She moved faster still.

"No, Phoebe." He caught her wrist. "If you don't stop now I'm going to come."

"Good." She pulled nearly to the ridged tip of his raging erection, then pushed back tighter still.

With a tortured curse he tore away from her, then let out another curse, and a third. She saw only his broad back and the rapid pumping action of his arm.

Then he expelled a huge breath and sagged. "Son of a bitch." He gasped for air. "Son of a bitch!" He looked over his shoulder at her. "Why did you do that?"

Phoebe's breathing was none too steady either. "I did it to prove that I could. Did you enjoy it?"

His eyes narrowed. His voice was a guttural growl. "What do you think?"

She smiled. Despite the exquisite frustration that had her in its grip, Phoebe felt an undeniable thrill of something else. Victory over him? Or perhaps this first proof of her control? She was so excited she could feel every place that her chemise touched her skin. Her nipples ached. Deep in her belly she was a boiling witch's brew of female need.

She'd just ruined the very erection that she'd so wanted thrusting furiously inside her. But it was worth it.

Mustering her shaky resolve, she forced herself to cross the room and collect his discarded clothing. "Here. You can get dressed now."

He stared at her as if she were a lunatic.

"You have to go now," she insisted, holding his breeches out to him. "We're done here."

"The hell you say. I'll be damned if we've even begun. We've got the whole night ahead of us. And I plan on doing to you exactly what you just did to me."

Despite the leap in her belly at that sensual threat, Phoebe managed to shake her head. There was much more at stake here than one night of passion. No matter how badly she wanted him, the fact was that James Lindford had been manipulating women all his life. Lots of them. Certainly he'd manipulated her with every meeting they'd had. But she'd just discovered that she could turn the tables on him. If he wanted her, he'd have to give her a lot more than merely one night of passion.

For whatever reason, she'd fallen in love with the arrogant oaf. He might have a few good qualities, but he had one huge flaw: he took women for granted. He made love to them, but he didn't *love* them.

But she'd decided to make him hers. And the only way to do that was to make him love her—or at least want her more than he wanted anybody else.

So she clamped down on the physical needs unmet inside her, and grabbed his cloak from the peg on the door. "Hurry up. I'm cold and tired. You have to go."

"I'm not going anywhere." He tossed his breeches at her and crossed his arms. "Give it up, Phoebe. We both know you don't really want me to leave."

No, she didn't. Not when he stood there naked with his legs apart and the fire behind him outlining his fla-grantly masculine form with licks of red and gold. But she wasn't letting him win this time. She snatched up his breeches once more. "Go home, Lord Farley. Go home with these on, or go home later with your legs naked for all the world to see what you've been up to."

"The hell you say. Throw them outside. I don't care. I don't need them right now. All I need is for you to finish undressing."

Phoebe glared at him. He was calling her bluff? Very well, time to change tactics. She marched past him and threw his breeches into the leaping fire.

"Bloody hell!" He yanked them out before they fully caught, and flung them onto the brick hearth. Then he turned on her, a large, angry man who happened to be naked and whose spent erection seemed to be coming back to life.

The thrill of battling him must have come at the cost of all her good sense, for instead of being afraid, Phoebe felt a surge of excitement. "Go home, I say. I don't want you here."

He began to advance on her. "We'll see about that."

Oh, dear! He was between her and the front door. So she dashed toward the kitchen and the back door. She was nearly out of the room when he caught the scooped back of her chemise. He just hooked it with one finger in the neckline. But it was enough to slow her down. She struggled away—he would not control her anymore! Then the fine lawn ripped and she hurtled forward, nearly stumbling into the table.

She whirled around. "You ruined my chemise. My very best chemise!"

"I'll buy you another," he growled, pouncing on her. He caught her around the waist, as if she were no heavier than the kitten he'd given her. Then he lifted her up and sat her on the table. "I'll buy you a dozen of them, and any other frou-frous your heart desires."

Phoebe tried to pry his hands off her. "You can't buy everything you want. You can't buy me."

"Even with sex?" He pushed her flat on the table, then loomed over her, bracing his hands on either side of her shoulders. "I know you don't want my money, Phoebe. It's one of the many things I admire about you. But you do like some other things that I'm able to do for you."

She glared at him. "Not tonight," she swore, knowing it was a lie. "Let me up."

"No."

She could feel the heat of him as he leaned lower. Though they didn't touch, fire leaped between them, and it was almost more than she could resist. But she knew that giving in was not an option. Not tonight. He held all the cards all the time. His desire for her was the only power she held over him, and tonight she wanted to see just how mighty it was.

When he leaned down to kiss her, she turned her head to the side. "I mean it, James. I don't want to do this. I want you to leave."

"Why?" He caught her chin in one hand and turned her to face him. "Are you saying you're not excited?

That you're not hot and melting for me deep down inside?"

She could hardly speak, so she shook her head. "Not . . . tonight," she barely managed to say.

For a moment she wasn't certain what he would do. She didn't think he would force her. Not that he would really have to. One kiss, one fingertip stroking down the slope of her breast, and she would be lost. She closed her eyes, and abruptly he pulled back.

She heard as he gathered up his clothes and dressed himself, but all she could do was lie there, gasping for breath. The kitchen table was no place for her to sprawl with a naked man in her house, but she just couldn't move. Only when she heard his heavy footsteps returning to the kitchen did she push herself upright. He stood in the doorway, dressed but disheveled. She'd never been the target of his anger, and she didn't like the way that he frowned at her.

"I don't know what game you're playing, Phoebe, but I don't like it."

She met him frown for frown. Was ever a man so dense? "I'm not the one who's the expert in games of this sort, Lord Farley. All I know is that tomorrow is my day off and I plan to do exactly what I want to do. Whether you like it or not."

He took that in for a moment, then said, "What should I tell the girls?"

"Tell them . . . I'll see them on Monday." It was awkward speaking of the children when she was so scantily clad. She tugged her chemise down to cover her bare knees, and felt it gap in the back where he'd torn it. "And tell them I love them."

He gave a curt nod, then he left.

Phoebe listened to the thunder of horse hooves carrying him away from her. She wanted to cry out for him to come back, but she didn't.

Instead she climbed off the table that had served nearly two hundred years of Churchill meals, and on stiff legs trudged up to her lonely bedroom. She'd sent him away tonight. But what about tomorrow night, and the next? And the next? She couldn't hold him off forever, even if for a few moments it had felt like a victory.

She'd thought that lust had infected her. But the truth was, love was far more powerful and debilitating than mere lust. She was in love, and only marriage could save her.

But not marriage to just anyone. Most certainly not to whomever Mrs. Leake imagined might be suitable for a girl like her. She was aiming higher than that. Much higher.

If she could not have James Lindford, she didn't want anyone.

She crawled beneath her bedcovers and closed her eyes, but that only made everything worse. She was aroused and frustrated, and though she tried not to, all she could think about was the night he'd made love to her here in her own bed. Every perverse moment was as alive to her as it had been then.

Unbidden, her hand crept down to her unsated sex and once more she imagined James there, touching her and kissing her. James, with his magnificent arousal at the ready to ease her every need . . .

CHAPTER 20

The return ride to Farley Park was a nightmare for James. It was too dark to spur his horse to a wild gallop, as his anger urged him to do. But riding slowly allowed him to think, and when he thought, it was of Phoebe, which aroused his unruly cock and made it painful to sit astride.

He should have stayed. No matter what she said, she'd been aroused and she'd wanted him inside her. He could feel it in the air between them, taste it, smell it, see it in her eyes.

But she'd told him to leave, and in a moment of fury and disbelief, he'd stormed away. Now he wasn't sure if that had been the right choice. He wasn't sure about anything, least of all Phoebe.

Bloody hell, but the woman was driving him mad!

The day that followed wasn't much better. With Phoebe absent, Izzy returned to her old, belligerent self. She hadn't behaved so badly in weeks. Meanwhile, Helen huddled in a corner, silently weeping into her handkerchief, and Kerry glowered at him—as if the girls' bad moods were *his* fault. To add insult to injury, it rained.

Even Catherine, who had perfected the art of never

noticing any of the upsets in her world, was beginning to show signs of strain. Her irritating friend had long since lost her temper.

"Don't you know what happens to girls who pout and frown?" Mrs. Donahue glared at Izzy as the carriage delivered them home from Sunday services. "Their faces get stuck in that ugly expression and nobody will marry them."

"You mean like this?" Izzy stuck out her tongue, pushed her nose up with one finger, and pulled her lower eyelids down with two others. "My face could stay like this?" She affected a horrified tone. "Oh, no. Then I'd look like you!"

"Izzy!" James snapped.

But the girl only scowled at him from across the crowded carriage, her face a mask of rage and contempt. "I don't want you to be my father. I hate you!" Before he could recover from the stab of guilt that shrill accusation sent through his heart, she flung open the carriage door, balancing herself for an instant on the threshold. Then she recklessly leaped out of the moving conveyance and onto the rocky ground.

James lurched to his feet. "Stop, driver!" But as quickly as James jumped out after her, Izzy was gone, scampering like a wild hare through the drizzle, making for the dreary woods and the anonymity of its shelter. At least she didn't look hurt. But that was small comfort.

"Son of a bitch!" he swore.

"Really, James," Catherine scolded. "There are ladies here. And a child."

That's my problem in a nutshell, he wanted to roar. Too many ladies and children demanding his attention when all he wanted to do was search out Phoebe and ease the distress that had showed in her face and posture when he'd seen her at church. Only he couldn't do that, not with everyone hounding him all the time, and always needing something from him.

With another muffled curse, he climbed up next to the driver, took over the reins, and started the team forward. First he had to get everyone back to Farley Park. Then he needed to lock himself away from all of them and think this mess through. Everything was out of control; his life was going to hell in a handbasket.

But it wasn't because of his children; none of this was their fault. He was the author of his own misery. The sole author.

He stared at the woods where Izzy had fled. He needed to know she was safe. No, not just safe, but happy. Right now she was neither, and so neither was he. And neither was Phoebe.

Though he was sunk in gloomy thoughts, handling the horses down the muddy, rutted road brought him some level of calm. He had to get this life he'd chosen back under control. Something had to change. He just wasn't sure what.

As if she sensed the beleaguered state of his thoughts, once at the house Catherine put all her considerable efforts into charming Helen. "Now, now," she said, giving Helen a hug. "I'm sure your father will locate your sister. Won't you, James?" She gave him a calm, confident smile.

"I've already called for a horse."

"You see?" She smoothed a wayward strand of Helen's fine, golden hair behind her ear. "Such a pretty little girl like you ought never to cry. It only makes your eyes puffy and your nose turn red. You don't want that, do you?"

Helen sniffled and wiped her tears. "While we wait for Izzy to come home, can we go get Leya?"

Catherine hesitated only a moment before answering, "Why, of course we can."

Only a moment. But it was long enough for James to recognize a disturbing truth. Catherine had warmed up to Helen. Who wouldn't? The girl had a sweet, malleable temperament. She was a pretty blond angel of a girl, not dark and exotic like Leya, or foul-mouthed and ill-tempered like Izzy. She was the perfect little lady, thanks to Phoebe. Catherine probably saw in Helen a younger version of herself.

But Phoebe loved Izzy and Leya too. Despite the problems of their heritage and upbringing, Phoebe detected in them the same goodness and potential that she saw in her own niece.

He was making a mistake marrying Catherine Winfield. All at once it was so clear to him. He didn't really want to marry her. Maybe he never had.

It made good sense on some levels. She would be an asset to his career and certainly she would make an impressive home for him in London. She'd probably give him beautiful children too, and he had no reason to doubt that she would love them.

But what about the children he had now?

It might not be fair to expect her to love his three motherless daughters. But when he saw how freely Phoebe loved them, it was hard not to fault Catherine for her lack.

"I'm going out to find Izzy," he said.

Helen looked up from her place beside Catherine on a settee. "Do you know where she ran away to?"

"No. Do you have any ideas?" He knelt down and opened his arms to her, and was amazed at how swiftly she ran to him. A tight knot of emotion twisted in his chest. What a sweet little kitten of a girl she was, this trusting child he'd gone seven years not knowing. He squeezed her against his heart. Thank God he'd been given this second chance! "Don't worry, sweetheart," he said, his voice thick with new feelings. "She'll be all right. She's a tough little character, our Izzy."

Helen circled one of her arms around his neck. "She probably went to find Phoebe," she whispered in his ear.

"Yes. She probably did," he whispered back.

She leaned a little distance from him and stared at him with damp, serious eyes. "If you see Phoebe, tell her to come home."

"I'll do that." He kissed her pert, upturned nose, and once more squeezed her to him. "I'll do that," he promised, reveling in the new pleasure of hugging his own child. One way or another, he'd bring Phoebe home to them all.

But first he had to find Izzy.

Something was afoot. Kerry observed Catherine as she stood with Helen in the window, watching James ride away. Then, Catherine collapsed on a settee, pressing a ridiculously frothy handkerchief to her mouth to forestall her tears. Tears!

For a woman not prone to emotional displays, it was most telling, and something in Kerry's chest turned to lead. He'd wondered how deeply her feelings for James ran. Now he knew.

"Shoo, child," Mrs. Donahue said, intercepting Helen as she made straight for the trembling Catherine. "Lady Catherine isn't feeling well. Now, now," she continued, turning her attention to Catherine. "You mustn't work yourself into a state, my dear. I'm sure Lord Farley will be back straightaway." The woman shot a cunning look at Kerry, then wrapped an arm around the wilting younger woman. "And I'm sure he'll locate the child. Izzy," she said, as if to convince him about how concerned Catherine was for the runaway child.

He knew what she was thinking: Since Kerry and James were such good friends, Catherine must always present the best face around him. But Kerry didn't fault Catherine for her lack of interest in James's natural-born children. In truth, he couldn't think of one well-bred society miss who would have responded any better.

What he did mind was that she still was in love with James, while James was so clearly *not* in love with her. She probably guessed the truth, if her tears were any indication.

He steeled himself against any display of his own feelings. For a short while, when she'd cried off from her betrothal to James, Kerry had actually been hopeful. Not that he had much of a chance with her. Although he and Catherine rubbed along admirably well, and he knew she liked him, he was well aware that she would never cross her father. Lord Basingstoke's expectations for his exquisite daughter ran much higher than a younger son with no political inclinations and such a modest income.

So he'd long ago resigned himself to admiring her from afar, consoling himself that she was in love with his best friend. But the very public dissolution of her betrothal had revived his foolish hopes—until she'd told him about her plans to follow James to Yorkshire, and asked him to go ahead of her and sound out the situation.

He should have stayed out of it. He could see that now. But he'd never been able to deny Catherine anything, and this time had been no different. Like picking at a sore spot, poking until it ached and bled, he'd come to Yorkshire to smooth the way for her with James. Then he'd stayed to squeeze every bit of personal pain out of his abject misery. Why couldn't she see how devoted he was to her?

Because he'd hidden his feelings so well.

But seeing her unhappiness now was too much to bear. He waved Helen over to sit beside him—anything to prevent him from going to Catherine. "I'm sure James and Izzy will soon return to us safe and sound. Perhaps a little wet," he added, smiling down at Helen.

From across the room Catherine whispered, "He cares more about the child than he does about me." There was anguish in every word.

"He does not," Mrs. Donahue countered.

"I'm afraid he might," Kerry said, unable to prevent the words.

Mrs. Donahue shot him a withering look. "Mr. Fairchild. If you don't mind, I am trying to comfort Lady Catherine—"

"By lying to her?" Kerry knew he should stop. He'd already overstepped himself. But he'd been holding his tongue for nearly three years; he didn't think he could hold it a minute longer.

Giving Helen a reassuring pat, he rose and stalked over to the settee, staring down at the wide-eyed Catherine, while ignoring her furious companion. "Do you want to be married to James Lindford? Not Viscount Farley, that fine, worldly fellow who wants to follow in your father's political footsteps, but James Lindford, the doting father of three natural children?"

"Of course she does!" Mrs. Donahue fairly shouted.

But Kerry saw the hesitation in Catherine's lapis-blue eyes. "No, I don't think she does. Be honest, Catherine. What *do* you want? You, not your father or your friend here."

"I . . . I don't know."

Kerry smiled down at her beautiful, confused face. "Hasn't anyone ever asked you that before?"

Slowly she shook her head.

Mrs. Donahue stood, insinuating herself between Kerry and Catherine. "This is ridiculous. Of course she wants to marry him. It was she who pleaded with her father to make this journey."

"Because he wants me to marry Percival Langley," Catherine burst out. Again she pressed the handkerchief to her lips. "He's heir to the Earl of Bexham, who is said to be very ill."

"Langley? Your father wants you to wed that nasty old goat?" Kerry advanced on Mrs. Donahue until she backed up. "No wonder she's here chasing James if Langley is her only other option—" Abruptly he switched his gaze to Catherine. "You have other options, you know. You needn't limit yourself to a choice between Langley and James."

Mrs. Donahue let out an ugly laugh. "If you mean yourself, Mr. Fairchild—and I'm sure you do—I can guarantee that Lord Basingstoke would never accept any suit that you might make."

"It's not *his* acceptance I want," Kerry bit right back at her. "It's Catherine's."

Into the ringing silence created by that outrageous admission, a small, childish voice ventured, "I think maybe that Mr. Fairchild loves you, Lady Catherine."

Kerry chuckled at Helen's sweet statement of such an obvious truth. Mrs. Donahue scoffed in contempt. But Catherine only stared at him, amazed, no doubt, at the effrontery of his declaration—and through a child, no less.

She ducked her head under his steady regard, then looked up, composed once more. When she stood, she was the elegant woman he'd admired for so long, every bit of her discomposure tamped down and put away. His heart pounded with dread. This was probably familiar territory for Catherine, dismissing a too ardent admirer, turning away the suit of an unsuitable man.

"Leave us," she said to Mrs. Donahue.

The woman gave Kerry a nasty smile. She, too, knew what was to come. Kerry braced himself as she hustled Helen out of the room and closed the door behind them.

In the silence he watched as Lady Catherine prepared herself to let him down. He saw her lick her pretty pink lips, and saw the rise and fall of her lovely bosom. "Is it true?" she asked. "Do you love me?"

He stiffened, locking his hands together in a painful fist behind his back. "I do."

She blinked, the tiniest break in her serene countenance. "All these years, when we've been such good friends. Why have you never revealed yourself before now?"

"Because you were waiting for James. I thought you loved him." He paused. "Do you?"

He held his breath. She met his challenging stare. "No."

"No?" Was he hearing her correctly?

"I . . . I like him. He's handsome and rich, and my father was very keen on him as a son-in-law—at least he was until this business with the children. Father became so angry he wanted me to make another marriage right away. He latched on to Percival Langley but I . . . I couldn't. So I came here . . ."

"Despite your reservations about James?"

She nodded.

Hope, wild and uncontrollable, leaped like a frantic creature in Kerry's chest. "Don't marry James, Catherine."

She made a helpless, fluttering gesture with one hand. "You make it sound so simple. But we both know it isn't."

"You mean Langley?"

"I mean my father. He said if James would keep the children out of London he might reconsider our betrothal."

"The hell with your father!"

Her eyes widened.

Kerry pressed on. "Marry me, Catherine. I may not have the title you seek, nor the money. But I'll make up for the lack in other ways. I swear, I will."

She studied him intently. "What ways?"

That took him aback. But it also fed the insane hope that had awakened in his chest. "I'll love you. Neither James nor Langley can promise you that. I've loved you for years. I always will. You'll be the most important thing in my life. The center of my world. My very life will revolve around you, Catherine. I swear it."

Once again tears glinted in her luminous blue eyes, but tears for him. Kerry took her hand in his, afraid to believe that he might actually win this beautiful, delicate woman for himself. "Marry me, Catherine. I know you don't love me," he hurried on. "But you like me—probably more than you like either James or Langley. We've always gotten on well, and I . . . I do love you. Don't let your father hobble you to any man who can't say that with utter conviction. Marry me."

She was silent so long he began to perspire. Then finally, "All right," in a soft, vulnerable voice.

"All right?" Kerry froze, hardly able to breathe. Had he heard her correctly?

"I'll marry you," she said with the beginnings of a smile trembling on her lips.

He bent down, drawn to those sweet, quivering lips, dying to kiss them after so many years of knowing he'd never have the right to do so. He needed to kiss her, to make certain this was not some dream he'd conjured in his fevered brain. But mere inches from his goal, he stopped. "When will you marry me?"

"As soon as you like."

"Tomorrow?"

She laughed, the prettiest, tinkling sound he'd ever heard. "That soon?"

"It's either that, or accept that I must compromise you."

"All right."

He *was* dreaming; he *must* be! But he was willing to gamble that the dream was real. "All right, you'll marry me tomorrow? Or all right, you'll let me compromise you?" He gave her a teasing grin.

She rose up on her toes until their lips were nearly touching. "I think . . . I think whichever one you prefer."

The cottage at Plummy Head was empty. No smoke rose from the central chimney. No life seemed to exist inside the stone walls. It wanted Phoebe for that, Phoebe to cook and garden and mind her small flock of chickens and goats.

James sat his restless horse in the front yard, ignoring the dreary drizzle as he scanned Phoebe's simple home. If she could make a happy home here, how much easier it should be for her to make a happy home where money and space were no object.

Then his eyes lit upon a trail of muddy footprints on the porch. Small, muddy footprints. Izzy was somewhere nearby. Not in the house, however, for the steps veered away from the door and back to the yard. Rather than chase her down, however, this time he wanted her to come to him. He wanted the same trusting hug from her that he'd received from Helen. He might not get it today, but perhaps he could begin the journey to someday deserving it from her.

So he dismounted and led his animal to the small

porch, then sat down on the top step. "Are you there, Izzy? Can we talk?"

No answer. He tried to determine which way she might have gone, but the rain had erased any trace of her direction. "I need your help, Izzy. I can't fix this family of ours without you helping me."

Again nothing. He racked his brain for something else to say, something that might draw her out—if she was even nearby. "I'm sorry," he called into the emptiness around him.

He strained to hear a response. Then from across the yard, from the brand-new goat shed, came, "Sorry for what?"

He squinted at the shed, unable to see her. But at least she was there, and she was waiting for an answer. He said the only thing he could think of. "I'm sorry I'm such a failure as a father."

"You should be sorry," the accusation came after a long silence. "You do everything wrong. Everything!"

James stared down at his clasped hands. She was right. He'd had good intentions when he'd taken her and her sisters in to raise. But so far nothing had turned out as he'd expected. He looked up at the goat shed. "Maybe with your help I could learn to do better."

Slowly the door of the shed opened and a slight figure moved into sight. Izzy, muddy and bedraggled. A rush of relief surged through him. But her chin jutted out, he noticed, and her arms were crossed, as belligerent as ever. "Whyn't you just go back to London and leave me and Helen and Leya here with Phoebe? Go on and marry that stupid snob and leave us alone."

He shook his head. "I can't leave, Izzy. You're my daughter, my oldest child. And Leya is my youngest, and Helen is my middle girl. Every one of you is special to me, and the thing is, I don't want to live anyplace that you three don't live also." He meant it. He could never go back to London without them.

"Well, I'm not going anywhere with you and that Lady Catherine. I'm stayin' here with Phoebe. So's Helen and Leya."

"So am I."

The words surprised him as much as they surprised Izzy. She stared at him across the splattered yard, disbelief clear on her face. "Are you bamming me?"

"No." He stood and started with measured tread toward her. "I'm not bamming you, Izzy. I'm not going to marry Catherine. And I'm not moving back to London. I think what I want to do is stay here and raise my girls all around me."

Izzy cocked her head. "And marry Phoebe?"

He chuckled. It was easy to answer that. "And marry Phoebe—if she'll have me." He stopped three paces from her. "I'm not sure she'll have me though. What do you think?"

She gave him a contemptuous look. "Considering what an idiot you've been, I'm not so sure."

That wasn't what he expected. "Will you help me?" he asked, realizing he wasn't just saying that. Maybe she could help him.

Izzy's face remained doubtful. "You want my help? Don't you know how to make a woman want you?"

"I know what to do with the wrong kind of woman," he muttered. He let out a groan. He couldn't believe he was having a conversation like this with a ten-year-old girl. But Izzy was not just any ten-year-old. She'd lived a hard life and seen things no child should see—things he'd make sure she never had to see again. "The thing is," he went on, "I've never dealt with a woman like Phoebe—the right kind of woman."

"Do you love her?"

He'd been avoiding that question. Every time it came up in his tortured thoughts about Phoebe, he'd avoided it. But now this too-wise child was asking him in her straightforward way whether he loved the woman he said he wanted to marry.

"Yes. I believe I do." He was amazed at how easily the truth came out. He did love Phoebe.

"Well, she hates you." Izzy crossed her arms as if daring him to contradict her.

He frowned and rubbed one gloved hand across the back of his neck. "So, how do I change that?"

"Well, you have to make her love you." Relaxing her pose, she ventured out of the doorway of the shed. "You have to give her something she really, really wants."

"I don't think gifts are what Phoebe wants from me—" He broke off when an idea occurred to him. "You do want her to be your new mother, don't you?"

"Of course."

"All right, then. Can we make a pact?"

"What kind of pact?"

He squatted down on his heels, putting them face to face. "It seems to me that we both want the same thing: Phoebe as my wife and mother to my children. Agreed?"

She shrugged and studied him a long moment with a wary expression. "Agreed."

"Then we need to work together to make that happen."

She tucked her chin against her neck and considered his words. Her eyes were far too old for her young years, he realized. If he did nothing else for her, he had to change that one thing.

"What do I have to do?" she finally said.

He stood. "The first thing we need to do is send Catherine home to London."

"And her ugly friend."

"And Mrs. Donahue," he agreed.

"But Mr. Kerry can stay, if he wants."

"Actually, I think he may want to accompany Catherine home, to offer her the comfort of his shoulder to cry on."

Izzy rolled her eyes. "If you say so. Men are idiots. That's what my mam used to say."

James felt a spurt of guilt. Yes, men were idiots. And he'd been the biggest idiot of all. About women. About his children. About love and loyalty and how to be happy. Trust a ten-year-old raised in the rough streets of Seven Dials to cut straight to the root of his flaws. But he could change; at least he meant to try. To Izzy he said, "Once Catherine and company are on their way, I'll talk to Phoebe."

"She'll probably say no," Izzy said.

"What do you mean? To my proposal of marriage? Why would she do that?"

"To get even with you for being so mean to her."

"Do you honestly think Phoebe would do that?"

Izzy considered a moment, then the tiniest smile curved up one side of her face. "No. She's far too nice to get even with you like that. Look how nice she was to me after I stole all her stuff. She doesn't even know everything I took."

"What else did you take?"

A guilty wave of color washed onto her face. "Once I picked her pocket—just to keep in practice, you see. I got a whistle and a watch. But I put them back the next time I came over."

James shook his head, but he had to grin. "It seems like her goodness must be rubbing off on you. But you're right, she was nice about you stealing the things she knew about."

But as they made the wet ride back to Farley Park

with Izzy sitting in front of him, guiding the horse with her small, sure hands on the reins, James knew he'd stolen far more from Phoebe than a bucket, and a watch, and a few other inanimate objects. What he'd stolen couldn't be returned, for he'd stolen her innocence. He'd also stolen her beloved child, at least that's how she must see it.

He couldn't undo any of that. The question now was whether he'd broken her heart beyond repair when he'd fallen back into a betrothal to Catherine, and whether he'd destroyed her ability to ever trust him.

He suspected he could coerce her into marrying him. She was, after all, practical. But as he considered that possibility, the truth about what he really wanted from Phoebe finally began to dawn on him. It was astonishing. Staggering. He wanted Phoebe's love when he married her. He wanted her smiling and happy and as eager as he now was to bind them eternally together. He wanted that more than he wanted a career in politics—or anything else for that matter.

As sweet as it had been, stealing Phoebe's innocence was a small thing compared to what he wanted from her now. For he'd resolved to steal her heart and never give it back.

CHAPTER 21

Church had been a dreadful affair. Phoebe had arrived early, hoping to avoid conversing with any of her neighbors, most of whom no doubt expected her to reveal all about life in the unusual Farley household. She'd managed to duck into the dark, ancient church without meeting anyone, and take a seat in her family's pew.

But praying for guidance in her dealings with James had done absolutely no good, for each prayer disintegrated into a pathetic plea to see him again. Today. Tonight.

She'd groaned and bowed her head, screwing up her face beneath the shelter of her hands. But nothing would drive out the thought of the cursed man. Then Mrs. Leake had entered the quiet church and slid into the Churchill pew to sit with her.

"Now, now," the woman had whispered. "Don't let yourself get so downhearted, Phoebe girl. I know you love young Helen. But the good Lord has something better in mind for you than minding other people's children. A husband of your own and a baby every other year. That's what He wants for you, and that's what I want for you too."

It had taken every bit of Phoebe's willpower to squelch the sudden urge to strangle the woman and run screaming from the church.

From that point the day had descended straight to hell. She'd heard the murmur that rippled through the congregation when Lord Farley and his children and guests took their seats in the normally empty Farley box. Izzy and Helen turned around to wave at her; Mr. Fairchild winked. Lady Catherine and Mrs. Donahue didn't acknowledge anyone, not upon their arrival nor their departure.

As for the viscount himself, thank goodness his back was to her throughout the service. She only had to keep her head bowed in prayer as he departed so as not to meet his eyes. But she'd felt that hard, blue gaze upon her.

Had he felt as keenly the weight of her own gaze during the vicar's rambling sermon? Had he prayed as hard for forgiveness as she had—and with as little success?

From the misery of the church she went to the misery of dinner in Mrs. Leake's overcrowded dining room. The meal was a noisy affair, with nearly a dozen guests besides herself. The butcher and his youngest son; a widowed farmer from Wickfield; a blustering, red-faced tradesman whom she suspected of being a smuggler. Mrs. Leake had never been one for subtlety, and today was no different. Phoebe felt like a milk cow being examined on market day.

Of the several single fellows consuming great quantities of Mrs. Leake's food, the one she most favored was sweet, simple Martin. At least he liked her for herself, not for the farmland and the sturdy house that came with her.

By the time Mrs. Leake's cook brought out a dessert

of rum cake and sweet cream, Phoebe's temples ached from the pressure of smiling while dodging questions about her scandalous employer.

"Have they reconciled yet?" Mrs. Leake asked, leaning to look at Phoebe. "Seeing as how they came to church together, it stands to reason they've reconciled. She and her friend have been visiting with him for nearly a week."

"Five days," Phoebe said. Then realizing how snippy she sounded, she added, "I suspect any announcement they make would be to their families first."

"But surely you suspect which way the wind blows," Mrs. Tinsdale said. "Servants always know what's going on in a grand household like that. Tha's what my sister says, and she's worked a dozen years belowstairs for the Earl of Fenham."

"A governess is more than a servant," Mrs. Leake put in. "Besides, our Phoebe is related to Viscount Farley now, being Helen's aunt and all. So you see," she said, catching the eye of each bachelor, one at a time. "Our Phoebe girl has quite come up in the world. Yes, indeed, she has."

Quite come up in the world. The words trailed Phoebe home, tormenting her more with every step along the muddy cart track. Yes, she'd quite come up in the world. Mistress to a wealthy peer. Wasn't that every girl's dream?

A quarter mile from Plummy Head it started once again to rain. But Phoebe didn't increase her pace. There would be no more dinners at Mrs. Leake's for her. No more making excuses why she'd rather walk home than be delivered in Malcolm Horstat's wagon. No more explaining why she'd rather walk alone than beside Denby Fulcrumb. No more silencing the fact that she'd rather beat herself senseless with a hammer than try to converse one more minute with Gordie Wilkins.

Spinsterhood had never looked so appealing.

But being James Lindford's mistress would be much more fun.

She groaned at her own perversity and swiped raindrops from her face. Then she pulled the brim of her bonnet to a steeper angle over her brow and slogged the last steep slope up to Plummy Head. It would be fun, yes, moments of fun sandwiched between days of despair.

Yet the thought of never seeing him again was its own sort of despair.

She was cold, wet, and miserable by the time she reached home. She removed her damp shoes and outer garments, built up the fire, and put on water for tea. While that heated she dusted and swept, and brought more wood in from the wood shed near the kitchen door. Anything to stay busy and not notice how quiet and lonely her cottage had become.

Once upon a time she'd dreamed of just this sort of solitude, to have no one making demands on her or telling her how to behave. Just the comforting crackle and pop of the fire while the rain beat fruitlessly upon the windows. But how quickly solitude turned to loneliness.

As the tea kettle began to shriek, she stared about the neat, lifeless cottage, and admitted the unwelcome truth. She was lonely. Last night had been lonely enough. Tonight would be even worse. She hated living at Plummy Head without Helen. But if she followed Helen, then she would put herself in the way of James Lindford and the same sort of emotional storm they'd fought last night.

It would also put her in the way of James Lindford's wife.

Again she sighed, facing a truth that she desperately preferred to avoid. Tomorrow she must go back to Farley

Park. Despite the dreadful battle she and James fought, each of them trying to subjugate the other, she must go back if she wanted to continue to be a part of her niece's new life.

"All right. I'll go," she said to the lifeless cottage. If it weren't raining so hard, she would go now so as not to suffer the endless, empty night that loomed before her. Since the weather made that unwise, she decided to stay busy by bathing and washing her hair.

It took time to heat enough water for a full bath, to stoke the fire and refill the pots and drag in the tub that hung on an outside kitchen wall. Dusk had fallen over the sodden land before she stepped into the steaming bath scented with dried lavender leaves. She sank down so that only her head and bent knees showed above the surface.

"Ahh." She leaned her head back, reveling in the pervasive heat. She would unpin her hair in a minute and begin the laborious task of washing and rinsing the waist-length tresses. But for a few moments she simply wanted to relax, to let the scalding heat of the water ease the tautness in her shoulders, and loosen the kinks in her neck. She would rest like this for just a little while, her eyes closed, her head comfortable against the tub's rolled rim. Just a few more minutes . . .

Smoke from the single chimney of Phoebe's cottage fled west on the salty wind gusting in from the North Sea. She was home.

Both anticipation and dread swept over James as he urged his animal on. He'd returned Izzy to Farley Park, letting her off at the kitchen door, then taking his animal to the stable. He'd had every intention of following her inside, then having a private conversation with Catherine. But once in the kitchen he'd been informed by the cook that Lady Catherine had retired to her room for the evening, requesting a tray be sent up for supper. Likewise, Mrs. Donahue and Mr. Fairchild had requested the same.

The cook indicated the three trays on the wide kitchen table. "Miss Helen said she wanted to take her supper down here with me. So did Miss Izzy. But since you're home now . . ." She trailed off, a question in her voice.

"That's fine. The girls can eat in the kitchen if they like."

"Very well. And yourself, milord? Will you take your meal in the dining room, or shall I prepare a tray for you in your study?"

James glanced at Izzy, who lurked in the shadows near the pantry, listening to every word. He gave her a wink. "You needn't prepare anything for me. I have to go out, something I need to do."

Then with Izzy's grin of approval to warm him, he'd gone straight back to the stables, saddled a fresh animal, and despite the weather, taken off for Plummy Head.

Now that he was almost there, however, he wasn't certain how to begin. Beg her forgiveness first? Propose first?

What he wanted was to seduce her first, to get her soft and willing to do anything he asked so that she would accept his proposal before she had time to think and remember how thoughtless and unintentionally cruel he'd been these last few weeks. How dense and obtuse and undeserving of a woman like her.

Most especially he didn't want her to think about his past history with women and what it implied about his future behavior. He was a changed man, though he had no way of proving that to her. But he was good at seduction—that was his only ace in the hole—and he knew how willing a partner she could be.

Just the thought of her firm, peach-toned skin, so responsive to his touch, made blood rush to his loins. He didn't realize his hands had fisted on the reins until his horse tossed its head and half-reared.

"Sorry, fellow." He petted the horse's neck, but it was easier to calm the blowing animal than to calm his own rising excitement. There in that unassuming little cottage waited the woman who would spend every night of the rest of his life in his bed. Calm be damned! The glimpse he'd had of her in church had tortured him all day. He'd not wait one more minute to be with her.

Across the rocky meadow they flew. The horse took the ancient stone wall with clearance to spare. It might have been merely a molehill for all either of them cared. "A generous feed bag for you when we return," James promised the horse when he flung himself down, then tethered the spirited animal inside the goat shed. Impatient, he nonetheless hauled up a bucket of water from the well before striding for the house.

He expected Phoebe to meet him in the doorway. Hadn't she heard the horse hooves on the hard ground? It was too early for her to have gone to bed. Then an unhappy thought struck him. Could Phoebe still be in town? Was it perhaps her new maid who'd built up the fire?

"No," he growled, willing away that unacceptable possibility. Ignoring the precepts of good society, he burst into the house without knocking. There he came to a sudden stop. From the bracing cold of the cliff-top winds to the moist warmth of the overheated kitchen, from fear of finding someone else in her place, to confronting Phoebe's dewy form asleep in a large tin tub before the fire, the transition was abrupt. He had the presence of mind to shut the door behind him quietly, but nothing else. He should leave and come back later.

Or leave and knock until she awoke and dressed, then let him in.

But it would take a far more saintly man than himself to turn away from the feast set before him now.

Phoebe at her most vulnerable. Phoebe at her most innocent. Young and exhausted and more beautiful than anything he'd ever had the privilege to view.

Her hair curled in damp ringlets at her temples. Her lashes cast perfect crescents on the creamy curve of her cheeks. Diamond beads of moisture gathered on her brow and in the hollows of her bare shoulders and throat. She deserved real diamonds, he decided, though he doubted they could be more flattering to her than the ones that adorned her now.

One of her arms draped over the side of the tub, and his gaze slid down the curving length, past dimpled elbow and elegant wrist to the curl of her lax fingers.

He sucked in a breath. This was perfection. The perfect woman who deserved a man far better than he. But he was not noble enough to forgo the gift handed to him now. He wanted her. He would always want her.

Without thinking he shed his hat and gloves, then shrugged out of his coat. He stepped nearer, bending over her to touch the water. It was cooling. He wanted it warm, for her and for himself. So spying another pot simmering at the hearth, he slowly poured in the water, careful not to burn her. He halted when she turned her head and shifted within the tub. But when her eyes remained closed, he resumed his task.

"I'm sorry for making your life so complicated, so hard," he whispered to his sleeping beauty, his future wife. "But I plan to make every bit of it up to you."

He was rewarded with the ghost of a smile, the faintest lift of those pink, succulent lips of hers. He suspected it was not his words that pleased her but rather the warming bathwater. But he didn't care. He emptied the pot, then with one hand swirled the water to spread the warmth around the tub.

One of his fingers grazed her knee; his thumbnail slid along her thigh. Blood rushed to his loins and he groaned. The heat was not enveloping just Phoebe. It had spread to him, gushing through his eager body in a fever of love and desire.

He went still at the thought. Love and desire. Not just desire; not even desire first and love second. Love was the fire burning through his veins, love for this one particular woman. Phoebe and no other.

"Phoebe," he whispered, crouching on one knee beside the tub. "Phoebe, wake up." He traced a line up her thigh and across her knee, then down into the water. His cuff became wet but he didn't notice. "Wake up, my beautiful soon-to-be bride. Open your eyes and see what you've done to me." *Hurry up, else I will rip my breeches for wanting you.*

Phoebe was warm and comfortable, and therefore unwilling to come back to wakefulness. She shouldn't doze off in the bathtub but rather should wash herself while the water still retained some warmth. But she had time, she decided in the one part of her brain that was marginally alert. She shifted in the tin tub and sighed. The water was still warm. There was plenty of time.

Something slid along her nose, light as a feather or a breeze. She wrinkled her nose and it departed, only to land upon her mouth. She wriggled her lips and it was gone. Then it was back, tracing the curve of her lower lip, then her upper.

It felt good. She let her lips part. It felt sensuous, like being kissed by James . . .

She opened her eyes, blinking her damp, clumping lashes. She was dreaming of James; was it any wonder?

Her every waking moment was filled with thoughts of him. Why wouldn't her sleeping self turn to him as well?

Again she blinked, and his face came into view. It seemed so real, him leaning over her with a smile lifting one side of his face, and the glitter of love in his eyes.

Love. She smiled back and her eyes drifted closed, filled with a contentment she'd never known. He loved her.

His finger smoothed over her lips again, and this time she opened for the kiss she so desperately wanted. "Kiss me," she whispered. "Please."

"With pleasure," he answered. His finger dipped briefly between her lips and she felt a jolt of pure pleasure. Oh, but it felt so good. Then his hand cupped her cheek and she curved her face into it.

So good. So real.

Too real.

It wasn't until he tilted her chin up that the truth struck her, as stingingly as one of her mother's slaps. She jerked fully awake, sitting straight up when her legs stiffened. The water sloshed over the rim of the tub. He grinned down at her suddenly revealed breasts, and with a horrified squeak, she sank down again, sending even more water splashing onto the floor.

He was here and it was no dream!

"Don't look," she ordered, caught somewhere between shock and anger and an utterly insane sort of joy. She crossed her arms over her chest. "Close your eyes."

James shook his head at each comment and instead braced his elbows on the edge of the tub. He was in his shirtsleeves, with one cuff rolled halfway to his elbow.

She stared at him in confusion. "How long have you been here?"

"Long enough," he said. "I needed to see you."

"To *see* me?" Phoebe rolled her eyes and let out a strangled laugh. "I think you've seen quite enough."

"No." He bent nearer and a lock of his hair fell across his brow. Ridiculous how golden his hair looked by firelight. He needed a haircut. He probably hadn't had one since his arrival in Yorkshire.

She closed her eyes against such perverse thoughts. His hair was not her concern. Let Lady Catherine admire its color and curl and length, not her.

She turned her face to the fire. "What do you want, Lord Farley? Is there a problem with the children?"

"Only that they miss you."

"You've wasted your time coming here, then, since I fully intend to return in the morning. I'll see them then."

"I didn't come on account of the children, Phoebe. Surely you know that."

She didn't bother with a reply. Of course she knew. He'd come for her, for the privacy her lonely cottage afforded them.

If only the idea didn't send such a powerful frisson of excitement humming along the surface of her skin. If only she could be angry and insulted at his assumption that she wanted him here. Instead she was flush with anticipation and passion. After their last confrontation here—

No, she wouldn't dwell on that. Heavens, but lust had overtaken every facet of her good judgment.

One of his hands dipped into the water and stirred little ripples against her protruding knees. "I have something to tell you."

She didn't want to hear it, not his reassurances about her continued place in his life after he wed, not his promises about the children or her position in the household or the depths of his regard for her. She'd already made her decision to return to Farley Park, and she wasn't foolish enough to pretend she didn't know where that would lead. If only he wanted her for his wife instead of his mistress.

She let her head fall back against the tub. *Don't talk. Just love me. Make love to me.* Unable to speak the words, she showed them instead by relaxing the defensive posture of her arms. His eyes fell to the peaks of her breasts, barely shrouded by the sudsy water. When he looked back at her face, his pupils dark and wide, she knew he understood her silent message. Unconsciously she parted her lips, breathing through her mouth in shallow pants. *Kiss me.*

She felt his hand move against her thigh, first the outer slope, then around to the sensitive inner side. With only the slightest pressure he parted her legs. Head, arms, legs, she now rested lax and open to him, supported entirely by the tub and protected hardly at all by the watery curtain that covered her.

"Do you have any idea how beautiful you are like this?" His voice was low and thick. Aroused. It excited her to know how easily she enflamed his passions. It was only skin, she wanted to say, the same familiar skin she'd lived in all her life. She knew she was far from the most beautiful woman he'd ever been with.

But for whatever reason, he admired her ordinary self, and under his admiring regard she always felt beautiful. She would always owe him a debt, if only for that.

He palmed the inside of her thigh, up and then down. She caught her breath as his hand glided over the web of curls that hid the entrance to her sex. She was so hot inside there, just inches away from where his fingers trailed.

The air caught in her throat, and she saw the faint, satisfied lift of his lips. But he didn't linger in the place where she already throbbed in readiness. Up the other thigh his palm traveled, up out of the water, over her knee and down her shin to her ankle. Hot and wet. Slippery.

"Are you warm enough?"

She nodded. Oh, yes. Just the sound of his voice drove her fever higher still. He palmed the underside of her foot, then lifted it out of the water. "Beautiful," he murmured. He bent to lap water from it, and Phoebe groaned. His tongue sipped at her hot, wet flesh—behind her knee, at the inner bone of her ankle, at the sensitive arch of her foot.

He draped that leg over the tub, then turned and gave the same carnal attention to her other one.

Phoebe slipped lower in the tub, until her chin dipped beneath the quivering surface of the water. She was half-floating now, anchored within the tub by her elbows, knees, and head. It was such a deliciously helpless position. But then, she'd been helpless against his appeal from almost the first moment they'd met.

"My water nymph. Did you wash yourself before you took your wet nap?"

Even if she had already scrubbed herself from head to toe, Phoebe would have lied. "No." She looked straight up into his eyes, breathless for what he intended to do next. "No, not yet."

"Good." He found the wash rag and the soap in the dish beside the tub. Lathering the cloth, he began first with her feet. Phoebe flexed her toes. Good gracious, but he made them insanely sensitive. Her toes, the space between them. Everywhere he touched became erotically charged. As he moved past her knees, down to the submerged parts of her, his other hand slid beneath the small of her back, lifting her until her belly floated just beneath the surface of the water.

"My mermaid." His head lowered to nip the tender

skin of her belly, and like an earthquake, everything inside her vibrated. Something in the very possessiveness of his behavior shook her to her core. As if he knew, he looked up, his eyes burning with blue fire. "Enough play. Let me get back to work."

Employing the rough cloth, he began to wash between her legs. Phoebe didn't notice when he moved both hands to the task. All she knew was that the cloth abraded her little nub of passion in the most agonizingly wonderful way, while his other hand explored the deeper recesses of her. In his finger went, so warm and slick that she cried out with pleasure.

"Do you like that, Phoebe? Tell me."

"Oh, yes." She sighed. "Oh, yes."

"Faster? Deeper?"

She nodded, struggling to breathe as he increased the pressure of his knowing finger.

"Lift your breasts to me."

She did it without question, arching up with her head thrown back so that her puckered nipples broke free of the water. The air was cool on her glistening skin, but his mouth was hot. Hot and fierce. He caught the near breast, sucking hard, and she bucked up against the jolt of excitement that shot through her.

Biting, sucking, almost hurting her, he drew her out, his mouth at her breasts, his hands at her womb. Fiercely he pulled lust from every part of her. He turned her into a creature meant only for this moment.

More and deeper and harder he pushed, until like a tidal wave it rose, from toes to knees to belly, to all the extremes of her being. It hit her like a wall of boiling water welling up from inside, like shock waves that came and came and came.

But even then he wouldn't let it end. He dragged her out of the water and onto the rug, somehow loosening his garments during the process. Looming over her like a predatory beast over his delicious prey, he lifted her legs high. He braced her ankles on his shoulders, then with his avid gaze watching her every reaction, he thrust his molten member inside her.

Again Phoebe came, in a rush of fire and water and electricity. She was swollen inside, so tight around him that every movement felt amplified a thousand times over. Like thunder roaring and rattling the heavens after the strike of lightning.

Yet still he thrust into her, gripping her hips in his hands and thrusting inside her with furious determination.

He was going to get her with child.

Why that thought should lodge in her brain at such a moment Phoebe couldn't say. But in the middle of their sexual frenzy she nonetheless was certain of it. He put too much of himself into it. He drew too much of her out of it. What else could possibly result?

What more could she possibly want?

She stared up through a haze of satisfaction and desire, of love and longing, and watched his face as he approached his peak. His eyes were narrowed to straining slits, but she could see the light of pure arousal in them as they fixed upon hers.

"Show me you like it," he muttered, even as he grimaced, trying to hold his own culmination at bay. "Show me one more time."

With merely those harshly uttered words he drew new earthquakes of pleasure from the deepest part of her. He might not love her, but he always put her pleasure first. Always hers. It was no surprise that so many women adored him. Did she really think she could run away from this man? Did she really believe she could live without him?

"I like it," she whispered, every word a groan catching in her throat. "You know I do."

His shirt hung loose. She slid one hand beneath it and up his chest. His heart thudded a maddened tattoo beneath the hot damp skin. The muscles of his chest worked to hold her to him as he raced to his peak. "I love it," she confessed, her eyes fixed with his in a moment of supreme honesty. "But what I love most . . . is you. You."

For a moment he faltered, just a brief hitch in the perfect rhythm of his lovemaking. She almost missed it, because it was followed by such a burst of frantic thrusting. He gave a guttural cry as he stiffened. His thighs strained, and every muscle on his chest and arms bulged as he half lifted her off the rug.

Phoebe felt the pumping of everything he had into her, a hot and possessive font of life. She cried out and clenched around him over and over, as if they must always be joined thus.

The bathtub climax had been incredible enough. Every time they'd been together it had always ended in a physical relief beyond her ken. But this time the release of emotions layered pleasure upon pleasure. The truth lay exposed between them now. She loved him and there was no going back on that.

With a final thrust he collapsed over her, trembling as if he'd spent everything he had. In the overheated silence that fell over the cottage, there were only the harsh gasps of their breathing, and the comforting pop and snap of the fire. It was the most perfect moment of her life: physical and emotional completeness. She luxuriated in the rare contentment of body and spirit, and felt him relax into it too.

She could stay like this forever, she decided—*if* they'd been on a bed instead of this lumpy rug over a hard stone floor and *if* he'd not been so heavy on top of her.

She twisted her shoulders, seeking a more comfortable position and he responded with an easy roll to the right. Now she lay on top of him in a naked sprawl of wet limbs and tangled hair. Her whole backside was bare and exposed.

But there was no one to see but them. Besides, the room was warm and she was pressed onto a wonderful, warm body. It was only a sudden bout of shyness that made her shiver. He knew she loved him now. Would that change anything between them? Would he even care?

She turned her head to the side, resting it on his chest.

"Is it true?" he asked. Every rumbling word vibrated in the aftermath of their lovemaking.

She knew what he referred to. She mustered her unraveling courage. "Yes. It seems that I do."

He said nothing, as if he were considering what to do about her and this unfortunate emotional attachment she'd formed. Panic seized Phoebe as the silence stretched painfully long. What happened now? What should she do?

Why couldn't he love her back?

She started to slide her legs off him, but his arms tightened around her. "Let me up, Lord Farley. I'm . . . I'm cold. I need my dressing gown."

Back he rolled, covering her with his overheated body, trapping her in place beneath him. "Don't ever call me that again. From now on I'm James to you, Phoebe."

Braced on his elbows, he cupped her face with one hand. With the other he fingered the unruly tangles at her temple and brow. She had no choice but to meet his probing eyes. "And from now on I'll keep you warm. I'll keep you warm always."

She managed a smile, though it must have looked more like a grimace, for he went on. "I will. And since you love me— You weren't lying, were you?"

She closed her eyes, utterly miserable. "I wasn't lying."

"Good. Under the circumstances, then, I think we'd better get married."

Get married?

Phoebe's eyes popped open. "You mean you and me? Us?"

"Yes, Phoebe. You and me. Will you marry me?"

She was dreaming, of course. There was no other explanation. It could not be this easy: She confessed her love and he immediately proposed to her.

He hadn't said he loved her.

She swallowed hard. She wouldn't let that be a requirement to accepting his proposal. She was too practical to expect him to love her. But she wanted him to. Desperately.

Did he still love Catherine?

The very thought turned her cold. Surely he couldn't. But she had to know. "What about Lady Catherine? Aren't you already betrothed to her?"

His eyes narrowed and a small furrow appeared between his brows. "Not for long."

That should have cheered her, but it didn't. He discarded women so easily. "Not for long?" She pursed her lips, afraid to hear the answer to her next question. "And how long shall you remain betrothed to me?"

One side of his mouth curved up in a knowing grin. "Not for very long at all."

CHAPTER 22

Somehow Phoebe managed to drag her utterly spent and naked self up from the floor and into her dressing gown. James remained where they'd lain, stretched out on his side upon the rug, watching her jerky movements. His front side was still damp from their watery frolic, and he had the sultriest, knowing expression in his heavy-lidded eyes.

"You haven't given me an answer, Phoebe."

"To what?" As if she didn't know!

"Will you marry me?"

She ducked her head and fiddled with the ties meant to hold her dressing gown closed. "Marry you? Or be betrothed to you?"

He rolled on to his back. "We can skip the betrothal and go straight to the marriage, if that's what you prefer. Of course, I'll have to obtain a special license so that we don't have to announce the banns." He broke off when he spied her gaping expression. "What? You don't think I have the wherewithal to obtain a special license?"

"You . . . You really mean it?"

"Of course. There are a few benefits to being a viscount, and one of them is that I know people who can do me favors."

"No, no. I mean about marrying me."

He sat up, staring at her. With his open shirt and disheveled appearance, he might have been the bailiff she'd once wished he was, attainable for a woman like her. She swallowed hard. But maybe he *was* attainable. He certainly sounded sincere.

"Of course I meant what I said. Why else would I say it? Wait a minute. Did you actually think that when I said I wouldn't be betrothed to you for long that I meant I would propose to you with the intent later to break off the betrothal?"

"You're planning to break your betrothal with Lady Catherine," Phoebe said, a trifle defensively. "And before, in London, she broke it off with you."

"But I'm breaking off with her so that I can marry you." He rose to his feet.

"But why?" Phoebe wrapped her arms around herself, afraid to believe him. If she let her hopes rise and then had them dashed, she wasn't certain she could bear it. "I've already agreed to be governess to your daughters, and it's obvious you can make me act your mistress no matter how noisily I protest." She blushed, but forged on. "Are you offering for me because you're afraid I might marry someone else?"

"Partly." He stepped forward; she stepped back. "But that's not the whole reason."

"You don't want to share me. Is that it?"

His jaw tightened and the muscle there throbbed. "I'll never share you with any man, Phoebe Churchill. Never."

"Well, if we are ever to become man and wife, I refuse to share you either. What do you think of that?"

Comprehension dawned in his eyes, comprehension and a shadow of guilt. "You're thinking about my past. But that's over with, and anyway, this is different."

"How can I be sure? How can *you* be sure? After all, I know I'm at least the fifth woman for you." Her mind rebelled at the thought. "But I could just as well be the fifteenth." Her hands tightened into fists. "Or the fiftieth."

The guilt in his eyes deepened. "I wish I could undo my past, Phoebe. But I can't. All I can say is that you overestimate my appeal. All those other women—" He lifted his hands, then let them fall to his sides. "Yes, I pursued them. I've always pursued what I wanted, including you. But I never lied to any of them. They always knew my intentions. I've only proposed twice in my life. Once to Catherine, and now to you."

She wanted to believe him. She wanted to believe every single word. But it seemed the nearer she came to having some part of this man, the more parts she wanted of him. At one point she'd been happy to be his mistress. Then she'd wanted marriage. She still wanted that. But now she wanted it with love. Love first, followed by marriage and lifelong fidelity.

The problem was, he didn't love her. He wanted her, perhaps more than all the previous women he'd wanted, and she knew he liked her. He also thought her the best candidate to mother his children. But none of that was the same thing as love. She drew herself up. "If you had married Lady Catherine, would you have been faithful to her?"

She'd caught him by surprise with that question. He shoved his hands into his pockets, then turned and paced restlessly before the hearth. "I would have tried."

Oh, God! Phoebe threw her hands up in despair. "Tried? You would have tried?"

He looked up, frowning. "Yes. I would have tried. I'm being honest, Phoebe. Isn't that what you want from me?"

"Honesty *and* fidelity."

"I'll be faithful to you."

"Oh, really?"

"There's a world of difference between you and Catherine."

"Don't remind me." It was her turn to pace the short limits of the parlor.

"What does that mean?" He caught her by the arms, forcing her to face him. "What does that mean?"

At his touch, the last of her control collapsed. Like the opening of Pandora's box, all her secrets and fears and doubts burst out to poison the air between them. "It means she's beautiful and rich, with the right family. Everything I am not. I have no family connections; no experience with the peerage. I may have learned manners at my mother's knee, but nothing to adequately prepare me for the duties attendant on becoming a viscountess."

A viscountess.

While Phoebe had daydreamed about herself as James's wife, not once had she imagined herself in the role of Viscountess Farley. The real possibility of it scared her witless.

That fast the tables of her emotions turned. She'd doubted his readiness to marry when it was she who was the one most unsuited to their union. Cold with fear, she shook her head. "I cannot accept your offer. I'm flattered of course, but . . . No. I can't marry you."

His grip tightened on her arms and he pulled her nearer. "Yes you can. You will."

"You don't understand." She bowed her head until her brow rested upon his chest. "I couldn't possibly do it."

She heard his harsh breathing; she felt the rise and fall of his chest against her forehead. "Tell me this: If I weren't a viscount, would you marry me then?"

She drew in a long, shuddering breath. "I have wished that you were a bailiff," she admitted in a low voice.

His chest began an odd, rhythmic shaking. It took her a long moment to understand. He was laughing at her! She raised her head. "It's not funny! I would make a very good bailiff's wife."

"But you'll make an even better viscountess." With the tenderest touch he cupped one of her cheeks and smiled down into her unhappy face. "Maybe this might help to convince you. As I said before, I've proposed marriage twice in my lifetime. But one thing I've never done before is vow my love to anyone. Not until now."

Now?

Not until now?

Phoebe wasn't certain whether he'd actually said those words, or her poor, desperate mind had just imagined them. *Not until now.*

"I love you. You, Phoebe." His glittering blue eyes searched her face. "I can't live without you. Haven't I proven that over and over again? I've chased you down every time you tried to leave Farley Park. I need you there with me. You and no other. And if you won't live with me there, then I'll live with you here. Or we can go live in the bailiff's cottage."

One side of his mouth lifted in a crooked grin. "Don't you see? I love you. Say you'll marry me, love. I'm begging you. You'll break my heart forever if you don't."

If she hadn't seen the truth in his eyes, and felt the insistence in his hold, those simple words might not have been enough to make Phoebe believe him. But how could a woman possibly resist a man like this? His avowal was so urgent, so sincere, that tears sprang into her eyes. "You really do love me?"

"I love you." He shook his head, as if he were as amazed by that fact as she. "I should have realized it sooner, and then told you the minute I knew. I'm an idiot, I know. But I do love you. And I'll be lover, husband, viscount, or bailiff to you. Whatever you want me to be."

When she still stared speechlessly up at him, he added, "And faithful. That I promise you above all else. My past . . ." He let out a long sigh and shook his head. "Maybe I was just waiting, practicing for the real thing. For you. It's so clear now. I've been waiting my whole life to find you, Phoebe."

A slow smile began to curve Phoebe's mouth. He meant it. He really did. A happiness unlike anything she'd ever known radiated through her. But after all the torment he'd put her through, she didn't want to give in too easily to the rogue.

"Practice?" she echoed, glancing at him askance. "Every one of them was just practice, you say. Well, I suppose, then, that the practice has paid off." Staring straight into his eyes, she slowly wet her lips with the tip of her tongue. "You are rather good at convincing a girl to do whatever it is you want."

His eyes had grown hot watching the teasing of her tongue, and she felt his body tense. To his credit, however, he wasn't sidetracked by her sultry behavior.

"But have I convinced you to marry me?" he asked. "Have I convinced you that I love you?"

On the inside Phoebe might be trembling from the effort to restrain her bubbling joy, but her conviction was as solid as the granite ground beneath Plummy Head. "Yes."

It was his turn to smile. He pulled her a little closer. "And you will marry me?"

She threw her arms around him. "Oh, yes."

James felt the difference the moment he drew Phoebe against him. Although she had willingly admitted her love for him, she'd been reluctant to marry him, enough to have him terrified that she would turn him down. But the willingness he felt now in her embrace erased any worry he'd harbored. Like sunshine her love poured over him, heating through him in a way he'd never known. Their lovemaking had always been wonderful. She'd been willing and eager, giving totally of herself.

But what he felt now in the strong, feminine length of her was much more than that. He buried his face in the tangled dampness of her hair and inhaled. Essence of Phoebe. He could get drunk on it. He wanted to drown in it. Essence of Phoebe. Essence of love.

"There will never be anyone for me but you," he murmured as unfamiliar tears stung his eyes.

"There better not be," she said, lifting her lips to his.

He accepted the offer of her kiss and reveled in the excitement she roused in him. But as he lifted her high and carried her up the stairs to her bed beneath the roof rafters, he didn't correct her misconception of his words. It wasn't a promise he was making to her, that there would never be anyone else for him. It was a statement of fact, of comprehension, of personal revelation. He would never want anyone but her.

He hadn't given up freedom or variety or even a political career when he vowed his love and fidelity. Instead he'd obtained everything he'd never had: contentment; satisfaction. Family.

Love.

EPILOGUE

The London Tattler—**April 28**
The torrid tale of Viscount Farley and his trail of broken hearts has taken an even more lurid turn. It appears the betrothal between the esteemed Lady Catherine and the rogue Lord Farley has not only been resumed, the marriage itself has already taken place. And in the barren wilds of Yorkshire, no less!

Lady Basingstoke is said to be prostrate with grief at the abruptness of the union. Likewise, Lord Basingstoke refuses to answer any inquiries about his daughter's sudden reversal regarding the indiscreet viscount.

One hesitates to speculate on the reason for nuptials so hasty as to preclude the attendance of the bride's family. But given the number of children previously fathered by Lord Farley, can there be any doubt?

The London Tattler—**May 3**
Even in a season replete with petty scandals and peccadilloes, the transgressions of some loom like mountains of sin over the foothills and errors of their compatriots.

I refer, of course, to the shameful conduct of Lord

Farley. Bad enough that he toyed with the affections of that light of the season, Lady Catherine Winfield. Worse came the news that he rushed her into a marriage without the consent of her devastated parents.

But the actual truth is so vile and unbelievable that the reader is to be forgiven for throwing down this paper in utter disbelief. Rest assured, the truth is as I write it. Lord Farley is indeed wed in a rushed country marriage rite—but not to Lady Catherine! He has wed a country nobody, a woman hired as his children's governess, who previously worked as a dairymaid!

Yes, dear readers, the new Viscountess Farley is a crude local from the vicinity of his country seat. One wonders how many children the man has hidden in the northern wilds, and why at this late date he feels the necessity to wed a woman of that sort when he has refused to wed any of his previous inamoratas.

As for Lady Catherine, his supposed bride, it seems she, too, is wed in a hasty ceremony, but to the Honorable Kerry Fairchild, youngest son of the Earl of Sanderly. It goes without saying that her doubly distraught parents are in seclusion.

The London Tattler—May 19

Were it not for my faithful readers' right to know the truth, this correspondent would throw his pen and paper away, despairing of the selfish willfulness of the younger set. How is Mother Britain to prosper in the hands of this pleasure-seeking generation who flaunt every precept of good society? Marrying without parental approval may do for the common folk, but it seriously undermines the English tradition of consolidating power in the most capable hands.

It appears, sadly, that some of the older generation

*are not immune to this infection of disloyaity to tradi-
tion. I refer, of course to the news that Lord and Lady
Acton plan to host a wedding reception for her son, the
widely reviled Lord Farley—he of the dairymaid wife.*

*I predict a spectacular disaster. Who of any note can
desire an acquaintance with such a man and his necessarily coarse wife?*

The London Tattler—May 21

*Lady Basingstoke was seen at Madame Henri's exclu-
sive dress shop yesterday afternoon. According to
sources not to be doubted, she was fitted for a magnificent gown to be worn when she greets her newly married daughter and son-in-law. One wonders about the
desperation of a poor mother faced with either losing
her beloved daughter to an impulsive marriage, or accepting the errant child with her poorly selected mate.
While Mr. Fairchild boasts a fine family name, he is a
far cry from the rich, titled fellow Lady Catherine might
have claimed. Lord Basingstoke continues mum on the
entire subject.*

*Meanwhile Lady Acton, mother of Lord Farley, is
seen at the races, at Vauxhall Gardens, and at every
breakfast, rout, and ball in town. Clearly she detects the
animosity building toward her son and his goat-girl
bride, and is trying to deflect it.*

The London Tattler—May 24

*My dearest readers, truth is now become stranger than
fiction, and certainly more lurid. It seems that Lord and
Lady Basingstoke have joined as hosts for the Acton
party. Their daughter and her husband are traveling
south with Lord and Lady Farley (and I use the term
"lady" rather loosely in the latter case). Plans now are
for both couples to be feted at the planned ball.*

Though it pains me to say it (cover your eyes, you gentler of my readers) it makes one wonder what else the two couples do in tandem.

The London Tattler—May 30

Portman Square has become a crowd of tradesmen and servants preparing for the Acton fete. A steady stream of riders, carriages, and strollers also progresses past the ornate Acton manse, especially since the ill-matched couple is purported to be in residence. Could it be that voyeurism shall trump good sense, and draw those who should know better to attend an event designed to honor those who have no honor? Rest assured, dear readers, that should that be the case, your faithful correspondent will not fail to report on every aspect of that party, no matter the personal affront involved.

The London Tattler—June 1

Finally it can be said. The rumors of Lord Farley's marriage to a goat girl were vastly overstated. The new Lady Farley, formerly Miss Phoebe Churchill, second cousin to Baron Kennington of Yorkshire, is a stunning woman, gracious despite the staring eyes of more than six hundred guests. As expected, Lady Catherine Fairchild, née Winfield, comported herself in the manner one has come to expect of such a winning creature.

The two brides wore complementary gowns: ivory and azure silk for Lady Catherine, cream and apple-green moiré for Lady Farley. Likewise the women displayed a friendliness that defied every attempt to see scandal in their association. They were often seen arm in arm circulating among their guests.

Not straying far from their sides, the two grooms appeared utterly in their element. It is with considerable relief that your correspondent notes a pleasant truth: It was plainly a love match that drove Lady Catherine so precipitously into a union with Mr. Fairchild. There can be no other conclusion.

As for Lord Farley and his bride, it can be assumed that his mother (the ageless, ever gracious Lady Acton) has taken the new Lady Farley well in hand, for her behavior at the crush was beyond reproach. Given Lord Farley's past history, it remains to be seen how well he will behave in the future. And there is, of course, the question of his several children—there are now said to be three of them in residence with him and his new bride.

The London Tattler—June 2

Rotten Row is never easy to traverse, however yesterday it was an absolute snarl. The reason? The new Lady Farley and her husband's three daughters were taking the air in her mother-in-law's fabulous open phaeton while Lord Farley rode attendance. They attracted attention wherever they went, for it seems everyone who is anyone felt compelled to expound upon the crushing success of the party they hosted two days previously. Even your loyal correspondent was so moved.

The true reason for the extravagant attention, however, was the three little girls accompanying the newlyweds. Lady Farley held the dusky-skinned baby on her lap, and it was plain to one and all that true affection exists between the two. As for the older two, they are a curious pair of kittens, pretty little blond girls who look remarkably presentable given their unseemly beginnings.

At one point Lord Farley took the two older girls down to the water's edge. It was then that Lady Farley informed her audience that her husband had arranged for her to legally adopt his daughters. An unusual ar-

rangement to be sure. But as a former governess, she seems uniquely suited to the task.

Your correspondent finds it quite singular to see such generosity of spirit in so young a woman. No doubt Lady Farley will inject fresh life into the sometimes staid world of society.

Only one unpleasant incident marred the afternoon: Some light-fingered jackanapes picked my pocket. My pearl-handled knife, a gold watch, and one pound six were removed from my person during the crush around the Farley phaeton.

When a person cannot be safe, even in Hyde Park and surrounded by the crème de la crème *of society, well, it is a sad day for Britannia. A sad day, indeed.*

That's all I have to say on the subject.